*This book is dedicated to
Lorrie Honisett*

1941-2016

Finally the complex operation at San Francisco City Hospital was over. Dr. Howard Gardner, Head of Cardiology, breathed easier. The procedure had not been an easy one. A young man named Michael had undergone heart by-pass surgery, major blood vessels had proved difficult, and there'd been extensive bleeding. Gardner glanced at Nurse Evans giving her the all-clear to apply wound dressings over the sutures, count the swabs and instruments, and tidy up. The surgeon nodded at his assistant, Dr. Chuck Hudson, as if to say 'job well done.'

Nurse Evans untied the blood spattered apron as Gardner stood with his back to her. Removing his face-mask, he snapped off the latex gloves and pulled off the green, blood spattered gown, the whole bundle going into the bin. Within ten minutes the heart surgeon had scrubbed, got changed, and was heading for the doctor's lounge. Hudson was already sitting near the cold water dispenser, flicking through an old copy of *USA Today* magazine. Gardner peeled open a milk chocolate bar.

"You OK, Howard? You look tired." Gardner took a bite of chocolate. "By the way, how's Amanda? Still talking to cases on her couch?" Howard's wife, Amanda, was a psychiatrist with her own private practice. He glanced at Hudson and smiled weakly. "Oh, and a good job in there," added Hudson.

"Thanks." Gardner hesitated. "Me? Yes, I'm OK. Amanda's fine, too. Just a few little problems at home but nothing that can't be resolved." Gardner eased an index finger into the side of his shirt collar and moved it back and forward as if to let more air into his lungs. Looking out of the lounge window he saw slate-grey rain clouds approaching as he played with the bracelet of his gold Omega watch. Swallowing the last of his coffee he scrunched the cardboard cup and threw it into the trash can. The chocolate bar wrapper, folded lengthwise three times and knotted, followed the coffee cup. Walking to the door he hesitated before departing. Placing his hand on the door knob he looked back at Hudson.

"By the way, Chuck, thanks for your help today," he added as he left, closing the door quietly behind him. Gardner was about to walk through the double doors at the end of the long corridor when Nurse Evans shouted after him.

"Dr. Gardner, we've lost him! We've lost Michael. He has just died in the recovery room. We did everything we could." But today everything wasn't enough.

1

"Hello, San Francisco Police Department. Officer Bates speaking. How may I help you?" Bates put his cardboard cup down before picking up the phone.

"Oh, officer, my son didn't come home last night. Sometimes he's late, but I waited up 'til three this morning before I fell asleep, and he still ain't shown up. I'm worried sick."

Officer Bates took down the necessary details – caller's name, address, contact number. Name and brief description of the missing person. The time was 9.27 am.

"He was going out with some friends – and there's a girl he was seeing. He said they were heading to a couple of bars down town, but he's a sensible kid. He would have been back at midnight . . . latest. I've phoned two of his buddies and both say he left them before ten pm."

Bates reassured her that the call would be logged and all the information she'd given him placed on the SFPD computer. Yet another MisPer to add to the growing list.

"Thanks, Officer, sure appreciate it." She sniffed. "Oh, I'm so worked up 'bout it. Bye."

Officer Bates had been sitting there at the desk wondering why his bitch of a wife had left him last week. He spat the pink bubble gum into the centre of the form he'd just completed on behalf of Mrs. Bauer, moulded it into a ball, and threw it into the trash bin next to his black police boots. Why do these pathetic, snivelling old women bother him with phone calls, he wondered. Her excuse for a son was probably sleeping off too many beers under some bridge, vomit down the front of his shirt. He'd be home soon.

Then he cursed his wife again as he took a sip of his Starbucks coffee. Bates was looking forward to a couple of beers himself after a day pen pushing and filling in forms.

2

"Have you seen this advertisement, Jane?" asked her mum, Jenny, flicking through the Keighley News. A pale Yorkshire July sun was bathing the kitchen wall. Jane had just heard she'd achieved three good 'A' level grades but if the truth be known, she wasn't certain about going on to university. At least not yet. Friends had sown seeds in her mind about taking out a gap year.

A slice of brown toast lay on the plate in front of Jane, her coffee getting cooler. The day wasn't planned. She might walk into town, meet some girl friends, maybe watch a film at the new Empire cinema. A new Squeeze CD had just been released and the HMV store would have some in stock. After the stress of her studies, Jane wanted to relax, take things easy, and, to use a phrase she hated, 'chill out.' Jenny passed the newspaper across the breakfast table, pointing out an advert. Jane picked up her toast and read it as she sipped her coffee.

Au.Pair.US
Fancy working as a Nanny in the USA? Up to 250 USD per week.
Board and food included, time off, 24 emergency hour care.
One year contract with option to stay a further 12 months.
Previous child care experience necessary, interest in children a must.
College tuition available in a variety of subjects.
Low initial outlay. What are you waiting for?
Telephone 0209 1211 9801 now for an informal chat.

Jane passed the paper back to her mum. "I'm not sure. I know I've got some baby-sitting experience, and I've helped out at Keighley primary school. But . . ."

"But what? You love children, I've seen the look in your eyes when you've cared for them, down at the play ground, pushing them on the swings . . ." Jane stood up.

"Leave it, Mum, I'm not cut out for that, especially in America. All those Yanks. Everyone saying 'awesome' and 'swell' all the time. No thanks." Jane ate her toast, finished her warm coffee, and slipped off the kitchen bar stool as Jenny's husband, Paul, came into the kitchen. He yawned and stretched. In need of a shave, but more in need of some tea. Strong.

"Morning both," he muttered as he popped a slice of bread into the toaster. "Everyone all right this happy morning?" Jenny gave him a look that suggested 'yes.' Jane grunted something that sounded positive and went upstairs to shower. "Anything in the paper?" he asked.

"Same old," Jane replied flicking it closed and passing the newspaper across the table to him. "It's all doom and gloom, the pound down against the dollar, Islamic State this, refugees that, and the NHS going down the pan." She giggled after she'd said the word 'pan' as a vision of a bed-pan entered her head.

"So what's new?" said Paul. "It's the same with the TV news. As bad as watching some of the soaps . . . they're enough to make you look for a high bridge with a nice parapet on the side. What I want to read is that some people at a comedy show had to be treated for split sides after hearing some damn good jokes!" He lightly trowelled his toast with a low fat spread followed by a dollop of crunchy peanut butter. A brief cascade of milk whitened his tea in a mug with 'World's Greatest T-drinker' printed on the side.

Paul had been a successful Biology teacher but was now involved with higher matters – setting examinations, proposing changes to curricula and syllabi. Taking a great science to the next plane; wanting children to enjoy biology, not see it as a tedious subject done in a room that smelt of formalin with unpleasant objects in sealed jars and a life size plastic skeleton gathering dust in a corner. And having them get involved in a practical manner. Collecting specimens, cutting things up, drawing and identifying what had been found. He was freelance, and in demand.

"You're right," Jenny replied, "we need *better* news! So what's on *your* agenda today?"

"I've got a meeting with Arthur Wells at the university in Bradford at ten to discuss the proposed amendments to the Yorkshire Schools Examination Board syllabus for 'A' level Biology. That'll take a couple of hours, then I'll get a sandwich before I head off to see the new Headmaster at Harrogate School. They're extending the new sixth form laboratories and he would like my input. These public schools are not short of a bob or two." That really meant that Paul would be able to up his charges for his consultation. He waited a moment to see if Jenny had any further questions. "And you?" he asked.

"Not much. Some housework as usual on a Monday. Dianah suggested a bite to eat at The Cookhouse in Haworth. It has a good write up on Travel Advisor. What time will you be in?" Paul looked at the kitchen clock, an old habit whenever anyone mentioned time. The black hands on the round white dial showed ten minutes to eight.

"Around five o'clock, say. Well, must get ready. I hope Jane has finished up there."

"By the way," said Jenny, "I saw an ad in the paper this morning, au pairs required in America. You know how Jane is undecided about the next year or so . . . but she didn't seem very interested. I mean, she loves kids, has had quite a bit of experience in child care, and I think it would do her good! There's a telephone number. A quick call wouldn't do any harm." Paul stood with his arms folded across his dressing gown covered chest. He listened to every word. A few seconds passed before he spoke quietly.

"Why don't *you* make a call. Tell them you're phoning on behalf of a friend, get some details, and then mention a few facts to Jane later. You could even tell a little white lie and say that Dianah 'knows somebody who looked into it . . .' Jenny paused for an instant, grabbed Paul, and kissed him on the cheek.

"Brilliant! You're a genius! And if I raise the subject over dinner, you'll support me?" He nodded and smiled. With that Paul went upstairs two steps at a time and reached the landing as Jane came out of the bathroom, her hair bunned up in a towel like a Sikh.

"That was quick!" said her dad, taking the mickey as she glided into her bedroom. Jane looked at him through a three inch gap, teasingly put her tongue out, and closed her bedroom door. "I'll get you later!" he exclaimed as he headed for the shower cubicle. Jane smiled to herself. She loved her dad and their relationship was solid.

Twenty five minutes later Paul was leaving the house, briefcase in hand. He'd kissed Jenny and Jane, then checked for his wallet, mobile phone, glasses and car/house keys. He zapped the Ford Mondeo and the blinkers flashed twice. It was a forty five minute drive to meet Arthur Wells and Classic FM on low volume played as he blew Jenny a kiss. Pulling off the drive Paul headed west, turning up the temperature setting to 20C. It had been a poor summer going by the number of times he had lit the barbecue in the back garden.

Precisely none.

*

"So she'll need a J-1 visa but can stay on for another 3, 6 or 9 months?" Jenny was telephoning a girl at the au pair agency in London. *"And all costs are covered, plus up to 250 dollars a week? Yes, yes."* A pause. *"Forty five hours a week for a five and a half day week, with a weekend off in every four. Yes, yes. Uh, huh. Helping with bathing dressing, homework . . . yes, Study? OK. Each nanny has to undertake study? Oh, right. Three hours a week isn't too bad. And a financial contribution towards that, too. Fashion, media studies, business and photography? Excellent. Orientation? In New York, wow! Four days, that sounds quite adequate. And a dedicated counsellor? Other au pairs? I see, there'll be other girls there, too? OK, then*

after the orientation session they each go their separate ways . . . Chicago and San Francisco and Washington. Goodness, that sounds glamorous." Jenny paused for breath. *"Basic costs? Oh, I see, the visa, a DBS check and international driving licence application . . . one hundred and ninety pounds. The airfare? Three hundred and ninety nine pounds. Yes, that's not too bad if you put it that way. Interview at the London Embassy? Grosvenor Square, yes. You can send more information on line? Yes, of course, all lower case. It's jenny.lester1948@ hotmail.com Thank you, I look forward to getting the details confirmed. And your name is . . ? Virginia. OK. Thanks. Bye."*

Virginia hadn't told Jenny during their telephone conversation that Jane would have to complete an on-line application, write a letter to any American family with which she may be put in touch, and after approval by the family, attend an interview at which she would have to complete a personality check. In most cases the parents of the host family wanted a phone conversation with the proposed au pair, or 'nanny' as Jenny preferred. A GP would have to provide a clean bill of health, and once all of this was sorted out Jane could be on her way to New York for her induction!

Jane could handle all of this decided her mum. She was made of tough Yorkshire stock! Jenny decided she'd adopt Paul's suggestion; have lunch with Dianah and use that as the 'white lies basis' for a gentle chat with Jane that evening. Paul would be in his study and there was nothing on television worth watching. There never is.

Yes, that would be the plan. Perfect.

3

"Well, what sort of a day did you have?" Howard asked his wife, Amanda, over dinner. They were sitting in their large detached house at 31, Adair Way on the Stonebrae Country Club complex in Hayward, a few miles outside of San Francisco. The property suited their needs, a four bedroomed detached house with a triple garage in an upmarket area with views across to the bay. The two children, Teresa, aged six, and Ryan, seven, were both in bed. Their neighbour, Myrtle Murray, had collected them from school and been generally helping out for the past month. Since Myrtle's husband, George, passed away two years ago, she'd been a great asset. The children loved her, and, despite being seventy five years of age, was quite fit and healthy. Myrtle always put it down to taking her vitamins and minerals, plus one large banana, every day of her life since she was knee high to a raccoon. She didn't tell anyone about her habit of the last ten years, the small glass of rye whisky taken every morning with her coffee was purely for 'medicinal' purposes.

"OK, apart from one patient," Amanda replied. Howard let her continue. "I've been treating this guy for three months now and I don't seem any further forward."

"What's his problem?" asked Howard casually, sipping his Shiraz. Amanda hesitated, normally she wasn't for talking about her patients. Confidentiality was key to her professional work. But when Howard asked, though, she owed him a reply. Putting a forkful of tuna salad into her mouth, she looked at him.

"He saw his parents burn to death in their house in Sausalito three years ago. No way could he get near them, and by the time the emergency services arrived the whole place was an inferno." Howard looked at his well-done sirloin steak and put his fork down.

"Hell, what an experience!" The tone of his response suggested he didn't want to pursue the matter. "Well, I see the weather forecast is looking good for the next few days . . ." Amanda knew it was time to change the subject. "Any news on the search for an au pair?" asked Howard.

"I had a call from the agency yesterday. They're hoping two newspaper advertisements in northern England will generate some interest. We should hear in about a fortnight. Poor Myrtle, she's been a rock for a while, but she needs a rest." Amanda stood up, collected the plates, poured her husband a little more wine. "What about your day?" she enquired.

"Same routine. Pretty much. A heart bypass op and an artificial tricuspid valve fitted to a sixty five year old. The valve patient had his daughter come with him, waited for hours just to hear if the procedure went OK." Amanda noticed Howard's eyes light up as he told her that.

"A little lemon mousse to finish?" she asked, hoping she could tempt Howard to tasting his favourite dessert.

"Just a small wedge," he replied. He knew that his wife could make good desserts, and he loved lemon mousse. Amanda brought the two bowls to the table and they ate in silence for a while, Howard savouring the tangy citrus flavour. He reflected on Amanda's work as a psychiatrist, often wondering how her work affected her? Did she horde the troubles of her clients, pigeon-hole them, sift through the detail . . . all those with a multitude of mental issues? Her Bible was the Diagnostic and Statistical Manual of Mental Disorders: Fifth Edition. DSMMD for short. Perhaps she'd go to sleep with psychological issues spinning in her head, trying to subconsciously solve a problem? But he knew she wasn't like that at all. Amanda was a perfectly normal loving wife and mother. She was a good woman, and Howard knew he was a lucky man to have a wife like her.

Well, apart from those little moments when they had their differences often relating to Howard's first marriage. His first wife, Priscilla, had fallen from a viewing platform on the edge of the Grand Canyon eight years ago. Priscilla, an Audrey Hepburn lookalike, had leant over too far to take a photograph and apparently lost her footing. He'd told her not to wear those silly shoes. The battered body was found at the bottom of the canyon the next day. Witnesses suggested that Howard was helping her up, his arm around her waste raising her too high, but nothing was ever proven . . . *'no malice aforethought.'* That's what the judge had stated.

Close friends were surprised how quickly he seemed to get over it, although Priscilla's sister appeared devastated. Some said they were crocodile tears. Howard had to identify the body, too. Priscilla's head had been neatly stitched onto her neck, with make-up applied. He didn't shed any tears at her funeral and his work as a surgeon did not appear to be affected. They were made for each other, some said. Yet less than eighteen months after her death he said 'I do' to Amanda Raskoff from Milwaukee. Tall, blonde, perfect legs, a Doctor of Philosophy. It was when Howard mentioned Priscilla by name that Amanda got those odd feelings, the type some of her patients mentioned to her on the couch. But she was trained. A psychotherapist as well as a qualified psychiatrist, and, despite having a Ph.D., she rarely used her 'Doctor' title. Amanda was capable of managing her own problems. No, it wasn't an issue for her, and she just hoped that as time went by Howard would forget about his first wife and never use her name again.

*

"Well, when you put it like that, it does sound an interesting proposition." Jane, her slipperless feet tucked under her, was reflecting on what her mum had been saying. A CD of light music from West End shows was quietly filling the room. "And you say Dianah knew somebody who went to the States to be an au pair?" Jenny nodded and smiled. "I've always wanted to go to San Francisco. Ever since I watched that programme on TV about the Golden Gate bridge and Alcatraz. And did you know that Chinatown has the largest population of Chinese outside of China?" Jane cupped her hot chocolate with both hands, sounding more enthusiastic.

"It's up to you, of course, but with the educational bit it would look good on your CV. 'Studied photography in California.' And there's the option of staying on for up to a further twelve months. Come on, you love children, and a family with two nice kids, plenty of sunshine and making new friends, as well as learning about the American culture. You can't lose!" Jane rested her head back on the soft leather settee, closing her eyes. She imagined the life. Perhaps two years on America's west coast, trips to L.A. and Las Vegas, a visit to the infamous island prison. And, studying in an American college on a part time basis, Jane wondered if she'd come back with an accent? Talk about side-walks, car wind-shields and elevators. Chew bubble gum, eat Ben & Jerry's ice cream and say 'Hi' to everyone she met. Not mentally ready for a three year university course in the UK, why not go and be a nanny?

There was Harry, however. She'd bumped into him in the cinema, spilling his popcorn. Jane had insisted on buying him another carton and, after briefly chatting with him, he'd pushed a business card into her hand as he shot off to see a different film. She'd texted him on the mobile number on his Lloyds Bank card three days later. It went from there. They met at the same cinema and saw *Spectre* starring Daniel Craig. Jane wasn't sure about all that gunfire and jumping from high buildings but Harry enjoyed it – an escape from the drudgery of bank work, he told her later. He was three years older than Jane and had joined the bank from the school sixth form. His father had been a manager at Lloyds, so Harry simply followed suit. Jane and Harry continued seeing each other for a while, and she did like him very much.

"I'm going to do it!" Jane jumped up, her mug thankfully now empty. "But what about the initial costs . . . flight, DBS check, visa, driving licence . . ." Her mother looked at her.

"Don't be silly. Your father and I have already talked about that. We're looking at about six hundred pounds. There's enough in the savings account. You just make sure you get a clean bill of health from the GP. You can apply on-line and if all goes well you'll need to get down to London for an interview at the American Embassy. We can work together on the letter that you have to send to the potential host families, and I could pretend to be the American mother. We could do a mock interview!" They both laughed, Jenny noticing how happy her daughter looked.

"Harry and I are going to that new Brewer's Fayre on Saturday evening, I'll tell him then. I'm sure he won't mind. Let him have his usual pint of lager shandy before I gently share the news." Jane went through to the kitchen, rinsed her mug and placed it on the draining board. Her dad came down stairs, asking what the excitement was about. She kissed him on the cheek. "Ask Mum, I'm going to watch television in my room. And Dad . . . thanks."

"So, the conversation obviously went well. It was a good job you'd chatted with Dianah and got all of that information." Paul winked. Jenny prayed that Jane didn't meet Dianah or she'd have to invent a story. She wasn't used to telling little white lies but it seemed to have worked. All she had to hope for now was that the 'i's would be dotted and the 't's' crossed.' Jenny was convinced it would all go without a hitch and soon they'd be waving their precious daughter off at Heathrow airport.

4

Dr. Chuck Hudson had just finished a minor operation on a young male patient who needed valve repair on his left femoral artery. Basically a minor procedure, Hudson, aged 29, had notched up over a hundred of these. As an intern at SFCH he wasn't quite ready for cardiac surgery yet. He was still learning from Howard Gardner, but stripping arteries and veins along with similar operations on blood vessels had become routine for him. The OR was like working inside a computer, everything was measured, monitored, calculated, checked – audibly as well as visually. The only potential error aspect was human. Nurses were on hand to help with the procedures, assistants handed him the instruments, someone moved the operating lights and the anaesthetist made sure the patient remained unconscious.

Hudson was a good looking guy. Six feet tall in his socks, brown hair always smartly cut, he had the resemblance of a young Charlie Sheen. When he'd joined the staff at the hospital two years ago several nurses fell for him straight away. One, Karen Bardock, an attractive brunette, used to leave notes in his locker, slipping them between the narrow gap in the door. The *billet doux* became more amorous. After a number of attempts Hudson took her aside one day and quietly told her he wasn't interested. He left it at that. Karen assumed he already had a girlfriend, maybe in another part of the hospital, or working in San Francisco – perhaps a lawyer or a university lecturer? Karen continued to watch Dr. Hudson from a distance, admiring his clean cut features and determined manner. As time went on, she came to realise that she never saw Chuck Hudson with other females in the hospital staff room nor the restaurant. 'A guy that good looking could not be gay' she'd say to herself. But one day another nurse, Angelina Renner, during a scrub for an impending operation, casually mentioned that Dr. Hudson was more interested in men.

"You look surprised, Karen. You mean you didn't know?" Karen rinsed the povidone iodine suds from her hands and dried them on a sanitised paper towel.

"Hell, no!" Angelina looked surprised.

"I thought everyone knew!" There was silence.

"What a waste!" said Karen. "Gay!" She gave Angelina a thumbs down.

Alone in her apartment that evening, and needing a drink, Karen opened a bottle of Chardonnay. She was alone, and, ironically, when Karen took her first slurp of Californian white that evening, a young man that she knew quite well was entering Quentin's night club just off Oregon Street.

The soft, warm, flashing pink neon lights at Quentin's welcomed anybody that was seeking a good time.

*

"Will you be OK? Are you sure you know where the embassy is . . . you've got the address . . . and the nearest tube station?" Jenny was doing her mother-hen bit.

"Of course! Look, the DBS was all right, driving licence application successful, I've had the interview with the agency and done the personality test. The family that I've spoken to over the telephone really want me! I can tell. It went so well." Jane was trying to reassure her mum that she did not have to worry. She showed her mum the black, leatherette folder which contained everything Jane needed for her US embassy interview. "It's all here . . . the full address, the appointment time, and the person I'm seeing." Jenny looked at her daughter and realised that her concerns were unfounded. Here was a mature eighteen year old preparing for an adventure. Nine O levels and three A levels later, she was ready for the next chapter in her life. Jenny flicked open the folder.

"Sorry, but I want to be certain that you're going to jump the final hurdle." Jenny was reassured when she saw the letter from a Miss Steinberger at the embassy. Chancery Building, Grosvenor Square, London. Jane had also made a note of the train times from Leeds to King's Cross and back, had a map of the underground system, and a short list of questions for Miss Steinberger already prepared. Also in the folder were copies of the various test results and the DBS check as well as the signed form from her GP to show she was medically fit. The interview was scheduled for Wednesday. Harry had been good about the news, wishing Jane all the luck in the world and he'd asked her to keep in touch. After a heart to heart about their relationship, they'd agreed that if someone else came along they were both free agents.

After an uneventful journey courtesy of Virgin, Jane alighted at Kings Cross and made her way to Grosvenor Square. The American Embassy was an imposing building. A gilded aluminium bald eagle perched majestically on top. Two fine bronze statues stood near the main entrance, one of Ronald Reagan, the other of Dwight D. Eisenhower. A young girl who looked about fifteen years old asked Jane to check-in, then issued her with an ID badge. She beckoned a security guard over who took Jane up to the fourth floor. The door to the interview room was opened by a Miss Steinberger who asked Jane to take a seat.

"Thank you for coming here today, Miss Lester. May I call you Jane?" Jane nodded politely. "Allow me to introduce Miss Rosentheim. Miss Rosentheim works for a branch of the CIA but there's no need to worry. She doesn't eat people!" Jane smiled weakly. After the offer of coffee, and a brief chat about the British weather, Steinberger began the interview process. There was nothing awkward or intimidating. Rosentheim made notes and seemed to be watching Jane carefully. Was she looking for unusual body language, any signs of discomfort?

Why was Jane applying to be an au pair in the States, what could she bring to the family for whom she'd work, and what plans did she have after her initial twelve month period, asked Steinberger? Jane answered each one confidently and positively. She loved children, was a committed individual, but was undecided at this stage about what to do after the twelve month contract. However, she added that she felt that she would like to stay longer to absorb American culture. The interviewer and the CIA branch woman looked at each other and smiled after the last remark. Jane had nailed it, hadn't she?

"And lastly, Jane, how did your telephone conversation with Dr. Gardner and his wife go?" Jane thought for a brief second.

"Fine! They both sounded such lovely people. Dr. Gardner has a sense of humour, Mrs. Gardner seemed keen to meet me, and their children, Teresa and Ryan, sound adorable!"

Steinberger closed the interview with a firm handshake telling Jane to expect a telephone call the following day. On the rail journey back to Leeds Jane felt slightly guilty as she sipped a cardboard cup of Costa Coffee. She hadn't been one hundred per cent honest during her interview. It was a question from Dr. Gardner that had concerned her. Why did he ask her about boys?

And specifically "What *type* of boys do you like, Jane?"

*

"So now that everything is in order, and Harry has given you his blessing so to speak, it's all systems go. Houston we have lift off!" Jenny was more excited than her daughter about the US trip.

"Oh, Mum, for goodness sake! I'm only going away for a year. Two at the most."

"Shall we go through the list again? Let's see . . . passport, airline tickets, joining details at JFK airport . . ." Jenny was cut short.

"Mum!" Jane looked at her mother like a teacher eyeing an unruly pupil. "Look, here, a complete list of everything I need!" Jane held three sheets of A4 paper stapled together at the top left hand corner. "Printed off yesterday, and double -checked!" Paul chuckled. "And dad has seen it and agreed it was fine!"

"OK, OK. I'm only trying to help. It's just . . ." Jenny hesitated, "it's just that I want to be sure you're going to be OK." She backed off, breathing out slowly.

"I know you do, but I'll be all right. I've spoken to the Gardner's and their children over the phone. There are seven other girls who'll be landing in New York at about the same time, and after the four day orientation course we'll all be on our way. I'll skype you twice a week and send a postcard from all of the places I visit. In fact I've printed off fifty home address labels – how organised is that?"

"Your dad and I will go down to London with you to make sure you get your flight, it's not far, and we could visit Aunt Maud in Bedford on the way back. Paul, what do you think?"

"If you like."

"No! Absolutely not! I've already got the train times to Kings Cross and the Piccadilly tube line goes all the way to Heathrow. One suitcase, a small rucsack and a handbag I can manage! It's an early start. The BA flight times are here. There's a Premier Inn at the airport and I've already booked a room. The other au pairs will land at JFK around the same time and we'll be met by Nancy who'll be holding a placard with Au.Pair.US on it. We're staying at the Belleclaire Hotel in Manhattan." There was silence. Both Paul and Jenny looked at Jane, mouths slightly agape for a few seconds. If they had any doubt at all about her ability to plan and organise, it had disappeared within the blink of an eye.

"Fine, you've convinced us that we don't need to worry. I shall sleep better tonight." Jenny took another sip of her red wine and laid her head back. Four days later, on 18 August, Jane was flying above the clouds over the Atlantic and enjoying a glass of orange juice and a light meal. A few hours later the 'fasten seat belt' signs came on, the captain made his usual announcements and the Boeing began to descend. Jane adjusted her watch to New York time – a quarter past twelve. They'd be landing in half an hour.

As planned, and promised, Nancy stood with her placard at one of the eight terminal exits at JFK. Jane made her way toward a group of five girls surrounding Nancy. 'Two more to arrive,' thought Jane as she approached her host. Nancy was holding a light blue lanyard with an ID tag.

"You must be Jane!" said Nancy, her teeth shining. Jane nodded. "Here, pop this name tag around your neck." The other four were already wearing theirs. "It'll tell us who you are, and gives us a sense of identity." Nancy quickly introduced the girls to Jane. "This is Jane from England. Jane, this is Nora and Dawn from France, Tina and Diane from Italy, and Olivia from Spain." All the girls shook Jane's hand briefly, genuinely pleased to meet her.

"Are we waiting for two more, Nancy? I read that there'd be eight of us," Jane asked.

"No, just one. One of the girls, Grace, phoned me yesterday. Decided not to come at the last minute. Oh, here comes the last one." Nancy scanned the human horizon and recognised Doreen from her photo. Doreen from Portugal was quickly introduced to the others, given her ID tag, and Nancy shepherded her flock towards the main exit.

A minibus with Winston Airport Shuttle written on the side was waiting. The driver, Hank, helped the girls with loading their luggage into the back of the vehicle. Nancy pranced around a bit like a mother-hen, clucking intently. Hank drove carefully towards Queens, crossed the East River and passed the imposing American Museum of Natural History in Central Park. Voices babbled in the minibus as the girls chatted excitedly.

Within forty minutes of leaving the airport the airport shuttle was pulling up outside The Belleclaire on West Seventy Seventh Street. Nancy jumped off first, then Hank lifted their luggage out and lined it up on the side-walk. Each of the girls collected their own case and walked into the foyer where Nancy had already sorted out their room keys.

"Listen, girls. I have your keys here. I'll give you thirty minutes to freshen up, do the minimum of unpacking and we'll meet in the conference room along the corridor." Nancy handed out the magnetic cards and each of the girls headed to their room. Jane unlocked her case. It didn't take long to take her clothes out, put them on hangers, and brush her hair. A change of blouse helped her feel fresher. She was looking forward to joining the group downstairs, but something nibbled away in her mind. Jane recalled Dr. Gardner's question about boys and she felt a little unsettled.

It made her wonder what the surgeon was like.

5

"Are you taking the kids to the park, Howard? I would like to finish an oil painting – it's been on the go for ages. Two hours and I'll be done." Amanda had sided away the plates and dishes, put them into the dishwasher, and generally tidied up. The regular home help-come-cleaner, Katie, came in on Mondays and Thursdays but not weekends. It was Saturday and the sun was shining brightly. They'd been to the shopping mall to look at some clothes for Teresa and Ryan, then had coffee and do-nuts in Starbucks. Amanda, who always liked to dress well, was wearing a light blue crew neck sweater, seamed leggings and wedge shoes. Her blonde hair was tied up in a ponytail, a pearl necklace hung around her slim neck and she wore a small pair of gold earrings.

"OK, if I have to. You and your hobby. Painting! I never really get to see the finished articles. And when did you last sell one?" Howard smiled at his wife as he made a few digs, but Amanda let it wash over her like a thick coat of paint.

"I didn't think you were interested! I'll give you a private showing sometime! And, I've sold two this year. One of the psychiatrists at the hospital bought one for 250$. Said it was an investment. One day I might be famous and it could be worth thousands!"

"Will you two stop bickering, we want to go to the park, don't we Rye?" Teresa chirped up.

"Sure do. Come on, let's go!" said Ryan proudly wearing his new dark blue jacket.

"Do you two realise that by this time next week your new nanny will be here? Guess who'll be looking after you, then!" Amanda chipped in. Howard sighed. It would at least give him more time to get onto the golf course, spend less time reading goodnight stories to them, and enable him to get out walking. He loved the outdoors, doing real walking in the forests, not the sort of things he could easily do with the kids. His favourite place was Muir Woods National Monument, twelve miles north of the Golden Gate bridge. It was in a secluded canyon with a myriad of hiking trails. Giant redwoods surrounded the walkers who passed between them, their trunks piercing the sky. Although he and Amanda loved each other, they'd always had an agreement that they'd give each other space. She enjoyed her watercolour painting, he loved golf and what he called 'trekking.' Decent boots, a wind-proof jacket, and his camera and binoculars were all he needed for a few hours in the fresh air.

"Yes, yippee!" shouted Teresa. "I'm really looking forward to meeting Jane. I wonder if she looks anything like Tarzan's girlfriend?" Howard had read some Edgar Rice Burroughs stories to his daughter and she'd loved them.

"Stop it!" said her mum. "You've seen the photograph of her and I couldn't imagine her living in the jungle with Tarzan! She sounded nice over the phone, too. Jane will be great, it's just what we need as a family, isn't it dear?" Howard smiled but said nothing.

"Come on kids, let's hit the trail! Hope the ice cream man is still there!" Ryan and Teresa were ready. They kissed their mum goodbye and followed Howard out to their black Audi Q7 parked on the drive. They jumped into the back and fastened their seat belts. "Be back in a couple of hours," he shouted to Amanda as he reversed off the brick paved drive and headed out of Adair Way towards Corona Heights Park. He blew her a kiss as they drove off.

Once upstairs Amanda got changed. She slipped out of her top and pants and put on a well worn, paint - splashed smock over a clean tee shirt. Dark grey jogging bottoms covered her long, shapely legs. The studio was one of the bedrooms at the back of the house, completely kitted out with a solid table against one wall, an easel, and shelving that held brushes, pots of paint and every conceivable artist's accessory. In a corner there was a tall, deep locker that held several finished paintings. The grey metal container was kept closed, a four digit padlock guarding the contents. Amanda wanted to finish a painting she called 'Despair'.

'Despair' showed a man hanging from a bridge, a dog lead around his neck suspending his limp body. His eyes were red, his swollen tongue was black. The lower part of his body was naked, socks around his ankles, one shoe was missing. Amanda wanted to touch up the metal bridge to show dark green paint flaking off the iron parapet, and darken the background . . . rain laden clouds threatening to soak the body. Her right hand moved as if conducting an orchestra, left to right, up and down. Her hobby was Amanda's method to relax. The time passed quickly. Amanda had made coffee around half past three, become thoroughly involved with 'Despair', and then just after four o'clock heard the front door opening.

"Mummy, Mummy, we're back!" Amanda quickly cleaned her brush, carefully pulled the painting down off the easel, and placed it in the locker. She shouted down that she'd only be a minute. Amanda was pleased with her painting; it gave her satisfaction.

The children's faces were ruddy. Tired out and ready for their tea, hugs were exchanged, Howard giving Amanda an extra squeeze as he kissed her.

"Hi, finished your painting?" Amanda smiled and nodded. She didn't need to say any more. "We've had a great time, haven't we kids? Ice cream all round, too!"

"Yes, daddy took us to the Bi-Rite creamery for ice cream and I had balsamic strawberry and Rye had honey lavender!" screamed Teresa with excitement. But Howard was a little concerned at the way Amanda looked at him.

"Are you OK, honey?" Her face was pale.

"Yes, I'm fine. I'll put the kettle on and make coffee," replied Amanda as she went into the kitchen. She hadn't taken her smock off . . . red, green and black paint streaks were smeared down the front.

And her fingerprints were visible at the sides where she'd held herself tightly.

*

"Girls, please!" Nancy had to raise her voice above the chattering of the au pairs. "I know we've nearly finished for the day, and tomorrow's the last day before you all leave the nest. We need to go through a few more items before we have a Q and A session to round off. So can we concentrate for another hour?" The girls were in a good mood. Two full days of taking notes, role play, and hints and tips from Nancy on 'how to be the perfect nanny' had put them in high spirits. They'd got to know each other well and Nancy had told them on several occasions how pleased she was with the group. They'd completed three written exams and all got marks over 72%. The Q and A session was a lively affair.

"What happens if I don't like the children?"

"Supposing their dad gets flirty?"

"Can I refuse to help with their homework?"

"Am I insured to drive the kids anywhere?"

"What happens if I'm ill?"

The questions went on. Nancy handled each one like a politician, sometimes giving a direct answer, but usually replying with "on the one hand . . . however, on the other . . ." Each of the girls chipped in with their view on a matter, which was useful, and left everyone satisfied with the responses.

"Remember, before you leave here to catch your flights to various destinations, you'll have the name and phone number of your Counsellor who should always be your first contact if you have any query. If any matter can't be resolved over the phone, you can always meet with her to discuss it. She can also put you in contact with other au pairs in the area." Nancy hesitated. "Can I mention another matter that none of you have raised. It concerns boyfriends."

Nancy went on to tell the girls about an incident where a complaint was made to the company and the au pair was asked to leave the next day.

"Mama mia!" uttered Olivia in her Spanish accent, looking around her at the others. They grinned.

"But I don't expect that from any of you!" Nancy looked at each of the girls. "Is that clear?"

"Yes, Oui, Si!" they chirped, sounding like a group of mischievous girls in the first form at secondary school. Nancy smiled.

"OK, OK. But I'm serious. Any boys, be diplomatic, tell the parents. Don't let boyfriends interfere in any way with your role. You will have free time . . . see your friends then. Remember, the parents are paying you, providing you with a small car for you to use, and generally helping you integrate into the American way of life. Don't abuse it!"

That evening over dinner in the hotel the girls chatted about the day's events. Tina seemed to be the joker in the pack, making fun of being caught red handed, or red faced, with a boy. Tomorrow lunchtime they'd be taken back to JFK on the shuttle bus to board flights to their final destinations. For Jane it was San Francisco. She'd checked her itinerary. Five hours and thirty seven minutes of aircraft seat hugging, on board meals and entertainment courtesy of American Airlines. And some sleep. Perhaps.

After a light brunch, the orientation course complete, full details of their destination families checked, contact numbers provided, the girls were as ready as they'd ever be. As usual, Nancy mother-henned them into the minibus, and on the return trip to JFK the girls had a whip round for their driver at Jane's suggestion. After all, American workers lived on tips she'd read somewhere, so why not their driver?

Hank was chuffed to get the gratuity, and the girls enjoyed his 'Gee, thanks, gals!' retort. Nancy wished them every success and looked forward to feedback once they'd settled in. All of the girls gently kissed each other as they headed for their respective gates. Jane's flight was leaving from gate 67 in just over two hours. Time to check in and get a coffee, use the washroom, buy a newspaper. She put her rucsack through into the hold with her suitcase.

As she sat sipping her Starbuck's, Jane scanned *The New York Times.* World news . . . European reports . . . political spin . . . west coast news. 'Body found in wooded San Francisco area.' Jane read the reporter's comments.

A body has been found in a wooded area north of San Francisco by two hikers who were on a walking and photographic vacation. Police believe the body had been laid in a shallow grave for about three months. SFPD are following up on a Missing Persons list. An outline of Texas is tattooed on the left shoulder blade. Anyone with any information is asked to contact SFPD on 415-315-2400 or email SFPDCentralStation@sfgov.org

6

A hundred and ten miles from San Francisco a Chevrolet compact headed south on route 101. Two young men, Andrew and James, both in their twenties, needed coffee. The fuel tank was low, the needle showed less than a quarter full. John Prine was on a CD singing one of his country songs – 'Sam Stone.' Andrew sang along to it . . . *'came home to his wife and family after serving in the conflict overseas . . .'* as James tried to sleep. A branch of the Union Bank of California had been robbed, the thirty thousand dollars in used notes now stashed in a golf bag in the car trunk. It had been so easy. Just walked in, ordered the customers out, and demanded the cash. No argument from the scared staff, bundles of one hundred dollar bills quickly put into cotton bags and brought round to the front of the cashier's desk. By the time they'd left the bank an alarm bell was ringing in the nearby police station, but about thirty seconds too late. Andrew kept singing to the radio . . . *'and the time that he served, had shattered all his nerve, and left a little shrapnel in his knee . . .'*

"Hey, there's a service station up ahead!" shouted Andrew, tossing his pony tail backwards. "Hey, Jimmy, wake up, I can smell coffee!" Andrew's passenger began to rouse himself, stretching arms and legs as if they were elastic.

"OK, Andy, no need to scream about it! I'm awake." Jimmy sat up and flicked his gelled black hair as he looked in the mirror on the sun visor. "I need food, too. Robbing banks is hungry work!" They both laughed. The car eased into the car park next to a McDonald's golden arches sign. Burgers and French fries would be fine, diet Coke to wash it down. Andy and Jimmy got out, locking and checking the doors and trunk before heading into the restaurant. It wasn't too busy, and they could see the car from a window seat. Jimmy put the tray down between them and the two soon began to munch on the mountain of molten cheese, fried burger, onion slice, tomato and shredded lettuce. Two hands were needed to hold the burgers. French fries, lathered in ketchup, were eaten in bunches. No words were spoken. Andy looked at his partner and smiled, a self satisfied reassuring smile through those green eyes of his. Smug.

"What are you going to do with your half?" asked Jimmy after a few minutes.

"Dunno. Haven't really thought about it. Maybe another car. I fancy a Mustang, red with white wall tyres. Perhaps a vacation somewhere. Find a chick, spend some on her. What about you?"

"Yes, pick up a bird. Treat her to a decent beefburger, you know, with extra cheese and pickle." Jimmy chuckled. Throwing their scrunched napkins onto empty plates, and gurgling the last of their cola drinks, Andy and Jimmy left. Putting on their sunglasses they walked across to the Chevvy and got in. The day was hot and the air-con blew a welcome breeze into their faces within seconds. They refuelled at one of the Exxon pumps, Andy paid cash, and they slowly drove away with just enough gas to get them back.

"Oh, shit!" said Jimmy looking in the rear view mirror. A police cruiser was right behind.

"For goodness sake stay calm!" The red and blue lights came on. Jimmy wondered whether to spin the drive wheels and take a chance on out-running the cops. "Pull over, just bloody pull over!" demanded Andy. The Chevvy pulled in, Jimmy lowered the window. A burly officer from the California State Patrol bent down to look first at Jimmy, then at Andy. Jimmy could smell his spearmint breath.

"Good afternoon, gentlemen. And where are you headed?" Jimmy gulped but stayed cool.

"San Francisco, officer. Is there a problem?"

"Yes. Your nearside brake light is out. Make sure you get it fixed when you get to Frisco."

"Of course, sorry about that. I'm certain it was OK this

morning. Sure thing, officer." Jimmy smiled. Andy did, too. The Chevvy drove away as Jimmy turned the air-con up.

"Holy smoke. I nearly saw my burger and fries again!" admitted Andy. They'd be in Frisco in an hour and a half. Time to grab the golf bag out of the trunk, share the cash, and dump the stolen car.

And Andy had to be back at work in a couple of hours.

*

The tyres of the American Airlines flight to SFO screeched on warm tarmac, wisps of blue-grey smoke floating up into the afternoon air. Jane had enjoyed the flight, watched a Tom Cruise movie, and managed a couple of hours sleep. She had texted Amanda before she left New York to confirm her departure details and her ETA. Amanda had replied to let Jane know she'd be waiting for her, with Jane's name on an ipad. The luggage came round on the carousel as Jane collected her suitcase first, then the rucsack. She'd been warned to be aware of pickpockets by her mum . . . at least a million times. There were some dodgy looking people standing near the carousel, hands in pockets, caps worn with the peak at the back. Jane ensured her items were stacked securely on the trolley as she headed toward the exit.

Following the yellow and black signs, Jane held her passport and visa at the ready, but it was an internal flight and they weren't needed. Security men and half a dozen armed police milled around, watching the comings and goings of a myriad of travellers. A few minutes later Jane walked out onto the large concourse, her eyes searching for her name. Placards and name signs fluttered like daffodils in the breeze, but then . . . there it was. *JANE LESTER.* An ipad was held aloft like a winning sports trophy by an attractive, slim woman dressed in a black suit with a pencil skirt. Jane could tell from the radiant smile that it was Amanda Howard.

"Jane!" Amanda lowered her ipad. "Welcome to our city by the bay!" She hugged the new au pair gently. "Do you want a hand with your trolley?"

"No, it's fine. Thank you." Jane hoisted the rucsack strap over he left shoulder.

"Did you have a good flight from New York?" Amanda, smiling, began to walk to the main door and Jane followed. She thought how well dressed she was, this woman who's two children she'd be caring for during the coming year. Silk white blouse, black leather shoes, a pearl necklace and matching earrings. Amanda's blonde hair was shoulder length, straight but neatly trimmed.

"No problems at all. It was fine." They were heading for a multi-storey car park where Amanda's Ford Taunus was parked.

"The children are going to love your accent, Jane! The way you just said ' it was fine'. Gee, they'll think it's great!" Jane giggled. Her accent? She hadn't given it any thought. But inevitably the English names for some things were going to be different . . . purse not handbag, windshield not windscreen, sidewalk not pavement, napkin not serviette, fanny not bottom, soda not lemonade . . . the list went on. In fact, Jane looked forward to learning a new vocabulary as well as experiencing new tastes and flavours. She might even pick up the American accent! How would friends in Keighley react to that? On the second car park level they arrived at Amanda's dark blue car. Jane lifted her suitcase into the trunk. "Get in, Jane!" chirped Amanda. "It's half an hour to Hayward, then we'll get you settled in before you meet the kids." Jane allowed Amanda to join the traffic and concentrate on getting in the correct lane before speaking.

"May I say that I'm looking forward to meeting Teresa and Ryan. They sounded bubbly over the phone and I'm sure I'll get to know them very quickly."

"Well, they want to meet you, too! Teresa has made a little heart from wrapping wool onto cardboard and put the letter J in the middle. Ryan's got a wooden rifle and he's written 'Jane' on the butt. You'll soon get to know them. It took our last nanny about three months before I sensed that she was OK with them."

"So you've had a nanny before? I don't think the agency mentioned that." Jane moved awkwardly on the leather seat.

"Yes. Caroline was her name, she came from Scotland. There was a little incident with Ryan – nothing major, but Howard thought it best we terminate her contract. Anyway, it's all over now." Amanda seemed to want to move away from the subject. "Do you have any questions before we get home? Anything you need clarifying?"

"No, not really." Jane hesitated and Amanda sensed something. She glanced at Jane. "Well, I read an article in the New York Times about a body being found in a wooded area near here. It's unsettled me a little, that's all." Jane's fingers were repeatedly intertwining. The tone of Amanda's voice changed slightly, became softer and reassuring.

"Yes, I heard about that. It's an area where Howard likes to trek. Rough paths and tracks going up through the woods. There's the occasional wooden cabin. All in all it's pretty remote, but I wouldn't worry about it, though. The police are quite smart and they'll soon find the killer."

'...soon find the killer...'

Jane suddenly saw a sign for Adair Way and breathed a sigh of relief. Thankful to be nearly at her new home for the next twelve months.

7

Jenny was busying herself in the kitchen of their Keighley semi-detached house. Despite cleaning out two food cupboards, checking the best before dates and piling some old tins ready to be taken to the tip, she couldn't help but think about Jane. She hadn't heard from her daughter for three days. Jenny tried not to worry; promised herself she wouldn't. But when a mother is separated from her daughter by thousands of miles in a strange country with an unknown family, the grey matter won't rest.

Paul had been upstairs working on a revised syllabus for GCSE Biology. He was on a committee that constantly sought to make the subject more interesting, liven it up, add some interest for the young enquiring minds. He had some ideas of his own. Add more practical elements to it, collect and draw plants and animals, have a day by a river to catch a jam jar full of wriggly things. But keep it simple. Get the pupils to want to ask questions. The why and wherefores of nature. Not see the subject as drudgery but develop enquiring minds. That's what it was all about *and* to develop more Ph.D. students in the future! He came into the kitchen where Jenny was kneeling down in a corner.

"Say one for me!" Paul quipped as he made for the kettle. "Fancy a drink?"

"Oh, please. My knees are killing me! I should have used your garden kneeling mat. Never mind, I've almost finished. Look at that pile! Fourteen tins out of date, eight packets of various dried foods and two Christmas puddings over ten years old!" Paul made two mugs of coffee .

"So why do we keep buying all this food when we don't eat it?" Paul asked, tongue in cheek.

"Cheeky monkey! It's you! I always have a list when we got to the supermarket, but somebody tops the trolley up with *'oh, I fancy some of this . . .'* Paul smiled. He knew

Jenny was right. He'd go off with a basket while she was in charge of the trolley. But as a scientist, Paul's policy was *'if it's tinned and the can isn't bulging, it's all right.'* And Jenny, as a non-scientist and downright sensible housewife, was of the opinion that if it was past it's 'use by' or 'sell by' date then there was only one option – it went out!

"Don't worry yourself over a few food items and dates," suggested Paul, "we'll watch what we buy in future, now that there's only the two of us." He could see Jenny was concerned about something.

"Yes, of course we will, but I can't help but wonder if Jane is all right? She did say she'd keep us updated but we've heard nothing for three days." Jenny was standing next to Paul, both hands clasped around the mug, being contemplative.

"She's fine! Surely you haven't forgotten how she got herself organised, sorted out the travel, told us about the induction course in New York . . . she'll be in San Francisco now. Met the family and getting to grips with looking after the children!" Paul wandered off. He had some thinking to do - biological in essence. Jenny put the packs into a strong plastic box that she lifted into the utility room ready for Paul to take to the local refuse facility tomorrow. She picked up her mobile phone. Jenny sent a text.

'Hi Jane, we're sure you're OK. Haven't heard from you since Monday. Hope all going well. Let us have your news when you can. Love you. Mum & Dad x'

Jane's mobile was switched off. She was busy with Teresa and Ryan. The children were lovely, and Jane was more than convinced she would establish a sound relationship with both of them. Howard, however, was working late, a difficult operation delaying him. Jane wouldn't get to meet him until later that evening. But by the time she'd helped with the children, had something to eat and finished her unpacking, Jane was feeling tired. After saying goodnight to the kids and Amanda, Jane went to her en-suite room. An early night was called for; the alarm clock was set for 6.30 am.

As Jane's eyelids became heavier she scanned the newspaper again. Although she didn't want to be reminded of it, the news of the body found in a wooded area north of the city jumped off the page again. The report specifically mentioned the Muir Woods National Monument. She'd check it out on her laptop tomorrow.

And Jane drifted off to sleep . . . her mobile still switched off.

*

McEnroe and Nelson Real Estate Agents on Twenty Fourth Street were busy. They'd handled ten sales of prime residential property per week on average during the past twelve months. Harry Nelson, the senior partner, was a happy man; profits were up fifteen per cent on the previous year. He'd started the business with Tommy McEnroe ten years ago and they'd recently celebrated a decade in business with a dinner for the staff in a restaurant on the first floor of the Mark Hopkins Hotel. Ten of them sat around an oval, mahogany table. During a brief speech over coffee and brandy, Harry thanked the staff, giving due credit to his partner, but especially to the salespersons and the office staff who had worked so hard to make it a bumper year for sales. He mentioned each by name and a small round of applause followed each 'thank you.' After the meal they adjourned to a side room where a free bar awaited them. Taxis had been ordered for midnight so no one had to worry about driving and risk being stopped by the SFPD.

Not only was there a decently stocked bar but Harry and Tommy had hired the best bartender in Frisco – Coke Solano. Coke worked freelance and his reputation for mixing the best whisky sour in the Bay area meant he was in high demand. His reverse flip of the whisky bottle, ice cube catch in the glass and the exact amount of lemon juice meant you always got the best drink in town. Some said he was related to Burt Reynolds – he had that mature, rugged look.

As the staff chatted, Harry and Tommy mingled amongst them, spending five or ten minutes with each one. Five guys and three girls giggled and sipped their drinks as talk of vacations, friends and the latest crazes, movies and record releases were discussed. It was early September. Halloween, Thanksgiving, which was always on the fourth Thursday in November, and Christmas, weren't far away. Talk of the Yuletide festive season didn't mean kicking snow off your boots before you went into the house. In fact there was only eight degrees Celsius difference between the average winter and summer temperatures. No cold winters here.

Two of the girls, Angelina and Bobbi, were talking about their plans for a forthcoming trip to Los Angeles whilst Lionel and Willy chatted about a new Harley Davidson motor bike that Lionel fancied. He'd seen a Road Glide in the showroom window of the dealer in down-town Frisco. The bike was amber-whisky in colour, had loads of extras, and if he got a decent bonus from the firm he'd be putting a deposit down pretty damn quick. Harry noticed one of the salesman, Andrew, staring out of the window across towards Alcatraz in the distance. Harry went over.

"Hi Andrew, you OK? You look deep in thought." Andrew, a smart young man with blue eyes, looked round quickly.

"Oh, hi! No, er, I mean, yes. Just thinking about things."

"Everything all right? Family. Home?" Harry focused on Andrew as he held his gaze.

"Sure, everything's fine," replied Andrew, glancing at his watch.

"Are you happy with working four days a week, Andrew? You know, you're one of our best salesmen. You could earn more doing an extra day, it's there if you want it." Harry was making an offer.

"Dunno. No, I'm OK with four days, thanks, Harry. I've got my ma to consider. She's not too well these days, and . . . since dad died . . ."

"Of course, of course." Harry swallowed, cursing himself for letting the conversation get to this. "You stick to the four days, that's not a problem. Hey, I must go and talk to Jerry over there," said Harry, making an excuse to extricate himself from Andrew's family matters. Andrew looked at his watch again. It was a fine watch. New. Large face, black numerals. And as he did so, Harry glanced back at the salesman, staring out of the window again, and wondered one thing.

'How could Andrew afford a watch like that?" It was a Jaeger-LeCoultre Rendezvous Night and Day Rose Gold and Diamond watch. A twenty thousand dollar timepiece.

Harry made a mental note to check Andrew's commission payments over the past year. He must be doing better than the senior partner thought.

*

"Hey, don't run, Ryan! We're not late, you'll be in time for school assembly." Jane was getting the kids into her car, a new four door, auto gearbox Honda Civic in light blue. The Honda had been ordered for Jane a week before she'd arrived and within a couple of days she'd felt confident about driving it. The built-in sat-nav was a boon; within seconds she could enter the address, automatically save it, and follow the map and the honey-sweet voice that told her when to take a left or when to make a U-turn. Her mother had fussed about driving on the 'wrong side of the road' and telling Jane that most Yankee drivers were useless. Jenny had her opinions about most things.

"I always sit in the front 'cos I'm older!" yelled Ryan.

"No you don't! We both get in the back!" squealed Teresa. Jane stayed calm.

"Now, listen up, and listen up good," she spoke softly,

surprised at the manner in which she'd got their attention. *'Listen up good'* . . . hadn't she heard that in some American film? "Today you're both in the back. It's our first trip to school and I'm going to see how well behaved you are." Jane had already made two dummy runs to Lexington Junior School with Amanda, a twenty minute drive away from Hayward. "If I think your both being good you can take turns in the front. If not, it's the back. OK?"

"Aw, shucks," chirped Ryan, "I wanna' be near the sat-nav and watch the map on the screen!"

"Don't give me that 'shucks' bit, Ryan. Come on, in now!" Jane's voice was firm and controlled as she held the back nearside door open for Teresa to get in. "And I'm not holding the doors open for you after today. Get it? You're both sensible young adults and you need to act like that." Ryan beamed.

"Gee, Jane, I don't think anybody's ever called me a young adult before! That's swell!" Both of the children hopped in, Teresa breathing in the newness of the interior . . . hints of apple wood, leather and vanilla. The rear door childproof locks were in the 'on' position as Jane closed her door firmly.

"OK, kids, safety belts on? A red light in front of me tells me Ryan hasn't fastened his yet." Ryan tugged at the belt and Jane heard the click as it snapped into place. "Let's go! School, here we come!" The children laughed as Jane reversed off the drive, put the gearshift into Drive and prepared to get to Lexington Junior as quickly and safely as possible.

"What about the radio, Jane? Mum always has the local Bay radio station on," quipped Ryan.

"No she didn't!" snapped his sister.

"It was on unless she had something important to say to us," retorted Ryan. "Traffic news, and important things happening in this area!" Jane coughed a pretend cough.

"Now listen, no arguing in this car. This car does not like arguments! We're going to name her *Serenity* and that means that when us three are in her there are no arguments!" Jane could so easily have said 'my car', but she wanted the children to feel some ownership. She'd used this psychology before when handling small children and it usually worked. There was a short silence.

"Sorry, Jane," said Ryan. Teresa echoed his words. "But what does serenity mean?" Jane could see his face in the rear view mirror, his little button nose screwed up.

"Serenity means peaceful or calm. Quiet, placid . . . no arguing." Jane looked at the digital car clock. Eleven minutes on the road, nine to go – all being well. After another short period without talking, Jane continued. "You said the radio was off unless your mother had something important to say to you? What did you mean . . . what sort of things?"

"Oh, just things about the family. Like if dad was having a bad time, or if we'd heard an argument they'd had and she wanted to tell us about it. Like it was over nothing at all and we needn't worry." Jane was slightly puzzled. She knew she had to be careful asking questions, especially so early in their relationship.

"Having a bad time? Does your dad have a bad time?" Jane's voice was mellow, gentle.

"Well, not really," replied Teresa, "but sometimes he gets angry over nothing. Mum has to tell him to calm down. He works long hours at the hospital . . . I think he gets stressed." Teresa's words sounded as if an adult was speaking them; her mother maybe? Jane pulled up alongside the kerb a few yards from the school gates, stopped the car and got out.

"OK, folks, we've arrived! Young adults out here!" She hugged Teresa and placed a firm hand on Ryan's shoulder. "You have a good day, you hear, and I'll collect you both at half past three this afternoon. Right where we're standing!" The kids were about to rush off when Jane spoke again. "And one more thing. Serenity also means keeping things between us!" She winked and they winked back. Jane watched them as they went into the school yard and headed for the main door. A black woman standing near the door gave Jane a wave as if to say 'hi, your new, aren't you?' Jane would make a point of getting to know her name. Maybe tomorrow?

Meanwhile, as Jane drove home she wondered what Teresa really meant . . . *'sometimes he gets angry over nothing.'*

8

It was true. Howard Gardner worked long hours. At 39 years of age he wasn't quite as agile as he was. Having moved from Baltimore General Hospital twelve years ago, two years before Priscilla died, his increased annual salary of nearly 300K dollars helped make up for the hard work he put in during the week. Cardiac surgery was a specialist field. A surgeon had to be more alert and focused than, say, the orthopaedic guys who pulled a few hips out of their sockets and glued new ones in – 'bone carpenters in hospital gowns' they were often called. No, the human heart and the associated arteries and veins was a delicate part of the human body. Working at 72 beats per minute on average, it was *the* organ that kept humans alive. Two thousand million beats in a lifetime, five hundred million litres of blood pumped.

By-pass surgery and cardiac implants had become routine, but he never took those operations for granted. Howard graduated from medical school at the age of 25, and he'd risen to become Head of Cardiac Surgery at the City Hospital. He loved his work and had a good team around him. The nursing staff, despite liking a joke and a prank from time to time, were dedicated. The 'work hard, play hard' motto should have been written on their foreheads. Gardner and Hudson's team, plus the nurses, had been together for three years. They knew each others skills and foibles during surgery. Rarely were words spoken, there was little need. Instruments, sutures, suction tubes, diathermy equipment, they were all on hand as soon as they were required. Chuck Hudson was growing in confidence. At 29 years of age he was learning his trade quickly. Howard Gardner was able to let Hudson perform some of the operations on his own but for the moment always stayed close by. Just in case. Hudson felt reassured when Dr. Gardner was there. Not intrusively, but near the operating table . . . to give advice if needed.

The nurses had become accustomed to Chuck Hudson being gay. In fact, although he'd felt insulted initially, he now took their comments with a smile. He didn't ignore them but went along with the idle banter. And as Hudson had not been seen with another man, in a 'relationship' way at least, nobody really got up tight about it. He was smart, well dressed and didn't smoke. He chewed gum and had perfect teeth. There was nothing not to like about the aspiring heart surgeon. And Karen, one of the OR nurses, still did not want to believe that Chuck Hudson wasn't interested in women.

"Some fine work there, Howard," said Hudson sipping his coffee in the OR staff room next to the doctors lounge at the end of another day. "That stent you placed so expertly should give that woman another five years at least." A dozen doctors and nurses relaxed as they wound down after a number of operations that had begun at 8.00 am. Gardner sometimes preferred to use the staff room instead of the 'Doctors only' lounge to mix with his team, to chat and bring a happy ending to their surgical labours. The nursing staff giggled seemingly about nothing at all. Howard munched on a crunchie bar, in need of a sugar fix. When he'd finished he knotted the wrapper and tossed into the paper bin three feet away.

"Thanks, Chuck. You did good, too, helping out the way you did. Won't be long before you'll be operating solo. But don't go looking for another job. OK? I need you here!"

"Nope. But, hey, I see you always knot your candy wrappers before you throw them away." Howard smiled.

"An old habit. I hate to see packets people have scrunched up slowly opening, in slow motion, filling a bin when they could have knotted it!" Howard looked at his Omega. "I'm off. Need to be in to say a proper 'hi' to our new au pair who arrived a couple of days ago. Her name's Jane and she's beautiful." Howard stood up, said his good-byes to those left in the staff room. As he walked out his cell phone rang. Checking the caller details he pressed the red button.

It wasn't important - he'd phone back later.

*

"Yes, Mum, I'm sorry! I know I ought to have called sooner but my feet have hardly touched the ground since I arrived! No, I don't leave my mobile phone on all the time. Do you have any idea how much it takes to care for two lively children, and help with their homework? And . . ." Jenny interrupted.

"Slow down, you'll burn yourself out talking to me, let alone helping the children! Now, take it easy! What are Teresa and Ryan like? Well behaved, I hope." Jane took a deep breath.

"Well . . . the kids are fine. Teresa can be mischievous but she's good at her homework. A bit untidy at times, but I'm working on getting her to sort out the drawers in her bedroom. Ryan, on the other hand, is straight talking, fun at times but hates homework. I've got to use a bit of psychology to get them to come round to my way of thinking, but it's early days."

"I'm sure you'll do a great job. What do they look like?" Jenny had pictured the two children in her minds eye. Curly haired all-American kids with freckles, just like she'd seen on adverts for popcorn.

"I'll send you some photos. I can send some with an email later. Of course photos don't give the whole story, but you'll see mischief in Teresa's blue eyes. Her blonde hair is like her mum's whilst Ryan has dark locks that are in need of a trim." Jane stopped herself, she could have gone on and on about the youngsters. "Listen, Mum, I need to go. I'll email you and dad."

"What about the parents? Are they nice?" Jenny persisted.

"Yes, good. I'm going now – I'll be in touch. Love you both. Bye." Jane knew she had to sever contact there and then. Her mum would have wanted lots of detail and Jane could pull that together and send an email tomorrow. Jane had always been able to talk to her mother, she was a good sounding board, but she begun to wonder if her mum should know about comments the children had made about their parents? About their arguments, Howard's anger – even mood swings? No, she would leave it. She did not want her mum worrying about family issues. Then there was the previous au pair, Caroline, who'd left before her contract expired. Amanda has said something about an incident between her and Ryan. But Jane knew her mother would be fretting over these incidents, and offering her daughter advice. No, she didn't need that right now. Jane could imagine the way the conversation would go . . . *"well, what I'd do if I was you is this . . ."*

Jane heard the children shout 'Daddy, Daddy!' as Howard walked through into the lounge where they were playing. Homework was finished, their supper nearly ready. Ryan was constructing a large *Lego* house with green and red bricks whilst Teresa was colouring an intricate parrot in her drawing book. Jane heard Amanda call upstairs.

"Jane, you there? Howard's home and would like to have a chat!" A chat? Hopefully nothing was wrong. Jane hadn't been there long. Because of his long work hours, Jane had to admit that she and Howard hadn't really made time for a conversation. He probably wanted to ensure all was well, didn't he? Jane came downstairs and entered the lounge where Howard was helping Ryan put the roof on the plastic bricked house.

"Hi, Jane, how's it going? Sorry I haven't made time to see if everything is OK. Amanda tells me you're happy with the children? Hey, let's pop into my study – leave the kids to it for a while." Howard held his right palm open to signal for Jane to go ahead. His study was the second door on the right in the large, open plan hall. The door was always kept locked. Even Katie, the twice weekly cleaner who also did the laundry, wasn't allowed in. "Take a seat." Howard pointed to a brown leather chair. "Tell me, Jane, how are you finding things here in San Francisco?" He smiled broadly. Jane tried to relax and took a deep breath.

"Everything is fine so far, Howard. I love the children with their odd little habits and I know I'm going to get on very well with them." So far so good, thought Jane.

"And the facilities here? Your room, the car, getting yourself around town?" Howard didn't take his brown eyes off the nanny. Jane noticed how dark his eyes appeared. She put it down to tiredness.

"Yes, it's all good. I love the Honda and I'm becoming accustomed to driving on the right hand side of the road. I must admit, though, the style of driving here is different from Yorkshire!" Howard maintained his smile and stayed silent, encouraging Jane to continue. He raised his eyebrows. "My room is great, plenty of space for all my things, and a good mobile phone signal!"

"Is there anything you're thinking of doing whilst you're here in California? You can attend a college course, you may know that. Maybe business studies, or fashion, or . . ."

"I'd like to do photography!" Jane chirped up excitedly.

"Sounds great! I'll get Amanda to make some enquiries at City College of San Francisco and see when you can start. The South East campus is on Oakdale Avenue. They do photography there. We also want you to have a good social life during your stay. You'll go crazy looking after the kids all of the time, you need to make friends while you're here. Amanda has some friends with daughters and she can introduce you." Jane didn't reply as she had images of mad Saturday nights out on the town. "And what about boys? Did you have a boyfriend when you left Yorkshire?" He smiled. Dr. Gardner's words from several weeks ago came ringing back in her ears. Why the hell was he asking her about boys? Jane composed herself and breathed out quietly and slowly.

"Yes, I had a boyfriend. His name's Harry but we decided that we'd split for a while. I'll probably keep in touch though." Jane didn't know where this part of the conversation was going. Howard detected a change in body language.

"OK, that's fine. None of my business really – just interested. Hey, look at the time . . ." He changed the subject quickly and stood up. Howard walked to the study door. "Come on, Jane, time to eat!" Jane got up, smoothed her skirt down and followed Howard. As she got to the door he stepped in her way. "And if there is anything I can help you with, you just have to ask."

9

You're making progress, but it is slow. This is a long tunnel you're walking through and we're not going to get to the end today. Some things may not be not clear. It's dark. Never mind. Walking along the tunnel is a challenge, the ground feels heavy, mud-like. Keep lifting your feet, but don't plod. Ease each foot upwards and forwards purposefully. You'll have to concentrate at first but soon it will become easier. Can you feel that now? You can. Good.

You seem concerned. Don't be, try to breathe easily. Relax. What are you thinking about now? OK, but we can explore that another time. Do not worry about it. These things happen.

After what you've told me I think we ought to wind down now. There are a number of issues that we can work on over the coming weeks. But remember, the tunnel is a long one and you won't come out of the other end until you have confronted the matters weighing on your mind. There will be times when you will feel upset, but you've got to be strong. Take another drink of water. Get off the couch slowly."

The client eased their left leg off the edge of the leather couch and stood up.

"I'll see you again next week. Thursday at 7.00 pm. Meanwhile, continue to take the medication I've prescribed. Two tablets twice a day with food. Be yourself and try to avoid situations that you find stressful."

They walked to the door. The client left.

10

"Come on Ryan, you can work that out. Which is the greater – three quarters or seven tenths?" Jane was in schoolmistress mode. "No, you don't just guess! Look at it from a percentage point of view. What's three quarters as a percentage?" Ryan nibbled on the end of a ballpoint pen.

"Why, it's seventy five percent." He beamed as if he'd discovered a new continent.

"So, what's seven tenths as a percentage?" Jane looked at him.

"Seventy! Of course, it's three quarters . . . that's bigger!" Ryan had his light-bulb moment.

"Well done! You see it's not that difficult, is it? Let's try another. If apples are twenty cents each and I buy six, and oranges are thirty cents each, how many oranges can I get if I have three dollars in my pocket?" Ryan grimaced. He took his pen and began to calculate. Jane saw him write down six multiplied by twenty. Result 120. He paused, changing the total to one dollar and twenty cents. The gnarled end of the pen was between his teeth again. Jane gave him time to ponder.

"I'm stuck! It's about ten oranges, I think." His button nose moved up and down in time with his eyebrows.

"You can't just say 'about ten, I think!' This is maths. It's an accurate subject!"

"We call it math. Not maths. Americans leave the 's' off the end. You don't know how to use some words!" He sounded clever. Jane responded promptly.

"Now then, Ryan. That's rude. Are you sorry?" She looked at him. He nodded as he held his head down. She could see he was. "OK, so what's three dollars less the one dollar and twenty cents you spent on the apples?"

"One dollar, eighty cents!"

"Good! So . . . ?" He wrote down one hundred and eighty and divided it by thirty.

"Six! It's six! Six oranges and six apples!" Ryan had

scaled his Mount Everest. "Thank you, Jane, I understand that now!" Jane left Ryan to tackle three other math problems while she attended to Teresa. She was struggling with words.

"Jane, I'm supposed to fill in the blank spaces to find the names of animals and it's difficult. Look here. Question number one says 'I am a mammal and I swim in the sea. Answer is D space L space H space N. It isn't a shark, is it?" Jane smiled at Teresa.

"No, it isn't. Try putting other letters in the spaces. So, you've got a D then an L. You may have a vowel, that's A, E, I, O or U, in the space." Teresa frowned, her small brain working away. Jane could tell it was hard for her but didn't interrupt. After a few more seconds Teresa shouted out.

"O! It's O because it gives you dolphin. D O L then the rest of it!" Jane told her how pleased she was. "Let me try the next one. It says 'I am a canine with a good sense of smell.'" Jane noticed B-O-D-O-N-. "What's a canine?" asked Teresa.

"It's a dog. Their big teeth are called canines. That's where we get our tooth name from – we have canine teeth . . ." Jane pointed to her right canine.

"Vowels don't fit. You can't put a vowel between B and O can you? Unless it's a BOO something!"Teresa giggled. A simple but lovely sounding little chirp like a sparrow. "Wait! It's bloodhound! Hurrah!" She was pleased with herself. Jane told Teresa she'd done well, it was important to encourage her at this stage. "I want to finish these three now. Can I?" Teresa was keen to complete her homework assignment.

"OK. I'm going to leave you two alone for five more minutes, then I'll be back." Jane left to pop up to her own room. She wanted to check on the schedule for the rest of the week. The children were due to stay on at school for an extra hour on Thursday and Amanda had left Jane two brochures on SF colleges and their courses. As Jane was about to walk upstairs she noticed a copy of the Chronicle with the date – 9 September – on a side table. A front page headline jumped off the page at her.

Headless Torso Found in Woods
by reporter Tom Lederer

SFPD have confirmed that they are having problems in identifying the decapitated body, aged between twenty and thirty, found at Muir Woods National Monument on 21 August. The head is still missing, and fingerprinting is virtually impossible owing to the decomposition of the body. The dead man was wearing light blue Wrangler jeans and brown boots but no shirt. The County Coroner, Abraham Sykes, estimates the body has been in the woods for four months, plus or minus a fortnight. The wrists were tied behind the body with green and white duct tape.

A tattoo of the state of Texas on the left shoulder blade may be a clue to the origin of the person. SFPD have told the Chronicle that they are in touch with the Texas state police and going through a number of Missing Persons lists. SFPD are asking anyone with information to call them on 415-315-2400. In particular, the police would like to talk to hikers who regularly use Muir Woods and may have been in the area during April or May. Anything out of the ordinary, vehicles parked in unusual places or individuals acting in an odd manner would be of interest to SFPD.

Anyone in the San Francisco area who may know of a missing male that matches any of the above description should call the SFPD number or email
SFPDCentralStation@fsgov.org
Anonymity is assured.

Missing male? No one had told Jane the body was that of a male! She had assumed it was a woman. Weren't all the bodies she read about in crime novels of young women who'd been out late at night on their own . . . followed by a maniac hell bent on squeezing the life out of her? Fingers tight around the throat, the victim's eyes bulging, tongue turning blue.

Obviously not.

*

Jane had just dropped the children off at the school gates. Homework was completed, their lunch packs filled, clean handkerchiefs pocketed, shoes polished. Jane had been looking after them for two weeks now and she was pleased at the development of their relationship. They took turns to sit in the front of the Honda Civic; Jane had suggested this 'alternate days in the front seat' strategy to Amanda first, who agreed without discussion. Jane felt that, with some of her initiatives being readily agreed to, life was going to be relatively easy over the next eleven months. But chickens were not being counted before they had hatched and it was still early days in the Gardner household.

As Jane turned to leave the school gates she spotted the black woman again, checking the children into the building. The woman waved. Jane responded. But the wave from the school step was a beckoning one as if to say 'come over here and say hi.' Jane felt that she ought to be friendly. Entering the iron gates which were still open, she walked over to the main door of the building.

"Hi, you must be Jane? I've heard a lot about you from the Gardner kids!" Jane wondered for a second what the words 'heard a lot about you' meant? "My name's Liza Freeman. I'm the caretaker here. Ain't you from England?"

"Yes, that's right. And I hope what you've heard has been all right?" Jane smiled but inwardly wondered what was coming next.

"Of course it has! Them two kids, why, they good as gold. Two good parents an' all. Pity the last au pair didn't stay long. She seemed OK to me. I think dem kids loved her but, well, something didn't work out for 'em. I don't know what happened, but every time I asks them they just clam up." Jane listened carefully but had no intention of passing a comment. "They say you's good at numbers an' words. Ya know, American kids these days, they gotta learn to read and write properly, then get a good education if they're gonna get a good job in this country. So, let me wish you good luck an' all. No doubt our paths will cross from time to time. And let me say this . . ." Liza hesitated and lowered her voice. "You can trust me, Jane. If there's anything I can help with . . . just ask." Right at that moment, Jane trusted her as far as she could throw her twenty stone frame.

"Liza, you're sweet. Thank you so much. I think I'm going to be OK but if there's anything, I'll let you know." With that Jane turned on her heels and headed for her car. She sensed that the eyes of Liza were boring a hole into the back of her head. How could she trust a woman that she didn't know? Maybe Jane would 'test the water.' Tell Liza something unimportant and innocuous to see if it got around the other au pairs or parents? If anything got fed back to her she'd know it was Liza that had let it out. The more Jane considered that, the more of a potential little game it could become. Jane would give it a try - this large black woman just might be an ally. After all Jane had so much more to learn. And would Teresa and Ryan clam up if Jane asked them about the previous au pair?

She would find out. But not just yet.

*

Jane was in her room putting away some clothes that she had washed and dried. It was Wednesday, the one day of the week that Amanda took off from her busy private practice. The day was mild with large patches of baby blue sky as Jane heard a gentle knock on the door. It was Amanda.

"Hi, come on in," said Jane as she closed the last drawer. Amanda was smartly dressed as usual – v-neck beige sweater, designer pants in yellow, and slip ons. A thin gold necklace with a small gold teddy bear hung around her slim neck.

"Hi, Jane. How are you getting on? I mean, really getting on? Is everything OK for you?"

"Oh, yes, it's fine. Thank you." Jane wondered if Amanda had an ulterior motive, or if Howard had made any comments.

"Good. We want you to be happy here, to enjoy your stay in America. You've kept yourself to yourself since you arrived but I think it would be good to make some friends. Socialise. What do you think?" Amanda had positioned herself on the side of the bed at an angle of forty five degrees towards Jane . . . non threatening, casual, relaxing. Jane supposed that was how she made contact with her patients. Amanda's voice was soft but firm.

"Why yes, that sounds fine," said Jane. "Howard said you've got some friends who have daughters."

"Did he now?" Amanda hesitated as if it came as a surprise but kept her poise. "Well, he's correct. Vida Honeywell has a daughter, Marie, who's your age and Rosemary Gless has a girl, Samantha, a year older. They both work down town, one for a lawyer, the other for a real estate agent and each has a small apartment they're renting. Maybe you'd like to meet them this week-end?" Jane felt obliged to say 'yes.'

"That sounds great!" replied Jane, hoping her smile looked genuine. "Where and when?"

"I've already spoken to Vida and Rosemary. The girls usually go down to Fisherman's Wharf on a Saturday morning. Pier 39 is a lovely spot with boutiques, restaurants, bars and cafes. There's even a shop that sells things for left handed people! Howard could run you down if you want?"

"No, I'd like to drive myself. It would be a challenge. The sat-nav will get me there. What time?"

"About ten thirty. There's a cafe called Leo's. I'll suggest the two girls meet you there!" Jane smiled and glanced at her open laptop. "I can see you've got things to do so I'll leave you to it." Amanda moved toward the door. "By the way, you may have heard whispers about the last au pair we had, Caroline. I told you that she'd left before her contract expired. It wasn't anything serious, but she had a boyfriend that Howard simply didn't like. She brought him round here one evening and they argued. He ended up calling Howard names before walking out. I guess what I'm saying is that if you find yourself a young man, be careful. There are some nice guys about, but some oddballs, too." Amanda closed the door gently.

Jane sat at a small desk on the far side of her room and looked out at a clear Californian sky. She tried to analyse what Amanda had said. Maybe Howard didn't tell his wife *everything*? Did Howard have something against au pair boyfriends after his experience with Caroline? Didn't Amanda say previously that Caroline had left because of some issue with Ryan?

Jane was looking forward to meeting Marie and Samantha, but she'd be careful what she said. Very careful indeed.

11

"Hi Andy. So what did you do with your share of the thirty thou?" asked Jimmy.

"Some new clothes. I needed a leather jacket. The other one I had was stolen from that club down town. The girl in the cloakroom denied I'd ever left it with her. Bitch! I felt like stuffing the ticket right up her nose. I spoke to the manager. Huh, a kid younger than me! Said he'd keep an eye out for it. Liar! If I catch anyone wearing it I'll knife 'em! My new jacket ain't going into no cloakroom. It's quality leather, Turkish made, and it cost me eight thou." Jimmy whistled long and slow. "I might use the rest to buy that bike. Saw one at the dealers. Fast. Sleek. Might give my ma some, too. An' you?"

"Just gonna stash it for now. Fifteen thou will last me for a while but we ought to think about our next job. There's a small bank up north that might be worth looking at. I can get a car again, something quick. Might even have a golf bag in the trunk!" Jimmy grinned; his bubble gum chewed rapidly. "Christmas ain't far off. Need some extra cash for that." He paused. "How's work going?"

"OK. Been busy with houses. You know." Andy looked at his expensive watch, purchased with the proceeds of a former heist. "Need to go . . . things to do." Andy stood up, straightened his tie, polished his shoes on the back of each trouser leg and tossed a ten dollar bill on the table. Coffee had been good. Leo's never let you down when it came to coffee.

Andy strode out into the sunshine, a light breeze coming off the ocean, blowing across Alcatraz that stood forlornly out in the bay.

*

Saturday morning was cloudy. The dark red paintwork of the Golden Gate bridge seemed to be duller than usual.

Jane had the whole weekend off, her one in four. Amanda had confirmed the meeting with Marie and Samantha. Leo's at 10.30 am. She'd had a light breakfast before Howard and Amanda were up and about, and checked on the children. Jane had free run of the house, at least as far as most activities were concerned. Amanda's art room was locked when she wasn't using it, and Howard kept his study secure. They'd told Jane that it was always the case, and had nothing to do with her being in the house. Clearly they didn't want her to feel those doors were locked only since she'd arrived. Jane did wonder if there'd been a problem when Caroline was there. Perhaps an item had gone missing, or something had been moved. A diary opened . . . a folder accidentally left open?

"Good morning, Jane!" Amanda breezed into the kitchen, hair tied up in a pony tail. She was wearing a loose, paint - flicked sweater and baggy jogging bottoms. Seeing Jane's expression Amanda smiled.

"I'm going to do some painting. Got one to finish off and I may exhibit two others soon. There's a gallery in town that allows artists to show their paintings every other month. Are you looking forward to seeing the girls?"

"Absolutely! From what you've told me they seem a bunch of fun. I can't wait to see what they're up to and hearing about their jobs."

"Are you sure you want to drive to Pier 39? As I said, Howard can take you and you could catch a bus back. The buses are pretty frequent between here and down town Frisco." Amanda didn't want Jane to have any problems on what would be her first venture into town.

"No. I'll be fine. Sat-nav has parking places listed. It'll be an adventure. If I get lost I'll phone you." I've got both of your private cell phone numbers. Only to be used if I'm desperate!" Amanda and her husband each had two mobile, phones. One private, the other for her practice and his hospital work. "See you later, Amanda, and enjoy your painting!" She grabbed her handbag and keys and got into the Honda. Her keyring had a front door key on it;

Amanda had told Jane when she first arrived that she could come and go as she pleased, and common sense should prevail on aspects of entering quietly if she came back late.

The destination was entered on the GPS. Reversing onto Adair Way, the sta-nav voice kicked in. Jane had the local radio station on low volume. Country music played. Kris Kristofferson was telling her about some guy *'wasted on the sidewalk in his jacket and his jeans.'* The run to Pier 39 was going to take under half an hour, and Jane felt pleased that she getting used to driving on the right hand side of the road. A blue and white sign with a large P indicated the parking area a few minutes from the pier. There was a space between a yellow Hyundai and a silver Qashqai. Her car slotted in nicely. Gear shift into P, handbrake on, engine off. She breathed a sigh of relief as she undid her safety belt. The day was brightening up, clouds had drifted away and the mist that often hangs over the bay area had cleared. All she had to do now was find the girls. She checked her watch. 10.25 am. Perfect. Suddenly she heard a voice.

"Hi, you must be Jane?" An attractive dark haired girl was stood next to her. "I'm Sam. Hi! Marie is over here." Sam pointed to a table under a wide parasol in the front of Leo's cafe. Marie stood up and, smiling broadly, gently shook Jane's hand.

"Jane, good to meet you! Welcome to Frisco, the city by the bay. The city of flower power – at least it used to be!" Sam pulled a chair out for Jane. "How are you getting on with the family . . . and the kids?" Jane remembered the promise to herself.

"Great! I love the children and of course their parents are *really* nice."

"Coffee?" interrupted Sam. "What do you like? Espresso, filter, latte . . ."

"Filter is fine, with hot milk if possible." Marie caught the waiter's eye and ordered for the three of them. Jane decided to take the initiative with the conversation, partly to avoid any more searching questions on the Gardner family.

"So one of you works for a real estate agent and the other for a lawyer. Let me guess . . . Sam you're with the lawyer. Marie you're in real estate." A complete guess but Jane prayed it was correct.

"Yep! Dead right! Who told you? Amanda?" said Sam. Jane shook her head and grinned.

"Call it intuition." She had to be sure not to say something inappropriate. Sam had that look of someone whom she could visualise in a lawyers office. Smart, good poise, clear diction, pleasant manners . . . Marie on the other hand was, well, ordinary by comparison. A plain face, short hair, a few freckles, one eyebrow slightly higher than the other . . . "No, a pure guess!" They all giggled like junior school girls. The waiter arrived with their order and placed the cups on the round, wooden table.

"So, Jane, you've replaced the other girl. Carol or somebody. Not sure what happened there, but she soon went after the little incident." Jane didn't reply to Marie's comment but sipped her filter coffee. It tasted good. "I know Dr. Gardner doesn't stand any nonsense. Mom said it was his decision to get rid of her. I only met her once, at a garden party."

"Caroline, her name was Caroline. No, I don't know what happened," Jane volunteered. She did not wish to get into a discussion on who said what to who. In any event, she didn't even know. Changing the subject she said, "This coffee is good!" Perhaps Sam and Marie were fishing; had their mothers put them up to it? Come to think of it, just who arranged the plan to have coffee? Jane thought it was Amanda, but perhaps Vida or Rosemary had proposed it? Either way, diplomacy was the key right now. Sam chirped up.

"Yes, Leo's is the best by far. Hey, that's good slogan for them! 'Leo's is best by far' or . . . 'Get the lion's share at Leo's.'" Again, they chuckled as if it were the end of a school term.

"But really, how are things going in Adair Way, Jane?" Marie was drawing her. Jane had to respond.

"They're fine. I'm getting to know Teresa and Ryan. She's a sweetie and Ryan is a typical boy! We do homework together and they're making good progress. Howard and Amanda let me get on with things, you know – the washing and ironing, taking the kids to school, helping in the kitchen and so on. Howard's also helping with suggestions on a college course. Amanda gave me two brochures that I haven't really looked at yet. I'd like to do photography. I think the City College may have something appropriate." Jane hoped that her summary was sufficient to keep the girls content for now. "But hey, that's enough about me for now. Tell me about your lives in Frisco?"

Marie put her cup down and began to tell Jane all about her new boyfriend called Arty Jennings, and her work at the real estate agents on Twenty Fourth Street. McEnroe and Nelson was the name. She'd been there thirteen months and did a load of secretarial stuff, including filing and copying and helping clients with details on properties for sale. She enjoyed popular music, especially boy bands, and had a poster of David Beckham in his soccer kit on her bedroom wall at home. Marie filled in a few more gaps about her schooling and vacations to other parts of the west coast and then her enthusiasm for sharing all that with Jane seemed to wane. Sam filled the gap of silence.

"My life is fairly quiet, Jane. I love photography, too, and used to collect match-books. From cafes and restaurants, you know. Ma said it was a fire hazard so I stopped. I began at Hardy & Davison Lawyers about fifteen months ago after I graduated from High School. My pa knew a senior partner there and he got me in. Pa passed away a while back." Sam hesitated as she looked into her cup, but Jane didn't press for details right then. "Country is my favourite music and I adore Garth Brooks. Don't know anything about soccer . . . who's David Beckham?" Jane laughed again. "Why don't I pay for the coffees and we can take a walk around the pier?" Sam offered.

"Hey, good on you, Sam!" quipped Marie, her thumbs working overtime sending a text to someone on her smart-phone. Jane and Marie got up as Sam paid the waiter and slipped him a two dollar tip. He winked at her, more out of hope than anything else. Marie put her phone away but suddenly suggested that they ought have Jane's cell phone number. Jane gave her number and the other two entered it into their Contacts list. Jane had been given a US cell phone by Amanda making life easier for her. Jane put their numbers into her phone.

They walked on, past another cafe and a seafood restaurant right on the edge of the pier. A guy on a stall nearby was carving wooden plaques, the kind you put on the front of your house to let people know it was 'Dun Roamin' or 'Worlds End.' A craft shop selling hand made jewellery was close to the Left Hand shop. The girls took Jane in to see the array of left handed gadgets . . . scissors, can openers, rulers. Jane was so surprised that she almost wished she was left handed! The three continued to chat amiably when suddenly Sam suggested meeting up the next day. There was a fairground over the bridge in Sausalito with special events taking place.

"Can I bring Arty?" asked Marie, "he loves fairs! I think he holds the world record for eating the most toffee apples in one day!" Jane winced. What sort of a guy was Arty? Big and fat? Gross with puffed out cheeks? An Oliver Hardy lookalike?

"What about you, Sam? Boyfriend?" asked Jane. Sam shook her head.

"No, not at the moment. I'm not bothered just now. Why don't we meet here tomorrow? Same time, same place. I'll drive and you can leave your car here, Jane. Marie will get a bus from her place. What do you think?" Jane agreed. It was her week-end off so she may as well take advantage – start living a bit. "And I'll ask Arty to bring a friend from the office. There's a guy called

Andrew. He's nice."

*

"I don't want to go to school today!" Ryan was getting agitated on the first day of the week. "You have all the fun at the week-end. I wanted to go to the fair, too!" He sulked, his lower lip larger than normal. Ryan *did not* want to put his shoes on.

"Listen, Ryan, it was my week-end off." Her tone was soft. "You know – a break away from things here. I met with some people who your mum knows and they invited me to go to Sausalito. We could go sometime. I know so far I've only taken you to school and to the local park but maybe next week you, Teresa and I could visit somewhere like Muir Woods – take a picnic!" Jane was working overtime on her child psychology skills. He relented a little. "But you have to be good. Teresa has been a perfect example this morning. Up early, showered and dressed, and . . ." Jane hesitated for effect, "has been reading her set book for this term – *Oliver Twist*."

"OK," he replied slowly sounding like the cartoon character Sylvester. "When can we go to Muir Woods then?" Jane eased his shoes on and Ryan began fastening the laces.

"Say this coming Saturday. I'll check it's OK with your mum and I'll go shopping then fix us a picnic with some nice goodies!" Jane listened to herself . . . *'fix us a picnic with some nice goodies . . .'* What was she going to sound like when she got back to Keighley? But she was in the US of A! The children wanted to relate to her and she with them. "I know you like Bi-Rite ice cream and we can take some popcorn. I'll make your favourite sandwiches – tuna and mayo with sweetcorn – and we'll take some chilled drinks." The picnic menu flowed from Jane's tongue like a stream.

"Coca-Cola, p-l-e-a-s-e!" urged Ryan, followed by Teresa adding 'Kia-Ora orange in small cartons with the hole in the top for the straw.' Jane had to concede, and she nodded and smiled at them both.

"You got it! Do well at school this week and I promise we'll have the whole day there, and I'll take my camera! I want some good pictures of you against those giant redwoods!" Ryan offered to take his rucsack to carry the 'provisions for the expedition', as he put it. So that was that. Jane had to get Amanda to agree, then she'd plan the excursion. She'd heard Howard mention Muir Woods National Monument so maybe he could suggest some places to walk. Jane was aware of the body discovered in the national park but she'd check out the location and avoid that part. In any case, there'd be black and yellow police tape sealing off the immediate vicinity and they would keep well away. She did not want the two children seeing the area where the headless torso had been found and have to answer their searching questions:

'Why didn't he have a head?'
'Why were his wrists bound with tape?
'What's a tattoo?'
'Do you think his mum knows why he's missing?'
'Will she be worried about him?'

Jane dropped the children off at school as usual. There was no Liza keeping an eye on the schoolchildren today but another woman, somewhat younger. Jane waited until the two youngsters were inside the main door and was about to stroll to her Honda when she heard a voice behind her.

"Hi! Didn't I see you in Sausalito yesterday? Aren't you the new nanny to Teresa and Ryan?" A black haired girl in her thirties was standing next to her. With short cropped hair, she wore faded jeans and a loose top over a blue tee shirt, her feet inside brown boots.

"Er, yes, I was there. Some friends invited me out for the day. Do I know you?"

"No, except that I do this school run with my daughter, Amy, and I've seen you around. My name's Jodie, Jodie Patterson. We were at the fair, too, and I happened to see

Marie Honeywell. I've known her a couple of years. We sort of fell out a while back over some guy. It's history now. I got married and Amy came along and here I am!" Jodie smiled and continued. "So you look after the kids of Dr. Gardner and his wife. Isn't she a psycho-helper? You know, treats those with problems up here?" Jodie index fingered her temple with a twirl. Jane felt a little uncomfortable, her face suddenly warm. Something told her it was time to go. She glanced at her watch.

"Goodness! Is that the time, I need to fly! The plumber is coming to mend the dishwasher . . . I need to rush. Nice meeting you, Jodie. Maybe I'll catch up with you again sometime." Jane turned and walked to her car parked a few yards away.

"And isn't it his second marriage?" Jodie raised her voice as she continued. "Shame about Priscilla. I knew her when I was a teenager, she was nice. Some say she didn't slip, though . . ." By this time Jane had started the engine and was pulling away from the kerb. She eyed Jodie in her rear view mirror, her image ever smaller as the Honda accelerated towards Hayward. Who the hell was this Jodie? What right did she have to begin to question aspects of the family for whom Jane was now working as a nanny?

Jane grew anxious. She did not know that it was Howard Gardner's second marriage. But so what? People did get married more than once. Some of Jodie's words echoed in Jane's head as she sped along the freeway, radio turned off.

'Some say she didn't slip, though . . .' Slip? Slip where . . . how . . . why? She had to put this woman's words out of her mind. If she didn't they'd fester and begin to pollute the relationship Jane was trying hard to build with the children's parents. Should she phone her counsellor, Melody Oppenberg? She'd been given Melody's details at the end of her induction course in New York with an open offer to call her any time. But there was an issue here. What if Jane phoned to say she'd had a parent at school make comments about the father of the children. So what?

Couldn't she handle that? On the other hand, if things developed as in 'go badly wrong', would Melody ask why Jane hadn't called sooner? It was a dilemma. 'Oh, sod it,' thought Jane to herself as she pulled onto the drive, 'I'll leave it for now.' She hurried into the empty house and closed the front door, resting her back against the frame. Jane exhaled slowly, telling herself that there was nothing to worry about.

She'd had a nice time at the fairground, been introduced to Andrew, and had her first taste of chocolate doughnuts and a 'real' strawberry milkshake. Marie and Sam seemed OK and she'd get to know them better over time. Sam had mentioned that she and her mum, Rosemary, didn't speak much but Jane didn't enquire further. And Arty wasn't gross as she'd imagined, despite his love of toffee apples! Jane went into the kitchen and made herself coffee – a caffeine boost was needed. Opening her purse she took out a business card.

Andrew C. Wilson
Senior Sales Executive
McEnroe & Nelson Real Estate Agents
Twenty Fourth Street, San Francisco
Te. 415-316-7211

Jane smiled to herself. He'd been polite, bought Jane a milkshake, and was good looking, his blue eyes twinkling as he spoke.

He'd even suggested that she might like to meet his mother.

12

"Now, *you* can do it. You did these yesterday – this math is not as difficult as you make out, Teresa. You know your multiplication tables, so, three times eight is twenty four. You told me that earlier. So, twenty four divided by three is . . . what?" Jane persisted gently but firmly.

"It must be eight!" Teresa said triumphantly.

"Yes, you see it's not that hard. Look at the next one. Thirty five divided by seven." There was a pause. Teresa yelled the answer. 'Five!' And so the math homework continued. Ryan, meantime, was listing a bunch of words under the headings of Noun, Verb and Adjective. As Teresa battled with her figures, Jane looked over Ryan's shoulder. He'd written three words in each column leaving eleven more to list. So far they were all correct.

"Jane, what about this one? Pulse? I mean is it pulse as in my wrist, or something you eat, or can you pulse something . . . I'm confused with pulse!" Part of her role as she believed was to be a guide, a mentor, to get them to work things out for themselves. Reach logical conclusions. Several minutes passed.

"OK, it must be a noun. Whether it's in my wrist or I can eat it, it must be a noun. You can't pulse somebody or something, can you? And it's not a *describing* word so it ain't an adjective." Jane corrected his English; from ain't to isn't. "Caroline didn't help us like this. She used to get mad sometimes. Dad told her off once when he thought she was being too strict. Caroline had been feeling low 'cos her boyfriend, Jake, had been told off when he came here. She asked me a question on my math homework and when I got it wrong she slapped my leg – hard!" Tears welled in his eyes.

"OK, OK, Ryan. Take it easy. Caroline has gone now. And you're certainly not going to get a slap from me – you know that, don't you?" She pulled him close. She lowered her voice. "What happened then, after your dad heard what went on?" Ryan whispered.

"He came in and told her to pack her bags – just like that. She went the next day. Dad said he'd have it in for her boyfriend. He doesn't normally get angry but Jake had said something to my dad when she brought him round one day. I think it was about his job . . . that you didn't need to be properly qualified to be a heart surgeon, he was just a butcher . . . something like that. I heard my dad tell my mom that he knew where Jake lived and he was going to sort him out. I've still got the mark on my leg where she stuck the ballpoint pen into me." Ryan pulled his shorts up and showed Jane his scar. She'd never noticed it before, despite helping bathe both of the children several times. Jane hugged him gently.

"You poor soul. Well you don't need to worry now, no one's going to harm you like that while I'm here." Ryan's left sleeve made a good substitute for a handkerchief. "OK, let's finish this homework, it's nearly time for bed. You can both have a cookie and warm milk but must promise to brush your teeth extra thoroughly." The kids wrapped up their work, tops were put on pens, books put away. Jane put her arms around the two of them. "Now listen, we don't need to go telling anybody about any of this, do we? Why don't we keep it our little secret? What do you think, guys?" Both smiled and nodded as they looked forward to a chocolate cookie. Jane prayed that they'd go along with her proposal. She didn't want to consider the consequences if Amanda or Howard accused her of some kind of collusion. There were almost ten months of her contract left.

Jane saw the children off to bed, double checking that teeth had been cleaned and ears washed; the normal routine. Once satisfied that they were safely tucked up in their beds, Jane went to her room. A few emails and texts to be sent, diary to be consulted for the next few days and the college brochure to be scrutinised. Jane had told Amanda she'd check the course and make some enquiries, but maybe she'd leave any contact with Andrew for now.

Give it a week or so, no need to rush these things. As Jane raked through a drawer looking for the City College brochure she spotted a brown envelope tucked inside the thin slit between the base and the back edge of the drawer. She opened it. In her hand was a letter to Caroline Sinclair from the au pair agency, dated May of the previous year, confirming her appointment with the Gardner family.

It showed Caroline's address in Glasgow, her mobile and land-line numbers, and her email address carolinepsinclair1994@bt.com

Jane couldn't help but wonder if she should contact Caroline. And if she did, what could the girl from Glasgow tell her about what he really happened at the Gardner's?

*

Howard had left home early. There was a meeting of senior surgeons at SFCH regarding a new procedural matter that concerned types of anaesthesia relating to operations. Some surgery could now be done using spinal anaesthesia, the patient remaining awake during procedures - some guy had even played his clarinet whilst undergoing surgery! But for each operation there would need to be a full risk analysis undertaken.

It was Monday and Amanda wasn't due to leave home until 9.30 am. She had her first client appointment at 10.15 am., a woman with chronic schizophrenia who was having her third treatment session. Jane had taken the children to school and was back just after 9.15 am. Amanda heard the front door close.

"Hi Jane. By the way, I spoke with Vida and Rosemary this morning. They told me you'd had a good time over the bridge on Sunday. You seemed to get on OK with Marie and Samantha?" Was Amanda fishing for something?

"Yes, I like them. They're good fun and we had a great time. Thanks for the introduction, by the way." Jane was about to start cleaning the children's shoes.

"Vida said Marie had brought a friend along, or at least

her boyfriend invited him? Andrew, wasn't it? I don't think I know of him . . . into Real Estate isn't he?" Jane avoided eye contact as she picked up a yellow duster destined to bring Teresa's shoes to a mirror shine.

"Something like that. We just talked about hobbies and music, mainly." Jane was beginning to think she was on a couch, somebody taking notes on her subconscious mumblings.

"Well, you'll have to see how it goes. What about college? Are you still set on photography?" Amanda may have sensed the subject ought to be changed.

"Yes. I'll contact them later today. I've got an email address for their main office so I'll make enquiries about enrolment. The brochure states that there are three intakes each year. Hopefully my Nikon camera will be OK, I can't afford to buy another one." The last touches were put to the pair of shoes.

"There is a good photographers on Fifth Street. Bausch & Hickock have been trading there for ever and they sell second hand cameras. Worth thinking about if the college tutor suggests a better model." Jane knew she could stretch to that if necessary. Her mum had ensured that there would be enough in Jane's bank account for her to use her debit card. Amanda looked at the clock on the kitchen wall. "I need to fly. Have a good day, Jane, and I'll see you later. Bye." Amanda grabbed her Taurus keys from the tray on the hall table, deftly picked her coat off a hook and was out of the front door in seconds. A minute later Jane heard the front door slam. 'Ooops,' she thought, 'what had Amanda forgotten now?' Jane looked into the hallway. Katie the cleaner stood there panting.

"Hi Katie. You look exhausted. What's up?" Katie took her headscarf off and shook her long brown hair right and left like a wet dog trying to dry itself.

"Nothing. I'm fine. It's the hill that does it. I'm not as fit as I used to be, and that cycle needs the chain oiling." The headscarf was hung loosely on a peg.

"You mean you've ridden here? What's wrong with the

car?" A sensible question, Jane thought. Katie stood with her hands on hips.

"Car! We ain't got one. No sirree. Just my cycle ol' Faithful. I get on Faithful and pedal like billy-o up to Adair Way." If Jane had closed her eyes she could have been listening to Calamity Jane. "Anyways, we ain't really got to know each other yet. I'm Katie Clarke. Cleaner extraordinaire who can wash and iron with the best!" Jane laughed out loud.

"And I'm Jane Lester, au pair extraordinaire! And it rhymes!" Katie giggled like a teenager. "Let's have a coffee before you get started," Jane suggested. Katie nodded in agreement. Soon there were two cups of steaming cafe latte in front of them, courtesy of the new coffee machine. "So, Katie, how long have you been working for the Gardner's?" Both sipped their coffee. Jane put Katie at around thirty years of age.

"Two years an' three months, not that I'm counting! I work for two other couples in the area and do odd jobs for an old lady further down the street from us. My ol' man, Clint, gets picked up from the end of the street and he's an engineer in the Anchor Brewery. We ain't got no kids." Jane instantly liked Katie. She was basic, down to earth, and what you saw was what you got. She guessed she was good at her job, probably good at anything she set her mind to. Dressed in blue jeans and a dark grey turtle neck sweatshirt she was your typical American outdoor girl - a wedding ring was her only jewellery. Perhaps she and Clint had tried for a family, but Jane wasn't going to ask.

"I love being with the kids," Jane offered to kick-start the conversation which was only going to be brief for obvious reasons, "and I get on really well with Howard and Amanda – they're both so kind. He must be good at his job – surgery and all that – and Amanda with her own psychiatry practice. It's a privilege to work for such a great family." Jane felt she had sown a positive seed. Katie sipped her latte.

"Yeh, they're fine. I don't ask too many questions about

things. I come here twice a week, Monday and Thursday, unless it's a holiday. Won't be here on Thanksgiving, for instance. She let's me get on with things. Both trust me with a key to the front door. Mind you, I had to give them two references from previous employers. Still, you can't be too careful these days. It's OK round here, smart area, but in other parts around Frisco you have to take care."

"How do you get on with Howard?" Jane asked as casually as she could before finishing her coffee.

"Well he's OK, I guess. Shame about his first wife, though. I recall meeting her once at the opening of a new store in town. She was lovely. I don't know, they seemed well matched to me but others said he had problems . . . something to do with accepting her beauty. I mean, she could have been a film star. Tragically she fell whilst they were on a vacation to the Grand Canyon. Cynics say he hired a good lawyer, even paid him well. The SF Chronicle featured the story. Maybe he was jealous? All the guys used to salivate over her good looks." Jane glanced at the clock on the kitchen wall. "They say he suffered severe depression after that . . . his eyes often look, well, dark to me. Course, he's over it by now. Hey, look at the time. Why I've got cleaning and dusting to do throughout! Thanks for the coffee, Jane. Maybe I'll catch you later?" Katie grabbed her cleaning materials from a cupboard in the utility room to get on with her routine. She felt a bit guilty at having allowed her tongue to wag so much but she needn't have been concerned.

Jane wasn't going to say anything.

13

Body in Woods Update
reporter Tom Lederer

Late yesterday SFPD revealed some additional information on the 'Body in the Woods' case. Further forensic evidence now shows that the fingerprints of the victim had been removed by a strong acid that had rendered them impossible to analyse.

A police statement indicates that the victim was probably killed by a blow to the head, followed by decapitation as there was little or no bruising to the body suggesting a struggle. The killer may have had some medical training as the incision into the neck was clean and exactly between two cervical vertebrae. Traces of alcohol breakdown were present in the blood, again indicating that the victim had probably been drinking but the degree of likely intoxication is unknown. The depth of the tape marks into the wrists was limited and suggests the victim did not struggle before death and therefore may have already been dead when the wrists were bound.

Narrow channels caused by boot heel marks of the victim were traced seven yards from the shallow grave indicating the victim was dragged a short distance, possibly from a vehicle. It appeared the area close to the burial spot had been swept using a leafy branch in an attempt to hide traces of footprints. The police are currently checking tyre tracks within a wide radius of the site which is still cordoned off.

Following their appeal for any witnesses, or for further information from the public, several new lines of enquiry are being followed. Two walkers reported seeing a large, black or dark coloured vehicle parked approximately two hundred yards away as they headed home after a day's hiking at around 9.00 pm on 1 May. Although the light was poor, one hiker thought that the numbers 4 and 8 and the letter A were on the licence plate.

Anyone with any information at all are asked to telephone SFPD on 415-315-2400.

All calls will be treated in the strictest confidence.

*

"Hi, Jane, it's Sam!" Samantha sounded chirpy. "Hope you're OK? It's just that Marie and I were thinking of going to see a film, *Bridge of Spies*, this evening. Are you free?" It depended on the time, Jane mused. The children would need to be put to bed first . . .

"I can be away from here at 7.30 pm, would that be in time?"

"Sure. We can meet you down town at, say, eight. There's a bistro off Eighteenth Street, The Wineglass, and the AMC cinema is just round the corner. There's a multi-storey car park two minutes walk away. How does that sound?" It sounded fine. She was certain Howard and Amanda wouldn't mind, as long as the kids were OK. And the attraction of an American cinema! Wow! Surround sound, deep comfy seats . . .

"If there are any problems I'll phone or text you. Otherwise I'll see you there . . . The Wineglass, you say?" Sam confirmed the meeting place and ended the call. Jane smiled, she hadn't been out much. Her evenings were spent mostly in her room, either watching TV or reading her novel. Her laptop gave her access to the internet, of course, and she'd trawl various sites looking at a variety of things, including the weather in West Yorkshire. It was grim in Keighley! Rain, thick cloud, average 13C - typical for early September.

Thinking of Sam and Marie brought memories of Andrew back. It was going to be a girlie evening at the cinema. She wondered if he was thinking of her at all? Did he have a girlfriend? A guy as handsome as he was, six feet tall with close cropped blond hair, blue eyes and manicured fingernails. Yes, he must have. She had loved the day at the fair, and Andrew had been a gentleman. His soft voice and polite manners made him the kind of guy she'd like to spend some time with. Even take her mind off Harry back in Keighley . . . not that she thought of him much at all these days.

Jane was brought out of her daydreaming by Ryan. He shouted that they were ready for the ride to school and he egged Teresa to get a move on. Howard was in his study, door ajar, but ready to leave for the hospital. Amanda was dressed smart casual; in her job it was important that her patients did not feel threatened in any way, and that included dress. No low cut top, no see-through blouses, no high heels, no bracelets that jangled and screamed 'look at all my gold.' Nothing that was going to be a distraction to anyone laying back to talk about their problems. Just plain smart. Simple as that.

Jane started the Honda and with Teresa in front this morning they set off for Lexington Junior. Oddly, the children were quieter than normal. No rat-a-tat-a-tat of chatter talking about the day to come, or what they had done the evening before.

"You two are quiet. What's up?" asked Jane, glancing in the rear view mirror at Ryan.

"Nothing . . ." Teresa replied slowly. There was something wrong.

"Come on, out with it! We talk to each other in this car. You know, between us . . . don't we?" Jane lowered her voice to encourage a reply from either of them. Ryan's voice came from the back seat.

"Well, mum and dad had an argument this morning. I'm surprised you didn't hear anything. He was going on at her about her painting. Said she should be spending her time on something more useful. Said she spent too much time in her studio. Then he told her that he thought her pictures were rubbish. She tried to explain that it was her hobby and he could go to hell."

"Ryan! You shouldn't use words like 'Hell.' Even if your mum said that word you ought to avoid it." This worried

Jane. If Amanda really did utter those words, what was this saying about their marriage? "Listen, all mums and dads have their little differences. Often it's best to say what you feel, let it out. Better than holding it in and it building up over time. Then the safety valve reaches its limit and, boom, something explodes. Try not to worry about it."

"What's a safety valve, Jane?" Teresa innocently enquired.

"Oh, it's just a device that stops something exploding, like if it gets overloaded."

"So was mum overloaded this morning, do you think?" Teresa's doe-like eyes searched Jane's face.

"Well, maybe she was. If she enjoys her painting then your dad shouldn't have a problem with that, should he?" The response had to be positioned to appear politically correct; Jane couldn't take sides on issues like this. Suddenly Ryan changed the subject.

"Anyway, when are you taking us to Muir Woods? You said we'd go soon. I'm looking forward to the picnic!"

"OK, it's deal. We keep this to ourselves and we'll go to Muir Woods to see the giant redwoods this Saturday!" The children screamed with delight. Jane prayed they'd forget the tiff between their parents and concentrate on school work today. Parents argued, it was part of living together for goodness sake. Argue, debate, talk it over, get on with life. OK? Then forgive and forget.

But as Jane saw the children to the school gate she was slightly worried although she tried to hide it. Liza was there again, her large frame nearly filling the door. She waved at Jane. An odd wave, arm high but sideways on, fingers curled inwards slightly as if to say 'don't forget to come and talk if you want to.' Jane waved back before turning round and getting back into her car. The radio had The Rolling Stones shouting about a honky-tonk woman but Jane didn't need that right then and switched it off. Her thoughts turned to the cinema. Visualising the big screen, a popcorn bucket in her hand, reclining in the armchair-style seat with a Pepsi-Cola in the recess on the chair arm, she let her thoughts drift.

That was until she nearly careered into an oncoming eighteen wheeler truck that missed her by inches.

*

Jane had enjoyed the film at the big down-town cinema. AMC had branches all over the States, a bit like Empire cinemas or the Odeon back in Yorkshire. But the surprise was that both Arty and Andrew were also there to watch *Bridge of Spies*. Arty was hanging onto Marie like a limpet while Andrew appeared to make up the party. Neither Sam nor Marie explained Andrew's presence to Jane, and Jane wasn't for asking why he'd turned up. But he was genuinely caring, checking that Jane was all right after her near miss in her car, and reassured her that some truckers had a reputation for careless driving. It reminded Jane of 'white van man' around the roads of Keighley. Jane decided that she would be more careful and *concentrate* on driving when she was out in her Honda.

After the film – Jane refused to call it a movie – Andrew offered to walk her to the multi-storey car park. She'd seen US films back home where girls on their own might be followed by a dark figure across the flat cement floor, the click-clacking of the girls shoes echoing around the half empty expanse as she kept glancing over her shoulder. She shuddered. Of course, Andrew's offer was accepted. He put his hand on her shoulder. Gently. It felt comfortable. They chatted as they walked into the car park. Jane had parked the Civic underneath a light for safety, the neon strip lighting making the car appear lilac rather than blue.

"So your from England, Jane? Gee, have you met Prince Charles?" Andrew was serious.

"No, not yet," she replied, "but I might do at some time in the future!" They both laughed as Jane noticed his straight white teeth.

"Have you enjoyed this evening? I mean, you didn't

have a glass of wine earlier, because you're driving, but would you like to do it again? You and me, I mean." They stood next to her car, Jane's back resting on the drivers door. Andrew's blue eyes were clear and intense despite the dimness of the surroundings. He took her hand, ever so softly. It was warm. Seconds passed. Jane felt as if her head was filled with cotton wool.

"Er . . . er, yes." She so didn't want the moment to take control. But it was happening.

"I don't want to rush you. Take your time, it's OK. I can phone you next week?" His breath was on Jane's cheek, the gum he chewed making it feel fresh. Clean. For a split second her legs wobbled.

"I don't know much about you, Andrew. I mean, you're nice but . . ."

"But what? Am I going to eat you?" He grinned, somewhat slyly. "You know my friends, know where I work. I've nothing to hide. I haven't got a girlfriend, if that's what you're bothered about." He was so reassuring, Jane was finding it difficult to say 'no.' He was kind and considerate. Those blue eyes were penetrating.

"Yes! OK! Let's meet again . . . cinema, whatever, I don't mind. As long as you realise my main commitment is to the Gardner family – especially the children. All right?" Jane was firm in her reply. Andrew leant forward and kissed Jane on the cheek – lightly.

"Good. You'll realise you've made the right decision. I honestly think we can get on together. Getting to know an English girl – wow – I like that! I'll call you soon. My mother will be so looking forward to meeting you!" And with that Jane got into her car and set the GPS for Adair Way, waving goodbye to Andrew as she took the ramp. He stood still, turning slightly as she departed. A kiss was blown from the car park, but Jane didn't see it as she concentrated on her route back.

Andrew smiled to himself as he checked his Jaeger-LeCoultre gold and diamond watch. It was time to go. He had a friend to meet for a beer. They had something serious to talk about.

14

Muir Woods National Monument spanned 554 acres of forest and trails that criss-crossed the area. Some of the tracks were hard, suitable for vehicles, others natural, those that walkers liked to follow. It had been established by John Muir, a Scot from Dunbar whose parents had emigrated to the US in 1849. He loved the outdoors, loved to breathe unpolluted air, and sit and look out over vistas of priceless beauty. The main trees were the giant redwoods – *Sequoia sempervirens*. The tallest had been measured at 75 metres.

Ryan and Teresa had never been there before despite their father being a regular trekker. They'd heard his stories about how beautiful it all was, the sense of getting away from the hubbub of the city, the fresh air that filled your lungs. It was all here. Teresa had reminded Jane to take her camera as well as the picnic with the goodies they'd requested and Amanda had suggested taking a tablecloth to put onto one of the benches scattered throughout the woods. Howard recommended a longish trek but Amanda rejected his suggestion, respectfully saying the kids were too young to go hiking long distances. He loaned Jane a detailed map and took time to point out two viewpoints that gave excellent views for miles around. Jane had done her own mental calculation as regards the size of the woods in square yards – two point three million, near enough. Wow! It wasn't as big as Yorkshire, but it was pretty damned big!

"What's in the hamper, Jane?" asked Ryan, eager to know if he was in for a treat.

"Mostly what you want! Tuna, sweetcorn and mayo sandwiches, Twix bars, crisps . . . ahem, I know you call them chips, doughnuts, peanuts in shells, drinks and . . ." Jane hesitated for maximum effect, "Bi-Rite ice cream! A full carton in an insulated bag." There were cheers of delight from the children. "And I've got hand wipes, napkins and the cutlery. We're ready!" Amanda and Howard kissed the children good-bye and told them to be good. Within minutes all three were in the Honda, a quick check on extra clothing, walking shoes and the camera, then they were gone. Amanda spoke.

"I'm going to do some painting. Got a picture to finish off . . . if you don't mind, that is?" Amanda had already decided she was going to her studio whatever the reply might be. Howard tolerated gardening and some of the shrubs and bushes out back were in need of pruning. He might take a look later.

"Go ahead. I'm just popping into the study for a few moments – need to check a couple of things, then I'll get outside. The garage could do with tidying up, too. Things everywhere – those tools ought to be racked properly." Almost before he'd ended his sentence Amanda had gone upstairs. She took another look at 'Despair' and two others. One called 'Bleakness' was of a naked couple washed up on a beach, arms entwined, their mouths stuffed with seaweed. Finishing touches had to be added to the waves to create the wispy whiteness of the pounding surf as it bombarded the golden sand. An observer wouldn't be sure if the couple had drowned or been suffocated, and how close they'd been in life. Lovers, perhaps? The third painting she'd titled 'Grief'. An elderly woman, shawl around her shoulders, was lying dead in a rocking chair, her wide toothless mouth agape. Her hands were clasped around a crucifix hanging from a black beaded necklace.

Meanwhile, Howard had unlocked his study and was sitting at his desk fiddling with a pair of scissors, a copy of the San Francisco Chronicle in front of him. He turned to page five and found the latest report by Tom Lederer on the headless torso case. Carefully he cut around the newspaper article. He placed it in a thin card folder along with some others, closed it and placed the folder in a desk drawer. Howard had a wide variety of news cuttings. All were connected with murders, fatal accidents, deaths – he considered that as a hospital surgeon he ought to keep abreast of such things as part of his ongoing, broad spectrum education. He didn't see any harm in that. No harm at all. It was time to prune some bushes. And maybe tidy the garage; the tools needed a clean, too.

His sweet tooth hadn't been satisfied at breakfast, only a boiled egg and a slice of dry toast. A Milky Way next to a box of paper clips beckoned him. The blue and white wrapper slid off easily and the light chocolate bar was eaten in three bites. Folding the paper, Howard knotted it and dropped it into his trash bin.

*

Jane had arrived safely at Muir Woods and parked the Honda in a space between an SUV and a sports car. She was getting the children's stouter shoes out of the trunk, an anorak for each of them as well as the map, when Ryan suddenly piped up.

"There's Uncle Chuck! Over there!" Jane looked in the direction of his little index finger. Two men were walking away from the car park, the slightly taller one wearing a bright red outdoor jacket. "That's Uncle Chuck in the red! Hey, Uncle Chuck!" The men continued on their way. "Dad never told us that Uncle Chuck comes here even though they work together."

Well, Dr. Chuck Hudson was entitled to hike in the Muir Woods National Monument as much as anybody else, wasn't he?

*

Jane had thought long and hard about contacting Caroline, but if she didn't, she'd never know what had gone on at the Gardner's. She could always reply negatively – tell Jane to go to hell.

To: carolinepsinclair1994@bt.com
12 September 2015
Subject: Hello!

Dear Caroline,

My name is Jane Lester and I'm the newish au pair with the Gardner family here in San Francisco.

I hope you'll forgive me for sending you an email out of the blue but I got your email address from a letter that the agency had sent to you. It was in an unsealed envelope in a drawer in my room – I guess the same room you had when you were here.

The children are great and so far things are going well. But as a new starter it's often useful to know a bit more about the family. Without divulging any secrets, is there anything of which you think I ought to be aware? Any hints or tips would be a bonus. Anything about the children?

I hope the weather in Glasgow is treating you kindly. It's dry and 58F here.

Thank you and best wishes,

Jane.

PS My UK mobile number is 07901 992735 if it's easier to send a text.

Jane clicked Send. There, she'd done it. Now she'd wait.

It was also time to email her parents. Jane sent a long message every week, usually on a Monday, with a precis of the week's activities – news on the children, the parents, what had happened. Her mother would respond. Paul was still up to his armpits in biological education. In any event, Jenny loved gossiping through the ether. However, Jane was pleased that she was adroit at speed-reading; a two hundred word email from her mum could be read in less than ten seconds with none of the gist of it lost.

So Jane began to compose her weekly missive. But there was no way that she would mention the headless torso case. Not when she'd been there with the children, too. And in sight of black and yellow police tape fluttering in the gentle breeze; CRIME SCENE DO NOT CROSS.

And neither would Jane mention Caroline Sinclair, nor the scar on the leg of Ryan Gardner.

15

"Hi Jane, it's Melody. Melody Oppenberg!" Jane's counsellor was phoning her from an office in Los Angeles. "How you doing?" Jane was busy tidying the children's rooms and had some washing to do for them. "I haven't heard from you in weeks so thought I'd give you a call. Everything OK?" Of course it was. Otherwise Jane would have called her – that was the deal. Your counsellor was there to help you if it was needed. If not, no call. Jane sat down.

"Hi, Melody!" Jane made an effort to sound upbeat and positive. "Yes, it's all going well! The kids are adorable and we get on good." Jane cringed at her pseudo American terminology. "Howard and Amanda are great, they let me get on with the job, and . . . so far, so good."

"Well, that *is* good to hear! Is there anything that you want to talk to me about? Any concerns about the job?" It sounded as if Melody was dangling a hook. And to be honest, this call had caught Jane off balance. With a number of things rumbling around in her head she didn't want to start babbling on about locked rooms, or the previous nanny, or what the cleaner or school caretaker had said.

"Melody, really, I don't have any concerns. Amanda and Howard have made me feel very much at home. I've got a car, the weekly allowance is paid every Monday morning in cash, and I'm keen to begin the college course on photography. No . . . it's fine, thanks."

"Well, be sure to give me a call any time. You've got my email address, too. The other au pairs that you met seem to be getting on fine. The nearest one to you is Nora Dijon who is in Sacramento. Remember her, the one with all the red hair?" Melody picked up on the fact that this was pretty much a one-way conversation. "OK, Jane, you be good and I'll call again soon. Well, I must fly. Bye."

"Bye," said Jane, relieved in a way that Melody had

ended the call. She smiled as she recalled the dippy redhead who she sat next to on the induction course. What a character! Jane thought of their first meeting and wondered how Nora had managed to get a job as a nanny at all! Silly habits, a constant gum chewer, forgetful, an untidy dresser, the list went on. 'But,' thought Jane, 'she might be good at being a nanny!'

Finishing putting some toys away, Jane picked up discarded clothes from the linen basket in each of the children's rooms and planned to do some shopping. The children had enjoyed the day in Muir Woods and no awkward questions were asked about black and yellow police tape. Jane had taken about thirty photographs with her digital camera and wanted to download them onto her laptop to show the children. She didn't have a selfie stick but had taken several using the ten second delay facility. Jane would be able to send some to her parents along with some of the front and rear of 31, Adair Way.

As Jane went into the utility room out to the back of the kitchen with an armful of the children's washing her cell phone rang. She dumped the pile of clothes on a side table and looked quickly at the screen. It was Andrew Wilson; she'd put his number into her phone straight after the fairground visit.

"Hello?" Jane didn't want to let him know that she knew who it was. Play the game.

"Hi, Jane, it's Andrew! Hope I haven't caught you at a bad moment?"

"No. Doing a bit of washing, that's all. You?" She clearly wondered what he wanted – just asking about her health, or was there more?

"Yeah, fine. Just completed the sale of a three million piece of real estate out at Oakland. A good deal! Keeps the boss happy. Mr. Nelson has just congratulated me on a job well done." Andrew was bragging. He'd done a little of that at the cinema but Jane let it wash over her. "Listen, we haven't really got to know each other much and I was wondering if you're free for dinner this Friday?" As it happened, Friday was a day off for Jane.

"Sure. That'll be fine. Where can we meet?" Another drive into the city was in prospect.

"You're not driving. Give me your address and I'll save you starting the car. I can pick you up out front of your place at, say, seven o'clock." Jane breathed a sigh of relief. No driving. A chauffeur!

"It's a date! I'll see you then."

*

"It's true! We did see Uncle Chuck on Saturday, didn't we?" Ryan was insistent. Teresa played with a doll that wouldn't keep its woollen hat on.

"OK, Rye, *maybe* he was there. He's never told me that he ever goes hiking, and certainly never said a dickie bird about Muir Woods," replied his father. Ryan looked at Jane for support.

"I've never met your Uncle Chuck, Ryan, so I can't comment. You pointed at some guy, or two guys together, but they didn't look round despite your shouting. I don't know."

"Well, I'll ask him tomorrow," offered Howard, "that'll put an end to the conundrum." Howard was scanning the latest copy of *The New England Journal of Medicine*.

"What's a conundrum?" asked Teresa. "It sounds like a relation of the skunk!" Laughter rippled around the room. Howard obliged by telling his daughter it was a query, a question, a poser. When she wanted to know the meaning of the word 'poser' he told her to ask Jane when she went to bed. 'Kids!' thought Howard.

"We've time to take a peek at the photos from Muir Woods if you want." Jane looked at the children. Teresa squealed and jumped up, her doll dropping to the thickly carpeted floor as its woollen hat fell off again.

"Why don't you take the kids into the other room, Jane," suggested Amanda. "I don't think Howard or I want to see them now, do we?" Jane took them by the hand and went next door. After they got settled, Jane popped upstairs for her laptop and within minutes the three of the were huddled together on the sofa. Jane set the 32 images to slide show and clicked on the screen icon. Ooohs and aaahs followed rapidly, interspersed with giggles and quips about how they looked and how much they had in their mouths during the picnic. Seven selfies showed bright, smiling faces and even Jane thought she looked good – her light blue North Face jacket standing out against the background of redwood trees.

"There, look, Uncle Chuck. In the red jacket!" Ryan had spotted a walker behind them in one of the pictures. "Get dad, Teresa, tell him to come and have a look! Quick!" Teresa was off the sofa in a flash. Seconds later Howard came in.

"OK, let's have a look!" He leant over Jane's left shoulder. "Just enlarge that a little." Howard screwed his eyes up and focused on the walker in the red jacket. "Well, I'd say it was. But I can't be certain. If I saw him walking I'd know. He has that gait, that amble – like a cowboy. I'll tell you tomorrow. After I've asked him." And Howard did ask Chuck at the end of a day's surgery at SFCH, over coffee in the doctors lounge. Chuck told Howard he'd never been to Muir Woods.

And he didn't own a red jacket.

16

One sunny Thursday morning Katie was carefully flicking a fluffy duster over porcelain figurines in the main living room. A light fog that had seen in the dawn over the city had lifted and Katie hummed to herself, happy in her work. Katie and Clint Clarke, both 28 years of age, were both born in Frisco and had lived there all their lives. Of blue collar status, Clint had left High School with five subject passes and enjoyed using his hands. He was good at DIY and Katie never needed to ask him to fix anything around their home. Electrical or plumbing, gas or pipework, he could do it all. In fact, his job at Anchor Brewery really suited him. He'd been promoted last year to Senior Engineer, having worked there since leaving school. One of the perks of the job was his monthly beer allowance – eighty bottles of any kind he wanted. He usually chose the Anchor I.P.A., a light beer, full of flavour.

Katie, was a fine girl – he loved her to bits as he often told her. They'd married at the age of 19 in a small, simple wedding ceremony at St. Jude's Church. Katie's parents turned up, but Clint's Ma and Pa didn't. His father was against the marriage from the first moment Clint told him that he thought Katie was pregnant. She wasn't. As the marriage progressed it became apparent that Katie could not have children and she wasn't interested in any new-fangled fertility treatment. Clint's pa hardly spoke to him for five years, but he mellowed a little over time. They still weren't close, and the Christmas card sent by his ma was just about the only communication between them.

Katie drifted from job to job, mainly doing waitress work in coffee bars. She made good tips, always drawing a smiley face on the bottom of the customers receipt with the letters H.A.N.D. *Have A Nice Day.* Her good looks along with her friendly manner worked wonders. She made over thirty dollars a day in tips which the boss was happy for her to pocket herself – she worked for it! Her weekly wage was around three hundred dollars, so with Clint's engineers wages they managed. He'd passed his driving test a year after they married and got a drivers licence but had never bought a car. His dad had an old Pontiac which Clint thought he might pass onto him, but it ended up on the scrapheap. They had enough friends who owned a vehicle and sometimes Clint borrowed one in exchange for a few bottles of Anchor IPA. Katie's cleaning and laundry jobs these days brought in less than they earned jointly before, but they were happy enough.

When Macy's opened a new store in Frisco a decade ago half the town turned out. That's where Katie first met Priscilla Gardner. Literally by accident. Katie stepped on Priscilla's foot and apologised sincerely but the then Mrs. Gardner didn't bat an eyelid. She told Katie not to worry. Her husband, Howard, who was standing next to her, was a doctor, and if anything was broken he'd fix it. It was only a little bruising. A few days later Katie bumped into Priscilla in a supermarket check-out and they chatted about the foot incident. Both laughed it off. Katie liked Priscilla and when she read about her death at the Grand Canyon it really knocked her back. Especially the parts of the report in the Chronicle that printed alleged comments by some visitors to the canyon that suggested they'd been arguing a little while before she fell. One person had told police they'd seen Howard smack his wife in a cafe about an hour before she slipped. But after the county coroner had finished his report it all came down to the shoes that Priscilla was wearing at the time. Some fancy sling-backs with a smooth sole.

And even now, Howard doesn't realise that Katie was the girl who stepped on his first wife's foot in Macy's store all those years ago. That she and Katie used to meet down town for coffee, became good friends. Priscilla was the kind of beautiful young woman who, once she got to know and trust you, would empty her soul. Katie often wondered what Howard would think now if he knew some of his dark secrets were known to his house cleaner. That dark side of him, for instance.

The fluffy duster had done its work. The porcelain figurines were in pristine condition. It was now time to get the vacuum cleaner out. Katie was still humming to herself as the sun began to go down. Tombstone grey clouds slowly rolled in from the Pacific.

It looked like rain.

*

Wednesday's traffic in Frisco was lighter than normal. A dark red VW Golf was heading north out of the city, its two occupants silent. Brooding. Each with their own thoughts. They had a plan, hatched a week before. Drive up to Santa Rosa, park the car outside the Union Bank of California, and do the business. This bank was such a pushover . . . their branches just did not seem to take security seriously. And the staff were always so obliging, especially when a 9mm Glock pistol was there to greet them, too. An old canvas shopping bag would hold about fifty thousand dollars when stuffed, and the staff would do that. If asked nicely.

It wasn't only banks that were there to care for you. Members of the public were so kind, too. At gas stations, for example. Pull in, switch off, get out, fill up. Pay inside. Leaving the car key in the ignition was such a bonus for the opportunist thief. Pretend to be busy near another pump, or use a trash can between pumps, or look at the daily newspapers, even tying your shoelaces. It wasn't difficult. The VW Golf had been parked without a steering lock. Asking to be stolen, or borrowed really. One of the occupants would leave it back in town later. After they'd taken care of business.

A few miles up the road the Golf pulled onto a dirt track about one hundred and fifty yards off the main road, a cloud of dust swirled around them as the driver braked hard. A pair of Arizona number plates soon replaced the

San Francisco ones, then the two young men drove on toward their destination. Jimmy was driving whilst Andy rested his green eyes. He leant back against the reclined, soft leather passenger seat, smoothing his ponytail as he slowly breathed out. The driver, Jimmy, occasionally glanced at his face in the rear view mirror. He so wanted that gelled hair to be just so, a little quiff on top, kind of Brian Ferry of Roxy Music, but younger.

These two young bucks had to be careful, however. Because they'd held up three banks now, they knew complacency mustn't set in. Each had to focus on the task in hand. The routine would be the same. Park close to the front door, leave the engine running, the passenger strolls in, gun in the bag, orders everyone down and tells the cashier to fill the bag – quick! A bank teller would be hitting an alarm button somewhere under the counter, or on the floor, and thirty seconds would be the maximum time to get the hell out of there.

Today was Jimmy's turn. He breathed rapidly, pulse rate around a hundred. Like an actor waiting to go on stage. But he was in control, nice and easy did it. And everything went well right up to the time he asked everyone to leave. As Jimmy eased the canvas bag under the grill he didn't notice that one of those laying on the floor had a handgun under his jacket. He never heard the click of the trigger as the guy pumped four bullets into Jimmy's right thigh, his pants instantly turning crimson. A piercing yell meant that Andy had no choice. He did what they'd discussed time and time again – if the one in the bank gets hit, the driver goes. Jimmy went down like a sack of pumpkins, clutching his leg in agony, his face creased like a squeezed dish-rag. The squealing tyres of the VW Golf left wisps of smoke as it sped away. East then south, towards Frisco.

Despite attempts by the ambulance crew, Jimmy Walters died on the blood stained floor of the bank. He had no ID on him.

And the person who fired the four rounds into Jimmy's leg was never traced.

17

From: <u>carolinepsinclair1994@bt.com</u>
15 September 2015
Subject: Hello 2 U!

Dear Jane,

Thank you for your email. First of all, I'm not back in Glasgow, but working in Los Angeles as a Teaching Assistant in a junior school.

I don't know what you may have heard whilst you've been with the Gardner's, but I'll be truthful with you. The Gardner family told me to pack my bags before my contract expired. I'd enough money saved up to stay in the States for a while and I didn't wish to return to Scotland. There's nothing much there for me, anyway.

I loved being in Hayward and had made quite a few friends in the area. At the beginning I got on well with the two children, as well as their parents. Amanda was OK about me bringing friends back to the house as long as I obeyed their rules and that was fair enough. I'd become good buddies with a guy named Jake Bauer. He worked in the kitchens at the Mark Hopkins hotel. Nothing serious, but he was good company.

He came back to the house one day and Dr. Gardner didn't like him one bit. Jake always wore a discrete golden earring and Dr. Gardner took exception to it – called Jake a girl. In the heat of the moment Jake told him he was nothing better than a butcher with a certificate. That was that! He was banned from the house. I ended up crying, and the children got upset, too.

But even before that the relationship between the family and I began to alter. Jake and I split up, he stopped getting in touch. Don't know where he is now, but he was a bit of a drifter.

I realise I'm giving you quite a lot of information, but

it's important you know the circumstances.

As far as Ryan is concerned, and it's the reason I was asked to go, he stabbed himself with a ball point pen and blamed it on me. His personality changed during my time there. For some reason he became disturbed and had restless nights. I went into his room one night when he was crying and he attacked me with the pen, missing my right eye by an inch. He then dug the point into his own leg and screamed. Amanda came into the room and saw the wound, blood covering the sheets, and he told her that I'd done it. Of course, that was the end for me.

I'm not certain if Ryan's condition is genetic – I'll leave that view at that.

I don't know how long I'll be in L.A. but it's a six hour coach journey if ever you want to pay a visit. My UK mobile is 07933 991 455 and US cell is 54-8251.

Best wishes,
Caroline.

Caroline had told Jane how it was. Jane read the email twice over. But was it really the truth? And where was Jake Bauer?

It also put a big question mark over whether Ryan was always honest. Or did he sometimes tell little white lies? Would he *really* have stabbed himself in the leg?

*

Jane had waited in the front porch until Andrew pulled up in a battered old Ford. He was dressed casually, with a charcoal sports jacket and grey flannel trousers. Jumping out of the car before Jane got to the passenger door, he opened it and bowed slightly as she got in, swinging in her long legs with one deft move. He hopped in. She smelt his aftershave, one that Harry used to use. Putting the car into gear they set off, the car jolting several times before the noisy automatic gearbox settled down.

"Filled her up with kangaroo gas!" Andrew had shouted above the rattle of the engine. They'd both laughed. He drove carefully, but more because the car wasn't capable of any great speed, Jane decided. Andrew told Jane that the car had been borrowed from a friend since he'd just sold his own – a 2012 Mazda 6 Coupe – and hadn't got round to looking at anything else, yet.

Andrew drove to Chinatown. Jane had told him when they first met that she enjoyed Chinese food although chopsticks were still a challenge. They parked in a side street close to *The Great Wall of China*, a restaurant with an excellent reputation. Or so Andrew said. The place was fairly busy, but a young Chinese waiter led the way to a table in a corner. The walls were covered in a yellow and red patterned paper bearing symbols that represented the signs of the Chinese horoscope; red and white paper lanterns hung from the ceiling. Soon after being seated two hotplates, a basket of prawn crackers and a bottle of complimentary still water were placed on the table. Andrew poured the water as Jane perused the menu.

"We can keep this simple, if you like . . ." She looked into his blue eyes. "Why don't you let me order a variety of dishes to start with like prawn dumplings, mini spring rolls, sesame toast. See what you like, and for mains I can recommend the duck and sweet and sour pork with one portion of fried rice between us." That was good, Andrew taking charge, being masculine, in control. Jane liked that.

The meal was delicious. Small starters were savoured and conversation flowed like a rocky mountain stream. Jane had loved the crispy duck, so succulent and full of flavour. Andrew told her of his work at the Real Estate Agents, his hobbies which included philately - mainly South American stamps, and his love of music. He'd been polite, though, and asked her about England, her childhood, and her parents. But as this was only the second time she'd met Andrew, Jane was a little guarded about some of the things they'd talked about. However, it had gone well and they had enjoyed each other's company.

Jane laughed at some of his comments and his odd little ways of making a pun out of nothing. A sharp mind, Jane thought.

If there was anything that Jane had doubts about it was the way that Andrew had briefly held her hand before the ice cream dessert course. She'd left it for a second too long, but eased it away smoothly. No words were spoken as they finished their meal. He'd offered to pay when the waiter had brought the bill on a small wooden tray, along with two fortune cookies. Jane hadn't seen these before but Andrew explained their significance.

"They're like your mini horoscope in a crispy shell. Open it – see what it says!" Jane had refused, saying she'd prefer the excitement later . . . if he didn't mind. He'd smiled broadly. He didn't mind. Not for Jane. On arriving home Jane had already decided that she'd give Andrew a peck on the cheek – it seemed the right thing under the circumstances. And that's exactly what happened, nothing more, nothing less. He'd helped her out of the creaky passenger door, walked her to the front porch and then thanked her for her company, saying he'd had a great time.

Jane remembered looking into his eyes just before he said 'good-night.' She had once read that the eyes are the windows to the soul. But as Andrew turned away she wasn't totally sure what she saw. Letting herself into the house, Jane closed the door quietly, eager to see what her fortune cookie was going to predict for her, and Andrew had to return the old Ford to his friend before it got too late.

Amanda had caught sight of Jane's friend when he'd arrived earlier and she thought she'd seen him somewhere before, but she couldn't quite place the face.

*

Police reveal more clues in headless torso case
reporter Tom Lederer

Detective Simon Rogers of SFPD, the Lead Investigator, held a news conference yesterday afternoon. Along with Detective Megan Harris they told gathered reporters from the media that progress was being made but could not reveal specific details.

Number plates bearing the numbers 4 and 8 and the letter A are being checked out by SFPD. A walker stated that they believed that a black vehicle bearing such a plate was parked in an unusual off-road position on 1 May. Police have stated that there are eighty seven number plates that have such a combination of numbers and letter in the SF area and their enquiries on identifying the owners would begin immediately. Two other reports now received also mention a grey Range Rover with a dent in the nearside front wing and a white Mitsubishi Shogun with distinctive black and silver alloy wheels that were parked near the scene. The Range Rover had the tailgate open, but no one was in the vehicle at the time. A man wearing a red outdoor jacket was seen in the vicinity and police are asking that person to come forward so that he can be eliminated from their enquiries. Deep ruts made by a distinctive and uncommon tyre brand found close to the scene are also being examined.

SFPD are following up on three reports of Caucasian males that failed to return home week commencing Monday 27 April 2015, but at this stage no further details are available. Once again, SFPD are asking members of the general public with any information at all to call them on the usual number 415-315-2400 in strictest confidence.

18

The children had been quiet again on the way to school. Jane didn't want to magnify any issues, so, rather than ask if there was a problem she left the radio on a low volume, the music soothing as early morning traffic to school snarled up. She hummed to a Patsy Cline song, one she knew from way back. Jane didn't want the local news on – no need for the children to hear any details on the headless torso case. Having read the recent Chronicle report was enough for her for now. Three reported missing persons in Frisco and eighty seven car registrations to check. The police ought to come up with something soon. No mention had been made at the press conference with regards to the tattoo – an outline of Texas. That was still a mystery.

Ten minutes before they arrived at school Ryan had said that his parents were arguing upstairs when he was brushing his teeth. Although they were in the bedroom with the door closed, he said they were making 'a God damned awful noise.' Jane didn't chastise him for his colourful language, but she recalled the words of the email from Caroline . . . *'I'm not sure if Ryan's condition is genetic . . .'*

Teresa had put her ten cents worth in, too. Said that her dad had mentioned a lady called Priscilla and she had heard her mum, several times, tell him not to use that name. But she thought he was drunk because it was a Saturday night and he'd opened an extra bottle of wine and drunk most of it himself. Teresa always knows when they've rowed because 'dad goes out the next day and buys flowers.'

Jane wondered what sort of relationship Howard Gardner really had with his first wife? If they were a genuine loving couple and she did slip from the viewing platform at the Canyon he'd miss her very much, be devastated. And yet Jane had been told that he didn't seem to grieve for her, during or after the funeral. And after

Priscilla died, how did he meet Amanda Raskoff? Did he know her before? Perhaps she was a friend of the family? Or maybe he met her at some social function – a party? Or was Dr. Gardner into on-line dating? There had to be several web sites which he might have accessed, registered, and then entered his details.

'Doctor in his thirties seeks attractive lady of similar age for friendship and fun'

And then, not very long afterwards, Howard Gardner answered the question 'Do you, Howard Clark Gardner, take this woman . . .' to Amanda Jeanette Raskoff, the leggy blonde, the psychiatrist with a postgraduate doctoral degree. Jane assumed Amanda hadn't been married before, no emotional or mental baggage to add to the marital nest. At least not of that sort . . . and Jane also wondered what sort of people became psychiatrists or behavioural psychologists or psychotherapists? Were they people with some strange mental issues that they were trying to resolve, and by asking questions of others laid in a recumbent position were working through their own problems in some indirect manner?

"Jane, we're here! You've passed the gate!" Ryan shouted loudly. Jane jumped. She'd been thinking about things so intensely that she hadn't realised they'd arrived. She braked and parked the car. A Chevrolet Impala sedan tooted behind her, having to swerve to avoid the Honda brake lights. Not recalling the journey for the past few minutes, she had been in a daydream; Jane could not remember driving through the two sets of traffic lights or making the left turn into the avenue where Lexington Junior was situated.

"Sorry, kids! Wasn't concentrating this morning! Here we are, let's go!" Jane helped them out and stood and watched them walk to the main door with bags over their small shoulders then turned and got back into her car but not before seeing Jodie again. Jodie gave her a look, an odd look, but Jane didn't want to talk to her. Jane forced a smile, more out of acknowledging her presence than a true greeting. As Jane drove back to Adair Way she remembered what Jodie had said the first time they'd met . . . that she knows Marie Honeywell. And Marie's mother is Vida, a friend of Amanda's. Jane tried unsuccessfully in her mind to forge a link between them, other than just friendship.

But was there more that Jane could find out? Maybe it was time to have coffee with Marie again, make some time during a working day. Ask a few innocent questions.

On the way back, Jane noticed every traffic light and every turn, pulling up safely on the drive a little after nine o'clock.

*

"Welcome to this new term for those who have enrolled on the photography module here at City College, San Francisco. I'm sure that, along with my two tutors Greg and Alex, you're going to have a great time. We can't promise to turn you into the world's top photographers, but you'll end up a whole lot better than you are right now!" There was a gentle wave of laughter around the lecture theatre as Gloria Rudetsky smiled at everyone present – all twenty seven of them. Jane was seated three rows back between a skinny kid with freckles who needed a good feed and a shave, and a chubby girl who seemed intent on getting into the Guinness Book of Records for the most sticks of gum chewed in one attempt. "I'll ask Greg to hand out this term's timetable. When you receive it you'll see that we have two tutorials lasting ninety minutes each for two evenings per week – Tuesdays and Thursdays – beginning at seven thirty. Sometimes we'll meet here, in Lecture Room Four, and at others it will be in the Photography Laboratory on the floor above. There we'll be playing with cameras, looking at how to set them up, and using computers to digitally change pictures, eliminate red eye, etc., etc. I hope those two evenings each week don't infringe on your social commitments too much." There was a rumble of pig-like grunts from certain parts of the group. 'Skinny Kid' looked at Jane and shrugged his shoulders, his yellow stained teeth suggesting he didn't like going to the dentist. "And one last thing – some of you *may* need to invest in a new camera, or at least a decent second hand one!" More groans.

Greg walked down the central aisle handing out timetables to each student. This first session on the course was really going to be a taster of what was ahead over the next nine months. Not everyone had brought their camera but others were loaded down with enough gear to join a David Attenborough wild life trip to the Amazon. Gloria wasn't going to have this first evening last for an hour and a half. Her objective was to put faces to names – their photo ID tags would be handed out this evening – and clarify any points that students may have. A show of hands indicated that there were a number of queries. Gloria answered every one in turn.

Each of the students were asked to introduce themselves, give their names, and one reason why they were sitting there right now. A variety of reasons were thrown up, from wanting to work for HELLO magazine to getting a better job to simply taking better photos. Human interaction being what it is, there was limited socialising, but Jane knew it would get better as time went on – it always did. Like water, human beings found their own level . . . their own comfort zone buddies with whom they could relate. PLU it was called. You mixed with People Like Us. Same ages, same interests, same income levels, same likes and hates, same most things. But as Jane looked around her she didn't think 'Skinny Kid' or 'Gum Chewer' would be on her list. In fact, Gloria told the group that they could sit where they wished for each tutorial. 'Great,' thought Jane.

After discussing focal lengths, apertures, lenses, zoom facility, pixels and a host of other photographic jargon, Gloria brought the session to an end. The students quietly exited the lecture room, some saying 'bye' to others as they left. Jane, so far, was pleased she'd chosen this course. Whatever she did on her return to Yorkshire, a proper knowledge of photography would always come in handy. But before going back to the UK, she wanted to take better pictures of the children, her friends, and any trips she may take in California. Maybe even in Los Angeles? Teresa and Ryan had asked to go back to Muir Woods, so Jane could use her newly developing skills to take better photos there. The sky was the limit – literally!

But as Jane headed for the car park, key and safety whistle in hand, she hadn't noticed amongst the emerging throng another newly enrolled student on a Creative Writing course that had been in the lecture room next door. Her name was Jodie Patterson.

*

19

Andrew Wilson was a nice guy. Really nice. Smart, good looking, a good salesman. Mr. McEnroe and Mr. Nelson were both very pleased with his performance. He'd been with the office for two years and was one of those guys with whom you'd happily share a beer. All of the others got on well with Andrew and he'd do anything to help. If you had a problem you didn't need to look any further than Andrew Wilson.

He'd interviewed well. Fifteen minutes of grilling by the two directors of the company had been handled by Andrew in a calm, professional manner. The usual questions regarding working on one's own versus as part of a team was text-book in response. And when they probed as to what he'd bring to the company he talked for ages until Mr. Nelson interrupted. The references he'd brought with him for the interview were near perfect and neither of the directors felt they needed to follow up on them.

Andrew never wore a plain shirt with a plain tie; always a patterned shirt with plain tie or vice versa and his choice of neck-wear was excellent. He said he loved the outdoors and was a keen hiker. There were few parts of the eastern coast of the USA to which he hadn't been.

A keen musician, Andrew told his buddies he could play the piano and his favourite composer was Schubert. He could play all of the ten symphonies that Schubert wrote including the incomplete eighth in B minor and the 'Great' in C major. However, most of his friends didn't like classical stuff like that and so he never got the chance to play to them.

Although his colleagues knew he had owned a variety of motor cars, Andrew preferred to take a tram to the office telling them he wanted to keep his vehicles clean and the mileage low. He'd talk for ages about all the latest models – saloons, SUV's, station wagons, sports cars, and knew his Tecalemit fuel injection systems from his Weber downdraught carburettors.

His parents had been very loving and kind towards him. An only child, he was spoilt by his mother in particular. He had a small laptop computer when he was eight years old and a pony for his thirteenth birthday. He'd left High School in Sacramento with top grades and had captained the soccer team. It wasn't difficult to imagine Andrew Wilson, now aged twenty five, as being the boy that every girl would want to take home to her ma. How proud many a daughter would be to introduce Andrew as their new beau!

And his colleagues in the office were sorry to learn that his father, George, had died of liver cancer four years ago. His mother was distraught, he'd told them. Her health had gone down hill since he'd passed away and he visited her every Wednesday to make certain that she was all right. She lived thirteen miles north of Frisco in a small house off the beaten track, and he helped her with her shopping and things. The house was wooden, with a corrugated iron roof and had two bedrooms. When it rained hard, water would drip into the kitchen, but the good news was that it plopped straight into the sink. It was adequate for her – she didn't go far these days. In the yard his father's old 1952 Plymouth was slowly rusting, tyres flat, hens roosting on the back seat.

Andrew had good physical health – strong and fit, he could still run a marathon. At least he'd told his friends that. But it was in his head that he'd had a few problems. Nothing serious, but there were mood swings, occasional fits of depression, talking to himself when he knew he was alone, and sudden bouts of anger that came out of nowhere. Clenching his fists for a few seconds became a safety valve for Andrew. It was the nail marks on his palms that he had to hide, especially when the bleeding started.

Then there was the psychiatric treatment. He'd been to see his own doctor who'd referred him to a clinic on the south side of the city. A series of therapeutic sessions were recommended, with appropriate medication. The clinician found this patient a particularly complex, but challenging one. And once all of the psychological debris was removed, pulled away like candy floss to leave a thin stick, the *real problem* was that Andrew Wilson was a pathological liar. And he hated a guy called Jake Bauer.

His therapist had been Dr. Amanda Raskoff.

*

"What do you think that Chinese proverb means, Marie?" Jane and her friend were having lunch in Leo's, a light blue sky overhead. Marie had a one hour break from McEnroe & Nelson and knew that Andrew had taken Jane out for dinner recently. She looked at the slip of yellow paper again. 'One candle can change complete darkness to bright, but someone has to light it.'

"I don't know, sounds weird, but did you enjoy the food? I love their hot and sour soup, and the beef with mushrooms and water chestnuts is delish! He's such a nice guy, isn't he? So popular in the office – and really good at his job!" Jane smiled, knowing how lucky she was to be seeing someone as nice as Andrew Wilson. Marie took a bite of her prawn mayo on rye and focused on the proverb again. 'One candle can change complete darkness to bright, but someone has to light it.' "Well, maybe it means you're in darkness just now and it's up to you to light the candle, you know, to brighten things up!"

"Marie, do you mind if I ask you something?" Jane hesitated for a second, "it's not that important but . . . do you know a woman named Jodie Patterson?" Marie seemed startled.

"Why, yes, I don't know her that well. Known her on and off for two, maybe three years. She's a few years older than me. Why, what's on your mind?" Marie put her half eaten sandwich down.

"It's nothing really. I met her for the first time recently at the school entrance when I dropped the kids off. She said a few things that made me feel uneasy – things about

Amanda. Called her a 'psycho-helper' which I thought was downright rude!" Marie grinned . . . she liked the way Jane said *downright rude* – it sounded so polite in a way. Very English.

"Let me be honest with you Jane. I first saw Jodie at a party nearly three years ago. We liked the same guy, a good looking hunk called Tex. She was dating him for about six months, then they fell out. She wanted to dominate the relationship, became aggressive, but things took a turn for the worse. She used to hit him, punch his head. I'd always had a soft spot for him – he was a really nice guy. Caring, thoughtful, but not her type. Then Tex and I became friendly and started going out. She hated that, ended up with some other guy that she could impose her will on, and married him. I think they have a daughter called Amy." By now Jane had eaten her tuna salad and a few crumbs remained on Marie's plate, the two bottles of water empty. "What I'm really saying Jane is that you need to be careful with Jodie – nice as pie one minute, crazy as a loon the next. If I were you I'd avoid her. My mum knows a bit more about her. I'll make some enquiries, but don't worry, I won't drop you in it!" Marie laughed softly. "Trust me."

And with that the hour was almost up, Marie had to get back to work and Jane had things to sort out in the house. Jane offered to pay for lunch, gave the waiter a twenty dollar bill and told him to keep the change – about one dollar fifty. He smiled leeringly, then winked. These Italian waiters were all the same, she thought. The two girls wandered away from Pier 39, Marie heading for the office, Jane toward her car parked nearby. They'd hugged before separating. Marie spoke.

"Jane, I hope you and Andrew get on well. He's a real nice guy. Genuine, talented, straight. And as for the fortune cookie proverb, I'd leave it to providence. Heck, it could mean anything – anything you want it to mean."

As Jane drove back to Hayward she considered what Marie had said. She trusted Marie, was beginning to like her. But Jodie Patterson was someone to be avoided.

*

Jane was starting to feel more at home with the Gardner family and was settling down into a routine. One week-end off in four, the thirty five hour week, and helping the children with their homework was an enjoyable challenge. The course at City College was under way, and she'd seen Andrew twice now, once for the Chinese meal and they'd been to the cinema again. He'd been kind, bought the tickets and popcorn, and paid for a hamburger and a coke. Samantha and Marie kept in touch with her, silly texts and facebook items about their latest exploits were being shared. Nothing was upsetting Jane too much, and when she took everything into account, it was all going well. What was the alternative in her life right now? Her first year at some British university! That could wait. Most of her friends from Keighley had gone straight to tertiary education after 'A' levels, but here she was, in the Californian sunshine, making friends, enjoying herself and learning about photography.

Then there was Andrew. Jane considered herself to be fortunate, although on reflection, she didn't know that much about him. He reminded her in some ways of Harry back home in Yorkshire, but Andrew was nicer. His neat, blond hair suited him, but if there was any criticism, it was that his finger nails were a little too long. Jane couldn't say anything – didn't know him well enough, but perhaps in time? From a few small comments he'd made she felt their relationship was moving in the right direction. He was looking for another car instead of having to borrow one, and he'd even mentioned part ownership of a small yacht berthed down at the marina. She'd never been on a yacht or sea-going vessel of any kind. A rowing boat on a large lake in Skegness during one of their holidays had been the limit of her experience. Jane mused . . . the Pacific breeze ruffling her hair, sunglasses perched on her head, long chiffon scarf blowing out behind her, Andrew by her side . . .

But Jane couldn't help but wonder about Andrew. Maybe he'd had a string of girlfriends, 'chicks' she'd heard them called, and for one reason or another the relationship hadn't lasted. Marie had sung his praises, but he came to the cinema a little while ago with Sam, Marie and Arty to see the Tom Hanks film without a 'chick' in tow. Perhaps he'd just finished with some girl but didn't want to mention it. He was lovely, and Jane did wonder what Amanda and Howard would make of Andrew when she finally got round to inviting him to Adair Way? She could picture it . . . 'Amanda, Howard, Ryan, Teresa, this is my friend Andrew . . . he's just bought a new car and he owns a yacht . . .' The Gardner family would be impressed. Really impressed. That would feel so good, thought Jane, her heart pumping a bit faster.

Suddenly, whilst doing the children's laundry, she stopped and asked herself what on earth was she thinking about? She'd been daydreaming – all of these thoughts were whizzing through her head. She wasn't in some film with Matt Damon or Leonardo di Caprio! 'Get a grip, girl,' she said to herself as if talking to somebody next to her.

"Jane? Are you OK?" Amanda came into the utility room. "Did I hear you talking to someone?" Jane felt stupid and involuntarily hung her head like a naughty schoolgirl. She was tempted to say 'No, miss' but resisted.

"No. I was just thinking about a few things – letting my imagination loose, I suppose you'd call it." Jane pulled a bundle of clothes out of the tumble drier. "I don't want to end up on your couch, though! Unless the therapy was free!" Jane gave Amanda a cheeky grin.

"I'm booked up for the next three weeks. You'd have to make an appointment!" Amanda jokingly replied.

"To be honest, I was thinking about my friend Andrew who picked me up that evening to go to Chinatown. We had a lovely meal. Maybe I could bring him here to introduce him sometime?"

And like a flash of lightning, Amanda remembered

where she'd seen him before. That young man that had opened a squeaky car door for their au pair, helped her into the old car, and taken her out on a date.

She wondered if he still had nail marks on the palms of his hands?

20

Chivers, the elderly doorman with a grey moustache smiled, touched his peaked cap, and greeted the man as he entered Quentins, the gentlemen's club. It was a cool evening but the small reception area at the entrance warmly welcomed it's members. The cherry pink wallpaper with red roses and gold cherubs added a *je ne sais qua* to the ambience. Crispin was on duty in the cloakroom.

"Good evening, sir. Are you well?" asked Chivers, his peaked cap at a slightly jaunty angle. The tall, handsome young man in his late twenties smiled in response. The member slipped a twenty dollar bill into the doorman's gloved right hand. "If you don't mind me saying so sir, you *do* look like a young Charlie Sheen." He'd heard Chivers say that a million times.

"Thanks. Have any of my usual friends arrived?" he asked, taking his coat off.

"Yes, the one you call Sloppy is here, sir. I haven't seen Mincing, yet. Is there any news on your other friend, sir, the one that went missing nearly a fortnight ago? Worked at the hospital, didn't he? The one you called Cutlass, as I recall." Chivers straightened his fingers as he stood to attention, aware of the nicknames that several members used to prevent their real names being known. "You seemed to get on well?"

"No, no news of him. I guess his family are concerned." The doorman nodded very slightly but said nothing. The club member handed his light coat to the cloakroom attendant, took his ticket, and strolled into the dimly lit lounge where a five piece band was playing *In the Mood*. The bar surface was illuminated with the subtle hue of small green and lilac lights around its perimeter. Down-lights at the rear of the bar gave a magical black and white effect as if one was sitting in a cave with Merlin the wizard. The club member sat on a cream leather barstool toward the left hand side of the bar and rested his leather shoe insteps on the chrome footrests. Quentins was plush. Opulent. They didn't let *anybody* become a member. As well as having a degree of financial soundness, prospective members had to have a level of panache and style. And, importantly, be recommended by another member.

"Good evening, sir. Is it the usual?" asked Jerry the bartender. The club member nodded, then looked around him. The place was getting busy. It was just after 9.00 pm. A few limp waves were exchanged between the man on the barstool and a handful of other members. The club member called Sloppy seemed busy chatting to an elderly gentleman on the far side. A tall glass edged with a slice of orange and filled with a golden yellow liquid was eased across the shiny bar, a little paper umbrella stuck into a pineapple chunk at the edge of the glass. This was a Jerry special; the bartender made up his own versions of a range of cocktails and spirits and most club members were happy to go along with his quirky style. His signature drink was a Screwdriver - best Russian 45 proof vodka and fresh Californian orange juice with a hint of pineapple juice.

"So your good friend, Cutlass, is still missing, eh? I should think you feel lonely, don't you? The number of times I saw you together on the other side of this bar, well . . ." The club member leant over his cocktail, then raised his head.

"Listen, Jerry, I don't know where he is and if you know your place, you'll keep any opinions to yourself. OK?" The bartender stood back. He realised he'd been too close to the mark and probably wouldn't get a tip tonight, but Jerry had worked Quentins Club for over five years and did well enough with gratuities. He'd observed all of the members in his time there, piecing various ones together, watching their body language, their little touches. It was irksome for a guy that was as straight as a die. The cocktail drinker was friendly with the young man called Cutlass, many knew that, but the member sitting at the bar right then didn't want to talk about him. One problem was that the two had been seen arguing a little while ago as they left the club just after midnight.

But the cocktail simply didn't taste right this evening. It was time to go – the feeling in the club just wasn't right. Another member put his hand around his shoulder and squeezed him.

"Come on, don't look so glum, there are more friends for you if you look hard!"

But the member wasn't interested. He had things on his mind; didn't even hear Chivers say 'goodnight.' Taking his coat he wandered back to the car park, started the grey Range Rover and drove down the ramp.

He needed his sleep. It was an important day tomorrow.

*

Detective Simon Rogers had been trawling through a list of registration numbers in San Francisco that included 4, 8 and A. The two walkers who had initially responded to the police request for further information had mentioned a large black vehicle, possibly a sports utility vehicle, parked close to the scene where the body was found. Rogers realised that the number may have come from outside of Frisco, but checking local license plates was a good starting point. Vehicles also get sprayed at body-shops so Rogers focused on larger cars that were any colour. He reduced the list to twenty four, eliminating 'mini' cars, medium sized saloons, station wagons and vans. He looked down the plates and corresponding owners according to the SF Motor Vehicle Drivers Licensing register. The list of vehicles included Mitsubishi Shogun, Nissan X-Trail, Audi Q7, Land Rover Discovery, VW Tiguan, Hyundai i35, Toyota Rav, Kia Sportage, and Ford Kuga. Then the owner listing – in alphabetical order beginning with Mr. Alan Beiderbecker through to Mrs. Valerie Yonge – nineteen men, five women.

Enquiries with the manufacturer of the green and white striped tape, a company called 3M, suggested it was a heavy duty type little used by the general public, accounting for a very small fraction of total tape sales.

Detectives Rogers and Harris were already considering some other leads, especially the three reported missing persons on the SFPD MisPer file. Three white men aged 19, 24 and 32 were still unaccounted for and were shown as having been reported missing from home during the week commencing Monday, 27 April 2015. The computer of each of the three were with the police IT department and although they'd been thoroughly examined before the end of April, a number of email addresses were being re-checked. Credit and Debit cards had not been used. Rogers and Harris had interviewed a total of ninety three family members, friends and acquaintances of the three men.

And Emily Bauer continued to wonder why nobody had been to see her about her son since she'd spoken to Officer Bates about six months ago? Living alone she had few friends and nobody to talk to about things like this. She kept his room clean and tidy, bed made, just in case he turned up one day. His laptop computer was on a table where he always left it. But nobody from the police had phoned to say they were looking for him. No visit, no news at all. She'd have to phone her old friend, Jemima, but Emily couldn't remember where she lived. She'd put an address book, which included phone numbers, in a safe place.

The little book also had an entry under C for Caroline . . . *Caroline Sinclair, Jack's friend. +44 7933 991 455 or 54-8251*

But poor Emily. Her senile dementia was getting worse. She just didn't know where that little book had got to, or where her son was.

She prayed he'd be home soon.

21

"Jane, I don't suppose you know much about Thanksgiving, do you?" Amanda had popped up to Jane's room. It seemed an out-of-blue question.

"Not really. Ages ago I went to see a film called *Trains, Planes and Automobiles* with John Candy and Steve Martin. It was about two guys who wanted to get home for Thanksgiving. They struggled with ice and snow and eventually made it, except that John Candy really didn't have a home . . ." Jane trailed off, sounding as if she was promoting the film to a group of visiting foreign film buffs. Amanda coughed gently; Jane stopped talking.

"OK, OK. Anyway, it's coming up soon. It's the last Thursday in November which makes it the twenty sixth of the month. Of course it's a family time. But on the following evening for the last four years we've had friends round for drinks and a finger buffet. Howard usually asks two or three of the guys from the hospital with their partners, and then there are family friends such as Vida and her husband, and Rosemary who's a widow. Last year we invited Katie and her husband. His name's Clint." Jane realised that Amanda was not aware she knew Katie's husband's name. "He brought twenty bottles of Anchor beer which pleased Howard! It would be so good if you could help with the preparation? We allow the children to stay up late, so you'll be around to look after them, won't you?" In other words, thought Jane, 'we'd like you home that night!' A trained psychiatrist. Certainly. Able to negotiate a deal. Absolutely.

Jane had read about Thanksgiving. The Plymouth Fathers, 101 Puritans, had set sail in the *Mayflower* to America on 6 September 1620 arriving on 4 December, and celebrated their first harvest in 1621 in Massachusetts. And that was how it all started. So it was the anniversary of their harvesting for which they gave thanks. Nearly four hundred years ago!

"And Jane," Amanda turned as she left her room, "Why don't you invite that friend of yours, what's his name? Andrew?"

"I'll ask him. I've only seen him a couple of times so I'm not sure what he's up to. But, thanks." Amanda closed the door, smiling to herself. She'd recognised Andrew Wilson when he'd picked Jane up, and she knew his problems. Since the time when Amanda was treating Wilson, she'd had some dental work done to straighten and whiten her teeth as well as rhinoplasty surgery . . . Amanda had never been happy with the shape of her nose. After a two hour, private hospital surgical procedure, and seven days of rehab, she was pleased with the outcome. Her hair was longer now so it was a fair assumption that Wilson may not recognise her, and she'd take great interest in seeing how he was getting on. Wilson was on her register when she'd worked at a clinic in the southern part of Frisco about eight years ago. He'd just left High School and, with an IQ of 95, had been labelled a failure. His attention span was short, he was a troublemaker according to the school Principal, and had the highest absence rate of any student in his final year. On the plus side, if there was one, was the fact that he was charming, smart, and handsome. And his ability to lie was his saving grace. If Wilson ever decided to set foot on the stage, with his charm he'd be a natural – a human melange of Noel Coward, Colin Firth and Roger Moore! But the theatre was probably the farthest thing from his mind right now.

He was missing a very good friend and thinking he needed to get out of town for a short while, get some real fresh air, somewhere out of Frisco. As he lounged in his one bedroom studio apartment, crunched empty beer cans on the floor and unwashed dishes in the sink, he suddenly realised he needed to his check his driver's licence. It was due for renewal, wasn't it? Andrew pulled out a small drawer in his bedside locker and rummaged about. He moved a few items, lifted out his contact lens box from Specsavers, and pushed aside a hairpiece. Then he laughed out loud.

Andrew Wilson never had a driver's licence.

*

The California Institute of Art was holding another bi-monthly art exhibition over the coming week-end. Amanda had four paintings that she planned to show. The gallery committee encouraged amateur artists to exhibit their work in a variety of media, entrance fee per artist was $25, and each exhibit was individually priced for sale. Applications had to be made three months in advance, and Amanda Gardner had recently received notification that she had been nominated to show her work. Amanda always favoured a single word for a painting title, and she'd named them *Despair, Bleakness, Grief* and *Dejection.*

Only ever wanting Howard to see her paintings when they were completely finished, that was one reason that she kept her bedroom-turned-studio locked. She couldn't trust him, or anyone else, not to go in and take a peek. Framed by an art shop in Oakland Amanda had put a lot of effort into the four paintings and was pleased with them. Her hobby had turned into a passion – it gave her so much satisfaction. Before ever she laid a brush on the canvas she'd close her eyes and picture the scene, what it was to look like, the message it had for the admirer. Although Howard had now seen the finished paintings, he rarely expressed much interest. He certainly didn't comment on the subject matter. What went through his wife's mind when she composed these paintings? And one of his problems was that he couldn't really *interpret* them.

"Are you really sure you want the San Francisco public to see those paintings of yours?" Howard asked over breakfast.

"What do you mean am I really sure? You make it sound as if I'll be ridiculing myself by exhibiting them!" There was a razor blade in Amanda's response.

"All I'm asking is, are they the right kind of art to

exhibit, with your name on each one?" Howard finished his toast and emptied his coffee mug.

"What is wrong with you? I honestly thought you supported my work, my creativity." Jane was with the children in the bathroom ensuring teeth had been brushed. "Well, I'm going to go ahead and do it whether you like it or not! You'll be laughing on the other side of your critical face when I sell all four! Bloody hell, Howard! Thanks for nothing!" Howard needed to get to work, and away from conflict with his wife.

"I think you're misjudging my comments. There'll be a report in the Chronicle, comments from visitors, and if you're not careful you'll be getting a reputation. Look at that picture of the old woman in a rocking chair holding a crucifix, mouth open . . . all gaga. What's that all about?" Amanda was not going to take the worm on the hook but she spoke harshly.

"Listen Howard, why don't you go to the hospital and do what you're good at and leave me to do what I do. I'm going to exhibit those paintings whatever you think. I tell you what, why don't you go and take a walk in Muir Woods over the week-end while I spend time doing something associated with culture?" The razor blade snipe had turned to a cut-throat approach.

"OK, OK, calm down. I'm off, see you later when you've cooled down. I hope you don't have any difficult patients today, that's all I can say." He bent to kiss her cheek but she turned away and he got the message. Was it him? Amanda couldn't take criticism, he thought. But then he was feeling out of sorts. There were things on his mind that had surfaced during breakfast. He didn't mean to take it out on his wife and he knew he'd regret it once he got to work. The florist, Roots 'n Shoots, would provide him with a nice bunch of flowers on the way home later. Howard said good-bye to the kids and Jane, then shouted farewell to Amanda.

But she didn't reply.

*

It wasn't the first time this had happened – an argument at the breakfast table. Amanda Raskoff had sometimes wished her medical course at the University of Wisconsin Medical School had continued after her second year, but it really wasn't for her. She'd done the whole anatomy and physiology bit, began studying causes of diseases, carried out the dissection of cadavers and even got into the chemistry of pharmaceutical preparations. But it was not what she really wanted. A dear aunt in Milwaukee that she loved very much had suffered from mental problems and as Amanda began to care more about her she became interested in matters affecting the mind. The medical school principal allowed her to change course and she ended up with a degree in Medical Science, not Medicine. After that she focused on Psychology and after a three year period of research she gained her Ph.D., and was so proud to be called Doctor Amanda Raskoff.

She took up an appointment with a renowned clinic in Milwaukee under Professor Cornelius Van der Walt who, as a young graduate, had himself studied under Sigmund Freud at his private practice in Vienna in the late 1930's. Amanda stayed there for two years before seeing an advertisement in *Psychiatry Monthly* for an opening in San Francisco. She applied and got it. So here she was working for herself as a Consultant Psychiatrist with her one day a week at the hospital. Her cases there were varied and complex, but her strength lay in delving back into her patients' mental history, unravelling the traumatic threads that intertwined in their minds. Yes, that was her forte.

But what nobody knew was that her first registered patient when she came to Frisco was a young hospital intern. A man with complex issues – his father had been a disciplinarian, his mother loved her other son more than him, and whose sibling had died in a freak accident. He had to be treated. Matters brought out in the open, sifted through, filtered to purify the debris in his head. If left untreated this young man was going nowhere other than down the drain. It was to be a challenge to the psychiatrist, but she wanted to help. He was good looking, had a sense of humour and she liked his style. With an IQ of 149, he was a very intelligent person.

And that client on her register was Howard Clark Gardner.

22

"I wish for one thing!" Teresa had just got into the back of the Honda for the school run. Her exclamation begged for Jane to ask 'What?'

"Well, it's mum and dad again. I don't know why they argue so much . . . why do you think they argue, Jane?" The nanny had to compose a response quickly.

"I've said before when you've mentioned this, Teresa. A lot of mum's and dad's have their differences, little things that they disagree about. And you know, it's better to discuss something than to bottle it up . . . so they talk about it and try to sort it out." Jane wondered if her explanation had come across adequately. "Why are you asking?"

"Mum and dad were talking about doing different things last night. They were in the bedroom and before I went off to sleep I could hear them through the wall. She wants to put her paintings into an exhibition and dad doesn't want to go to view them. He says he'll go to Muir Woods for a walk all week-end." Jane knew that she had to give Teresa a satisfactory reply before she and Ryan were unloaded at the school gates. Ryan piped up.

"Teresa, stop worrying so! Mum and Dad have argued for a long time. So from time to time they get excited about something – so what? So do we, don't we?" A perfect response from her elder brother. Teresa yawned as she grabbed her bag.

"Yeah, guess so. OK, I'll stop worrying 'bout it. But I don't like falling out with you, Rye." Ryan smiled at Jane as he opened the car door. He realised he'd achieved his objective. Jane helped Teresa out and took her hand. "Jane, what's a divorce?" Teresa asked out of nowhere. Jane didn't need this right now. She stopped and crouched down next to the little girl.

"Now listen," Jane said soothingly, "there isn't time to talk about this now. If you clear your little head while you're at school today there'll be a treat at tea-time for you. And it's a surprise! I know you'll like it!"

"Yippee!" shouted Teresa, her thoughts now immediately turned to Bi-Rite ice cream and the possibility of balsamic strawberry flavour. Ryan shouted for him to be included, too, and Jane nodded as she waved them off into the school yard. Looking around, she couldn't see Jodie Patterson, nor did she want to. Jodie was one human being that was best avoided, Jane mused to herself. But as she turned Liza gave her a 'have you a moment?' wave from the main door. Jane locked the car and wandered over.

"Hi Liza, how are you?" Liza said she was fine. It seemed a stock-in-trade reply from half the American population, Jane had noticed. *'I'm fine, he's fine, we're all fine . . .'*

"Hi, Jane. Listen, I don't want to worry you but did you know that your predecessor, Caroline had a boyfriend? I think his name was Jake something . . ." Was Liza fishing?

"Did she? I never met her so that doesn't mean anything to me, I'm sorry." Jane's secondary school am-dram skills from the pantomime season were being tested.

"Oh, I thought maybe Ryan's parents may have mentioned him? Anyway, he went missing a while back and some say he drifted up north to Canada. Others think he and Dr. Gardner had an argument or somethin' and well, things may have happened."

'Come on Liza, I haven't got all day,' Jane's inner voice was ticking . . . Jane kept eye contact but said 'nowt', as Yorkshire folk did sometimes when faced with an open comment.

"Well, whatever happened to him, somebody I know said they'd seen him around the city. His appearance had changed, shorter hair, no earring, smartened himself up a little. Strange thing is – he ain't gone back to his ma, but she's losing it anyway." Jane glanced at her watch. How long did she want to listen to this monologue?

"Anything else, Liza. I really have to go," Jane almost

pleading with her.

"Er, OK, just thought you'd be interested that's all. Hey, I must go, too. The bell is about to ring. Bye, Jane." And with that Jane found herself standing at the door alone.

There was a problem, however. And that was that Liza's *'somebody I know'* comment was possibly made by a phantom friend who, although usually reliable with information, probably used a white stick.

*

Marie had asked her mum about Jodie Patterson. Vida Honeywell had worked in an pig abattoir named But's Cutz in Frisco some years back. A guy called Phil Butler had set the business up twenty years ago and wanted a catchy name. It seemed to work. Vida had moved from large scale cutting and sawing of carcasses to preparation of cuts of meat ready for the butchers shops and supermarkets. Whole pigs would be hooked up to a slow moving, overhead suspension system. As each animal passed over a large wooden bench they were lowered, the hook removed, and the pink carcass laid out for an operative to get to work. Each leg was removed for gammon and fore hock cuts, back taken off for prime bacon cuts, the collar that provided those big chunks for roasting sliced away, and finally the head was taken off. A selection of cleavers and long bladed knives, sharpened to razors, were in racks to perform the tasks.

They worked rapidly, each of the six operatives on a line having, on average, six and a half minutes to perform their dissections. Hand-carts would contain up to twenty legs or backs or flanks. Heads were used for ears, cheeks and snouts that were sent to a factory on the east side of Frisco and made into pies, along with the minimum amount of pork to satisfy the US Food and Drugs Administration specifications. The interior of the factory was air conditioned and 99% sterile.

Vida showed promise when promoted to Administration

Operative. She became more involved with procedures, liaised with pig farmers, and implemented some new methods that increased efficiency. As a result she soon became Assistant Administration Manager and took on recruitment responsibilities. The factory employed two hundred and fifty staff but the drop out rate was high. Neck ache and back ache kicked in, degrees of boredom combined with lax attitudes toward cutting and slicing resulted in voluntary departure or the sack. However, those that put in the effort were well paid and bonuses were good.

One day Vida Honeywell interviewed a young girl for a position on the main cutting line. Her name was Jodie Ringer who had just been fired as a waitress in a down town coffee bar for fiddling the till. Vida never found out about Jodie's misdoings and when she was offered the job, Jodie accepted it. So she went through the training and learnt all there was to know about cutting up pig's bodies. Jodie also got to know about the better cuts of bacon – top back and long back rashers. When she married Grant Patterson eight months after starting work at the abattoir she knew exactly what slices to put into his sandwiches as a treat on a Saturday morning, with lashings of brown sauce. After a session drinking Michelob beer most of every Friday night it was a pick-me-up for her husband, but then he had an iron constitution.

But it wasn't until Vida noticed some discrepancies in the daily weighed-in and weighed-out figures from the hand-carts to the end of products section since Jodie joined that she had to take action. Vida had asked Jodie to stay behind one evening and to open her shoulder bag before she left. Jodie refused. Vida called a security guard who opened her bag and found two large, well wrapped hocks, two collars and a pack of oyster cut bacon. That was it, Jodie was given the sack on the spot, paid wages she was owed minus the value of the meat cuts, and told to get out. Jodie was escorted to the main door of But's Cutz but not before telling Vida that she hadn't heard the last of this!

And although the security guard had searched her shoulder bag, he hadn't looked in her black leather handbag. Inside she had a razor-sharp knife with a nine inch blade.

*

The three white males reported missing in April had all been checked out. The fully clothed body of one of them, aged 19, had been found in the bay, trapped eight feet down near the north side of the Golden Gate bridge. The left ankle of his bloated body was wedged between rocks, and presumably he had been looking for something he may have lost. Nobody was sure, but two US Navy divers had been on an exercise and discovered his bloated hippopotamus-like remains. Most of his face and neck had been food for the fish; his dentition confirmed his identity.

The 32 year old had fallen out with his girlfriend and taken his own life. Parts of his body were found on a large, open trash tip on the outskirts of the city. Apparently he'd crawled into a refuse skip after taking an overdose, died in there, and ended up being mangled in the masticating rollers prior to mixing with loads of other household debris. An intact femur along with some other bones, and his head, were accidentally stepped on by a City Refuse worker raking through the rubbish. These were sufficient for the police to ID him and inform his parents and ex-girlfriend of the devastating news.

To date, the whereabouts of the 24 year old man were unknown. His name was Jed Aldrin and he had a long, white scar on the inside of his right leg from a serious motorcycle accident four years previously. The body in the shallow grave wasn't him. Detectives Rogers and Harris continued to struggle to identify the decomposed body despite further enquiries with the states bordering Texas. Ongoing interviews with drivers of vehicles that had plates showing 4, 8 and A were nearly complete.

When the two detectives got back to their office after

having spoken to twenty one of the twenty four owners in the Frisco area, there was a message for Simon Rogers from the forensic pathologist who had been re-examining the headless torso. The detective was handed a folded piece of paper from an assistant. He opened it. The message simply read: *Tattoo added to body after death. Dr. Ken Jones*

And yesterday a young policeman that had been keeping guard on the shallow grave had found a chocolate candy wrapper in the undergrowth within a few yards of the grave. Glancing casually at the low shrubbery he'd spotted the wrapper tied in a knot. Without picking it up, and uncertain of its significance, he phoned the station and a Crime Scene Investigation Officer arrived soon afterwards to bag and label it. How could this have been missed after an initial search of the area?

And one key question that Detective Rogers continued to struggle with was: 'Where the hell was the head?'

23

"Well, I'm not sure it was worth paying five dollars to look at this stuff, Bertha!" Her husband, Bernard, was standing looking at a painting entitled 'Boy on a Bicycle.' "Our granddaughter could have done better!" He was wearing a shabby coat, scarf with at least one hole in it, and a pair of shoes ready for the trash bin. They had travelled over 35 miles to Frisco that morning to view the art. Wandering around the exhibition where ninety three pictures were displayed they found some of the frames were more interesting than their contents! At least that was Bernard's opinion.

Between 9.00 am on Saturday and 4.00 pm on Sunday over two hundred and thirty people had paid to look at the exhibition in two halls. 'The Seaside,' 'Rear Garden,' 'Through a Lens,' . . . the titles signalled a wide variety of subject matter as visitors came from far and wide throughout California, aged between 9 and 90. A cafe at the rear of the hall, where two girls served hot and cold drinks and a selection of snacks and biscuits, was certainly kept busy.

Amanda's four entries, submitted under her maiden name, were shown separately; one in hall A, the other three in hall B. Jim Salsa, one of the organisers, spent his time wandering around both halls and people watching. He wanted to observe how long visitors were spending at each picture. It was intriguing to see younger people spending most time looking at pictures that were of nature, or the outdoors, or of children whereas the more mature visitors seemed to prefer the *complex* displays . . . those that demanded concentration, working out what the artist was trying to depict. The message, even. If there was one.

"Let's have a coffee, Bertha, I need a caffeine fix after wandering around here." Bernard tugged at his wife's sleeve and they headed for the cafe. Bertha, dressed as if she'd come off the set of a 1930's film, found two chairs in the corner whilst her husband got the drinks. He picked up a twin pack of Doritos to go with the coffee. As a retired pensioner, Bernard had to keep his energy up; Bertha just liked eating biscuits. Setting the tray down and offloading the drinks and biscuits, Bernard removed the art exhibition brochure from his inside pocket and perused the list. He'd become interested in art about ten years ago and loved to study what he called '*decent'* pictures.

"There's some odd stuff here, Bertha. I mean, look at this one. It's called 'Grief.' I've spent ages scrutinising this one. The dead woman with her gaping mouth is clutching a crucifix on a black beaded necklace, the rocking chair long since stopped. Look closely and you can see a black cat asleep in the corner of the room. The woman is dressed in old fashioned clothes, all dark, and the wedding ring is broken." He hesitated as he slurped his coffee whilst Bertha opened the Doritos and popped a whole one into her wide mouth. "Seems to me the artist of this picture is possibly painting somebody in her previous life, or an image of an individual that she hates. The grip on the crucifix is telling me that the dead woman desperately sought salvation as life slipped away from her . . . she died a slow death, probably in prayer. The open, toothless mouth, reveals emptiness – a metaphorical gap in the life of the artist. The broken wedding band is making a distinct statement that all is not well. Dark clothes clearly signifies mourning . . . not necessarily of the dead woman, but of a part of the life that may be ebbing away from the artist . . . what's her name for goodness sake?" Bernard glanced down the glossy page. "Here it is. Amanda Raskoff. Hmm, that name sounds familiar. Maybe we've seen her paintings before somewhere? But it leaves me concerned . . . the depiction of the corpse, the brush strokes . . . the way you almost expect the dead woman's eyes to suddenly open and stare at you!" Bertha crunched her Dorito and finished her coffee. "I'd say Raskoff has some problems, and uses painting as a safety valve to handle her inner feelings. I need to take a look at the other three of hers to draw further conclusions, but, well, there's an issue there." Bertha smiled to acknowledge her husband's monologue and chipped in with 'Yes, dear.'

A guy with a blue baseball cap who was sitting next to the retired couple was so tempted to tell Bernard that he was spouting gibberish and 'to shut the hell up,' but he held his tongue as Bernard swallowed the last mouthful of coffee, stood up and returned the tray and crockery to the counter. He gently gripped Bertha's sleeve – it was time to look at some more pictures.

The dude in the blue baseball cap didn't realise that he'd been listening to Bernard Cromwell, retired Professor of Psychology at Yale University and author of seven books on the psychiatry of the mind and the inner self. Not only that, but also an acknowledged expert on psychoanalysis.

He'd once been a Visiting Professor at the University of Wisconsin, too, where Miss Raskoff had been his student.

*

Jane's relationship with Ryan and Teresa was becoming solid. Firm. Bonding was taking place. Jane had kept an eye on Ryan after reading Caroline's email comments. Despite her accusation of his behaviour, stabbing himself with a pen, restless nights and being disturbed, Jane had not seen this in him. He was behaving sensibly, taking on the responsibility of the elder sibling and had adopted a sense of self-discipline. No longer would Jane find underpants under his bed, socks strewn all over, clothes tossed randomly over chairs and shoes left with knots in the laces. And Teresa was turning into a young lady in the sense of her improved manners, deportment and attitude to her parents. Sometimes Jane wondered if Teresa imitated her? If she did, it was a compliment to the au pair!

Jane had considered visiting Caroline but decided it may be best to leave it for the time being. There was no hurry, and other things might spring up in the meantime that Jane might want to explore when they met.

Andrew had phoned Jane several times for a casual chat. She felt he hadn't been too forward and she liked that. In fact, Jane was beginning to feel that she ought to take the initiative in going out again. She could call him tomorrow and suggest a trip out somewhere. He may have bought another car by now – he'd considered a sports coupe. Not only that, but Andrew had that yacht down at the marina! Jane could offer to make a picnic and the basketwork hamper that Jane had used with the children would come in handy.

Jane's mum had emailed again yesterday with news, beginning with the weather as usual – squally showers had covered most of Yorkshire, rain sweeping in from the west, then news on the neighbours who'd bought a new Citroen C4 in an awful colour, and bits and pieces on what she and Paul had been up to. They'd just come back from two nights away in Northumberland bought on an offer on the internet; half price, with full English breakfast. The small hotel near Lindisfarne was ideally situated for the nearby island, and the chef had spent the last five years at one of the top London hotels. Or so the blurb said. Her dad, Paul, was one of the world's great sceptics, and suggested the chef hadn't been further south that the *Angel of the North* in Gateshead!

All of this news made Jane a little homesick, but it kept her in touch with reality – with what was happening in and around Keighley, and the activities of her parents whom she loved dearly. In turn, she tried to send informative emails with a few photos attached – the children and any place she'd been. Jane was aware that she hadn't mentioned Andrew to them and had mulled over in her mind just what she could say. Clearly, she'd let them know how charming he was, so well-mannered, and that he was excellent at his job. Not only that, but because he was so well paid he wore good clothes, was looking for a decent sports car *and* had promised a day out on his boat. And if she knew anything at all about timepieces, she'd be able to tell them that he wore a Jaeger-LeCoultre gold and diamond watch.

The sad thing was, Jane hadn't really noticed his watch. At least not yet. Her parents would be impressed – she could hear her mum now . . . *'hasn't our Jane done well for herself?'* And if Jenny Lester did say that, she'd add . . . *'and I hope she's careful.'*

Jane had her head screwed on properly – her folks had seen to that, with a sprinkle of sound Yorkshire acumen. She was nobody's fool. But as Jane was planning to see Andrew again, police in Santa Rosa were asking questions about a photograph found in the back pocket of the jeans worn by a bank robber who'd tried to steal cash from the Union Bank of California. The photo was of a man with green eyes and blond hair, a long pony tail just visible. On the back was written: *To my best buddy Jimmy from Andy. With love.* The Santa Rosa police were using computerised photo-match techniques to try to establish the identity of the green-eyed man. They believed it was only a matter of time before they found out who he was. The scanning equipment could be linked to all photographs used for any ID purpose within the state of California and it wouldn't take them long. Hair style, forehead and nose shape, eye socket detail, lip fullness, chin roundness, and neck width as a ratio to the broadness of the head . . . and the bonus for the police was that his name was Andy. No, it shouldn't take long to identify him . . . then they could begin to search for him. For Andy. Or Andrew.

They had already identified the dead bank robber. An inscription on the back of a Rolex Oyster Chronograph he was wearing read: Jimmy Walters 15.2.1993

24

"I don't care if you used your maiden name or not, you didn't sell any pictures so why don't you just accept it?" Howard's voice was raised. He and Amanda had eaten early. A salmon steak and salad, and both had had a difficult day. The children were upstairs with Jane, homework their main priority. Amanda had dealt with a particularly difficult psychiatric case late in the day but she wasn't for backing down. Her husband had taken one of the nurses to task about handing him the wrong instrument during an awkward procedure, and Chuck Hudson hadn't helped by defending the nurse during the surgery. So there they were . . . unstoppable projectile meets immovable object in the Gardner household.

"You don't give me much credit, do you . . . "

"Credit! What the hell do you expect? I don't know why you waste your time slapping colours on paper, or oils on canvas . . . or whatever you slap on what!" Howard knew he was over-stepping the mark. Sometimes he didn't know why he got so uptight. But those little niggles had been in his head for some time now. Those small beeps, like someone sending morse code signals - dots and dashes - or the tap-tapping of a branch on the window during a windy night. He never had them when he and Priscilla were together. They'd just developed. He couldn't quite remember when, but it was probably soon after he'd started his treatment – when Amanda Raskoff was his psychiatrist, his therapist. And although he'd had fourteen sessions of treatment, he couldn't recall any of them. Howard often wondered if she'd used hypnosis, but once, when he suggested it, she bit his head off. Torn a strip off him.

"I do not slap anything on! If you knew anything about art, you'd realise how much of the body and soul of an artist goes into creating the image on the paper or canvas!" Amanda's hands were on her hips, legs slightly apart.

"OK,OK, all I'm saying . . . "

"I know what you're saying. You're jealous! That's it! It's you all over." Amanda walked across to her husband and leant over him as he sat at the table. "Just because you've no hobby where you need talent, there's no need to take it out on me. Hiking in the woods – huh! Call that a skill?" Knowing the kids were upstairs, Amanda kept her voice low whilst ensuring that Howard got the message – loud, or not so loud - and clear. After a short period of silence her words became a whisper.

"All right, so I didn't sell any pictures." Amanda had calmed down. She looked Howard in the eye. "So? I got pleasure from exhibiting them and being there amongst fellow artists. The two days passed quickly and I met some interesting people. There was no harm in that, was there?" She smiled, wanting to diffuse the situation. Amanda let a few seconds pass. "Would you like a drink? Let me get you a gin and tonic." She was trying hard.

"There's something you need to know." Howard's voice was relaxed, any anger gone. Amanda stopped half way to the kitchen. Turning, she saw worry in Howard's face. What was it? What did he want to tell her? She knew that when he came out with *that* specific sentence it was bad news. Amanda returned to the dining table.

"What is it? Tell me." She wondered if he'd been brooding, worried about whatever it was he had to tell her? Building up inside, simmering, about to boil over. Amanda sat down.

"The police came to the hospital today." Howard paused, swallowed hard and then spoke slowly. "It was between operations. Lunch time. They wanted a private word. Two detectives. I had to use my office." He was leaving Amanda hanging. "They wanted to know where I was on Friday, 1 May . My every movement by minute during the day up until midnight, I mean . . . hell! Every minute!"

"Why?" asked Amanda.

"They're following up on vehicle plates that contain 4, 8 and the letter A in the Frisco area. There was a report in the newspaper some time back. A black SUV having a plate with those digits and letter was reported as being seen near to where the body was found up in Muir Woods, the one in the shallow grave. Ours fits the bill, so where was I on 1 May they're asking?" Did the SFPD actually believe that her husband, a respected heart surgeon at the City hospital had murdered someone and decapitated the body? "Hell, I always used public parking areas when I go up there. There's no way it was anywhere near the spot where they found the body."

"I'll get you a large gin and tonic," she suggested. He nodded, and Howard wondered if they had any more questions for him. Just routine they'd said. Standard procedure they'd said.

"There's something else . . . " Amanda searched his face, not expecting another bombshell. "The wrists of the guy were bound with an uncommon, industrial type green and white tape. You might have read it in the Chronicle recently. We had a roll in our garage a while back but it's not there now. At least I think we had." Amanda shrugged her shoulders.

"I don't recall seeing that," she replied as she went into the kitchen, plates in hand.

Howard yawned, and after saying good-night to the children he decided on an early night, his drink half touched, ice unmelted. Three more important operations tomorrow, but he was restless. The shadows under his eyes were becoming darker.

*

Jane had taken a seat in the lecture theatre, the dark haired girl next to her giving her a warm smile. Looking around her she couldn't see 'Skinny Kid' or 'Gum Chewer' anywhere. Maybe they'd packed it in – too much for them? Sometimes people registered for a course to get out of the cold night air, sit in the warmth and doze a little. Check out the others in the class, see if there were any chicks worth talking to – get a free meal off them, scrounge a few cigarettes. Any drug pushers were a bonus, a snort of cocaine here and there. Then you could always borrow a few dollars with the promise to pay the lender back soon. But you never did because you didn't turn up any more and the tutor wasn't allowed to give out your name and address.

This was the third lecture on the Photography course and, so far, Jane was pleased with her progress. Gloria Rudetsky was enthusiastic about the subject, explained everything clearly, and the practical sessions with Greg and Alex were really interesting. Gloria had shown twelve photos on the large screen at the front, then she went through them one by one for the class to critique each one. Comments such as 'too much sky', 'subject too centred,' 'poor composition' and 'too much included' were made. Jane realised that a lot of her photos were in all of those categories. The students were told to spend a little more time composing their shots – not to quickly point and shoot. Focus on the key subject matter, but take a longer look at what was showing on the screen of the camera – create the picture, frame it with tree branches or a wall, don't always have the subject dead centre, obtain a balance . . . and so on and so on.

The task for each student before the next session was to take ten 'composed' photos. Gloria gave them her college email address and they had to send their best three to her the day before the next session. Students were pre-warned that Greg, Alex and her would review them and show their top ten list on the big screen, as well as the ten that needed critical comment – in other words, the worst ten bordering on rubbish. Thankfully, all would be kept anonymous! In the coming weeks they'd be getting more familiar with their cameras, using a manual setting instead of having it on automatic, opting for different focal settings and exposure times, and once downloaded – changing what was shown on the computer screen. Gloria had assured Jane that her Nikon Coolpix P300 was perfectly OK so there was no need to buy another camera.

The evening at the college had passed quickly. The girl that had been sitting next to Jane introduced herself as Louise. She seemed pleasant; short black hair, dark brown eyes, not an athletic build but she looked as if she worked out. Louise said she had only just moved to Frisco having worked for the *Arizona Republic* newspaper in Phoenix, but she'd been interested in photography for a number of years. She was now an Assistant Reporter on the San Francisco Chronicle, always carried a camera with her, and was on the course to improve her skills in that area. Jane was tempted to ask her if she knew Tom Lederer, but then she obviously would, wouldn't she? And this evening wasn't the time to start talking about any news items. In any case they might be confidential, or tomorrow's headlines. Reporters surely wanted to keep things to themselves, didn't they? Jane and Louise left the college together, then split at the main door as they exited into the cool night air. Louise hitched her hood over her head.

"Jane, here's my card . . . just so you know who I am. Call me Lou. It's been lovely to meet you. See you next week." Louise headed off in the opposite direction as Jane shouted 'thanks' down the dimly lit street after her. The car park was one level below the street and, feeling it was safer, Jane took the concrete steps down rather than use the lift. Her shoe heels had steel tips and made a clicking sound as she headed down to her car. 'Why didn't I wear my rubber soles tonight?' she asked herself. Looking around she heard the sound of footsteps, but she couldn't see anyone. Her safety whistle was in her hand along with the car keys. Just as she turned a corner an arm shot out and grabbed her by the collar of her jacket, the other hand of the assailant twisted Jane round, and pushed her against a stone pillar. Jane tried to squeal but a gloved hand was instantly over her mouth, stifling her cry.

"Don't make a sound!" Jodie Patterson was holding Jane in a mole-wrench grip, her warm breath on Jane's face. The neon lights on the ceiling glinted off a sharp nine inch knife blade . "You think you're so high and mighty, driving around in your little car, acting all smart. You ignored me at the school gates, just couldn't be bothered to speak, could you? And being British, you consider yourself so much better than the Americans, with your talk and fancy words. You're no better than that other nanny, what was her name? Caroline. Oh, yes, she thought she knew it all. But she was naughty, wasn't she? Getting too friendly with the doctor, been seen in his big black car one night. They didn't tell you that, did they? You know____" Suddenly, Patterson's grip loosened as one of her arms was pulled behind her back, an arm round her neck as the knife dropped to the concrete floor. A good Samaritan held Jodie Patterson firmly; she was unable to move.

"One more move from you and I'll break your neck. Understand?" whispered the person who'd appeared out of the corner shadows, face partly hidden. A nod to Jane didn't need to be spelt out. With her vision misted, Jane ran to the Honda, got in and left the car park as quickly as she could. Her drive back to Adair Way was a nightmare. She didn't know what to make of the last five minutes. Why had Patterson attacked her? Jane hadn't done any harm to her, had tried to be civil. She blinked continuously to clear her eyes, traffic lights becoming blurred as she exceeded the speed limits along the road back to Hayward. And what had Patterson said about Caroline? *'Getting too friendly with the doctor . . .'*

Jane parked about fifty yards from the entrance to the Gardner household. She turned off the engine, and then the headlights. Tears uncontrollably ran down her cheeks as she searched for a tissue. Was Howard Gardner going to start getting too friendly with her? Jane had been sitting there for some minutes when, through damp eyes, she saw kaleidoscopic red and blue lights as a SFPD cruiser pulled up behind her.

*

The little old lady with the grey hair-bun took the steps one by one using her stick for support, went through the glass door and shuffled along to the desk. A tubby police officer with a neatly trimmed moustache sat on a high stool on the other side, hair gelled flat like patent leather. He looked down at the grey haired visitor.

"Yes, ma'am, can I help you?" Officer McGraw held a ballpoint pen in his right hand, seemingly glued to his fingers.

"It's my boy. You ain't never told me 'bout my boy." Her voice was raised. "I phoned here some while back, spoke to an officer, then zippo! I've kept his room tidy and all, case he walks in. The officer said he'd help . . ." McGraw held his hands up, palms facing the old lady.

"Whoa, there. When did all this happen?" Emily Bauer got closer.

"'Back in April. Phoned here, spoke to one of you lot, then I ain't heard nothing since! I know my memory ain't what it used to be and the days pass so quick. I just thought someone'd be round to tell me they'd found him." McGraw listened to every word that came from Emily's thin, lilac-grey lips. Her beady eyes seemed to draw him in like a hypnotist.

"Let's start again, er . . ."

"Mrs. Bauer, Emily Bauer."

"Right." Officer McGraw turned to one of his colleagues, a short guy who looked like Tom Cruise with sideburns. "Harry, can you take Mrs. Bauer here to the interview room and take down some details about her missing son?" Officer Ladd obliged, taking Emily by the arm and helping her the few yards to IR1 down the corridor. They both sat down and Ladd made notes on the details of her son. When it came to body height and weight she had no idea but gave Ladd their doctors address. He'd been to see a nurse at the clinic about a year ago for a check up – they'd have those details there. Name, date of birth, any distinguishing marks were all noted by the policeman. When they were finished, Emily was escorted to the main door of the police station whence she made her way home. Ladd entered the information onto the computer, adding to the list of others who'd been recently reported missing. He then checked the doctor's phone number and made a call to obtain her son's physical data. Ladd entered five feet nine inches and 168 pounds. The only mark on her son's body was a slight scar, an inch long, on his right cheek – Ladd had entered that in the appropriate place on his screen. And being a conscientious police officer, Ladd sent an email to Detective Simon Rogers informing him of the latest addition to the MP list. It was standard operating procedure. Within twenty four hours Detective Rogers was sitting in Emily Bauer's home, a cup of white instant coffee with one sugar taking the dryness from his throat.

"So, your son Jake didn't come home after he went out with friends on the night of the 23 April. Are you certain it was that night?" Rogers had a notepad in his left hand.

"Sure. It's my sister's birthday, and, she always reminds me that she shares the birth date with Mr. Billy Shakespeare. He wrote some plays or whatever, didn't he? Anyway, she'd invited me round for a drink but, well, I wasn't feeling too good so I stayed home. Jake left here around seven o'clock, said he was meeting his buddies for a couple of beers, then he's always home before midnight." Rogers scribbled notes.

"Mrs. Bauer, we're going to put Jake at the top of our priority list. As soon as we get any information we'll be in touch. Does Jake have a laptop computer or ipad?" She nodded and said he had a laptop. "Do you have the names of any of his friends? Those he saw regularly, went out with . . ."

"Can't say as I do, he had quite a few. John somebody. He talked about a guy named Jimmy. Oh, there was a girl he was seeing. Oh, what was her name . . . Caroline. That was it, Caroline. She was nice, brought her here once. She worked as a nanny in some part of Frisco. I think her number is in a little red telephone book I've got but I don't know where it is." Rogers sipped his coffee.

"Can I take a look in Jake's bedroom?" Mrs. Bauer nodded. Glancing around the room he noticed a pile of magazines, some sports equipment and an open design wardrobe containing a variety of shirts. There were receipts for a Sony micro-cassette recorder and a pair of headphones pinned to a cork-board, and three pairs of shoes under a dresser. Nothing really out of the ordinary. Returning within a few minutes, Detective Rogers took out his card and handed it to Mrs. Bauer.

"Mrs. Bauer, give me a call if you find the book. Or if you remember anything else that may be of help. Meanwhile, we're going to pull out all the stops to find your boy." Emily looked out of the window. "Before I go, do you think I can take his laptop, you know, just to check things?" Again, Emily nodded." Do you have anything personal of Jake's that I may take away, you know, to help with our enquiries. Something like his toothbrush, or hairbrush?" Emily went into Jake's room and was soon back. "By the way, does Jake have a bright green shirt?"

"No, not that I know of. Here, take this." Rogers noticed a few blond hairs on the hairbrush. He thanked Mrs. Bauer as he took the computer and brush, finished his coffee, then saw himself to the door. Emily Bauer wondered why the detective wanted Jake's hairbrush. Maybe he was a shut-eye or a psychic . . . you know, hold it and get some vibes – tell him where he was?

But Rogers was heading back to the police mortuary, he had something that Dr. Ken Jones would find interesting. And the IT guys could examine his computer, look at emails, view Favourites/History – see what Jake Bauer had been up to before Thursday, 23 April. Had he been searching any unusual web sites?

In addition, the reported grey Range Rover that may have had bodywork repairs to a dent and a white Mitsubishi with rare black and silver alloy wheels were being followed up. The police also had some information not made available at any of the press conferences to date, and that was that three hairs and some bright green fibre had been found on the body in Muir Woods.

The bright green fibre was shown by spectroscopy to be to a fabric known as Nylon 66.

25

Chuck Hudson and a hospital porter named Kris Roberts had been in a relationship for the past four months. The surgeon had noticed the good looking porter on a number of occasions, wheeling patients in and out of the operating room. It was the eyes that did it to begin with, the remainder of the face masked. Roberts had brown hair and hazel eyes. One of twins, Roberts didn't like to talk about his brother who'd died recently but Hudson never pushed him on the matter. He was tall and walked with a swagger. Hudson had noticed him more as he walked out of the OR, his body moving rhythmically underneath his sterile overall. With his reputation as an upcoming surgeon, the last thing Hudson wanted was to be talked about in the hospital corridors – or anywhere else for that matter. He had a desire to meet with Kris Roberts, but it needed to be outside of the City Hospital. Their relationship within the walls of the medical building would be strictly professional. It was sure to be spotted by Karen or Angelina or any of the other inquisitive nursing staff.

So Chuck Hudson had, over a Michelob beer in a nearby bar after work one evening, suggested to Kris Roberts that he might like to join a club. Quentin's. There they could meet in private, talk, drink, have a bite to eat and some fun. Quentin's had been established in 1965 and proved to be popular with many men in Frisco who enjoyed the company of other males. No women were allowed in, except the employed cloakroom staff, whose incessant chatter could be eardrum rattling. No menopausal problems to be vented, no gossip or bitchiness about the latest fashion trends. None of that. Just good, honest men's talk. About cars and motorbikes and boats . . . any *real man* stuff. And Roberts was interested in motorbikes, as his twin brother had been. Not just any type of bike, but *trial bikes*. Those with high frames, nobbly tyres and a gutsy performance that could be ridden through mud, over boulders and across waterfalls. They were *real* bikes.

The problem was he couldn't afford one, not on his wages at SFCH. But Dr. Hudson, being kind and thoughtful, had offered to get Kris a trial bike. Not new, but a good second hand one. Maybe a Honda or a Yamaha. Kris had laughed at that and Chuck liked his manner - soft and gentle. But more important than that was to get Kris membership of Quentin's. At an annual fee of $500, Kris shook his head at the suggestion, declined the offer. In his persuasive way, however, Chuck ignored the rejection and told him he'd cover his first year. Another Michelob later Kris, and after Chuck had described the club, agreed to join. Kris was amused to hear of the nickname concept; nobody used their real name. Chuck knew then that he had a name for his friend. A kris is a large knife with a wavy blade used in Malaysia so he'd name him Cutlass! Chuck would propose him – a formality – and he'd be a member in under a month.

So that's how it worked out. Chuck arranged for the delivery of a Yamaha motorbike to Kris' place and soon Cutlass had his membership card to the prestigious Quentin's Club. The two hospital staff were able to keep their relationship private, meeting up three or four evenings per week at the bar for a cocktail made by Jerry, the bartender. On week-ends Chuck would suggest short trips out of Frisco, and outwardly these two were just a couple of guys who were good friends. There were scrambling events held in parts of California and Chuck bought a small trailer on which he could transport the motorbike. He already had a tow bar on his Range Rover, with wired-up electrics, so it was no big deal to push the Yamaha onto the back and secure it with three strong nylon tapes, hand tightened with ratchets. Chuck would watch Kris, dressed in blue and white leathers, on his scrambler when he was competing, the spinning rear wheel throwing up stone chips as the exhaust blew out wispy, blue-grey gases.

And the two friends enjoyed each others company for sixteen weeks and three days. Chuck Hudson was a man of precision – he kept a diary – and wrote a daily entry from the first day they'd made that special contact as their eyes met. But the doctor was also a jealous person, feelings deep rooted in his soul. As long as he had his own way, he was happy . . . wanted to be in control, have friends around him agree with his decisions, didn't like to hear the word 'no.' And the stupid hospital porter just couldn't see that with his very own motorbike bought as a gift, he really should have been more aware of his actions towards the doctor. Shown more affection. Should have played the game, been good, well behaved. Understood the rules. But no. Kris was in close contact with Richard, another hospital porter, and trying to play him off against Chuck. Kris was clever, Chuck gave him that. Not clever in the high IQ sense, but clever in a subtle, underhand, cheating way. The problem was that Kris was getting a thrill from playing this game of his, maintaining eye contact with the surgeon when he came into the OR with another patient. Eyes that met for a moment too long. Not that anyone noticed.

And when Kris wasn't able to go out with the doctor, because of a supposed cold or 'flu, he'd be holding hands with Richard in some other gay bar in the city. When Chuck found out from a fellow club member at Quentin's he was livid, close to exploding. But even the most jealous person, with strong inner willpower, can control that like an overworked boiler getting up a head of steam, building up to an eruption, the safety valve designed to allow the escape of excessive force.

Chuck suggested that he and Kris spend an evening at Quentin's as he had a birthday surprise for him. Jerry had concocted a special recipe for a cocktail that he'd named a *Cutlass Cutie.* Kris couldn't resist that – a cocktail named after him! So he agreed and Chuck offered to pick him up at his apartment at 7.00 pm so that the hospital porter could enjoy a few *Cutie's*. It was a date. Chuck got showered and dressed in a smart pair of trousers and beige cotton jacket. A few generous dabs of 'Pour L'Homme' made Chuck smell irresistible, at least he hoped so. Likewise, Kris made a good effort, and Chuck greeted him with a gentle slap on the left thigh as his partner for the evening got into the tan leather front seat of the Range Rover. They drove down town, Chuck parked up, and the friends went into Quentin's.

"Happy birthday, Cutlass!" shouted a group of buddies as Kris walked into the lounge bar. One of them was called Doug, nicknamed Jess. The bartender, Jerry, was already tossing his cocktail shaker and almost ready to pour the first of his *Cutlass Cutie's* for the birthday boy. A blend of gin, vodka, vermouth and lime juice was poured over crushed ice, topped off with a green olive. Kris sipped his cocktail as others patted him on the back and made comments about his age, 25, and his partnership with Chuck. Everyone laughed out loud as the raucous remarks continued for some time, especially from Jess who was up from San Diego. Chuck knew he had to put on an act because he had something important to discuss with his buddy that evening. Not only that, but he'd bribed Jerry to make up an alcohol-free cocktail. Same colour, same bouquet as the *Cutie* with an olive. Chuck would stay sober.

And so everyone had a good laugh, jokes spreading like mist under the Golden Gate bridge on a damp day. Until Chuck suggested that he and Kris take a quiet double seat in the corner, out of earshot of the rest. They chatted amiably until Chuck asked Kris about Richard. Kris gulped, his Adam's apple visible beneath his open shirt collar.

"Come on," Chuck egged him on, smiling, "you can tell me. Who's this new friend of yours, then?" Kris had drunk four *Cutie's* by this time, his cheeks were warm, his head slowly spinning.

"Jus' a friend, it's no big deal. We work together so, you know, we're around each other all day ___ " The doctor's attitude changed, the charming smile gone. "Wassa matter with you?" slurred Kris across his empty glass. "Don't like it, do we, when I have another pal to play with?" hiccuped Kris. Chuck Hudson nearly flipped, but not in front of the other club members. Not now.

"Hey, yeah, you're right. It's no big deal. But you've had enough here, and I don't want to be responsible for you being unfit for work tomorrow." The charm returned. Chuck forced a smile. "Let's get you home and you can have an early night – sleep it off before morning." Kris tugged his sleeve away from Chuck's light grip.

"No! You can clear off! It's my birthday an' you can take a jump! I'm staying here!" Kris stood up but fell back down onto the double seat, his hand on his forehead. "Jeez, those cocktails were strong . . . what's in 'em, dynamite? No, you go, I ain't for missing out on my party. An' anyway, you ain't got me my present, yet!" Kris was raising his voice. Another club member came over.

"Cutlass, I think you've had enough. Why don't you let Doc take you home?" Kris stumbled slightly, steadying himself on someone at the next table, who told him to 'go drown yourself.' As Chuck helped Kris out of the lounge bar their conversation continued into the foyer and out into the night air. Chivers had said 'goodnight' to both of them, giving Chuck a glance that spoke volumes. The bickering continued into the car park and inside the Range Rover until Chuck screamed.

"Shut the hell up, you two timing piece of dirt!" He fired up the engine and the vehicle left the parking area at speed. Kris, without his seat belt on, flopped from side to side like a puppet. Two miles outside of the city limits, Chuck pulled the SUV off the road and down a dirt track, stopped the car and killed the lights. It was pitch black. As Kris began rabbiting on about the lack of his birthday present Chuck removed a syringe from it's wrapper. Kris never felt the fine needle go into his thigh through the thin material of his flimsy trousers and in three seconds the syringe barrel was empty, its clear, anaesthetic fluid now circulating very rapidly in Kris' bloodstream.

"Hey, what the hell_____" Kris slumped forwards, unconscious, his head hitting the dashboard.

Chuck's eyes became accustomed to the starlit night. He'd considered taking the heavy duty polythene sheeting out of the trunk, wrapping Kris in it to suffocate him and dumping it somewhere. But that would mean getting out of the car, struggling with the body, getting girt and dust on his clothes, all potentially traceable. Chuck waited. He heard a car drive past the end of the track, it slowed but didn't stop. He had to think this through, get his story straight for the police. They would come asking questions.

After a few minutes, his breathing back to normal, Chuck started the engine, put the headlights on, and drove down to the railway sidings. Some freight trains would be leaving the station in the early hours, heading out of Frisco with their heavy loads. His mother had always told him that it was 'dangerous to play near the trains.' She was right. Hudson parked in the shadows of a brick rail building and waited.

26

Jane had dropped the children off at school. There was no sign of Jodie Patterson. Jane was now seriously beginning to consider her role with the Gardner's as their au pair. She'd been there about six weeks. The police had been kind to her when they'd pulled up behind the Honda a couple of nights ago. She'd been honest, well almost. Telling them she'd had a bust up with her boyfriend over nothing, they believed her and wished her good luck. But Jane now had the nagging worry about what that Patterson woman had said regarding Caroline Sinclair. Not only that, but Jane still didn't know who her rescuer was in the car park. When she rewound the thoughts in her head, Jane couldn't be certain if it was a man or a woman who'd come to her aid. And what had happened after she'd driven off from the car park – did the good Samaritan beat the living daylights out of Jodie Patterson, give her a piece of their mind? Even kill her?

Jane thought long and hard about her position. She didn't want to get drawn into some Mafia-come-gangland scenario. She was there to do a simple job – care for the children. And she enjoyed that; Ryan and Teresa were close to being model charges. They were improving in all spheres, including homework that they detested to start with but which they now enjoyed. Jane saw growth in their personal development, correct use of sentences in conversation and the written word, and general all-round behaviour. In fact, there was now a comfortable routine for her in the household and she was getting on well with Katie. Because she'd been quite busy, Jane was aware that she'd neglected to contact Sam and Marie, and hadn't spoken to Andrew for a while. She ought to phone all three of them soonest. Texts and emails were fine, but Jane was really a 'talking person.'

Jane had also thought about Melody Oppenberg, her counsellor. They hadn't spoken for some time. Would it be politic to call Melody for a chat, even ask her what she knew about the history of au pairs in Adair Way? If Melody didn't know, she'd probe – ask Jane why she was enquiring and Jane wasn't the world's best liar. Then there was Nora Dijon over in Sacramento, the red headed dizzy au pair that Jane had met on the induction course. She was the closest other au pair to Jane. Was it worth phoning her?

Had Caroline really been seen in Dr. Gardner's car with him? Jane began to wonder about Caroline's dismissal. Had the nanny and Howard been having an affair and Amanda had found out? Perhaps some story was concocted and Amanda demanded that Caroline went or else? What Jane needed right now was someone she could turn to, somebody honest and reliable who knew what had happened. But who could she trust? Katie? Sam? Marie? Andrew? Liza? Even Caroline herself? Why not take a Greyhound bus up to L.A., meet with Caroline, play the innocent. Jane suddenly realised that Melody Oppenberg was based in Los Angeles. Two birds with one stone? For sure, Jane wanted some answers, the questions spinning around in her head like clothes in a tumble drier. Jane's cell phone rang but she didn't recognise the number.

"Hi?" she answered, omitting her name until she knew who it was.

"Jane? It's Lou. San Francisco Chronicle. Are you OK? Did you get home OK? I've had a problem getting your number . . ."

"Hey, whoa, slow down. I'm fine, thanks, Lou."

"I had to ask Gloria at college. She was reluctant to give me your number – privacy and all that – until I explained what had happened."

"What do you mean 'what had happened?'

"Well, it was me that grabbed that woman in the car park, the one who attacked you. I realised after we parted that I'd given you an old business card and ran back to give you a new one. I guessed where you were parked and as soon as I got down one floor I saw she'd got hold of you. It didn't look nice." Jane recalled the shadows had made it difficult to recognise who'd gone to her aid. "My judo lessons came in handy after all! Black belt. I also told her I was a reporter on the Chronicle, said I knew who she was, and that there'd be an article in the newspaper if she repeated it ever again, as well as being reported to the police. Except I told one lie."

"What was that?"

"I didn't know her from Eve!" Jane gasped. Lou had grabbed her assailant with no fear, protection kicking in when she saw that her new-found friend was being assaulted. Jane told Louise who the woman was, giving her some background detail to their first meeting at Lexington Junior School.

"Well, I think I scared her enough for her to leave you alone. She won't want to appear in the pages of our newspaper for harassment or intimidation. I've got connections with the detectives at SFPD, so, you know . . ." Jane felt relieved. "If there are any other issues with her, let me know. OK? I didn't get to give you my card so here's my email address." Jane wrote it down. LousePArcher@sfchronicle.com "Send me an email and let me have your cell number. I must go, phones are ringing all over the place here. Bye, Jane." So Lou had come to her rescue in the car park! And with a black belt in judo who knows a few detectives in the police department Louise Archer could be a useful ally. But Jane would need to get to know her better before broaching the subject of Dr. Gardner and the previous au pair. Jane's phone rang again. It was Andrew's number.

"Hi Andrew! How are you?" She wanted to sound lively.

"Hi, Jane! Been meaning to call you for a few days, but been busy. You know, the hectic life of a salesman!" Andrew laughed. "Listen, there's a Halloween party coming up end of October. Wondered if you're up for it? There'll be plenty of people there, including Sam, Marie and Arty. Should be good fun. What do you say?" Wasn't this just what Jane needed right now? A party to look forward to, let her hair down, have a few drinks.

"Yeah, great. Count me in! Let me have more details nearer the date, but it sounds good."

"Are we seeing each other before then, though? Time for another Chinese? There's a good place that's been recommended. Be nice to try it with you. And we can talk about that day out on the yacht." His smooth, syrup tone and perfect intonation made her instantly agree.

"That's fine!" she almost shouted.

"I'll pick you up in my new car on Tuesday at eight o'clock. OK?"

'New car. Ooh, that will be nice,' thought Jane. She felt so lucky. And she wondered if the restaurant would give out fortune cookies?

Andrew Wilson had yet to decide where he was going to get a car from, but it wouldn't be a problem.

*

The hair taken from Jake Bauer's hairbrush had been subjected to DNA testing. Detective Simon Rogers had been busy with other police matters – a number of thefts, a murder in one of the hotels, a missing wife who'd walked out on her husband after a row, a series of drug raids on pharmacies. Rogers and his colleague Megan Harris were kept busy in Frisco and neither had been back to the lab, nor heard from Dr. Jones on the results.

Rogers, 32, had been in the SFPD for ten years. A cop with good experience, he was six feet tall with close cropped hair, aquiline nose and dark eyes that gave away his Hawaiian heritage on his mother's side. His father had been a cop before him and retired only five years ago. Single, Rogers had been fond of Megan Harris for some time now, but she never wanted to mix business with pleasure. He always sent her a Valentine's card and a red rose in February but Megan ignored it, pretending not to know it was from him. She'd take the mickey by telling Rogers that she'd received the card and rose and wondered who'd sent them. He never let on! His handsome features were an attraction, but for now she'd keep him at arms length. She knew that if ever she let her barriers down her resistance to his smooth manners would be zero.

Harris, at five feet, four inches, was a dead ringer for Dolly Parton but with a lower centre of gravity, her blonde hair her own. Tougher than Alcatraz rock, she had an excellent record for solo arrests within the city, her gym club membership well worth her annual subscription. In a t-shirt, she had a figure to match any Miss USA, and her tanned legs were as smooth as polished walnut and about the same colour.

Both reported in to Lieutenant Marty Kluisters, a tough ex-Marine who was married to Letitia. Kluisters was hard but fair. If you tried to pull the wool over his eyes you'd be kicked hard, but play the game with him, get your job done, and he was as nice as pecan pie – but not as sweet. Kluisters was under continual pressure, his headaches managed by a regular intake of *Tylenol*, his indigestion neutralised with *Pepsidol*. The detective was anxious to solve the murder of the headless torso found in Muir Woods. He'd heard about Mrs. Bauer reporting her son lost, and the 24 year old male Caucasian, Jed Aldrin, who was still missing. He had car thefts aplenty on his plate, recreational drug use was escalating, four unsolved homicides and there seemed to be a spate of domestic violence sweeping across parts of California, including San Francisco. Police work! He loved it and hated it at the same time.

By the end of today, Kluisters' boss wanted to know if the body in the police mortuary was Jake Bauer or not. Where the hell was Ken Jones, the head pathologist who was getting the DNA results from forensics? Kluisters used the internal phone and dialled 114. No reply. He dialled again as Simon Rogers and Megan Harris entered the building. Rogers headed straight to Forensics and heard Ken Jones on the phone talking to Marty Kluisters.

"Yes, I'm sure. Absolutely. The hairs taken from the

brush are a not a match. Yes. Certain."

"Doc, did I hear right?" asked Rogers. Ken Jones nodded.

"The DNA profiles don't match. The body isn't that of Jake Bauer."

Rogers looked at Megan Harris. He would have put his month's wages on it being Mrs. Bauer's son. Was Bauer still alive? The IT guys were still trawling the laptop computer – and the detective was waiting for news. A link, some connection that would give a clue to Jake Bauer's whereabouts. An unidentified headless torso and young Bauer still unaccounted for. Megan Harris shrugged – more a reaction saying 'we'll have news soon' rather than 'we haven't got a clue.' Rogers was about to ask Megan if she wanted a beer in Mitch's Bar two streets away when a guy from Information Technology stuck his head around the door.

"Excuse me, Simon. I've been looking at emails on Jake Bauer's laptop. There's something I think you need to see."

*

It was quiet. Silent. Two big locomotives were situated at the railhead, twenty two fully loaded trucks linked to each one. Security lamps shed their ivory coloured light across the yard, a few dark areas where shadows were cast across the tracks. Nearly midnight, Chuck Hudson didn't need to wait any longer. He eased the Range Rover a little way in front of one loco. Going round to the passenger door he eased Kris Roberts out, handling him like he was lifting a roll of heavy carpet. Lowering him gently, Hudson pulled him across the first rail, tugged a little more, and then placed his neck on the next track. Hudson pulled a note from his jacket pocket. Having noticed Roberts' writing style from the porters notes he'd written in the hospital, Hudson had already prepared a suicide note.

Hudson slipped the note in Roberts' jacket pocket and

then climbed back into his car in the shadows, aware of possible CCTV cameras or Security Guards. He started the Range Rover engine, kept revs low, and slowly took the long ramp back up to the main road before putting the headlights on and driving home. It was a quarter after midnight, an hour before the first loco was due to pull out of the railhead. The body was laid about a hundred yards from the engine cow-catcher, hopefully far away enough for the driver and fireman not to see it – they'd be too busy checking the cab; steam pressure, water level, fire, coal. The heavy engine wheels would slice through the neck on one side of the axle, and the lower limbs on the other. The crunching of bones, splitting of muscle and tendons and then spurting blood would go unnoticed by the crew as the iron giant headed north. It got daylight around six o'clock and that's the first anybody might notice a body on the rails, blood coagulating on the gravel chippings around the sleepers. With a suicide note in his pocket, telling the finder that he was tired of life, this was how he wanted to end things. Kris didn't want to be a burden to anyone so, despite it being his birthday, this was the only way out for him.

Hudson had calculated that by the time Roberts' body was found, the anaesthetic injection would not be traceable in the blood stream, but alcohol from the cocktails would. Of course, there were witnesses at Quentin's – saw and heard them arguing, but Hudson was now clear on his story when the police came calling. He'd picked his friend up, driven to the club, gone in and celebrated his birthday with a special cocktail that Jerry had made. Kris had enjoyed the drink and had several but Hudson would tell the police he wasn't drinking alcohol that night. They'd had a slight disagreement about a cash loan and it had got a little out of hand. Roberts didn't know when he'd be able to repay the $1,000 so they argued. Being inebriated, Kris wanted to party on, but Hudson was firm and urged that he took him home. Other guests would confirm the events. He'd tell the police that he dropped Kris off at his front door, and then drove home. Hudson would tell the police he was back at his place by . . . He'd decide on a time that fitted in with the time they left the club and the estimated total journey.

'That piece of crap. Nobody messes with me . . .' Chuck Hudson was still very annoyed with his unfaithful boyfriend, but within half an hour those sixty inch wheels of the loco would have sliced through Kris' body, and he wouldn't have felt a thing! That made the doctor smile. 'Such a shame,' he thought. Still grinning he parked his grey SUV in its allotted space, locked it and quietly opened the front door of his apartment. It was now 1.50 am and time to get some rest; after such a busy night he was weary. Setting his radio alarm for 6.30 am Hudson got into bed and put the bedside light off, but not before wiping that red stuff off his lips. He was tired but found it difficult to sleep. There was something niggling him. Was there some little mistake he'd made? No, couldn't think of anything, and reassured himself it would all be OK. The suicide note was short and sweet. The police would find it in the morning.

Kris Roberts could go rot in hell.

27

Marie's mother, Vida Honeywell, and Sam's mom, Rosemary Gless, had been friends for a long time. Within a few months of taking up her new post in Frisco Amanda had met Vida and Rosemary, but quite by chance. Amanda was finding her way around the city, using landmarks like the TransAmerica building to guide her around, and getting used to the north to south and east to west street layouts. One damp Saturday morning she'd been driving down an Interstate highway when her front nearside tyre popped. She'd pulled over onto the hard shoulder, turned off the engine and sat there for a few seconds. Did she have a spare? A lot of new cars didn't. If there was one in the trunk, did she have a jack to change the wheel? And apart from that, how the hell *do you* jack up a car and remove the problem wheel?

Suddenly there was a tap on the window. Out of nowhere a woman was looking at her forlorn face. Amanda had powered down the window. Was it someone who was going to ask her why the heck she had stopped on the roadside – a hazard to traffic?

"Hi, you look as if you need help? I'm Vida Honeywell. My friend Rosy is with me in my car behind. Can we help?" And that became the start of a long friendship. A prayer by Amanda Raskoff had been answered by Vida and Rosy. Not only that, but Rosy had the spare wheel and jack out of the trunk, car lifted and wheel changed before Amanda could say 'alloy wheel fitted with a tyre.' Amanda had made to assist but these two angels of mercy had attended to the matter as Amanda had stood ambered in the flashing car indicators reflecting off the wet tarmac.

So that was it, phone numbers exchanged, coffee planned, and their friendship had begun. Amanda had met their daughters and they'd hit it off immediately. Vida and Rosemary's families were invited to the wedding of Amanda and Howard, enjoyed the reception at the Marriott

Hotel and they kept in touch. Just because of a flat tyre. But that's life.

As Amanda's relationship with Rosemary Gless developed it turned out that there was something irritating Rosemary, like a burr under a horse's saddle. It was the stepson from Rosy's second marriage to Geoff. His name was Doug. Geoff had died of pancreatic cancer some time ago and Doug moved away but it took about six months before Rosy raised the subject with Amanda; she couldn't hold it in any longer. Especially when Amanda asked Rosy if she was OK and Amanda could tell that she wasn't. When the two of them were having coffee one Saturday morning at Starbucks on Seventh Street back in early April, Rosy had burst into tears.

"I don't know how much more I can take of this. Geoff hasn't been gone long and that no good son of his wants to know how much he's getting from Geoff's will. The answer is nothing. He left everything to me. Doug is a waster." Amanda placed her hand over Rosy's.

"Hey, there, there. It can't be that bad. Where is Doug now?"

"He phoned me from San Diego where he's been working in a bar. He's arriving at my place tonight around seven. I'm dreading it. I know he'll be banging on the door until I let him in, then he'll want to stay. What am I supposed to do?" Rosy took out a small handkerchief and wiped her eyes, then blew her nose. Rosy lived in a fairly secluded, mid-sized detached house up on Nob Hill fronting onto Richmond Avenue. It held many fond memories of her time with Geoff. He'd been a successful chemical engineer with the Exxon Corporation ever since he left college with a good degree. "I've nobody else I can really turn to. I mean, Vida is kind but I don't want to get her involved. I feel I can talk to you Amanda, that you understand." Being a psychiatrist had some benefits, but the role could be a burden. Everybody believed you were going to be a saviour for them.

"Rosy, listen. Why don't I come up to your place at

around six o'clock? Then I'll be there when Doug arrives and we can talk to him together. You know, strength in numbers. You could diffuse the situation by having his room ready, his favourite meal ready to heat up, and a couple of bottles of beer. Ask him about his journey, how long he wants to stay for . . . that type of thing. What do you think?" Amanda maintained eye contact. The tears had stopped. After some thought, Rosy replied.

"If you're sure, I'd welcome that very much. Maybe you could stay for an hour or so, make sure, in you're professional opinion, if he's sound of mind. You know, not loopy or anything like that." Amanda smiled but said nothing. "OK, well, I'll see you later." Rosy stood up, closed her purse and walked to the door. She turned and waved at Amanda as she slipped out through the glass door.

Amanda sat there for a little longer, a mouthful of coffee still in the bottom of the cup. She wanted some quiet time to think about this. Rosemary had not described Doug in any detail and it was wrong for her to make assumptions about his character. She was quick to read people, see from their eyes what may be going on in their head, and look for body language signals. Needing to eat early, she'd just tell Howard that she was going to see Rosemary for a girlie chat and she'd be back home by eight thirty latest.

Amanda finished her coffee, put on her light coat and left the cafe. Right now Ryan and Teresa were with Howard in the park where he'd buy the inevitable double cones of ice cream and push them on the swings until his arms ached. Amanda would tell Howard about her evening's plans, make sure the children were all right, and start some preparation for the evening meal. But first there were some clothes stores and shoe shops deserving of her attention. She'd seen a pair of blue satin Manolo Blahnik shoes with a square diamante buckle; they would be a perfect match for one of her evening handbags.

. . .

An hour later, and nearly four hundred dollars lighter, Amanda drove home. The smart, bag with upmarket store logo containing her satin shoes was on the floor behind her. But a hundred yards from home her Ford Taunus suddenly developed a slight clattering sound from under the bonnet. Cursing under her breath, Amanda placed the gear stick into neutral and coasted the last few yards to 31, Adair Way. The car clock showed 5.28 pm. Phew! What a relief. Howard's Audi Q7 was parked on the double drive so he and the children were home. Entering the house she told Howard about the car problem, then her plans for the evening. After giving her a quick kiss, and not taking any notice of the shopping bag, he took control of the 'Taunus situation.' Amanda hugged the kids and went upstairs to her bedroom. Howard didn't need to see her shoes – he wouldn't be interested anyway.

Within half an hour a mechanic had arrived from the garage down town where they held an account for all three cars. A good looking young man in grey overalls and Mr. Fixit on his back in orange letters rang the bell. 'Here to look at the Ford,' he smiled at Howard as he spoke. Howard gave Mr. Fixit the keys and left him to it – no point in hovering over the mechanic. Apart from being able to check the oil and water levels, Howard knew very little about cars, let alone engines. In ten minutes the door bell rang again and Ryan rushed to open it. 'Dad in?' asked Mr. Fixit. Howard appeared behind his son. The bad news was that the Ford Taunus would have to be towed into the garage for the engine to be properly checked. Worse still, it couldn't be done until Monday morning first thing. So Amanda's plans were fast disappearing. That was until her caring husband suggested she take the Audi Q7. Amanda hadn't driven it very much, it was too big for her, but she instantly accepted his offer.

After the meal, a home made beef lasagne with a chicory and red pepper salad, Amanda put on some make-up, cleaned her already white teeth, and left. Entering Rosy's address in Nob Hill into the GPS system after starting the car, Amanda carefully eased off the driveway after checking and adjusting the rear view mirror. She waved to Howard and the children as she turned right and headed east. *At the end of the road make a right turn . . .* said the female sat-nav voice in a very sexy tone. No wonder her husband used sat-nav a lot, even when he knew where he was going!

Amanda worked out her strategy as she drove towards Nob Hill. She would use her smile, the firm handshake, some positive opening remarks about his physical features, questions such as 'do you enjoy being a barman in San Diego?' Yes, it would be all right. And she was supporting her friend Rosy. Amanda parked up about a hundred yards from Rosy's house – she felt she needed a short stroll and the evening was pleasant. But what she didn't expect to hear was Doug's voice as she stood at the front door. He had arrived earlier than planned and was arguing with his mother. As the first and second rings of the doorbell had gone unanswered, Amanda tried the handle and found the door unlocked. Letting herself in quietly she heard Doug shouting, almost on the verge of having a fit, and using words like *bitch, cow* and *parasite*. Amanda entered the kitchen to see Doug holding his mother's collar tightly, her face pink. Amanda threw down her handbag and rushed at Doug – he had to be pulled away; Rosy was being strangled.

"What the hell . . . who the hell . . ?" he shouted. Amanda pulled at Doug's muscular forearms, making little impression, but then he turned and grabbed Amanda with both hands, pulling her face close to his. She smelt a mix of whisky and cigarettes on his breath. "So, the bloody cavalry has arrived, has it? What do you think *you* can do, you bitch, you scum-sucking pig!" Amanda couldn't breathe, she felt her legs growing weaker as he tightened his grip, her silk scarf acting as a noose around her reddening neck. "I've only come for what's rightly mine. Damn you! This old bag isn't having it all!"

And then suddenly, out of nowhere, two curved prongs of a heavy claw hammer split his skull wide open.

28

"Hi, Melody, how are you?" Jane decided to make a timely phone call to her counsellor. There wasn't anything that she really wanted to talk to Melody about, but Jane simply decided that it was an opportunity to touch base – say 'hello', ask how she was, tell Melody that all was fine with the Gardner's. Except that it wasn't as good as it could be.

"Oh, hi Jane. Is all well with you? I was going to give you a call, but you've beaten me to it!" Jane didn't know if Melody was telling the truth. People often said that, lying, in their defence. "How are the children – Ryan and Teresa?"

The conversation ping-ponged for a few minutes. But it was long enough, Jane had done her diplomatic bit, told her counsellor she was fine, and becoming a nanny in the USA was the best decision she'd ever made. Melody in turn would be telling her next in line that Jane Lester in San Francisco was as happy as an Easter bunny! Jane didn't mention Caroline - if she decided to go to L.A. she'd already decided not to tell Melody.

Jane had taken a call from Louise at the Chronicle. Lou asked Jane how she was, and the suggestion of a meeting over lunch was proposed. They were both slowly getting to know each other and Jane surmised that Lou must be a busy girl wondering what news stories Lou was dealing with right now – items would be arriving on her computer throughout the day, phone calls made, leads followed up. Was it a case of filtering out those juicy stories that the public really wanted to read? After all, that's what sold papers, wasn't it? Lou would also be party to a lot of information on the headless torso case, other missing persons, and a whole raft of matters that affected the Frisco population. Not only that, but she'd have access to retrospective news, the data probably stored on discs in their offices. Jane might want to get to know Lou better.

Then there was Sam, who'd been at Hardy & Davison

Lawyers for almost eighteen months. Jane wouldn't ask anyone to divulge confidences, but . . . over a casual coffee, Sam could be asked if she might be able to check a few things. Jane didn't have anything specific on her mind, but was just contemplating a few possibilities. For example, Katie had mentioned that there had been a number of reports in the Chronicle on Dr. Howard Gardner in connection with the death of his wife in that awful accident at the Grand Canyon, and that he'd hired a good lawyer. Was it Hardy or Davison? And could there be anything else?

The Thanksgiving date was approaching, but it was Halloween before then. Jane knew Amanda had already started her preparation for the party that took place on the evening after Thanksgiving, and Jane had been commandeered to help. Halloween was yet to be clarified, but Andrew had invited Jane to a party – she just needed the venue and time. He hadn't mentioned whether they were dressing up, but it would be fun Jane had thought to herself. A long black cloak, pointed hat, maybe a makeshift broom like the ones that witches are supposed to fly on, and some scary make up. Yes, time for a little fun – some escapism.

Jane was also contemplating that six hour bus ride to L.A. to see Caroline. Google had indicated that it was 341 miles from Frisco, but of course the bus would be stopping at a few places en route, a good way to see some of the state of California, though. Caroline hadn't suggested staying over with her so if the journey was going to be made Jane would need to consider booking a room on a Saturday night. A small motel would suit her fine; she could afford a few dollars to pay for a room and treat Caroline to a meal that wasn't too expensive. An early Greyhound bus would get her there by mid afternoon. After freshening up she could meet Caroline for dinner, then make the return trip the next day. A couple of magazines and her current paperback would help pass the time, and she'd be back in Hayward by around six pm on

Sunday.

Meanwhile, Jane had to care for the children. Both of them were growing and developing. It was so rewarding, thought Jane, and only after a relatively short time. Even Amanda had passed a positive comment only a few days ago that had boosted Jane's ego, and Jane wondered if they might ask her to stay beyond her twelve month contractual period. But that was a long way off and she had other things to think about. Her frown turned to a big smile when she saw Andrew's name come up on her mobile phone screen.

"Hi, you big hunk of handsomeness! Been thinking about you! Have you got your new car, yet?" Jane hoped her verbal gush had made him turn red, especially if he was in the office.

"Miss Lester? Is that Jane Lester speaking?" Jane froze. Who on earth was using Andrew's phone?

"Er, yes. Who is this____?"

"Detective Simon Rogers, San Francisco Police. We need to talk."

*

An IT colleague of Detective Rogers, known to his colleagues as Gabby, was peering at the screen of a Toshiba Satellite C660 laptop computer. The Inbox of Jake Bauer's emails was open. The last one sent was dated 23 April 2015. Prior to that there were over three hundred emails languishing in Inbox, Trash and Sent messages. The majority were run of the mill messages to a variety of friends. Mrs. Bauer had already given the police the names of three of Jake's buddies, all of whom had been interviewed. Their stories had all tallied in terms of what he was doing on the evening of the twenty third. Jake had met a group of friends at a bar in town, *Billie's Beer Garden* off Thirty Third Street. Caroline Sinclair had been there, and three other girls. After a few beers they'd all left at the same time and headed down to another bar called

Clooney's, two blocks away. It seemed the group were not causing any trouble. Bartenders had been interviewed and nobody was reported as being intoxicated, and there were no comments as regards bad language. It wasn't a special occasion. They were just a bunch of buddies chatting and catching up on stuff over a few beers and cocktails.

"Take a look, Simon. On the day he went missing he sent four emails – three to a Caroline Sinclair, and one to a Jimmy Walters. I've checked on both of them. He's the guy shot in the bank robbery up at Santa Rosa a couple of weeks back. The girl here was an au pair girl with the Gardner family. She refers to her job as a nanny and in a previous email gives the address of the house in Adair Way." Gabby paused to let Simon Rogers read the content. "Here it suggests that they'd had an argument. Bauer is accusing her of becoming too friendly with the father of the children. She'd replied, this email here, saying he's being over-sensitive and Dr. Gardner, *Doctor, no less,* is just being friendly. It looks as if he'd visited the house a few times. The last email from Bauer to Sinclair is a 'let's kiss and make up' kind of message." Rogers eyes scanned the screen like a buyer on the New York Stock Exchange searching for a good share deal. "He invites her to the gathering at the beer garden so he can make amends for a few things he's put in previous emails. See here, she then replies agreeing to the night out . . . maybe thinking she'll be safe with there being a few of them together. He even said he'd bought her a little gift . . .now ain't that sweet?" Detective Rogers moved away from the desk. He was thinking.

So, Sinclair had met Bauer at the beer garden around seven. Others were either already there, or they joined them a little later. There were approximately eight or nine in the group, they didn't cause any disruption, and they moved onto Clooney's around eight thirty. Mrs. Bauer has already told us that her son was normally home midnight latest, but maybe usually around eleven or so. One of the Clooney's bartenders said he recalled Bauer and Sinclair being on good terms, hugging and laughing, although he looked as if he may have been taking something, some drug, maybe. His eyes were red as if he might have been crying, but he couldn't be certain.

The group left the bar at 10.12 pm according to a CCTV camera near the front door. They were chattering away and everyone seemed happy. Of those we've interviewed, they've all said that the group broke up outside Clooney's, Bauer and Sinclair going off arm in arm in an easterly direction. Nobody, however, was certain as to how Sinclair had travelled into town, nor how she was going to get back to Adair Way. So, was Sinclair the last one to see Bauer alive? Where did they go to as they walked away from the group?

For sure, Bauer had not sent any emails, made any phone calls, nor used his credit card since Thursday, 23 April 2015. At least *not* using *his* laptop or *his* mobile phone. He might even have got *another* credit card – people did. No, Bauer had vanished. There was no evidence that he was dead, but had he run away from something? One email from Sinclair had mentioned an argument with Dr. Gardner. Had Bauer come to a sticky end, buried somewhere, or cut into pieces and fed to the fish down in the bay?

As Rogers mulled these issues over in his mind he knew there were three things he wanted to do quickly. One, talk to Caroline Sinclair. Two, have a discussion with Dr. Gardner. Three, go and see Mrs. Bauer and ask a few more questions where, if he was lucky, he might get a white instant coffee with one sugar. Before he left the office, Rogers glanced at the SUV list again in connection with the headless torso. He and Megan Harris had narrowed the owners down to five – all of the others had alibis as regards their whereabouts on the evening of Friday, 1 May. Of these five, there were two Audi Q7's, a Hyundai i35, a Range Rover and the fifth was a VW Tiguan. The name 'Gardner' jumped off the page immediately - Dr. Howard Clark Gardner, registered owner of a black Audi Q7. Registration plate GTA-204-138. 'Hmm, interesting,' thought Rogers. He dialled a cell phone number.

Detective Harris picked up a few seconds later.

*

Jane had agreed to go to the SFPD Central Station offices at 766, Vallejo Street at the request of Detective Rogers. Immediately after his call to her on Andrew's cell phone she had called McEnroe & Nelson to be told by Mr. McEnroe that Andrew had been arrested half an hour before. A detective and two policemen had entered the Real Estate agent's office and, having established Andrew Wilson's identity, took him away. So, here was Jane going to talk to the detectives about her boyfriend – not understanding why he'd been arrested. But whatever the reason, she felt confused. Her mind was racing as she entered the main reception area. Within minutes a woman approached her.

"You must be Jane Lester," asked Megan Harris. Jane nodded. "Please follow me." They went down a corridor, turned left, and entered a small, brightly lit, square room. Jane sat opposite Rogers and Harris, a uniformed police officer, arms folded, stood at the door. Having been offered a coffee, Jane tried to relax but found it difficult. Rogers began the conversation after turning on the CD recorder. Jane sipped her coffee but realised her hand was shaking. She slowly put it down.

"First of all tell us what you know about Andrew Wilson, Jane." Rogers was straight faced, but smiled at the corner of his eyes. Jane would start at the beginning, but not before asking why she was there. Rogers explained that Andrew had been arrested in connection with a bank robbery in Santa Rosa. Gasping, Jane had taken out a handkerchief and wiped her nose. She had a bad feeling about this.

"Why are you asking me about Andrew? He has lots of

other friends . . ." Harris put her hand up as if stopping traffic at an intersection.

"Jane, we need to ask a few basic questions. We know you and Andrew are good friends. You'd seen each other, been out together. And you'll recall how you answered Andrew's cell phone when my colleague Detective Rogers called you on it. We recorded your reply." Jane felt her cheeks turn red. She knew that there was no point in bluffing – she'd be caught out. Telling lies would make it worse; getting her facts mixed up. So with that, Jane told the detectives her story. Everything. Well, almost everything.

But the SFPD only told Jane as much as they wanted to. *Not* how they'd found Wilson by using the photo in Jimmy's back pocket, matching the image to an application for a bus pass. *Not* that he was a compulsive liar. *Not* that he didn't have a driving licence. Few details were given out on the robbery when Jimmy was shot, and the police *did* believe Jane when she told them she didn't know anyone by the name of Jimmy Walters. And Simon Rogers felt that he didn't have to mention two items found in Andrew Wilson's apartment – a pair of green contact lenses and a blond wig with a pony tail. A simple but effective disguise when he and Jimmy were busy helping banks off-load their cash.

Lastly, after a few more brief questions, Detective Rogers asked Jane what she was doing in San Francisco. In his somewhat naive eagerness to get her to talk about Wilson, he hadn't asked that fundamental question. And when Jane told him what she did, he really believed that Christmas had arrived early.

It was time to talk to Dr. Gardner again.

29

Megan Harris had been working hard on the headless torso case. The body still lay in the morgue, the clothes that the victim was wearing were still bagged and in storage – jeans, boots, socks, underpants. No shirt. No cell phone or wallet; the crumpled green and white binding tape cut from the wrists still sealed in a polythene bag. The three hairs and the green nylon fibres were potential clues to the murderer or murderers, but they were waiting for someone and something to be matched against. Her colleague Rogers, as Lead Detective, was planning to see Dr. Gardner and she knew that his meeting would potentially yield some significant information.

Harris wondered about the tattoo of Texas. Was it a red herring, there to fool the police? Did the dead guy come from Texas, or was there a band called 'Texas' or perhaps there was some other relevant connection? Enquiries with the state police had led nowhere. And Dr. Ken Jones had said the tattoo was inked onto the skin *after* death. Close examination of the outer layer of the skin indicated that the black dye had not penetrated the epidermis as was normal with the art of tattooing. And then, through the thin plastic of the specimen bag, Harris looked at the candy wrapper found by the on-duty police officer near the shallow grave, still tied in a knot just as it had been found. A *Hershey Creamy Milk Chocolate Bar with Almonds* manufactured by The Hershey Company in Pennsylvania. Megan Harris ran her tongue over her teeth and gums imagining the taste and velvety texture of the smooth, dark chocolate. But what was this wrapper doing very close to the burial site? A pic-nicker? A litter lout? Somebody emptying a ruc-sac? A hiker, maybe? The glossy surface of the wrapper had been checked for finger prints but none were found. Some materials just couldn't hang onto fingerprints . . .and an old waxy Hershey bar wrapper was one of them. And was it really relevant to this case?

Meanwhile, a security guard down at the railhead had telephoned the police to say that he'd found what seemed like a suicide note next to the track. It was written on pink notepaper that had a small red heart with a blue line through it in the bottom right hand corner – a logo for a medical company, perhaps? The police asked about a dead body, but there wasn't a body anywhere – just the paper fluttering in the early morning breeze.

CAN'T TAKE ANY MORE. MY LIFE IS OVER. THERE'S NOTHING LEFT.

A glum emoticon face was scrawled underneath the message.

*

Jane had taken a phone call from Sam say how surprised they all were at the news of Andrew's arrest. They could not believe that he'd been involved with bank hold-ups. Jimmy Walters was known to a few of Andrew's friends, but Sam had never met him. Arty, Marie's boyfriend, had been out for a few beers with Andrew and Jimmy, and Arty had remarked that there was something odd about Jimmy. One eye was looking outwards; kind of squinting. He was no target for the front cover of a magazine but Arty had said he'd have looked good in westerns as a baddie. Mr. Nelson and Mr. McEnroe were both shocked when the two detectives had entered the premises and asked to speak with one of their employees. Less than five minutes later they'd handcuffed Andrew Wilson and eased him into a waiting police car parked right outside. Simon Rogers had kept the detail brief, not needing to explain much to the two owners of the real estate agency. But the photo on Wilson's annual bus pass application to the City Council was a perfect match to the one found on Jimmy Walters. One thing that Sam didn't question was whether Andrew was the kind of guy who'd play baseball for both sides . . . liked to alternate with both teams from time to time.

Jane tried hard to concentrate on her day after that call.

She had some washing to do for the children, make their beds, tidy up. She had been out taking some photographs near the Golden Gate bridge the day before and wanted to download them onto her laptop – then change the tint, or move the main focus of the photo, or . . . well, just try to be creative in readiness for the next class at college. There was also that incident with Jodie Patterson that gnarled on in her head. Being grabbed in the car park only happened in American films, didn't it? Jane could still feel Patterson's clammy fingers on her neck, the touch of butcher's cold steel against her throat. It seemed clear to Jane that Jodie Patterson had a problem, festering inside her cranium. Why? Jane didn't know, but there was something very odd about that woman – a person that she didn't want to meet outside of the school gates – or anywhere if it came to that! She had Lou to thank for getting her out of that mess. Hell, what would have happened if Lou hadn't turned up? And then, as sometimes happens, the very person that Jane had been thinking about was calling her. The phone was chiming, the screen showing *Louise Archer – Chronicle.*

"Hi, Lou, I was just thinking about you! How are things?"

"Hi, Jane, yes – fine. Listen, it might be useful to meet up? Have coffee . . . somewhere quiet?"

"Sure," said Jane, realising her voice sounded a generation away from her Keighley roots. "Where and when?"

"There's a cafe called The Four Barrels Coffee Shop on Valencia Street. Can you make eleven this morning? The cafe will be fairly quiet then, and there's a recess at the back of the place with just a few tables. There are a couple of things that might interest you." That call was a blessing in disguise. It took Jane's mind off her domestic chores, as well as thinking about Andrew. Finishing what she was doing, Jane decided to leave her laptop photography plans, finish up in the children's bedrooms and get ready to drive into town.

Louise hadn't indicated what was on her mind, but Jane assumed that she may have some news on an upcoming event, a circus in town, a mystery Halloween ball at a swanky hotel? For certain, Jane wouldn't be seeing Andrew for a long time and wasn't sure if she wanted to go to the party that he'd planned to take her to, even if some of her other friends were going to be there, too. No, she'd leave that for now and focus on her cafe latte in town, with a cinnamon doughnut, maybe? As Jane drove towards the city her thoughts started to wander. Not only about her scrape with Patterson, but what Patterson had said about Caroline. Jane was still concerned for Ryan and Teresa as they still occasionally mentioned arguments between their parents as she took them to school. How well did Jane really know Howard and Amanda? The more she thought about them, the less she knew. And was there a reason why Amanda's so-called art studio was kept locked, as well as Howard's study? Maybe not . . . Jane told herself not to become paranoid. Then there was the body in Muir Woods, the police still seemed no further forward in identifying the headless torso, but news snippets in the Chronicle or on TV kept the case in the public eye.

Jane pulled into the car park space on the second floor between an Explorer and a Chevy Compact, switched off the engine and checked her watch. 10.47 am. Perfect. It wasn't far to Valencia Street, then she'd look for the coffee shop. As Jane clicked the Honda Civic key fob to lock the car, she spotted a man and woman getting into the lift about twenty yards away. She couldn't be certain, the light was poor, but from the back it looked like Howard Gardner and Jodie Patterson. The lift doors closed quickly. Too quick for Jane to be certain. She climbed the concrete steps briskly, exited onto the main concourse, and looked in all directions.

There was no sign of either of them. Then she doubted herself; it probably wasn't them at all.

30

1 May 2015

"Holy smoke, what the *hell* have you done?" Amanda was breathing heavily as she moved away from the blood oozing onto the kitchen floor. The claw hammer had made a large cavity on the top of the skull; bone fragments and some small lumps of grey brain matter lay scattered inches from his head. She put a hand on her neck; it felt warm where Doug Gless had gripped her tight for what had seemed an eternity. A few moments longer and Amanda would probably have been sitting in the big psychiatrist's office in the sky.

"Oh, my God," screamed Rosy, "this wasn't supposed to happen! Shit, shit, shit!" She was panting hard as she eased her way around the body to take a look at her stepson's face. She bent over him, his eyes were wide open, the check shirt blood-soaked. "What the hell are we going to do?" Amanda wondered about the use of the word 'we', but dismissed it instantly. They were both involved here – no passing the buck, no one blaming the other. Doug was attacking Rosy in a very aggressive manner as Amanda came into the house, she ran to help Rosy and Doug turned on Amanda whom he would have killed. Rosy had to protect her friend so the two pound tool had to be brought down on his head with all the strength she could muster. Simple. At least in the way that it had happened. But not so simple now.

"We've got to get him out of here, dispose of him, scrub this floor . . ." Rosy's mind was working overtime. "And get rid of the hammer, too." Amanda began to calm down. She needed to be rational. Think things through.

"Rosy, sit down here," Amanda pulled a kitchen chair from under the table. "Do *not* step in that blood!" Rosy slowly eased herself onto the chair, hanging onto the side of the oak table for support as her fingers gripped the wood, her knuckles blanching. "Let's think about this now. We both know what's occurred – and it just turned out the way it did. He was hell bent on killing you, then me, and you hit him with the hammer. Right?" Rosy's face was sallow as she slowly nodded. "We've got to do something with the body. We certainly can't call the police. Their forensic team will piece the events together and, well, we'll both be in for it . . ." Silence hung too long in the air, but it was useful to reflect on events. After a while, Rosy spoke.

"Let's take him up to Muir Woods! Stick him in a hole out of the way. Maybe the wild animals will chew at him?" Amanda wondered if Rosy had been watching too many 18 rated films lately. But the clinical psychiatrist had a thought. It wasn't a pretty one, but it was feasible. Amanda sat down and looked at her watch. It was 6.32 pm. It wouldn't be dark for a while longer, sunset was at 8.01 pm, but if they were to put Rosy's plan into place, they'd have to drive to Muir Woods after dusk.

"Rosy. Listen to this and tell me what you think." Rosy gulped from a glass of water that Amanda had poured out for both of them. Amanda outlined a plan, and she needed Rosy's agreement to carry it out. Amanda proposed that they burn off Doug's fingerprints. There was a demijohn of sulphuric acid in the garage that Geoff used to use for cleaning rusted metal parts and other jobs. That would make things more difficult in case they tried to match the dead body to anything with which Doug may have touched in the house. The thought of hacking his hands off made Amanda swallow hard.

Doug's shirt had a motif stitched onto the right hand side of the chest – with his initials DG. That had to go. Rosy chirped up and suggested taking his shirt off altogether – they nodded in agreement.

Amanda decided that, if his wrists were bound, it might make it look as if he'd been tied up before being killed – a planned execution rather than a sudden murder. Rosy pondered the idea then, surprisingly, smiled slightly. Amanda rushed out to the garage where she found a reel of wide, striped adhesive tape. Then, between them, they bound his wrists as tightly as possible.

"I've got another idea!" exclaimed Rosy. "A tattoo – I saw a film once where they tattooed somebody's arm to make it look as if they were from another country! A foreigner! It foxed the cops for ages!" Amanda stood up.

"Does Geoff have any black paint in the garage, Rosy?"

"Black paint? Maybe. But I know he's got some inks . . . black, even Indian ink. The sketching he used to do." Perfect, thought Amanda. Rosy fetched the pot of ink and then, at Amanda's suggestion, got some needles from her work basket. Amanda selected a knitting needle to begin with, then a finer pointed one. "What you gonna do? A bunny rabbit with big ears?" Rosy almost chuckled. Looking around her Amanda spotted a souvenir from Texas on a cupboard top, an outline of the state with three big wooden cubes that were used as a calendar. Why not? Amanda used her artist's skills to 'engrave' an outline of the Lone Star state, Texas, a millimetre or so into the epidermis on his left shoulder blade. Now that ought to confuse Sherlock Holmes, thought Amanda . . .

"Wait a minute," Rosy had put her hand on Amanda's arm. "If Doug's reported missing and his body is found it won't take long to identify him. His dentition . . . I know he looked after his teeth and regularly saw his dentist here in Frisco." A few seconds of silence followed as Rosy's eyes flashed around the kitchen like a lighthouse beam. "Could you pull his teeth out?" She stared at Amanda.

"I'm no dental surgeon, Rosy! Do you want me to use a pair of pliers, for goodness sake?" The two women stared at the body for a while, minds working overtime. Blood had stopped its gradual movement across the floor, a large semicircular pool lay under Doug. "You'll be asking me to decapitate him next!" Rosy smiled.

"That's right! Do it!" Amanda gasped and looked at Rosy as if Rosy had instantly become deranged. "You told me you'd been a failed medical student, done two years of dissecting cadavers – so, *you can do it*!" Amanda sat on one of the chairs to get her breath and take stock of the whole matter. Hell, she was sitting in a friend's kitchen with the body of Rosy's murdered stepson laying in what was starting to look like a crimson jelly. His skull was part-caved in, his fingertips red raw from acid burns, and wrists secured with the striped duct tape. This had to be a dream, didn't it? Amanda was jolted from her unreal thinking when Rosy spoke.

"Well? Do it, Amanda!" Rosy carefully held a sharp serrated knife out in front of her, handle towards Amanda. Amanda stood up and grasped the riveted wooden handle firmly. Between them they dragged Doug's body a short way across the floor away from the darkening, congealing blood.

"Rosy, you know I think a lot about you, and if we go through with this it absolutely must be our secret, do you understand?" Rosy nodded. "No, I mean *our secret*. Nobody, but nobody else must know."

"Cross my heart and hope to die!" replied Rosy, right index finger crossing her chest.

And with that their work began. Rosy looked on as Amanda recalled her student days, then, using a hacksaw that she'd gone to fetch from the garage, began to sever the spine. A dull rasping sound competed with their heavy breathing as the blade slid between the third and fourth cervical vertebrae. Push - pull, push - pull, push – pull. Tugging at his scalp, the head came away easily, the neck muscles bright red with the empty carotid arteries and veins dangling like snotty cat gut. Rosy then took over. Now wearing her household rubber gloves, and holding Doug's scalp, she gingerly placed the head in a wide, double layered plastic grocery bag. Every item used was individually wrapped in newspaper and bagged in heavy gauge polythene, secured with more of the striped tape.

Rosy began to wipe up the blood from the impervious, tiled kitchen floor. Old towels from the garage that had been used by Geoff to mop up all kinds of liquids came in very handy. Again, each of these was bagged twice. The body of Doug was rolled in a three by two yard old carpet remnant from the garage to prevent the dripping of any remaining blood. Then Amanda and Rosy carried the body into the hall where it lay until Amanda walked to her car. It was now getting dusk as Amanda quietly drove the Audi to the front door. Ten minutes later, both women praying that nobody was looking out of their windows, the loaded carpet remnant was eased it up into the back of the Audi, its lights not yet switched on.

Back inside Rosy made certain that everything was ready for disposal. The plan now was to drive past a couple of restaurants that used back street trash dump-bins and drop various bags in. The severed head bag was put to one side and Amanda volunteered to take care of it. The carpet would need to be disposed of, and the kitchen would need a thorough hot water and disinfectant clean, but Rosy would do that on her return. Amanda told Rosy to get into the car while she did a final check inside. Minutes later, Amanda, having locked the front door, climbed into the driver's seat and started the engine. She passed the door key to Rosy and gave her a reassuring smile. God, that was difficult.

It was 8.15 pm and it would be pitch black when they arrived in the woods a dozen miles out of Frisco to 'do the business.' A snow shovel, along with a pair of heavy duty gloves in the back of the car, would come in handy. All they had to do now was hope that their idea went as planned.

Low cloud intermittently masked a silver moon as they slowly drove away from Nob Hill and headed north.

31

"Dr. Gardner?" Detective Rogers asked the question as Howard answered the door bell. "How are you? May we come in for a few minutes?" It had been nearly two weeks since Rogers and Harris had seen Gardner in his office at the hospital. Howard was surprised at their visit, thinking that the detectives would have phoned first to check that he was at home. But then the 'surprise element' was one the police liked to employ. Howard took them to his study, unlocking the door swiftly using the key on a ring on his belt – where it usually stayed. He'd quickly informed Amanda about the presence of Rogers and Harris.

"So what can I do for you, Detective Rogers? I thought we'd gone over things before?" Howard was sitting behind his desk in a relaxed style.

"Well, you'll recall that two hikers reported seeing three vehicles parked within a few yards of the shallow grave on the evening of May first. We've had alibis from the owners of the other two, but you haven't yet confirmed where you were between the hours of, say, six o'clock and ten o'clock that evening. You had stated that you were at the hospital during the day – a Friday – but we'd like to know your movements after you'd finished surgery."

Howard explained that he'd ended the final operation of the day at around 4.30 pm, then had a quick coffee with his fellow surgeon Dr. Hudson. He'd arrived home at about a quarter after five and his wife came into the house at about half past five saying that her car had just broken down outside of their home. A mechanic arrived shortly afterwards but the car had to be towed into the garage on the Monday morning to get a new part fitted. Detective Harris made notes as Howard spoke. Howard concluded by saying that he was home all evening.

"And your vehicle – the black Audi Q7. The licence plate contains the numbers 4 and 8 and the letter A – as reported by the hikers. In the San Francisco city area there are only two vehicles that match the vehicle style – an SUV – and the numbers and letter of the vehicle index." Rogers waited for a comment, not taking his eyes off Dr. Gardner for a second. "Was your vehicle home all evening, too?"

"Well it certainly wasn't mine – have you checked the other SUV?" Rogers didn't respond to that question.

"So, Dr. Gardner, where was *your* vehicle that evening?" Howard was about to say that it was parked on the drive but then suddenly remembered that Amanda had borrowed it to see a friend. He had to be honest, telling Rogers the truth about his wife's time away from the house for a few hours. Howard recalled the date because there was a programme on TV about 'May Day' that was hosted by a girl called Miranda who looked remarkably like his wife. Harris kept scribbling notes. Rogers asked about Amanda's departure and return times. 'Approximately 6.00 pm and 10.30 pm' answered Howard.

"And the striped industrial tape we asked you about before? You did tell us that you had some in your garage but then you couldn't find it. Any idea where it is?" Rogers tone was even . . . matter of fact.

"No idea, I'm afraid I haven't. The tape wasn't important, there was only a bit left on the roll, may have gone out in the trash. Used it for bits and pieces . . . can't really remember."

"Well, if you do recall anything you can let us know." Rogers paused. "We'll need the name and address of the friend your wife visited that evening, and if you don't mind we'd like to examine your Audi right now. We've got a forensics guy sat in the back of the car. Discretely of course. It's just routine; it won't take long. We'll have to talk to your wife sometime but we'll leave that for now. Oh, and we'll want a quick word with Dr. Hudson. Is he at the hospital tomorrow?" Howard nodded uncomfortably, swallowing a build up of saliva as invisibly as he could. "I understand that you have an au pair girl called Jane Lester?" Howard sat up, then nodded again. "Do you know a man called Andrew Wilson?"

"Wilson. No, I don't think I do. Why do you ask?" Rogers briefly explained the situation. It didn't mean anything to Howard, except that he knew Jane was seeing some guy. Without saying any more about Wilson, the detective continued.

"Have you had any other au pairs working for you in the last few years?" Howard told them only one, Caroline Sinclair, but prayed he didn't ask about her boyfriend – the little bastard that had once told him he was no more than butcher with a certificate. Rogers didn't ask, he didn't have to. Harris closed her notepad and the two detectives made a move.

"If we could have the keys to your vehicle, Dr. Gardner? Shouldn't take more than a few minutes. He'll just take a few photos, fibre samples and material swabs from inside the Audi. The neighbours won't suspect a thing!" Rogers smiled for the first time that evening. "Oh, by the way, do you eat Hershey chocolate bars?"

"Yes. I quite like them along with a few other different ones, they keep my sugar levels up!" Howard grinned briefly. "Why?"

"Oh, no real reason – just wondered. Thanks for your time Dr. Gardner. We'll be in touch."

The last thing that Howard Gardner wanted was gossip in Adair Way generated by nosy neighbours. But by the time he'd poured himself a glass of Jack Daniels in his study and taken a long sip, Harris was ringing the door bell to hand his car keys back to him. She smiled enigmatically and left. Howard locked his study, then took his glass into the lounge where Amanda was watching TV with a glass of wine. There was a programme about cooking the perfect pasta with home - made cheese sauce. Amanda lowered the volume as she turned to look at him.

"What was all that about?" Howard wasn't sure where to start. But he certainly had some questions for his wife.

And why the hell did Rogers want to know about Hershey bars?

*

Jane had met Louise as planned. The Four Barrels Coffee Shop was good – everything focused on the dark brown bean. Photos of coffee pickers in East Africa, packs of ground coffee to purchase, mugs with 'I love coffee!' printed on them. Jane was amazed at how quick they served the drinks. One guy took the order, another made the coffee, then it suddenly appeared on a tray as Lou swiped a plastic card to pay. Twenty five seconds from 'I'd like a cup of...' to carrying the two cups to a vacant table at the rear of the cafe. This was America, after all.

Lou had opened the conversation, asking Jane how she was and enquired after the children. Small talk. Jane gave a half minute reply, but detected that Lou's body language was saying 'let's move on.'

"Listen, Jane, there are some things you ought to know. I've been going back through some old copies of the Chronicle on the computer as well as chatting to a friend in SFPD. I entered the name Patterson and there were over fifty listings for that name, of which forty four were related to Jodie Patterson. Let me try to summarise what I found or else we'll be here all day." And with that, Louise began. Her story unfolded . . .

'Jodie Patterson had been brought up in a care home, abandoned by her parents, both alcoholics, when she was three years of age. Four different families had looked after her between the ages of three and seventeen. Unable to keep a job for long, she'd moved from job to job – either getting fired or just walking away from it. Fourteen court appearances were listed, with two resulting in short jail sentences and seven turned into community service. She's also spent a year as a manager of a brothel.

Married twice, her first husband allegedly left her after being maltreated, and little is known about her current husband. She has a daughter named Amy. Jodie was sectioned under the US Mental Health Act five years back and treated for a variety of conditions. She's probably still on medication and suffers from serious mood swings, real mood swings. Able to hold a sensible conversation one minute, ready to cut your throat the next - as per the car park experience.

No one was sure why she started the course at the college a while back, maybe craved social interaction, but it's understood she's quit. So, hopefully, you won't see her again during your Wednesday evening photography course. As you're aware, her daughter attends Lexington Junior – so obviously you can expect to see her there again sometime. You ought to ignore her – but nicely!

But, and here's the interesting thing, Jodie was a friend of a girl called Caroline Sinclair who worked as a nanny to a local family. She, and this girl Caroline, would go out together with the children. Once Caroline had left the kids with Jodie for half an hour or so. She'd bought them an alco-pop each. 8% alcohol in a cherryade flavoured drink! They were very ill! The parents decided not to press charges, but clearly they were livid and Caroline was lucky not to get fired!'

So this was the news from Louise. Jodie Patterson was someone to be avoided. Hell, what a background! And friendly with Caroline Sinclair . . .

The two girls had left The Four Barrels and stood for a few seconds on the pavement, busy with people hurrying along, the temperature about mid fifties. As Lou was about to go, she had turned to Jane with a final comment.

"Rumour has it that Jodie and Howard became friendly when he first moved here from Baltimore. Maybe that's why Howard didn't fire the au pair?"

32

Jane was pressing the children's clothes, a cup of coffee perched on a table near the ironing board. She was beginning to feel as if she was in a film. An actress with a small part, but certainly on the credits that would roll up at the end. She'd come to San Francisco to be a nanny – look after two lovely children, integrate with an American family, study, travel . . . perhaps find a young man for companionship, even love. But Jane reflected on her time in California. A little over two months – that was all. Her contract was for a year with the option to increase it for another twelve months. But would she even be in San Francisco for that long?

The more she pieced together details about Amanda and Howard, the less some things made sense. Locked rooms in the house, arguments that disturbed the children. Jodie Patterson seemed to be a screwball, a vile tongue, physically intimidating and an all round waste of space. Yet had Jane seen her and Howard together in the car park? Lou said they were friendly. Some questions still needed to be asked. Answers provided.

The two children were a beacon of light in the mistiness of her current existence. They kept her going, were her raison d'etre for being there, and provided a welcome challenge for Jane. Their relationship was blossoming, no question. She was aware of their likes and dislikes, their little foibles, how to get the best out of them, and they were learning from Jane which gave her a huge sense of satisfaction. She loved them.

Then there was her boyfriend, Andrew. What a strange guy he'd turned out to be. At first Jane did not want to believe what some of her friends were saying about him. But as facts were released it became apparent that he was the bad apple in the barrel. And a liar! All sweetness and charm over Chinese food, acting as her chauffeur . . . the invitation to his virtual yacht in the marina, the one that only existed in his head. He didn't even have a driving licence! And his relationship with Jimmy Walters! Hell, driving out of town to rob banks in disguise! Green contact lenses and a wig! The question for Jane now was 'did she want anything more to do with Andrew?' He was locked up, awaiting trial. She could visit him, make an appointment – see him behind a glass screen . . . and there was the fortune cookie proverb *'One candle can change complete darkness to bright, but someone has to light it.'* The small piece of yellow paper was still tucked inside her diary.

Amanda's friends Vida and Rosemary had provided early friendship for Jane via their daughters Marie and Samantha. And when Jane thought about them she knew that Sam could hold some answers to questions about Howard Gardner. She *must* make that phone call to Sam very soon.

Oh, and there was Caroline Sinclair . . . the au pair with a clouded history. There was an offer from Caroline to visit her in L.A. A Greyhound bus journey, overnight stay, back the next day. Not difficult. Caroline would be able to fill in some gaps – as long as she told the truth. Jane decided to take another look at the emails from Caroline, maybe read between the lines . . . and ask about Jake Bauer. The poor guy was still unaccounted for, but did Caroline miss him? Of course, Jane wouldn't say anything about her little talk with Lou. She'd play her cards carefully, hold the aces to her chest.

As Jane folded the last of the clothes she'd ironed, her cell phone beeped twice. One new message. It was from Sam.

Hi Jane, time for a chat? Lunch tomorrow? There's a bistro in Sutter Street. It's called 'Gaspar.' Can you make noon? Lol, Sam x

It was time to light a candle.

*

Chuck Hudson allowed himself a wry smile as he bit into a muffin. The fresh brewed coffee smelt good as he poured himself a cup. Ready to set off for the hospital, he listened to the local radio news expecting a report on a body found on the tracks – another suicide in this city, another troubled soul who couldn't handle life and all it brought with it. The debt, the misery, the loneliness. But any news on that subject never came. It seemed to be all the usual local news, followed by the weather . . . 55F and light cloud. But no suicide near the railhead. Not to worry – the cops wanted to keep it quiet. They would have identified the body and found the note. All pretty straightforward. There'd be something on the news later – Dr. Hudson merely had to wait. Yes, there'd be an announcement about Kris Roberts . . . a guy who'd had enough and couldn't take any more.

It was a 7.25 am and the washing up had to wait. Dr. Hudson had a busy day ahead of him. He'd always been a busy boy. Ever since he'd been adopted by a couple who couldn't have children. As an orphan, Chuck Hudson had been confused about his sexuality. From the age of three, little Chuck was dressed as a boy, but sometimes as a girl. Despite that, he was an intelligent child, always doing well at school, avoided sports, but came top of his class every term. Good results at High School and entry to Harvard Medical School was taken as a given. He was a brilliant student. But there was something hidden away in his psyche, some deep seated matter that perplexed even his own self analysis.

Dr. Chuck Hudson didn't consider himself a killer. No – he wasn't one to take a life. He'd been trained to save lives – he was a medical doctor after all. But when it came to young men, he had an unhealthy interest. And because he'd killed two other men he knew a body left on a railway track wasn't a big deal. The strange thing was, he always felt that he was a woman when he dealt the final blow. He *was* a woman when the last breath was expelled from the lungs of his victims. Chuck always liked to put lipstick on before the end, and look into the eyes of his victims.

His face was the last image they'd ever see on their dying retinas before meeting their Maker.

*

"Good to see you again, Jane. Are you OK?" Sam sat down next to Jane at the table in Gaspar's bistro. Jane smiled wanly, not wanting to let Sam know how she really felt.

"Yes, not bad. Keeping busy as you might expect with the children . . ." Sam offered to get the drinks as she waved to a waiter. Sam asked for two slim-line tonic waters with ice and lemon, the waiter gliding away to get their order.

"You sure . . ? I mean you look a bit washed out if you don't mind me saying." Jane explained that she'd been busy and that a few restless nights hadn't helped. She told Jane that an aunt in England was very ill and prayed that the lie didn't show in her eyes. Sam gently held Jane's hand for a second, then let it go. Jane found her look difficult to interpret, and wanted to move on.

"Listen, we don't have long," suggested Jane, "you know I spoke to you briefly a little while back about Howard Gardner?" Sam recalled Jane asking a few questions and had made some discrete checks in the file relating to the court appearance of Dr. Gardner after the death of his first wife, Priscilla. Sam paused as the waiter placed their glasses in front of them, along with the check.

"This must remain strictly between the two of us, Jane. Is that clear?" Jane nodded, feeling as if her primary school teacher, Miss Kelly, was addressing her. Sam continued. "And don't ask me how I got this information. I've spoken with someone who works in my office and that's all I can say. Howard was represented in court by an attorney called James Atkins, an old and trusted friend of Blake Hardy, my boss. They were at Yale together, and both enjoy golf . . . so, Hardy got Atkins to defend

Howard. And . . ." Sam hesitated, "all three of them are members of a society called the *The Choirmasters*, a sort of California Mafia. I guess your equivalent is the Masons – you know, not *what* you know but *who* you know." Sam tapped the side of her nose and grinned. "Howard allegedly offered Atkins a $25,000 back-hander if he was found not guilty! Rumour has it that Atkins spread some of that cash around the courtroom, so to speak." Jane gasped, then took a sip of her cool tonic water, absorbing what Sam had told her. "So, Howard was found to be innocent of any attempt to push his wife from the viewing platform at the Grand Canyon. Verdict was *Misadventure.* And Howard emphasised repeatedly that her shoes were to blame . . . as well as reaching too far over to take a photo. Atkins poo-pooed three witness statements from that day after they had all failed to remember what type of jacket Priscilla was wearing, and the colour of her hair."

Sam continued, adding that, allegedly, Howard Gardner was a Jekyll and Hyde character. Really nice one moment, totally different the next. Another source had told her that he'd undergone psychiatric assessment and analysis but his treatment had finished some time ago. And, despite being a competent heart surgeon, he was known to have a 'short fuse' which, apparently he was able to control. Most of the time, anyway.

Jane concluded that Howard Gardner was someone to keep at arms' length. She had to be civil, however. After all she was the nanny to Howard and Amanda's two children with nine months left on her contract. Jane knew her role within the Gardner household; she simply had to keep her 'nose clean,' get on and do what she was paid for, and try to enjoy it. There was no point in phoning Melody, her counsellor. She'd probably take matters the wrong way, even ask Jane to leave if she felt there was a hint of danger to Jane. If she did phone Melody it would just be to say 'hi' and let her know all was well.

So, the meeting drew to a close. Sam paid for the drinks and both girls left the bistro together. Jane thanked Sam very much for her time and for her 'confidential' information. Had she underestimated Sam? Jane was tempted to ask her exactly how she'd got all of the information, but decided not to pry – it was a deal between them, and Jane had agreed up front that the details would be kept confidential. Scraps of data were coming together, the jigsaw puzzle starting to take some semblance of a complete picture. But there would be some pieces that would require closer examination for Jane to be able to ease them into place. The straight edged parts of the puzzle formed the border; now it was the tongues and grooves that had to be slipped together.

Sitting in her room Jane logged onto the Greyhound.com web site. A return ticket was purchased on line from the bus station, at the junction of First Street and Folsom Street in San Francisco, to East Seventh Street in Los Angeles. $29 for the fare was little price to pay to meet Caroline Sinclair for a chat, talk about things, see why she left the Gardner household. There'd be so much to discuss.

As Jane closed down her laptop her mobile beeped twice. It was a message from Sam. It read *Halloween party cancelled. Speak soon. Sam x*

'Thank goodness for that,' thought Jane. Was she bothered about the party? No. Had she other things to think about? Yes. And she certainly didn't want to meet a masked Michael Myers walking along Adair Way in the cool, early hours of the morning, serrated hunting knife in one hand with killing on his mind.

33

Jane had emailed Caroline with the option of two weekends when she would be available to travel to L.A. She was due for a break on October 17 and 18 and again on November 14 and 15. The first dates suited Caroline better, November being busy for some reason. Jane remembered that Amanda was still planning her 'Friday after Thanksgiving party' that would take place on 27 November and be relying on Jane to help out. So . . . the October weekend was better anyway. To maintain a good relationship with Amanda, Jane checked that it was OK with her before replying to Caroline. And it was. But Jane had to be careful, she didn't want Amanda nor Howard to know exactly why she was going! But Jane had to be reasonably honest . . . tell them she was going to L.A. to see another nanny. She'd call her Irma. It was sort of true, keep details to a minimum and get her story straight from the beginning. The Greyhound bus, a small hotel, meet up with Irma, have dinner, catch up, stay over, and back on the Sunday afternoon.

The Travel Inn on South Westlake Avenue in downtown L.A. was booked for the Saturday night, £47 sterling equivalent. It wasn't far from Caroline who was residing in a rented apartment on Potrero Drive in Monterey Park. So, it was all planned, and Jane was looking forward to it in a strange way. She knew some things about Miss Sinclair, but there was more to learn. Deciding she ought to make a few notes, Jane wrote down half a dozen headings to jog her memory – an old habit when revising for her school and college exams. It was easier to memorise facts when they were written down, visualise them in her mind's eye. She wasn't going to have the note book on the table over dinner, though . . . didn't want to come across as a reporter from the 'Daily Gossip.' No, Jane would keep it handy and, if needed, would use it as a prompt when she went to the Ladies to 'powder her nose.' On reflection there was still the option of asking Melody about Caroline, but Melody would start asking questions, begin probing, and Jane didn't want that.

But there was *one* little thing that niggled at the back of Jane's mind. Supposing something happened to her on her trip to L.A? If nobody except her and Caroline were aware of the meeting, and Jane went missing, who would know she was in L.A? Perhaps she ought to tell her mother? Give her mum a few facts – hotel, times of the journey . . . But her mum would worry, get concerned, even nervous. Jenny Lester's mind would start to work overtime. Her daughter on a bus alone, travelling very nearly the distance from London to Edinburgh on her own with strange people. Vulnerable. Perhaps sat next to a drug addict or a pill popper? No! Jane would leave it. Take the risk – she'd be all right. But wait, there was Lou from the Chronicle. Lou had taken the time to talk with Jane, feed her a stack of information. Wasn't it only courteous to tell Lou that she was heading south to Los Angeles? Yes, she'd do that. It was good manners after all, and it would be an olive branch – show Lou that she really wanted to be friends.

As Jane left her room around mid morning she saw Katie polishing the bannister and flicking a feather duster at several large ornaments in the three recesses down the staircase. Katie glanced at Jane.

"Hi, Jane, au pair extraordinaire!" Jane chuckled, recalling their exchange when they first met. Jane said 'hi' and asked Katie how she was. Katie replied positively – she always did in her Calamity Jane sort of way. "By the way, have you left an dirty washing around these parts lately?" Jane frowned.

"Dirty washing? Certainly not! What on earth do you mean, Katie?"

"Well, seems that no matter how much I use my furniture polish and floor cleaner an' all, I detects a slight odour . . . like clothes that needs a good clean, maybe underclothes . . . seems to be coming from one of the rooms off the landing up there." Jane couldn't smell anything other than a hint of lavender from Katie's cleaning.

"No, can't smell anything unusual, but I'll check the kids bedrooms. Ryan may have slipped a half-eaten sandwich under his bed or something? Anyhow, Katie, must go, I've got some things to attend to . . ." And with that Jane popped back into her room for a few seconds to collect her mobile phone. But as she came back out Jane noticed there was a slight odour. Nothing really obnoxious, and it reminded Jane of the field-mouse that her dad had caught in a trap in their garden shed when she was about six years old. It had been dead for over a week, or so her dad had told her. A sort of smell of, well, an old piece of cheese, or a drain that needed unblocking.

Musty, mouldy. Not nice at all.

*

Detectives Rogers and Harris had been sifting through the file on Missing Persons, and the one they now had open on the desk was on the Gardners. Forensics had given Rogers a report on the Audi Q7. There wasn't very much for the detectives to get excited about. Howard and Amanda had been asked to attend the police station to provide a sample of saliva for DNA analysis, and several hairs found in the vehicle only matched the DNA of the Gardner's which was now on their database. However, there were four fine nylon bristles that Forensics matched to a cleaning brush brand called StevieD, similar to those sold by automotive outlets. Traces of an ammonia cleaning solution, Sav-U-Wash, were also discovered along with several blue denim fibres, the type of fibres used in a range of jeans products sold throughout the US. Rogers wondered if the Gardners were fastidious owners or perhaps the vehicle had been cleaned recently?

The Forensics guy who'd travelled to the Gardner's house with Rogers and Harris had rolled each of the four tyres over a 3mm deep sheet of contact material with mild adhesive properties like a giant post-it note pad. The convoluted tread patterns of the 19" Audi *Continental* brand tyres did not match any of those found in Muir Woods near the crime scene.

The detectives had asked Amanda about her evening out on 1 May. No real issues . . . she'd left home around six ten pm, arrived at the home of Rosemary Gless twenty minutes later, chatted about 'girlie' matters, had two glasses of fresh orange juice, and then took her time driving home. The Audi was parked back home at 10.28 pm, Amanda stating that she remembered looking at the car clock digits just before she switched the engine off. Rogers made notes but had no specific questions for Amanda, who'd used her psychiatry training to 'manage' the interview to go in her favour. However, Harris chirped up, asking when the tyres were last changed on the Audi Q7. As Amanda was about to reply, Howard intervened, saying that the tyres had been on the SUV for at least two years – their mileage being relatively low. Amanda didn't butt in, and it was left at that.

Meanwhile over at the Gless household in Nob Hill Rosy had long since cleaned the kitchen and the surrounding area. Not only that, but once she thought the place was like a new pin, Rosy phoned an industrial cleaning group called Buttfield Cleaning Utilities, BCU, that specialised in the cleansing of a wide range of stores and warehouses as well as those more difficult to clean places like garage workshops and greasy hotel kitchens. Rosy had been totally thorough in wiping away the blood and picking up small fragments of skin and chips of bone from where Doug had been fallen during the dispute over what he thought he was owed. Every crack in the tiled floor had been scrubbed with a toothbrush and strong bleach, and every cupboard surface, horizontal and vertical, had been wiped down with a strong disinfectant. Every single item from toothbrush to scrubbing brush, from wet cloths to drying paper towels were disposed of. Rosy had got rid of these items over a period of three weeks, dropping them into public waste bins, restaurant trash cans and her own rubbish that was collected weekly.

Rosy had also employed *Green Tree Gardening* to remove the four feet wide tarmac path from the front door step and replace it with a cream coloured pebble surface to a depth of six inches. It would have been difficult to ask BCU to power hose the tarmac footpath when it appeared fairly clean, and now the original dark grey surface had gone. It was October 11 so it was nearly twenty two weeks since Rosy had committed the murder of her son. But no questions had been asked, no police visits made, no neighbours enquiring about anything . . . so Rosy at last began to relax. If anyone asked about Doug, well, he was living and working in San Diego and enjoying life. Rosy would say that she visited him from time to time but that he wasn't bothered about coming to Frisco.

Rosy met up with Vida and Amanda once or twice a month for coffee down town, had joined a card group that played bridge every Wednesday, and enjoyed her garden. There was always something to prune or plant or feed, and the roses were a delight almost all year round. Rosy had just received her invitation to Amanda's 'Friday after Thanksgiving' party and was looking forward to that. There'd be people there that she knew, but also some new faces. The Gardner's always entertained well and one never left their home hungry or dry.

Whilst Detective Rogers was going through some notes in his office, the Gardner file still open, Rosy was putting on the kettle to make some tea when she heard the front door bell ring. Glancing at the kitchen clock she noticed it showed 4.55 pm. Rosy rarely got anybody calling at this time, but she walked through the wide hallway and answered the door.

A guy, about twenty years old, was stood there in a loose grey jacket over a light blue tee shirt with dark blue, baggy jeans that seemed to stay up by willpower. A black *New York Yankees* baseball cap held in a mop of blond hair, curls sticking out either side. Nipping at his right ear lobe was a small gold earring. Rosy noticed that there was an old Chevrolet pick up parked at the end of the drive, green and rust in colour. She could see the outline of a girl in the front passenger seat.

"Hello, can I help you?" asked Rosy.

"Er, yup. You Mrs. Gless?" he asked with a slight stutter.

"Who wants to know?" Rosemary was slightly on edge, the visitor not over-friendly.

"My name's Ollie, I'm a friend of Doug. We ain't seen him for a while, kinda six months or so, and we recently got this address here in Frisco from his landlady in San Diego." Rosy swallowed gently as she kept her eyes fixed on his. "Wondered if you know where he is, that's all?" The girl in the front seat of the pick up got out and ambled slowly towards the caller on the step, hands on her stomach which was bulging and shaped like half a watermelon. She looked at Rosy with doe eyes.

"I gotta find him 'cos I'm carrying his baby," she drawled in a Southern accent. "My name's Cissie."

34

'Good morning San Francisco. I'm Jim Cashin and here is the eight o'clock news on this sunny morning here in Frisco on SFRS. We have breaking news coming in that a doctor from San Francisco City Hospital, a heart surgeon called Dr. Charles Hudson, has been shot and killed in a drive-by shooting near to the hospital main entrance. According to eye witnesses a grey coupe, possibly a Ford or BMW, slowed down and the driver was seen to put his left hand out of the open window and fire two pistol shots at the doctor. Again, eye witnesses say he fell instantly, one bullet hitting him in the head, a second went into his upper body. The car sped off eastwards but so far no one has been able to confirm any details of the licence plate. Dr. Hudson was a well liked surgeon at the hospital and so far we do not have any motive as to why anybody would want to kill him.

We'll bring you more information on this as it comes in. Now for other news . . .'

Howard Gardner was just parking his Audi in the staff car park at the City Hospital when he heard the news on the car radio. Chuck Hudson dead? No, there must be some mistake. Perhaps somebody who looks like him, or a visitor – wrong place, wrong time. But not Chuck? Howard rushed round to the front of the hospital as fast as his legs would carry him to be confronted by a crowd that had quickly gathered. Two SFPD cruisers were already there, red and blue lights strobing the morning air. One of the policemen was trying to maintain crowd control whilst two others made room for a stretcher that was being carried to where Chuck lay in a pool of blood. His limp body was lifted onto the stretcher, covered with a blanket, and taken inside. Within five minutes the onlookers started to drift away leaving two janitorial guys to sluice away the dark red liquid with a power-jet. In under ten minutes everything was almost back to normal. Except that it wasn't normal. The six feet tall, brown eyed doctor who resembled Charlie Sheen was dead.

Not only that, but a hospital porter called Kris Roberts had handed in his notice. Roberts had been off work for a couple of weeks – a bad dose of flu, apparently – and had posted his resignation to HR only two days before.

*

Jane told Amanda that she was visiting an au pair girl named Irma Randolph who lived in L.A. She didn't need to say any more than that. It was her week-end off, to which she was entitled, and wanted to go visit Irma for a girlie chat and to see how she was getting on. They'd met briefly during the training course in New York and 'hit it off', according to Jane's story. Amanda asked Jane to be careful on her journey to L.A., and to keep her handbag close to her. *'Don't trust anyone'* was Amanda's advice, and for Jane to keep her mobile phone switched on all the time. Jane had done her packing on the Friday evening – just enough for an overnight stay – and included her phone charger. She had her credit card along with two hundred dollars in cash to see her through until Sunday. The latest *Hello* magazine and her crime thriller novel would keep her company on the journey.

Amanda had offered to give Jane a lift to the bus station on First and Folsom where the L.A. bound bus, number 6845, was leaving at 9.45 am. Scheduled arrival in L.A. was 5.25 pm and Jane would take a taxi to the Travel Inn. In an email to Caroline, Jane had suggested having dinner close to the Travel Inn and she'd pick up the tab. Caroline proposed eating at an Italian restaurant within a mile of the motel, Luigi's, where she'd offered to play chauffeur, proposing to pick Jane up at 6.00 pm, then dropping her off back at the Travel Inn after they'd eaten. And talked.

So that was that. The week-end was planned, everything would turn out OK, and Jane would be back in her own bed on Sunday evening. On the Saturday morning Ryan and Teresa had hugged Jane as if playing big brown grizzly bears, telling her to be careful because they wanted to see her smiling face again the next day. The children had really bonded with Jane, and for her, looking after such good children wasn't a chore at all. The three of them got on very well. As Jane hugged the kids she couldn't help but think about the email from Caroline . . . and her words *'he stabbed himself with a ballpoint pen.'* She was going to have to be careful when discussing 'Adair Way matters,' and especially Jodie Patterson and her relationship, if it existed, with Howard. Then there were a few other matters that Jane needed to discuss to try to complete her mental jigsaw puzzle, hoping the pieces would fit together by the time she was back in Frisco.

*

Jane had been dropped off at the Greyhound terminal an hour before departure – normal procedure. Bus 6845 departed San Francisco bus station on time with 28 passengers on board. The big ten wheeler, 50 seater MCI vehicle complete with wi-fi and electrical outlets slowly pulled away minutes after Jane had placed her small bag into the overhead locker and settled back. She was sitting next to a woman that Jane estimated to be in her seventies who introduced herself as Lucille. Jane began flicking through her magazine, the passing skyscraper skyline disappearing as the bus headed east and then south to join Interstate 5. The semi-arid landscape of California spilled across the vista, turning from grey to golden.

Bus 6845 pulled off Interstate 5 and slowed as it passed the Welcome to Avenal sign, named after the Spanish for 'oat field' which they said looked like golden silk when they first arrived. The bus eventually came to a halt at the bus station. There was a coffee machine and, after checking her change, Jane fed a dollar and fifty cents into the slot. In seconds a cardboard cup was full of hot, steaming coffee. She decided to call Lou, let her know where she was, how she was doing. Within seconds, Lou had answered her cell phone.

"Hi, Jane, where are you? Got there yet?" Jane had told Lou her week-end plans a few days earlier, given her the motel name and number in L.A. as well as Caroline Sinclair's details. Jane told Lou about the trip so far, and that she'd call or text her when she got to the Travel Inn. Without spelling it out, this was Jane's safety net. If anything happened to her whilst she was visiting Caroline at least somebody would know where she was and what she was doing. Harry the driver quickly checked his human cargo and then 6845 was on its way, southwards to San Fernando, desert and scrub on both sides but Jane was feeling sleepy and closed her eyes. After a few more stops Jane yawned and looked at her watch, it was five o'clock. She'd soon be arriving at the bus station at 1716, East Seventh Street in down town Los Angeles. Her journey had seemed a long one, and yet it didn't. Seven hours and forty minutes. Jane had seen most of *Hello* magazine and read over one hundred pages of her book, and in it the detectives were still on the trail of the murderer, a spooky guy called Chrissie Weeler. As Jane began to collect her things together her fellow traveller, Lucille, spoke in a quiet voice.

"We haven't really made time to talk, my dear, have we? What with you an' your reading an' me with my thoughts . . . you seem a nice girl to me. What you doin' here in L.A? Visiting friends?" Jane looked at the old lady, grey hair in a bun and thick, rimless glasses perched on her nose with willpower.

"Er, yes. An old friend I haven't seen for a while." Jane didn't want to get into a conversation now. Not when she was getting off in five minutes and needed to grab a taxi to her motel.

"Well, you have a good time, ya' hear," Lucille exclaimed. Jane reciprocated the wish and smiled as Lucille winked at her.

"Travel Inn, South Westlake, please," requested Jane as the cab driver left the rank two minutes after the Greyhound had arrived.

35

"Nope, don't know where he is. He left home last year, said he was getting a job in San Diego working in a bar or something? He doesn't keep in touch. Kinda loner, really." Rosemary's face was straight. The two callers on the front step eased forward slightly as Rosemary kept her cool, a hand on the inside door knob. These good-for-nothings weren't coming in. No way. In any case, Rosemary had a visitor who was sitting in the kitchen with his coffee. If she called out, he'd come running. The baseball bat in the umbrella stand was within easy reach – if she needed it. Cissie spoke.

"Yup, he worked as a barman for a while, but he got fired for putting his fingers in the till. I was a waitress at a Howard Johnson restaurant in town. I remember when he called in for a Coke 'n burger one day. We hit it off right away and then started dating 'bout seven months back. I was renting a one room place and he came to stay for a while." Cissie fondled her rotund belly. "And this is his! He told me he was coming to Frisco to sort some business, didn't say what but it was something to do with what he was owed?" She paused as if expecting a comment. Rosemary shrugged. Ollie chirped up.

"Cissie here asked me to help her out. We've driven here hopin' to find him, I mean, he's got to take responsibility for the baby, ain't he?" Ollie gargled with some phlegm at the back of his throat as he tipped the peak of his cap upwards. "He's gotta be around here somewhere? Do you know any of his buddies, you know, where he might be staying?" Ollie took a step closer, his dilated pupils cross-wired on Rosemary's face.

"Look, sorry guys. But I just don't know, right? He's a drifter. He could be anywhere . . ." Doug's mother suddenly realised that she ought to sound concerned. "But hey, if you find him ask him to get in touch. As his ma I still love him, warts an' all." Rosemary smiled a rehearsed smile. "I've got some stew on the stove so I must go." She began to close the door when Ollie put his hand up to his ear, imitating a phone, little finger and thumb outstretched.

"You gotta number we can dial if we see him? Ya know, keep you informed an' that."

"Phone's been out of order for months now. Use a cell phone but that's being repaired. Sorry." Rosemary prayed she sounded convincing.

"OK, we'll just have to come back if we get some news." Rosemary slammed the door and laid against it, breathing heavily. She didn't want those two anywhere near her home. Without twitching the curtains she watched them get into the rust heap on four wheels and slowly drive away, thick exhaust fumes polluting the clean Nob Hill air.

'Would they ask the cops round here?' wondered Rosemary. No, they wouldn't do that, just because a friend was missing. The police would have too many questions for them. Ask Ollie for a driving licence, vehicle insurance, name and address . . . and Rosemary could make up a story that she was being harassed. She'd *over-egg the pudding*, tell the police that this so called Ollie was a pest and a down right nuisance and his female friend was making up this whole thing about her son getting her pregnant. What a load of bullshit that was . . . that's what she'd tell them.

As Rosemary's blood pressure was returning to normal, helped with a glass of warm milk, her male caller chatted about weather and his plans for a long vacation. Rosemary found herself being charmed by his gentle manner, his easy going way, the hazel eyes. As he finished his coffee, the telephone rang. Picking it up her mind raced, wondering who it could be? Over the past couple of weeks she'd expected *that* call from a detective, or from some person in authority asking awkward questions. 'Where were you on..., when did you last see your boy..., what was his last address..., a neighbour said they'd seen..., can we come over and take a look at your house..., perhaps look in the garage..., check things out...,'

'Hello?' She tried to sound as normal as possible despite images of black and white SFPD cars parking up on her drive.

"Rosy, it's Amanda." There was a sense of urgency in her tone. "Are you OK?" Before she could reply, Amanda quickly continued. "I've just heard from Howard. Apparently they've cleared out Chuck's locker at the hospital and found love letters between him and Kris Roberts! And a few notes from the female nursing staff, too. It looks as if Roberts is now their number one suspect for his murder!" Rosemary felt the blood drain from her face, her arms beginning to show goose-bumps.

"Ah, right. Well listen, keep me informed . . . I need to go now as I've got things to do . . . bye." She replaced the phone on its cradle and turned to the smart, brown haired young man that she had met last year at Amanda's garden party just after Thanksgiving.

"I'm so sorry but I'm going to have to throw you out," she smiled a perfect fake smile. "Something's come up and I need to go." He stood, zipped up his dark blue leather jacket, and moved to the front door.

"Thanks, Rosemary, good to see you again . . . and thanks for the coffee!"

Her male caller casually strolled down the footpath, got into his silver grey BMW coupe, fired up the engine and drove away, but not before he'd given Rosemary a wave and blown a kiss. She felt she needed to talk to somebody about things and thought of her daughter, Sam. But they hadn't spoken for a while, and this wasn't really a mother to daughter scenario was it? No, she'd bottle things up for a while.

Kris Roberts' BMW left a trail of light grey exhaust fumes as his car pulled away from Richmond Avenue.

*

Detective Simon Rogers was poring over some files on his desk. Several missing persons, four murders, and two cases of fraud, other reported incidents. Life wasn't easy for Rogers at the moment. He seemed to spend every waking hour on police work. OK, it was his job, but occasionally his mind drifted – he could see palm trees swaying on the beach down in Florida. He quietly sang a Johnny Cash song, Orange Blossom Special. *'I'm going down to Florida, get some sand in my shoes . . .'* Rogers was whisked out of his reverie as Megan Harris came in, smelling as sweet as ever.

"Don't give up the day job, Johnny!" she laughed, "unless you're looking for a change of career. But with that voice I'd have second thoughts!" Simon Rogers grinned. He knew she was one for a joke at his expense but he'd get her back later. "Here I've brought you a coffee." She placed the cardboard cup on a coaster depicting the Florida Keys. "What you up to, Simon?" Rogers flicked open a red folder where he'd placed a lime yellow sticker to keep the page.

"I was just thinking about the headless torso case. We've got some information, with a couple of things to follow up very soon, but we don't have specifics on the body . . . as in height and weight. At least they're not here. Did Doc Jones mention that in his report?" Harris turned on her computer, asking for a minute while she brought up some details.

"Yes, here it is. I think it was filed under 'Clothing' rather than with his anatomical information. It says . . . height estimated at six feet, five inches allowing for a normal head size that would match the stature of the bone structure. Weight one hundred and seventy seven pounds, allowing for blah-blah-blah. So there it is." Rogers reviewed the other parts of the autopsy. Neck lacerations strongly suggest the use of a sharp serrated knife, possibly domestic, and the marks between the third and fourth cervical vertebrae were possibly made by a hacksaw blade. The tattoo was drawn on the skin after death, and there were no fingerprints that could help identify the corpse. The clothing was not unusual or out of the ordinary, but . . ." He hesitated. Harris looked up from her desk.

"Yes?" she asked.

"Well, it may not be anything, but I saw an ad on TV last night for Wrangler jeans. Nothing unusual there. But they mentioned how the company listened to what the customer wanted – 'made products for you' was how they put it. I logged onto their web site this morning and hit a few keys that took me to their market research strategy. Said they always checked out new designs and styles before they were launched to the great American public! A new style of jeans, with two inch turn ups and different pocket design with tungsten studs was being test marketed in California. San Diego to be precise. Three stores in town were selling the new product for a six month period to assess sales potential." Harris never took her eyes off her colleague.

"So? You getting into marketing now as well as country singing?" Rogers didn't smile this time. Putting his coffee cup down he stood up and walked to the window and gazed out at the cloudless sky.

"The headless torso was wearing a pair of those jeans. He's either from San Diego or he shopped there. It's a start. All we have to do now is find his head."

"Good detective work, Simon. I've got an update, too," Harris added. "The StevieD brush bristles are from an industrial cleaning machine, they're twice as long as the bristles Joe Public can buy in retail outlets in Frisco. The Sav-U-Wash cleaning solution isn't common, either. So I've been checking places where motorists could get their cars valeted . . . visited eleven in the area. Only two use *both* StevieD industrial *and* Sav-U-Wash. I checked the records of each for the last six months and guess what? The car dealer Pete Hardison Inc. out on the east side of the city valeted a black Audi Q7 on 4 May! A woman, who waited for half an hour while the job was finished, paid cash for the job. The guy I spoke to described her as a well dressed, leggy blonde who spoke in an educated manner."

"Do they log the registration numbers of vehicles they

clean?" Rogers tossed the crumpled cup into a bin and congratulated Harris on her investigation. She shook her head.

"No, but he thinks he'd recognise the woman again. One other thing," Harris hesitated, "he said she watched him clean the Audi, got close up, and she lightly munched on a chocolate bar while she waited. He thought that seemed odd with a figure like hers."

"What kind of chocolate bar, did he say?"

"No, he wasn't sure. But it was kinda' flat with a dark brown shiny wrapper – he recalled that bit. Oh, and another thing." Megan Harris dug out her notebook. "Right next door to Hardison's is a tyre dealer, Wheeler and Howison. I took an urgent phone call as I left Hardison's – didn't have time to check the tyre guys, but I'm going there now." Harris picked up her bag and cell phone and headed for the door. "Back soon!" she said. As Harris closed the door the telephone burred twice before Rogers picked up.

"Detective Rogers." A receptionist on the main desk at the police station told him there was a woman who demanded to speak with him. Rogers asked for the call to put through. He repeated his rank and name, then hurried downstairs.

"Detective Rogers! I ain't heard from you in ages. I've given you all the details you wanted, names 'n things, an' you said you'd keep me updated! Why, he's been missing since Billy Shakespeare's birthday. Just where the hell is my boy, Jake?" Mrs. Bauer was persistent if nothing else.

Simon Rogers knew he had to find some answers. And soon. After placating Mrs. Bauer, he returned to his office. Scooping up his phone, he checked his underarm holster and badge, and slipped his jacket on. It was time to go.

36

Jane had checked into the Travel Inn and unpacked a few things. Caroline would be here in about half an hour. Just time to freshen up with a quick shower after the journey, change her blouse and skirt, and put on a dab of lipstick and a spray of perfume. As she went to turn on the shower tap her cell phone beeped twice. Message! May as well check it now, Jane decided. Was it her mum? It would be around breakfast time in Keighley. Or was it Sam? Asking if she'd arrived OK? Perhaps Marie had texted, but she hadn't been in touch with her for a while. Jane hoped that it wasn't Caroline, cancelling the plan to meet . . . Jane hit Open Message on the screen.

Hi Jane,

Hope all OK. Can't talk right now but need to chat to you about Caroline Sinclair. Can't put it in a text. Please be careful. You cannot believe what she says. Take care-please!

Lou x

*

Howard Gardner had had a busy day at the hospital. He rarely worked on a Saturday, but a patient who needed a heart transplant was on the operating table. All the talk was about the shooting of Chuck Hudson and chatter and gossip about the letters found in his locker. Howard needed to be strict with his staff. Cardiac operations still had to be carried out, patients prepared for surgery, taken to recovery afterwards, brought to the Cardiac Care Unit and nursed back to health. But he couldn't stop the whispers in the corridors or the staff room. It wasn't every day that a hospital surgeon was murdered near the front entrance of a big hospital.

The police worked with discretion. The case was being handled by Detective Shaun Pomfret, an experienced policeman with over twenty five years service with both the LAPD and then with the local city police force for the last ten years. Pomfret was two years from retirement and his wife, Alma, couldn't wait for him to finish. His love of Dunkin' Donuts had given him a good paunch and his receding hairline went farther back each month. She had always wanted to travel and promised herself that once Shaun had 'hung up his handcuffs' they'd be off to Oklahoma to see her two sisters, then to the Big Apple and Washington DC.

Pomfret had interviewed around fifteen staff at SFCH. All vouched for Dr. Hudson's integrity and skill as a cardiac surgeon. Two of the nursing staff, Karen and Angelina, had told Pomfret that they had a crush on Hudson, but after realising he was gay, left well alone. Both of these had intimated that Chuck and Kris Roberts seemed to be on friendly terms, and Karen had told Pomfret that she'd heard they visited a club called Quentin's. Nobody could really say what the relationship was like between Hudson and Roberts – they'd kept it very discreet – but it was strongly suggested that they were an 'item.' Pomfret knew he had to visit Quentin's and make some enquiries. Clearly, if the surgeon and Roberts had some form of break-up, perhaps Roberts had a reason to put a bullet into his gay lover. Hudson's wallet contained a business card for a lawyer in Glen Park in the northern part of the city and a telephone call from Pomfret soon revealed that Chuck Hudson had filed his Last Will & Testament with his legal representative about six months ago. Further details had been lodged with the Cypress Lawn Cremation Society – and he wanted his ashes to be scattered in Muir Woods.

Howard landed home at a little after 6.00 pm after another hectic day. A seventy two year old man had received the donated heart of an RTA victim and a replacement aorta operation had been challenging. Howard was pleased with the outcomes, but missed Chuck Hudson by his side. As he entered the house his nose told him Amanda had started preparing dinner – pasta with home made meat balls and a green salad lightly coated with a low calorie French dressing. Caramel ice cream was for dessert, mainly for Teresa and Ryan, and a bottle of Californian white wine was cooling in the fridge along with the usual diet cokes.

"Hi dad!," shouted Ryan as he came through the front door. Ryan was in high spirits. He'd got an 'Excellent' grade in Maths at school and gave credit to Jane for helping him so much. Howard hugged Ryan and congratulated him, but not before giving Teresa a cuddle and whispering 'I love you.'

"Dinner will be up in five minutes, guys," said Amanda to the trio. "Go wash hands and get ready." Ryan continued to beam like a lighthouse beacon and then suddenly asked about Jane.

"I wonder if Jane is enjoying her week-end away? Hope she's all right?"

"Of course she's OK," their dad replied. "She's meeting up with another au pair to catch up on things, and anyhow, she deserves some respite from you two!" Teresa and Ryan giggled, fully understanding the point their dad was making.

"I miss her!" shouted Teresa. Ryan added 'me too.' Amanda brought the warm plates into the dining room with the bowl of pasta and meat balls and a wooden bowl of mixed salad. She poured the drinks, making sure the children got theirs first, then two glasses of white wine in front of her and Howard. After family conversation – friends, school, the weather, aunts and uncles – they ended the meal, Ryan turning his index finger around his ice cream bowl to finish every last bit. Amanda was pleased that they'd enjoyed it; being a mother and a psychiatrist had its benefits, each one complementing the other in a way.

"I'm not gonna have Jane read me a story tonight," offered Ryan. Teresa pulled a face that said 'nor me.' Howard was tempted to make the offer, but there was something he wanted to talk to Amanda about.

"Sorry, but it's an early bedtime tonight, kids," Howard chipped in. "Jane is enjoying her time off so why don't we just take it easy – she'll be back tomorrow and we'll give her a warm welcome when she gets here! Maybe string some balloons up at the front gate?" The children yelped like puppies at the idea. Amanda left Howard to do the washing up as she herded the two upstairs with the plan to let them watch some TV in their rooms. Saturday nights were good for cartoons on three local television stations and Amanda knew they'd be happy watching those for a while.

Washing up finished, Howard had poured himself a Remi Martin brandy and settled into his favourite leather recliner. Amanda occasionally enjoyed a Bloody Mary, so Howard had made a double for her, with a dash of Worcestershire sauce. Sitting comfortably with some low volume classical music coming through the Blaupunkt speakers, Howard turned to his wife.

"So, honey, do you mind telling me what you've been up to? Is there something you're not telling me? The cops have been at the hospital today. Some balding guy asking about Chuck, and then that Rogers with more questions. Apart from the enquiry about Chuck, Rogers was asking me about the car. Something about it being cleaned? New tyres? Hell, I've never bothered about getting it cleaned – it doesn't get that dirty, for goodness sake! And the tyres were OK. Have you been honest with me about where you were on 1 May when you borrowed the car? You said you'd been to see Rosemary. Did you really see her? I know I've had my problems, my head and all, but isn't it time you were totally honest with me."

Amanda knew she had a challenge. It was imperative that she got her story straight. She'd been rehearsing details in her mind for the last six months. So far the police seemed no nearer to identifying the headless torso and, with any luck, Doug Gless would remain an unidentified person forever, but she ought to be vigilant. Amanda stood up and went over to her husband. Kissing him on the cheek, she bent down and whispered in his ear.

"Of course I've been truthful with you! But don't you remember that *you* asked me to get the tyres changed? So I did! I showed you the receipt for four new tyres fitted at the start of May. Look why don't we have an early night? See what Mister Teddy Bear can do for us between the sheets?" Amanda sounded convincing.

Howard had *never* asked his wife if she'd enjoyed *that* evening with Rosemary Gless, what they did and what they discussed. When she'd got home that night he'd said he was tired, had things on his mind. The following morning, a Saturday, Howard had left home before breakfast to go sea fishing with an old friend from the golf club.

And maybe he did ask his wife to change the tyres?

*

"Caroline?" Jane opened her motel door to a girl who looked older than her twenty years. Dressed in a skirt that needed a press and a light brown blouse with one button missing, Caroline looked like somebody who'd dressed in a hurry. Her attempt at colour co-ordination would have left Gok Wan wretching, and the single string of pearls didn't match her earrings. A hint of cigarette smoke hit Jane's nose as Caroline reached forward for an expected hug.

"And you must be Jane! Hi, welcome to L.A." Jane stepped outside onto the walkway that ran along the front of the motel block. If it hadn't been for the text Lou sent, Jane might have invited her in for a few minutes, or made the hug a little firmer. "My car's over here." Caroline led the way across the car park to a small, two door compact Dodge sedan. The two of them hopped in and fastened their seat belts. "I'm so glad you came, it's great to meet you! Italian OK?" Jane nodded and forced a smile.

"Perfect!" The Dodge engine was coaxed into life after two turns of the key and the two girls drove out onto South Westlake Avenue as Caroline mumbled 'Luigi's, here we come.' Various parts of L.A. were pointed out by Caroline as they tootled along, the traffic light for a Saturday evening. Luigi's was less than five minutes away. The car bounced over the low kerb as Caroline stopped close to the main entrance and next to a flashing neon sign that read 'Trattoria Open.' Jane closed the creaking passenger door and followed Caroline into the cool, dark interior. A waiter with his *Antonio* name tag greeted the two diners with 'bonjourno' and showed them to a red and white cloth-draped table in the corner. The ambience in Luigi's was good, subtle lighting with lots of dark wood and a carved wooden staircase that led upstairs to another dining area and the toilets. Paintings of parts of Italy covered the walls; Jane recognised the Leaning Tower of Pisa and the Colosseum in Rome. As they sat down, Jane handed Caroline a brown envelope.

"Here, this is yours." Caroline looked puzzled. "It's the letter I found at the back of the drawer in your room!"

"Of course, it's how you got in touch . . . thanks." Caroline tucked it into her handbag. Jane quickly took the initiative to start the conversation. She smiled.

"So you're working as a Teaching Assistant? That sounds fun!"

"Well, it's OK. Been there nearly five months. When I told them I'd got good grades in English and History at A level they were happy to take me on, and a place at Glasgow uni when and if I return." Caroline switched the questioning. "And what about you? How are things in Hayward?" Antonio handed them a menu each and placed a jug of water on the table, two slices of lemon bobbing on the surface. Jane had anticipated this obvious query and gave a diplomatic response. She told her how much she enjoyed being with the children and their development –

not that she felt Caroline gave a fig for their progress. 'How did Jane get on with Amanda and Howard?' Whoa! She'd need to be a bit more careful here. A factual reply was the best option, and Jane didn't say anything that Caroline wouldn't have known or been aware of. Antonio interrupted the dialogue as the girls placed their order, with an agreed portion of garlic bread to share for starters.

"Did I read about some doctor being shot at the main hospital? Dr. Hudson, wasn't it? That must have set Howard back quite a bit. I think they got on really well." Jane told Caroline about the incident, avoiding an opinion and almost quoting the news reports on the matter. A few minutes later the pungent garlic bread arrived, pizza shaped, sliced into six portions and lathered with garlic butter. Caroline waited as the waiter poured the water into their stemmed glasses.

"Caroline, can I ask you something?" Jane posed with a segment of garlic bread as if waiting for a photograph to be taken. "It's about Ryan . . . you know, about that scar on his leg. I know you said he did it himself, but do have any reason why he would do such a thing?" Jane's eyes never left Caroline's face.

"It was as I mentioned in the email. Poor little soul." She sounded compassionate, but Jane wondered if she meant it. "For some unknown reason he'd been acting oddly for a week or two. Not wanting to do his homework, feeling listless, etcetera. When I went into his room he lunged at me with a pen, just missed me, and then stabbed himself! Just like that! His mother heard the cries, came in, and he said I'd done it." Caroline bit off a piece of crusty baked bread, being careful not to let the butter drip down the front of her blouse. Jane swallowed her mouthful, but, not wishing to sound like a lawyer, carefully posed the next question.

"Did you ever meet a woman called Jodie Patterson?" Of course, Jane knew the answer, but wanted to know more.

"Jodie? Why yes. First met her at the school in my first

week there. Didn't know much about her, but crazy as a loon, some said." Caroline smiled. "Did *you* meet her?" Jane was honest to a point, telling Caroline how she'd met Jodie Patterson, but omitted any comments on the evening class photography courses. Jane took a flyer with her next question.

"And how did Ryan and Teresa get on with Jodie?" Jane sensed that Caroline didn't like the enquiry, but grinned.

"Fine, just fine. She was always kind to them, bought them an ice cream or drinks when we were out. Things like that." So she didn't *deny* knowing Jodie, but Jane couldn't ask about the cherry alco-pop without giving Lou's confidential comment away. There were two pieces of garlic bread left when Antonio came to ask if they'd finished. Both girls looked at each other as if to say 'do you want any more?' but neither did so he whisked the plate away as only Italian waiters can. Jane continued to be aware of what and how she'd asked questions, the tone of her voice slowing and being lowered at the appropriate moments.

"Caroline, if I ask you anything you are not comfortable with, you will say so, won't you?" A nice touch, Jane thought; helps lower the thresh-hold of volunteering that extra bit of information otherwise held back. Caroline nodded. 'Of course,' her eyes said.

"Your boyfriend Jake. He's still missing isn't he?" Jane continued. "You put in your email something about him and Howard having an argument? I realise this is a crazy question, but do you think he had anything to do with Jake's disappearance? Strictly between us two, of course." Another barrier lowered. Caroline took out a handkerchief from her handbag and gently wiped her nose as Antonio came with two plates, spaghetti bolognaise and a lasagna. Deftly he sprinkled parmesan cheese and black pepper from a canon-like wooden pepper pot over both dishes, silkily moving away afterwards.

"Jake wasn't really my boyfriend. We got on well

together, went to a few parties and such. He mixed with a strange crowd, but in Frisco they're all strange, aren't they?" She brightened up at her last comment and put a forkful of twirled spaghetti into a spoon and began to eat. "I wanted company, liked being with people. Sometimes I felt that the four walls of the Gardner household were crushing me. I was surprised when Howard made the comments he did about Jake, but then he'd had a drink. He also told me later that Jake reminded him of the brother he once had! Blond, tall and good looking. I thought that was strange." Caroline rambled for another minute or so. "Do you have a boyfriend?" Jane had expected the question, and decided on the truth. She told Caroline about Andrew, how she'd met him, what he did and then how she'd discovered his dark side. It also reminded Jane to make some enquiries about Andrew – she didn't know if a date had been set for his trial yet. But Jane omitted details about a wig and green contact lenses, it sounded too far fetched. Jane pursued the questioning.

"So, Caroline, do you think Howard did anything to Jake? Got rid of him somewhere? You know . . . he is a *surgeon*." Caroline put her fork down and wiped her nose again. Jane wasn't certain if it was for dramatic effect.

"Perhaps."

37

Caroline went on to tell Jane a lot more than she'd expected. The way in which Howard became friendlier with her, asked her to go directly to him with any issues in the home and not bother Amanda who was a busy woman. Caroline also mentioned that Dr. Gardner seemed very well informed on what was happening in San Francisco, as if his brain was wired up to continual news access. Sometimes when he needed to go out to refuel the car, he'd ask Caroline if she wanted some 'fresh air' and he'd take her along, later telling Amanda it was at Caroline's request. She felt he was beginning to have a hold over her, a Svengali effect. Howard asked why she bothered with a loser like Bauer; there were much better guys around. And it was never totally clear to Caroline who had made the final decision on the termination of her contract, but she told Jane that she believed Amanda was becoming jealous of her relationship with Howard. On 10 May Caroline was told to get out of the house, seventeen days after Jake was last seen. Caroline confessed that Howard had made advances to her one evening when they'd both gone out to collect a KFC family meal from a downtown restaurant. She'd felt herself succumbing to his charm when she pulled herself away from his wandering hands.

One evening when the children were in bed and Amanda was out, Howard had taken Caroline into his confidence and told her about his first wife, Priscilla, the two whiskies he'd drunk having loosened his tongue. 'I loved her but she didn't do what I told her. The bitch argued too much, wanted her own way all the time. She had to go. But I didn't kill her. She loved the Grand Canyon. She was too close to the edge.'

"Would you like the bill now?" asked Antonio, interrupting the intriguing storyline. Jane glanced at her watch. It was nearly 9.30 pm! Where had the evening gone?

"So, Caroline," Jane whispered, "do you believe that Howard Gardner had it in him to kill Jake Bauer?" She nodded.

"I do. Because I wasn't playing ball with him, he may have murdered Jake to get back at me . . ."

As Jane's hair lay down the soft pillow she reflected on the evening with Caroline. Guiltily, she hadn't given her enough credit for being a straightforward, decent and honest person. Caroline had virtually opened her soul, kept nothing back, and admitted that she had been out a few times in the Audi with Dr. Howard Gardner – hence Jodie's comment on that. She didn't lie about knowing Jodie, but Ryan had lied about being stabbed by Caroline. When Jane asked a direct question – 'were Jodie and Dr. Gardner having an affair?' - she said 'no.' And when Jane pushed her luck and asked if Jake and Patterson were ever lovers, again the reply was no. But the addition of 'not as far as I know' on a number of occasions was interesting. Howard could indeed have been the killer of Jake Bauer, his whereabouts still a mystery. And right now Dr. Gardner, it seemed, was the only one to have a motive.

*

"Amanda, it's me! I couldn't talk when you phoned. You'll never guess who was sitting in my kitchen. My God, was I scared when you told me who the police have now identified as their prime suspect? It was Kris Roberts! I met him at your party last November. I don't recall giving him my address but he says I did. I made an excuse about having to go somewhere and he left. There weren't any problems . . . but when I now think that there was a murderer drinking *my* coffee in *my* house and being as nice as you like, well, I shudder all over. I've gone cold just telling you about it now." Rosemary hardly took a breath as she shared her news about a killer who came to call. "Not only that, but when he was here I answered the door to a young couple looking for Doug. Asking me *where* he is, and the girl, whose name was Cissie, claimed she's pregnant with his baby! Obviously I told them I had no idea of his whereabouts, but the guy might think about asking the police to help find him. They'd got my address from a notebook or diary they'd found. If they go to the police, they're going to come round here and start asking questions, aren't they? Holy Moses, I just don't know what to do. And as if that isn't enough, if any of my neighbours saw Kris Roberts, or his car parked out front, once it gets on the six o'clock news . . . hell, I'm done for!"

"Rosy. Stay there and be calm. I'll come over as soon as I can."

Amanda had to think over this whole situation. Ponder exactly what happened on the evening of 1 May. Nobody else knew she was there but Rosemary and a stiff in the mortuary - a headless torso who had been discovered with his wrists bound, a tattoo of Texas on his left shoulder blade and who was wearing a pair of Wranglers, underpants, socks and boots when the body was found.

She *had* told Howard she was going to Nob Hill, left soon after, went for a drive and then got home. And of course he believed her.

Because he always believed what Amanda told him.

*

It was late Monday morning and Katie, who was in the house alone, had been cleaning the place since 9.00 am. Recalling that she'd mentioned an unpleasant odour to Jane, who apparently hadn't noticed anything at first, Katie's keen sense of smell was suggesting that her janitorial skills were falling behind par. She prided herself on sweeping, mopping with a citrous-smelling disinfectant solution, followed by dusting and polishing until your face could be seen reflected in most surfaces. She'd been at it for almost three hours, with all rooms nearly done except for Amanda's studio which, as usual, was locked. Katie had tried the door but to no avail. Getting down on one knee she put her eye to the keyhole. Little could be seen – an easel, some jars containing paintbrushes, a paint palette. But Katie's nose picked up an odd smell. Ripe cheese mixed with old socks, a hint of something that may have been there for a while.

Should she tell Amanda or Howard, or leave it until one of those two, or the children or Jane mentioned it? By the end of the day, someone would make a comment. Jane said she was going to check Ryan's room for a discarded sandwich or burger. Perhaps he'd ashamedly bundled up a pair of his underpants that were in need of a good wash and stuffed them where nobody could find them? Whatever it was, Katie decided that to say nothing was bad practice. She'd leave a note in the kitchen where Amanda would find it when she came in later.

Meanwhile, Detective Rogers had gained approval from his boss, Marty Kluisters, to take a plane down to San Diego to save time driving the eight hour journey. The Southwest Airlines internal flight only took an hour, fifty minutes and Simon Rogers would be there and back within the day, a hire car getting him around the city. Kluisters had decided not to involve the police down there, these were just some routine enquiries by one of his detectives. Rogers' objective was clear. He'd already checked out the addresses of three stores test marketing the new Wrangler jeans – with two inch turn ups – and had questions for each of them. It was a long shot . . . how many pairs had they sold? A hundred, a thousand, ten thousand? With no way of identifying the torso buyer, apart from estimated height and weight, it would be difficult. Did they pay cash or use a card? Forget the cash buyers, but a list of credit or bank card names could be a starting point.

The first store, The Schultz Emporium, was an old style outlet that was trying hard to go up-market. The new Wranglers were targeted at the male 18 to 25 age group, and previous research had indicated that 48% of the stores' customers were in this bracket. During a typical week in the second quarter of the calendar year, and the marketing had begun on 1 April, just over fifteen thousand customers entered the store. Plenty of foot traffic for the jeans company! But not everybody wanted jeans with turn ups!

The second outlet, Sutton's, had similar figures, and the third, Charlie's Clothing Store had even more customers coming through the doors – typically eighteen thousand per week. But Detective Rogers wasn't having any luck. Even with the size, 34 inch waist and 34 inch leg, none of the staff could positively recall anybody of the height and approximate body size buying such a pair. Was he going to have to tell Kluisters the air fare was wasted? A helpful girl named Evelyn in Charlie's went through the sales by size, they'd done that in the other stores, too, but she spent time staring at a computer screen in the office, Rogers hovering over her right shoulder.

"Let's see, Detective, so far we've sold eight hundred and twenty three pairs of the new style . . . hmm, 34 waist and 34 leg, let's see, hmm . . ." Rogers didn't go to church but he was praying hard. "And . . . ah, here it is. Six pairs to date." Rogers uncrossed his first two fingers behind his back. "And . . . three paid cash, the others paid by credit card."

"Can you let me have the card details of those three people? Are there any other staff who may be able to add anything to these sales . . . I know it's a long shot."

"Since the beginning of the test marketing we've had three sales girls focusing on the Wranglers. The jeans company want customer comment feedback as well as sales data and they were interviewed just a few days back, after our six month test period. Stay here I'll see if I can get each one to pop in." Evelyn left Rogers looking at staff rota on a small notice board – Jenny, Dolly, Maud, Dawn, Audrey, Alison, Jemima . . .

"Detective, here's Dolly. She'd been involved with the sales of the jeans." Dolly, blonde and about five feet, one inch tall smiled broadly. 'Hi! Nice to meet you!' she said to Rogers as if about to enter a beauty competition, her standard-wear blue and white striped blouse revealing a little more cleavage than normal. Rogers talked with Dolly for a few moments, Evelyn ever-present and listening carefully. There was no joy there, and she was followed by Maud, then Audrey. Meanwhile, Evelyn had brought up the credit card details of the three purchasers of 34/34 jeans.

    Anthony J. McGraw
    Lewis S. Heppel
    Douglas P. Gless

"Can you recall anything at all about McGraw and Gless, Audrey. It says here you served both these guys? I see the sales were both in April so it's a few months ago . . ."

"What do you think I am? A mastermind? Brain of America? Gee, we get loads a' guys here buying all sorts every day. No way!" Audrey was nothing if not direct, even blunt. Rogers was disappointed but understanding. "You finished with me now?" Evelyn nodded and Audrey left the office. 'Blast,' thought Simon Rogers. Evelyn gave him a sad smile. Within a few seconds there was a knock on the office door. It was Audrey.

"Sorry to bother you, but I just remembered somethin'. There was a guy, 'bout the size you're saying. He bought a pair of new jeans with a credit card. Funny thing was, it's odd what you do notice . . ." Rogers waited, "he didn't have the first part of his left index finger, 'cos I recall he had a slight problem putting his pin number into the machine. Like, he used his middle finger. Huh, strange . . ."

Laying in the mortuary five hundred miles away was a headless torso.

His left hand lacked a complete index finger. The top inch was missing.

38

"So how was your week-end with Irma?" asked Amanda casually the following morning. Jane had just finished sorting out some washing and ironing for her and the children. She'd arrived back around 9.00 pm on Sunday evening after an uneventful Greyhound trip back from San Diego and after saying a quick 'hi' to Howard and Amanda had gone straight to her room; Teresa and Ryan having been asleep for almost an hour. Anticipating her enquiry, Jane had semi-rehearsed her response.

'Good journey . . . nice motel . . . good Italian restaurant . . . great to catch up with Irma . . . laughs and giggles . . . restful night . . . pleasant trip back . . .' That just about did it, with a few gaps filled in and am-dram skills to the fore. Experienced psychiatric counselling would enable Amanda to pick up little nuances, inflexions in the voice, rapid eye movements, the scratching of the nose – give-a-way signs that might have suggested Jane was being miserly with the facts. The real honest truth was that Amanda Gardner didn't care whether her nanny had enjoyed her week-end or not. She had other things on her mind, like Rosemary Gless prattling on about her stepson.

"Oh, that sounds great," replied Amanda with a smile. "Well I'm pleased you got there and back OK. Did you meet anybody of interest going to or from Los Angeles?" Jane suddenly remembered Lucille, the old woman who'd spoken to her on arriving in L.A.

"No, pretty much kept myself to myself!" laughed Jane, desperately trying to appear casual. "Met a nice old lady on the bus but we didn't talk much."

"You'll never guess what . . ." Amanda changed the subject. 'What?' queried Jane. "Howard has started playing bridge . . . at the golf club, with an old friend called James Atkins. They were at Yale, I think he studied Law while Howard was busy cutting up cadavers!" Amanda chuckled. "Twice a week, too! Still, it will get him from under my feet on those evenings – I can relax and concentrate on my painting . . ." *James Atkins* mused Jane, a name she'd heard before, but where? Atkins, Atkins – that was it. The lawyer that had defended Dr. Gardner in the trial of his wife's death at the Grand Canyon. The dishonest lawyer? "Anyway, Jane, I've got things to do, so if you'll excuse me." And with that Amanda Gardner picked up her coat and headed to the door.

"Amanda, what about the note from Katie . . . ?" Jane's voice tailed off as the front door banged. That would have to wait. Amanda quickly reversed her Ford Taunus off the drive, spinning the drive wheels slightly indicating she didn't want to hang around.

Jane made herself a milky coffee. It was mid morning, the children's laundry had been organised, and she wanted some 'me-time.' Sitting down at a kitchen stool she lovingly held the warm cup with both hands like a long lost friend. The slowly spinning caramel coloured froth was mesmerising, wanting to suck her in like a mini whirlpool. Taking stock of the last forty eight hours, she tried to piece things together – complete her mental jigsaw. 'Bloody hell!' she exclaimed out loud, surprising herself at the her voice in the silence of the house. It was as if another person had just uttered those words.

And so Jane reflected. From her arrival at the airport to meeting the family, from Andrew Wilson to Jodie Patterson, from Sam and Marie to Louise . . . and her meeting with Caroline Sinclair. The headless torso, the disappearance of Jake Bauer, the murder of Dr. Hudson . . . so much had happened in such a short time. She sipped her coffee, froth sticking to the sides of the cup but deftly removed with a teaspoon. She was still going to the photo classes at college, loved looking after the children and had made some friends in Frisco. Her driving confidence had improved and Jane had even been contemplating another year on her contract.

But it was Dr. Howard Gardner that caused concern; the things the children had said about arguments between him and his wife, but more of a worry was Caroline's answer to Jane's question – 'could he have done it, killed Jake Bauer?' 'Yes,' she'd replied. And Jane was certain she'd seen Patterson and Howard together, and Jodie was now living on her own. Then this latest news that the respectable Dr. Gardner was starting to play bridge on two evenings a week with Atkins! Were things beginning to stack up, or was Jane getting five when she added two and two together?

'Bridge, my backside,' thought Jane, but she paused for a second to think about how her own personality was changing. This wasn't the Jane Lester that had left a chilly Heathrow airport on 18 August, was it? Had said good-bye to her parents back in Keighley? She felt herself 'hardening up', a phrase her dad might have used in a kind way when she needed motivating.

Glancing at her watch, Jane wondered where the last twenty minutes had gone. There was some shopping to do, the children's rooms to tidy, a photographic assignment to complete before the next evening class and a few emails to send to friends, not forgetting her mum and dad. Rinsing her cup, she replaced it on the wooden tree at the end of the granite work surface. And she had to call Louise again. Jane had left two voice mail messages on Lou's cell phone but so far there'd been no reply. Maybe she was busy on a news story?

Across town, Rosy was wiping away a tear as she spoke to Amanda in the lounge on Nob Hill. The tension was clear in her voice, Rosemary's hands quivering as if stuck in a snowdrift without gloves. She continued to bombard her friend with gripes about the police visiting her – more questions about Doug. The what, where, why and when?

"What we did was horrible and when I look back I wish to God I'd never hit him with that hammer." She stopped suddenly, staring at Amanda. "You did get rid of that clawed hammer, didn't you?" Amanda nodded. "And with no fingerprints and no head, there's no way they can identify him, is there?" Amanda smiled and shook her head. "Gee, I just wish to God it was all a dream." Rosemary rambled on for another half hour, but much of what she said passed over Amanda like a gentle wave on a sandy beach. "And the head, for goodness sake, you got rid of the head, didn't you?" Amanda held her hands up, palms facing Rosy as she nodded and smiled. "And, after we got back, I don't even remember what time you left here!" Rosemary wiped her nose.

"Listen," Amanda spoke softly after a short pause. "This all took place nearly six months ago. Don't you think that the cops would have been asking questions? They'll have reached a dead end by now. Sorry, no pun intended! There's no evidence! And as for the hammer and Doug's head, of course I got rid of them. You asked me to, and have I ever let you down, Rosy?" Amanda Gardner sounded as if she was discussing a new banana and walnut loaf recipe, not the horrific murder of Rosy's stepson. "If the police do come round, act normal, stay cool, and only answer their questions . . . don't go offering up extra information! OK? Get your story straight – when you last saw Doug, when you'd last been in contact, the same as you told those two that visited you recently, that Cissie girl and her friend. And two downbeats like that aren't going to visit the police." Amanda continued, Rosemary becoming calmer, more composed. "So don't worry, right?" Amanda finished her mini sermon and stood up. She hugged her good friend. "Be strong, be brave. You'll get through this."

Amanda was aware that she'd used 'you'll' instead of 'we'll' as she spoke her last sentence. Leaving the house, she got into her Taunus, and headed home. The very last thing Amanda Gardner was going to allow was to be implicated in the murder of Doug Gless. Rosemary was a close friend, but sometimes the time came when your own survival was way more important.

'Sorry, Rosy, but I actually don't remember being round here very long on that Friday evening. Did I see Doug? Why no. Yes, you and I chatted for an hour or so, then I

decided I needed some sea air and drove up the coast road for a while. Parked up over the bridge...listened to the car radio. Driving up to Muir Woods? I don't think so. If anything was disposed of, why, you must have done that yourself using your Buick station wagon in the garage. With a friend who helped you dig the hole and dump the body. Maybe the one who called in for coffee recently? He's strong. It would be easy for you both. By the way, how *is your amnesia treatment coming along?'*

39

Detective Rogers had phoned American Express and obtained the address of Doug Gless. He was renting an apartment in a run down suburb of San Diego, and when Rogers knocked loudly on the door another door, eight feet away, slowly opened.

"Yes, can I help you?" An elderly grey-haired woman in a dressing gown, cigarette dangling from the corner of her mouth, eased her door ajar about six inches, a heavy chain preventing it from opening any further. Rogers explained who he was, flashed his ID, and enquired about Doug Gless.

"I rented him the room for about a year. Ain't seen him for a while, maybe 'bout six months. I gave him three months then boxed his stuff up and put it in the basement. He owes me a couple thousand dollars!" The smoker who hadn't yet dressed was the landlady, Gertrude.

"Mind if I take a look at the box?" asked Rogers. Gertrude grunted, turned around, fumbled with something that made a jingling sound, then handed Rogers a door key. She told him to go downstairs where he'd see shelves along one wall stacked with a number of boxes and one marked DG in black contained his belongings. Going down two flights of cement steps, Rogers squeaked open the rusting metal door, pulling a light switch on as he went in. In seconds he'd spotted the heavy brown cardboard box tied with thick string. Slipping the loose string off, Rogers soon found what he wanted – a dog-eared spiral notebook that contained names and addresses, a dirty comb and toothbrush and a couple of photos showing a young guy, probably Doug himself, with a girl. Placing all three in separate specimen bags, he put the top back on, eased the string over, and returned the key to Gertrude. He placed the items into his briefcase and handed her a note of what he'd taken. Rogers left his business card with Gertrude, who gave a phlegm filled cough as she shut her door. The heavy chain clunked back into place.

By 6.25 pm Detective Rogers was sitting at the desk of Lt. Marty Kluisters.

"Good work, Simon," Kluisters said. "What next?" The ex-marine was straight to the point as ever.

"Toothbrush and comb are with forensics, and the names in the book include some with a cell phone number next to them. There's an address here in San Francisco, up Nob Hill, and a couple of addresses of places he may have worked – a bar called 'Mitzi's' and another named 'JR's'. A Ho-Jo restaurant is listed with Cissie in brackets next to it. Guess it's a girl's name? Some guys names here, too. Marlon, Donald, Ollie and Jerome. All with numbers next to them."

"Any progress with the info? How far have you got?"

"Well, two of the cell numbers are dead. I tried a third and it rang continuously. The fourth one, registered with AT&T, belongs to Oliver Jackson. A nasal-sounding voice on the mail answering service told me to leave a message. He called himself Ollie, and he'd get back to me. I didn't bother leaving one. As far as the Nob Hill address is concerned, Richmond Avenue, the property is owned by a Mrs. Rosemary Frances Gless. Quickly checked her out. She lost her husband a little while back. She has a daughter, Samantha, who works for a lawyer in town. I'll go check Mrs. Gless out in the morning after I've spoken to Forensics – told 'em it was important."

"And if the DNA matches, you'll have some sad news for her." Marty Kluisters could be the epitome of the under statement. Rogers nodded. "But how the hell did that guy, if it is him, end up in a shallow grave in Muir Woods? And where's his damned head?" Kluisters stood up. "Bloody good detective work, Simon. Fancy a couple of beers before home time?"

And Katie still hadn't had a response to the note she'd left for Amanda about the unpleasant aroma upstairs.

*

"Jane! It's Lou! Sorry I haven't been in touch sooner but I've had the mother of all 'flu bugs! Laid me low since Saturday – I was going down with it when I sent my text about Caroline. Thought I was dying!" Louise was sitting at her desk in the newspaper offices, turning gently on her leather swivel chair. "Had to get the doc to call and he prescribed some Tamiflu. But that's enough about me, how did your evening go?" Jane gave Lou the bare bones of her L.A. trip saying that basically it was fine and they both had a frank conversation about a range of issues. Despite Lou's warning shot about Caroline, a brief chat over their cell phones wasn't the best way to share what had been discussed. However, Jane did tell Lou that *she* felt Caroline was honest about things and might have a had a raw deal with the Gardners. Jane recalled Lou's *'you cannot believe what she says'* part of the text that was still in her messages Inbox.

"Jane, let's meet! Tomorrow? I'm free between one and two." Jane proposed Gaspar's in Sutter Street having had lunch there with Sam. Lou agreed, she'd see Jane at 1.00 pm. "Be really good to catch up!" ended Lou and hung up. Jane wasn't sure if it was her, or if Lou was still recovering from her 'flu, but she sounded different. A little matter-of-fact, business-like somehow. Perhaps she was stressed over a news story, had a deadline to meet, an editor on her back? Jane paid it little attention, she knew Lou had become a good friend. But just after she'd ended her call to Jane, Lou's cell beeped twice. The Inbox had a new message.

See you at bridge class.

*

Amanda was furious, but tried hard to control it. Thankfully the children were upstairs doing their homework. Having seen the note from Katie, Howard had phoned a domestic cleaning company, SnowWhite, to come and take a look at their property to check out the smell. It wasn't anything to get concerned about, and he knew Katie took her work seriously. But Howard hadn't mentioned it to his wife, only to Jane, who said she'd be in all day when SnowWhite were due to call. Two guys turned up, showed their ID, and Jane had let them in to take a look. The equipment they brought in included a machine that looked more as though it ought to be on the next Apollo space mission. It could detect a wide range of chemicals from as little as one part per million, and could differentiate household odours such as those given off by onion, garlic, and fruits and vegetables from ammonia, methane, sulphurous and aldehyde-type odours, the latter associated with death and decay. Supposing a dead rat had been lodged in a pipe? Or a mouse stuck in the air vent somewhere? Maybe a bird had flown into a window and fallen into some guttering where it was rotting, maggots growing nicely in its putrid flesh? Howard was anxious to find out. As a surgeon he'd seen death many times, on and off the operating table, but this wouldn't be good in his own home if any visitors dropped by!

"So why the hell didn't you tell me these guys were coming? And, and . . . you gave Jane permission to let them into my studio! Bloody hell, Howard. I told you never to use that spare key! OK, it's not meant to be Fort Knox, but I prefer to have nobody – repeat nobody – going in there!" Amanda had blown a fuse. Jane was standing within a few feet of Amanda and feeling as guilty as if she'd stolen a white stick off a blind man.

"Calm down, Amanda. I forgot to tell you. OK? I sometime forget things. You weren't going to do anything about it so I made a call from the hospital two days ago. Katie was concerned! And I gave Jane permission to let them in, but only if they honestly felt they needed to. And they did! I guessed where you might have left the key, and the machine, whatever it does, picked up a relatively high concentration of some chemical from around the edges of your studio door. They had to gain entry. A key was better than busting the door off its hinges,OK?" Amanda appeared to be cooling off, but she knew she'd have to find a different place to hide the spare key. She braced herself.

"So what did they find, someone's dismembered body? A severed head?" Amanda laughed nervously.

"I was here when they brought out the body," Jane said. Amanda gripped the granite worktop." *'Body?'* "It was a dead chipmunk, a young one. Been stuck in a narrow ventilation duct that runs between the two external walls for up to a month. Their machine was clicking like mad as the nozzle picked up the smell." Jane smiled gently in an attempt to diffuse the tension. Sitting down Amanda had relief written across her face.

"So that was it? A bloody chipmunk!" Amanda slowly breathed out and headed for the wine rack. "I need a glass of wine! Howard do you want one?" Her husband nodded and grinned at her. She poured two large glasses as Jane walked to the kitchen door – she needed to attend to the children. "Sorry, Jane, didn't mean to go off the handle. You only did what Howard asked you to do. But next time . . ." Amanda didn't need to finish her sentence.

"Yes, I know," replied Jane. "It could have been worse! And Katie will be relieved." Amanda was going to go and check her studio after she'd finished her wine, wanted to be certain that nothing else was touched.

Nothing.

40

Detective Megan Harris had been to Wheeler and Howison's to check out the tyre fitting on a black Audi Q7, no license plate listed, that had four new Continental's fitted on 4 May. She'd been shown a copy invoice for the work – tyres 265 50 R19 at $235 each, fitting charge $25 per wheel including balancing, and new valves at $9 each. Total bill $1,076 - cash paid. A young tyre fitter remembered the attractive, well dressed woman who'd waited for the work to be done. He'd wondered why she wanted new tyres when the ones on the vehicle still had enough tread for another twelve months of motoring at least. Harris asked if the tyres that had been removed may have been kept but the reply was 'no.' The tyre fitter couldn't recall the brand of the old tyres, and all removed tyres were collected monthly by the local environment department and disposed of appropriately. They were long gone.

Back in his office, Simon Rogers had phoned Forensics first thing the following morning after his trip to San Diego and it had been confirmed that a DNA test showed that Mrs. Gless was going to get some real bad news that day. Rogers decided he'd drive to the house around 10.30 am with Detective Harris and hope that Mrs. Gless would be home. A phone call was no way to break such information – it needed to be done face-to-face in her home. Rogers had done this many times before, and Harris would be the ideal foil to be there to console . . . and put the kettle on.

At the next desk, coffee cup next to his computer, Detective Pomfret was going through a file on Kris Roberts. Kluisters had asked him to get a better profile on the hospital porter who'd recently handed in his notice and who was still being hunted by police. Enquiries had shown his rented apartment was empty, and a call had been put out to all units on a silver-grey, two-door BMW with license plate KR 210885. Staff at the hospital had given Detective Pomfret, the lead detective on the case, names of Roberts' friends as well as the address of Quentin's Club. He was heading there in ten minutes, but Roberts could be anywhere by now; he had a brother in Fresno and a sister who lived somewhere in southern California.

Rogers cell phone began to warble. He didn't recognise the number, somebody who needed a Kleenex tissue spoke.

"Hi, did you try to call me? I'm Ollie Jackson. Who is this?" Simon Rogers gave minimal details, but asked Ollie if he could call by the police station as soon as possible. Reluctantly Ollie agreed. If the detective could speak with Jackson before he drove to Nob Hill, a few more useful details might emerge But it wasn't going to make the visit to see Mrs. Gless any easier.

Meanwhile, Jane was finishing off tidying the kids rooms over in Hayward and then decided to check her emails. She was seeing Lou at 1.00 pm and didn't want to be late. After sending up to ten within the last couple of days, she wondered if there'd been any replies. Her parents, friends in Keighley, and one each to Sam and Marie with photos of the kids attached. She hadn't spoken to Sam and Marie for a while and they may just have replied with some news. Jane logged on, clicked her Inbox, and saw four unopened emails. There was one from Caroline and three others that could wait. As Jane would be seeing Lou later for lunch, Caroline might have something of interest that Jane could share with her.

Dear Jane,

It was lovely to meet you last Saturday. Thank you for your company and listening to my nattering! As we shared some common issues it made a great change for me to be able to chat about things which otherwise get stored up in my head.

I hope I didn't say too much, I mean, I tried to answer

your queries as best I could. What we discussed must stay between us, as you said over our meal. Take what I said about Dr. Gardner with a pinch of salt. Basically he's a good guy, a wonderfully talented surgeon who lives under his wife's control, at least that's how I saw it.

But there's something else I forgot to mention. I'm not certain if Dr. Gardner was unfaithful to his wife but there were two occasions when I overheard him talking to someone on his cell phone. It was what I'd call lovey-dovey. He mentioned wanting to see more of her. I think he called her LuLu or something like that, and I recall he jokingly said something like 'I hope it doesn't get into your newspaper.'

Maybe it's nothing, but there's no harm in you knowing. Be careful.

Love,
Caroline.

Jane sat down and breathed deeply. 'OK, OK,' she told herself. 'Two things can be done.' Cancel lunch with Lou . . . or, go ahead and meet her at Gaspar's as arranged.

She knew what she would do.

*

The Cypress Lawn Cremation Society had a reputation in Frisco for giving people a good send off – 'Heaven Here We Come' was their motto, and nothing was too much trouble. Chuck Hudson's stepfather and stepmother had been informed of the tragedy and hospital staff who had worked closely with Dr. Hudson were given leave of absence to attend the funeral service on what turned out to be a damp October morning. His coffin was carried into the chapel where the hired pastor churned out a few words saying what a good guy Chuck had been. He added a few extras gleaned from a brief conversation with Howard Gardner and made his two minute eulogy sound very convincing . . . the usual stuff. His step-parents stood silently at the front. No hymns, no words from anyone else, but a few tears were wiped away as the coffin slowly moved on a silent conveyor belt, heavy velvet curtains closing behind it to the strains of 'Abide With Me' played by a small, dumpy lady wearing an all-to-obvious wig. Among the congregation were Lt. Marty Kluisters and Detective Pomfret, eyes peeled for anybody who didn't appear to fit in. Was Roberts going to be there? Collar turned up, a pair of shades on?

The group of about twenty left the chapel and walked outside to the rear of the building where several bunches of flowers were laid out, some with a simple message such as 'We'll miss you' or 'Lots of love.' Howard had a quiet word with Mr. and Mrs. Hudson while the two detectives remained vigilant as others talked quietly in huddled groups, a combination of idle gossip and honest words for the murdered doctor. After some five minutes people began to move away. Howard Gardner and the nursing staff, including Karen and Angelina, had to get back to the OR for an important heart operation, Amanda had a clinic, and generally . . . well, people had things to do. Neither of the detectives noticed anything out of the ordinary, and no sign of the ex hospital porter.

Hudson had left his final wishes with his lawyer, in conjunction with Cypress Lawn, and his ashes were to be scattered in Muir Woods, a map having been left with the cremation society. A representative from the society would take the ashes the following day and, anyone wishing to be there were to meet at the West Car Park at precisely 11.00 am. It was felt that there'd be hardly anybody there, no one being able to make the time to stand around while fine white granules were sprinkled across the ground, heavy winds permitting. In fact, the C.L.C. Society had to carry a wind-speed gauge; wind velocity above 20 mph would prevent the final remains being laid to rest. San Francisco council eco rules!

The gunmetal clouds along the coast were lifting the

next day, the light drizzle had stopped, and with hardly any breeze the ashes of Dr. Chuck Hudson were taken to his final resting place. The urn, safely in the hands of a young man dressed in a dark suit and sitting in the front of a Cypress Lawn black limousine, was making its way north out of the city. As it approached the West Car Park and stopped, an unmarked police car pulled in behind it and parked twenty yards away. Detective Pomfret, on his own, was making it his business to take a last look, see who turned up for the final laying to rest. His wife, Alma, had given him a good breakfast a few hours earlier, and the two large coffees with a chocolate doughnut he'd consumed in his office were making him feel a bit sluggish. Hudson's step-parents who'd driven the 295 miles to be here had just arrived. Pomfret rolled out of his car and followed the two C.L.C.S. Representatives, the pastor and a woman wearing dark glasses, who'd got out of the black limo. Hudsons parents were a few steps behind. They slowly walked up the track leading from the car park, Shaun Pomfret following them at a discreet distance. A handful of other walkers were out trekking but no one seemed to take much notice of the darkly clad group led by the pastor who'd taken the service at the crematorium the day before.

Arriving at a tall sequoia tree, the party stopped. The young man passed the urn to the pastor who held it in both hands for a few moments and then, with heads bowed, he said a quiet prayer. Handing the urn to the woman, she removed the lid and scattered the ashes across a small area, gently shaking the urn from side to side as if putting flour onto a baking board. Hudson's step-mother was being comforted by her husband as Pomfret watched from a hundred yards downhill, searching the woodland for signs of anyone else, anybody who could be taking an interest – *perhaps an unhealthy interest*. He saw a man, maybe fifty yards away and standing perfectly still, watching the short service at the foot of the giant redwood. Pomfret began to move in an arc, keeping his eyes focused on the solitary male visitor, his right hand moving to grip the butt of his handgun, but within seconds the man had gone.

As Pomfret was about to make his way back down the trail he noticed a small piece of black and yellow plastic ribbon not far from where the ashes had been scattered, only about twelve inches long, that was stuck under a heavy fallen branch. He picked it up. The letters DO NOT CR were clear to see.

41

Gaspar's was quite busy but Jane and Louise found a table against the far wall away from the door where the cool Frisco breeze didn't quite reach. After initial pleasantries and a hug that was more of a gesture than genuine, they both ordered a sandwich with side salad and a portion of kettle chips to share, non-carbonated water to drink. Louise opened with Jane's expected question.

"So, how was it? What sort of a girl is Caroline?" Lou smiled; at least the corners of her mouth angled upwards slightly.

"Caroline's great. She picked me up as agreed and we ate in a lovely Italian restaurant close to the Premier Inn. I offered to pay for the meal, it was the least I could do – after all it was my suggestion to get together." Jane held back on detail.

"What did you talk about?" Louise took a bite of her ham-on-rye open sandwich. "There must have been so much to discuss . . . her role as a nanny, the Gardner family, the kids, people you both know . . ." It really sounded as if Lou was fishing, a big net ready to drag in all the minnows. "How does she feel about being sacked by Amanda?"

Sacked by Amanda!

"Pretty cheesed off."

"And the incident with Ryan? I mean, that was pretty bad, wasn't it?" *Incident with Ryan!*

"Yes, it was."

"I think she liked Howard, he was good to her, wasn't he?" *Good to her!*

Lou seemed to know an awful lot about what had happened up until 10 May when Caroline had departed, and that left Jane feeling very uncomfortable. Was it the time to hit her with what she knew about Lou.

'No, let's play along for now,' decided Jane.

"Well, we talked about all sorts, actually, but I don't

remember all the details. Caroline ordered two cocktails before we started eating, then we got through two bottles of red wine, and . . . the gorgeous waiter brought an Italian liqueur, Limoncello, with the bill!" Jane surprised herself by her string of lies. "Oh, while I remember, do you know anybody called Jim Coughlan?" Jane came straight out with the question.

"Jim Coughlan . . . no, can't say I do. Why do you ask?"

"Well, Caroline mentioned him in passing, that's all. Read something about him. Said he was the editor on the *Arizona Republic* where you said you worked." Louise coughed and wiped her mouth with a napkin. Lou did not reply. Jane gently popped a few kettle chips into her mouth. She was in the lead now. 'Fifteen – love' from the tennis umpire.

"Listen Jane, I've just remembered, I've got a meeting with my boss in half an hour and I need to finish off an article on diabetes. Here, take this." Lou dropped a ten dollar bill on the table as she stood up. Jane kept her seat.

"And, oh, Lou, daft question, but do you know how many cards each player is dealt in bridge?"

"Bridge? No idea! I don't like cards! Must fly. I'll be in touch soon. Be good!" Lou left quickly, smart-phone in hand, heels clicking on the tiled floor. Jane finished her lunch with a satisfied grin and paid the bill. $18.25 wasn't bad to reach that point with Louise Archer, a girl she thought she could trust. Jane realised she'd probably lit the blue touch paper and it might be only a matter of time before the firework exploded. But Jane chuckled to herself – Limoncello with the bill. Ha! Not only that, but Jane had just invented the name Jim Coughlan! Louise didn't even bother to tell Jane the real name of the editor, and Jane wondered if Miss Archer ever worked in Phoenix at all? Jane didn't need to be a Miss Marple or a Hetty Wainthrop either to realise that Louise seemed to know far more about Caroline's history with the Gardner's than she ever would have gathered from general conversation.

But as Louise walked back to her car she was texting,

both thumbs working overtime on her smart-phone screen.

...

As a reporter, Louise Archer had known Dr. Gardner for some time. She'd covered a story on improvements in surgery in San Francisco but, after a half hour interview, it seemed that she hadn't lost much time in making her affections known for him. The heart surgeon had given her his cell number so that she could get updates on future surgical developments. But Dr. Gardner had stressed that she shouldn't call him unless she needed to. At least he was pretty sure he'd said that. But as Jane headed back to Adair Way, the sometimes forgetful Howard Gardner was already planning his next move.

*

Detectives Rogers and Harris parked the unmarked, dark blue cruiser thirty yards along the avenue from the home of Rosemary Gless. Ollie Jackson had called into the police station in Vallejo Street earlier and told Rogers and Harris what he knew about Doug Gless. He was pretty sure that Doug was going to see his Ma, told Ollie something about his Pa passing away and how much money he was going to get. Not only that, but Ollie wondered if Doug was running away from his responsibilities with Cissie who'd gone into the station with him and Rogers saw for himself her six month bump.

A watery sun struggled to break through the clouds as Rogers rang the bell. They waited for ten seconds, then rang again. There was no car on the drive. Their eyes met and each asked one another the same question without speaking. Nobody home. Harris stood back and looked at the upstairs windows – no hint of a curtain twitch. Rogers nodded toward the car to say 'let's go' when the front door opened slightly.

"Hello, may I help you?" Harris noticed the horizontal

door-chain. Was Mrs. Gless a nervous person? Rogers introduced himself, then Megan Harris. "Yes, please come on in, Detective." Act calm, she told herself. The chain was clinked off the inner socket. Rosemary Gless led the way into the lounge and offered the two detectives coffee or tea after they'd sat down. They asked for coffee, both milk no sugar. Within minutes Rosemary was back with a tray. Meanwhile, the two visitors' eyes were searching the room for any tell-tale signs of her son . . . any indication that he was here. On the sideboard were two photographs of Rosemary, one with a guy who Rogers assumed was her husband Geoff, and another of Rosemary and Geoff with a young man that Rogers recognised from a photo in the basement box. It was Doug.

"When was the last time you saw your son, Doug, Mrs. Gless?" Rogers opened the discussion.

"My *stepson*, Doug. He was Geoff's boy from his first marriage," she hesitated, "but of course I always treated him like my own. Well, let me see. He came to see me about a year ago. He was doing odd jobs in San Diego. Sometimes he phoned me, reverse the charges, but he wasn't one for keeping in touch."

"Do you know a young man called Ollie Jackson?" asked Harris. Rosemary shook her head. "Or a young woman called Cissie?"

"Er, no, the names are not familiar. Should they be?" She sipped her coffee. Megan Harris explained the visit of the two of them to the police station but didn't say they'd been invited there. "Oh, those two? Er, yes, they called here recently . . . enquiring about Doug, but as I said, I haven't seen hide nor hair of him for a year or so." She smiled. *Stay calm and only answer their questions.* Rogers chipped in.

"When your husband passed away, did he leave anything in his will to Doug?"

"No. Oh, wait. Yes. Sorry. On his death Doug was to inherit ten thousand dollars." Rogers asked if Doug knew that. "Er, I'm not sure . . . he probably did."

"So if he did, wouldn't he come here to make enquiries about his inheritance?" Rogers was persistent. Rosemary could feel she was being pushed into a corner.

"Yes, you'd expect that, but, well, as I said, he hasn't been here for some time. He did phone a while back, maybe beginning of May, said he might come up to Frisco. Also said I could wire the money to a bank account in San Diego, but, well, I just never got around to doing that." Harris finished her coffee and putting the cup down, opened up.

"Don't you think it's strange that if he was due ten grand, he'd have been chasing you for it?" A nervous laugh came from the thin lips of Rosemary Gless.

"He wasn't short of money, always able to pay his way. I think he had a credit card that he tried to pay off monthly, and his jobs were well paid – cash in hand, you know." *You're saying too much.*

"You said 'wasn't' just then. Did you mean isn't? And 'had' a credit card . . . do you mean he hasn't got one now?" Rosemary swallowed hard as she replayed Harris' question in her head. She explained her incorrect reply as being due to lack of sleep. The smile was wearing thin, her lips losing their dull glow.

"Do you have an address for him in Diego?" Rosemary shook her head, emphasising that their contact was only by telephone. *Why don't they leave me alone?*

Further questions followed. Rosemary tried to discipline herself, keep her answers short and to the point, just as Amanda suggested. After another five minutes, Rogers asked if they might take a look around the house. There was nothing to hide – Rosemary was confident of that. As she carried the tray back into the kitchen, the two 'tecs followed her. Harris noticed how clean the kitchen was, in fact it looked updated - considering the age of the property. From the kitchen, Rogers walked into a conservatory at the back, then returned and took a look into three other rooms.

"Shouldn't you have a search warrant or something?"

asked Rosemary. She'd watched NCIS a few times. Rogers diplomatically told her that technically she was correct, but this was an informal check. However, if she wanted this to become an official, documented search of the whole house, Rogers would go through the proper procedure. "Er, no, it's OK. Take a look, sorry, just on edge that's all, er, I mean 'cos of my fatigue and that."

"What's through there?" asked Harris, looking at a strong door leading off the kitchen.

"Leads into the garage, car's in there and a few bits and pieces. Bit untidy, but go ahead, take a look." Rosemary sounded pleased with herself, she had nothing to hide. Both detectives went through the door into a wide garage, a ten year old Buick station wagon parked in the middle, and plenty of room to walk around it. Shelves were on two walls, boxes of nuts and bolts laid out along them, old jam jars containing hooks, screws, nails, door knobs . . . Tools were hanging regimentally from large plastic coated metal U-hooks, and it gave Rogers the impression it was a 'man's place.' An iron vice was securely attached to a workbench, two rolls of striped strong tape beside it, and there were more jars of liquids, red, black, yellow – and a demijohn marked 'Danger Acid.' His eyes scanned the whole place. Seemed pretty normal. A small Bosch fridge was in one corner, purring away gently, and a fan set in the fixed window allowed air to be expelled or sucked into the garage, keep it ventilated. Rogers was about to leave the garage when he looked more closely at a row of stainless steel tools. All were clean, polished, except for one in the middle. It was duller than the others. He took a closer look, almost drawn to it. If Rosemary's husband kept such a tidy place, was even proud of his tools, why was this dirty?

Rogers didn't touch it, and silently pointed it out to his colleague. Harris shrugged.

They were looking at a large claw hammer as the fridge continued to hum gently.

*

"Come and sit down, Mrs. Gless, there's something we need to talk about." Rogers ushered Rosemary into the lounge and she sat down. "I visited San Diego recently. We had a lead on a pair of jeans Doug bought in a store, a new style being test marketed there. We found that he'd bought a pair using his Amex credit card, an unusual pair with two inch turn ups, size 34 waist, 34 leg." Rosemary listened as though a radio story was being read to her. "I saw his landlady and had access to some of his things. Some hair was taken from a comb for DNA analysis, and there was a photo. Is this Doug with his girlfriend?" Rogers knew it was Doug from the photo on the sideboard. "Can you confirm if this is Cissie, the pregnant girl who called here?" Rogers genuinely wasn't certain. He handed the photo to Rosemary who stared at it for a few seconds before a tear began to fall down her cheek. After she'd wiped a few tears away, Rosemary handed the photo back to Simon Rogers.

"That's Doug OK. But it isn't the girl who came here. It's his sister . . . she died in a car accident four years ago. He always carried this with him after that." Rosemary braced herself. "And I have to tell you that Doug is gay. He never looked at women . . . there's no way he would have got her pregnant. She's a downright liar." Megan Harris knew what was coming, and went over and stood behind Rosemary's armchair.

"Before we came here today, our Forensics department checked the DNA from Doug's comb with a sample taken from the body found up in Muir Woods found on 21 August this year. We have reason to believe that the body is that of your son, Doug." Unblinking, Rosemary Gless focused on the family photo on the sideboard. "I'm very sorry, but as a matter of procedure you'll have to come to the mortuary to identify the body. Our car is outside, and Detective Harris will take you there now while I wait here." Rosemary was silent. *How the hell did it come to this?* Helping Rosemary with her coat, she put on her shoes and Harris held her arm as they walked out to the cruiser just along the avenue. Within a few seconds of the door closing, Detective Rogers made a call to Jim Bell in Forensics.

"Hi Jim, Simon here. Can you send two CSI guys out to Nob Hill – 29, Richmond Avenue – as soon as possible. Yes, bring the usual kit, including the luminol. I'm here now and I'll stay 'til they arrive. Thanks. Bye." Rogers went for another look around the garage while he waited. He pulled a pair of blue nitrile gloves from his jacket pocket and went across to look at the claw hammer again. And the rolls of tape.

But before the Crime Scene Investigators arrived, Rogers got the biggest surprise of his life.

42

"Oh, Jane, but we want to go to the funfair on Saturday, don't we Teresa?" Ryan was putting Jane under pressure. Ten miles south of the city a funfair had been set up for the autumn and winter season. It wasn't a big one, but there were chair-o'-plane rides and dodgem cars and well . . . all of that, plus the food and drinks cabins to satisfy every child's taste and fancy. Jane knew she hadn't given enough time to the children of late, just the basics – help with homework, the journeys to school (with the odd glimpse of Jodie Patterson from a distance), washing and ironing, and the general teaching of good manners and bonhomie that she'd created as their nanny. That's what she was there for, after all!

"All right, calm down Ryan. I'll check with your mother and if she says it's OK, we'll go. The weather forecast isn't great, but if it stays dry it's a deal." Ryan beamed. He'd won. Had Amanda passed a 'psychology gene' onto her son? Was that possible? Jane wondered if this young man would turn out to be a manipulative individual, but if so, she prayed it would be in a positive way. Jane realised that she had a narrow road to run, doing her professional role *and* keeping the children happy. She wondered to what extent Ryan had tried to 'work' Caroline round to his wants. When he didn't get his own way did he resort to evil tactics like stabbing himself in the leg and saying that the au pair had done it?

"Jane, look at the time!" Teresa was standing in the hallway, fully dressed, school-bag in hand. But Jane had lost track of time; it wasn't like her. Although the morning was the same as any other, she'd had her mind on other things, like her brief lunch meeting with Louise Archer, for instance. Jane's knowledge now put her in a difficult position. And if Louise and Howard were that friendly, and they both knew that Jane was aware of their relationship, she was vulnerable. *'Why not have it out with Dr.*

Gardner?' Jane thought to herself. Confront him alone, just let him know what she had found out. What could happen after that? OK, she'd get fired? But Jane was doing a good job for the Gardner's, Amanda had told her that several times. If Jane spilt the proverbial 'beans' on Howard, it could be the end of his marriage – his second marriage. He couldn't risk that. He wouldn't risk that *and* his professional standing at SFCH as head of cardiac surgery would he? But Howard would now know that she'd been to see Caroline in LA, and not Irma as she'd said. Not only that, but he'd be aware of Jane's meeting at Gaspar's. "Jane, did you hear me? Come on!" Teresa was walking out of the front door, Ryan close behind. Jane picked up the Honda car keys and dashed out, the clouds beginning to part as San Francisco came to life on a cool October morning.

On the school run the children chatted about this and that, and Ryan was already planning which rides he'd go on at the funfair. Teresa was more interested in selecting an ice cream or two, her mouth watering with the expectation of a large Bi-Rite cornet. She told them that they'd have to do well with their homework until Friday, and keep their rooms tidy! This psychology worked both ways.

In a suburb of Frisco that same morning, armed police had surrounded a condominium in which they believed Kris Roberts was holed out. Detective Pomfret had been to Quentin's and several of the members he'd spoken to had mentioned a guy called Lee Jepson. He and Roberts were very friendly – in fact, Chuck Hudson would get jealous whenever he saw Lee and Kris together. Pomfret had been given Lee Jepson's address on the east side of the city and he was paying him a second visit – he hadn't been satisfied with Jepson's denial of the whereabouts of Kris Roberts. Things he'd been told didn't stack up. A two door, silver grey BMW was parked out back under a heavy tarpaulin sheet and Pomfret had obtained Kluisters permission to take four policemen armed with automatic rifles to take up position in front of and behind the condo. Pomfret wanted to talk with Roberts about the murder of Dr. Hudson – he was still prime suspect – and despite newspaper and radio pleas for him to come forward, he'd never showed.

Pomfret banged on the door. A pinhole of light appeared in the door as someone opened the peep-hole. Before he could knock again, the door burst open and a guy with a handgun barged past knocking the out-of-condition detective to the floor. Pomfret was winded and needed time to catch his breath. The guy was lean and fit and in seconds he was sprinting out of the front door of the condominium and across the grass toward the main road. Seeing an armed policeman, he aimed in his direction hoping to scare him off but, despite the helmet, a bullet hit the officer in the forehead and he crumpled like a lead weight. He kept on running, now side-stepping the morning commuter traffic, until he was out of sight, a narrow side street providing an ideal getaway. Cars squealed to a halt as two of the armed officers gave chase. It was too risky to start shooting now. But these cops were fit, too, and despite body armour and carrying their weapons, they chased the fleeing man until he ended up in a cul-de-sac half a mile from the condo. Being trapped and with nowhere to run, he turned and stopped, his breathing heavy and laboured. The two policemen walked slowly toward him. 'Put your gun down, Roberts, and hold your hands up in the air' yelled one of the cops.

He stood, feet apart, hands by his side. Time slowed as he eyed both policemen. But before either of the two cops could get near enough the barrel was under his chin, the trigger pulled. At such close range his scalp erupted into the morning air, bone fragments flicking from his skull like a soft-boiled egg being smashed with a metal spoon. Brain tissue spattered like thick porridge over a nearby yellow Hyundai.

Later examination of the bullets from the handgun, a Smith & Wesson .45, showed it was not the one that was used to murder Chuck Hudson. And the guy who had committed suicide that morning wasn't Kris Roberts but someone called Dick Webber to whom Jepson was offering a bed for a while, a straight guy up from Santa Rosa but with a criminal record. A guy waiting for the cops to come calling. He'd grabbed the gun, which Jepson kept for personal protection, and ran when he suspected the police were after him. Lee Jepson was taken into custody and told police that Roberts had confessed to him about Hudson. Kris Roberts had left Jepson's place two days previously and Lee Jepson swore that he had no idea of Roberts' current whereabouts. Although Jepson couldn't believe it, Kris Roberts had also told him that Hudson had tried to kill him by giving him an injection and laying him on the railway tracks to get decapitated by a freight train. And in the interview with Detective Pomfret, Lee Jepson also mentioned a woman that Roberts saw sometimes; nothing sexual or anything like that, just a woman who understood what being male and gay really meant. Jepson told Pomfret her name was Rosemary and she lived on Nob Hill. Pomfret had made a note but it didn't really seem that important.

Jepson denied knowing anything about Webber's criminal record. He'd met him in a bar on Fisherman's Wharf a while back, and being down on his luck, he'd offered him a bed for which he paid Jepson one hundred dollars a week – cash. Kris Roberts' car was impounded and Jepson's gun was now in police hands. The room that Lee Jepson allowed him to use had been thoroughly searched. There were few signs of any personal belongings . . . except for a dirty T shirt and a pair of old socks in a basket. But the police did find a receipt under the edge of the carpet for a Kahr KM9 handgun from a gun store in the city. A follow up investigation proved Kris Roberts was the purchaser, and the bullet removed from Hudson's skull matched the KM9. Roberts was still out there.

Armed and dangerous.

*

Within fifteen minutes two guys from Forensics had parked up in a plain, white van. To minimise attention from the neighbours, both were in denim boiler suits and carried a black hold-all each. They looked just like workmen that turn up to mend the boiler or check the gas fire. Simon Rogers was sitting waiting for them, wiping his brow with his handkerchief. He opened the door to let them in.

"Bloody hell, Simon. You OK?" asked Mitch, looking at Detective Rogers' ashen pallor.

"Let's get straight to the matter, guys. Follow me." Rogers led the way into the kitchen and through into the garage. The back door of the Buick was raised, but he motioned to the fridge in the corner. "Take a look in there!" The one called Mitch quickly donned a sterile over-suit and elasticated cap, slipped on a pair of powder-less latex gloves and went over and cautiously opened the door. The inside light came on, and, apart from a few cans of Budweiser beer, he was looking at a head. Poised and upright, as if it was about to say something.

The gruesome face could be seen through a double layer of heavy gauge polythene. The blue eyes were open, lips bared to reveal ivory coloured teeth, and congealed blood was blackened on the forehead where matted hair hug like wisps of thin liquorice ribbon.

"Oh, shit!" shouted Mitch as he recoiled from the open door. He'd seen a lot in his five year career with SFPD but this made him gasp. Carefully lifting the package out from the middle shelf, Mitch passed it to his colleague who bagged it, holding the head carefully as if it were a Ming vase. Few words were spoken as Rogers then went to the rear of the station wagon. He pointed to marks on the floor mat. It had to be dried blood, a deep red against the light brown of the rectangular fibrous floor. The next ten minutes were spent taking samples from the Buick and then, along with the claw hammer and a number of hacksaws, all of the items were placed into standard evidence bags.

Simon Rogers looked at the kitchen and remembered the remarks of Megan Harris – how clean and updated it looked compared to the rest of the house. The forensic duo swabbed the floor and cupboard surfaces with luminol, the result of which would be that the smallest amount of blood would show up. Even a single drop.

Eighteen minutes after entering the property, the two denim clad, boiler-suited men walked nonchalantly back to their van, popped their bags into the back, and drove away. Simon Rogers needed a drink, something cold. He went to the fridge in the kitchen and, with his hand about to open the door, shuddered as he quickly decided that a glass of tap water would be fine. Gulping it down, he saw Megan Harris coming up the path with Rosemary Gless. The latch key clicked and they walked in.

"Yes, it's him." Rosemary volunteered. She broke down, the tears being absorbed by a large handkerchief; one that may have belonged to Geoff. Rogers gave Rosemary a few moments to compose herself.

"Mrs. Gless, we're going to have to go down to the station for you to make an official statement. Whilst you were at the mortuary we had two CSI guys take a quick look around here. They've taken away some items, but we'll explain more down at the station. Is there anything you want to tell us right now?" She took a deep breath and looked at her watch.

Tell them only what you have to.

"Can I use the phone? I promised my friend, Vida Honeywell, I'd call her around now. She'll be wondering why I haven't phoned." Rogers shook his head.

"I'm afraid not, Mrs. Gless. But you can call her later."

Down on Vallejo Street Rosemary Gless began her story. The two detectives listened intently. She'd already mentioned some things, but they'd want her to start again. See if she was saying the same thing. Always a useful way to check a story.

Would Rosy tell them what *really* happened?

43

"Howard, you've always been honest with me. I need to ask you a question, maybe a few." Jane, having plucked up the courage, was standing in the kitchen. It was 3.45 pm and the children were upstairs doing homework. Howard had come home early for two reasons. One: No important surgery that afternoon that required his services. Two: An architect was due at 4.00 pm to help draw up plans for an extension on the rear of the house – a big job that needed planning permission. Jane realised her window of opportunity was probably about fifteen minutes.

"Sure, go ahead, Jane." He smiled the reassuring smile of a hospital doctor but Jane wondered if it was genuine. She'd gone through the questions in her head a thousand times . . . now she couldn't remember them. Pulling her thoughts together, she opened her dry mouth.

"Were you seeing Jodie Patterson a while back? I'm sure I saw you in town with her?" Howard maintained his smile, telling Jane that Jodie's aunt had been in for heart surgery three months back, and she'd called the hospital to speak to him about the results of her recent check up in the Cardiac Clinic. Howard had to go into town to see his financial adviser and suggested a quick coffee so he could give her an update. Yes, they parked in a multi-storey, yes, they had coffee in the shopping mall. 'And . . . is there a point?' enquired Howard. Jane blushed slightly.

"I'm sorry to have jumped to conclusions. I did think I'd seen you and Jodie and wondered if . . ., oh, never mind. But you are on friendly terms with Louise Archer, aren't you?" How did Howard maintain that smile, wondered Jane.

"Ditto situation. Louise came into the hospital for a chat regarding an upcoming article for the Chronicle. Updates on surgery, new techniques and so on. I gave her my cell number in case she had any follow-up questions. In fact she's had some emotional problems, and I've suggested she book a few sessions with Amanda. She needs the professional counselling that I can't give – I'm only a cardiac surgeon." The smile was Gioconda-like. "But this is just between us two, yeah?" Jane nodded. Hell, what else could she do as Howard lightly placed his hand on her shoulders. She left it there.

"And you've decided to take up bridge! So Amanda tells me. Are you *really* doing that? I mean, why take up bridge?" It seemed Jane's last chance to have Dr. Gardner mince his words, get his reply wrong, avoid eye contact, scratch his nose . . .

"Why, yes! I've promised myself for years that I'd like to be good at something other than surgery. My golf is trash, I don't enjoy hiking as much as I used to, and a day or two out in the bay on a yacht still turns my stomach. So, with maths being a strong point, I decided I'd have a go at that! You can come with me if you want – every Tuesday and Thursday evening at the golf club. Open to the public! I can introduce you to Jimmy Atkins, my old buddy from Yale! Louise knows him and she's *also* thinking of playing with one of her Chronicle colleagues! I'm sure Amanda wouldn't mind! What do you say?" The front door bell rang before Jane could reply as Howard slowly removed his hand from her shoulder.

"Hope that's cleared things up, Jane. Must go, these architects charge by the minute – the meter's already running! By the way, Amanda has cancelled the party on 27 November – didn't think it appropriate with what's gone on lately." With that Howard left the kitchen, still smiling, as Jane stood there feeling the biggest fool in the state of California! She went upstairs with her metaphorical tail between her legs. 'Sod it!' she said to herself, 'have I made an absolute idiot of myself or what?' She wanted to lay on her bed and cry, but tough Yorkshire stock won over self pity, and she went to see how Teresa and Ryan were coping. She breathed deeply, pinched her cheeks to add some colour to them, put on her *own* smile, and opened Teresa's door.

"Hey, Teresa, how are you getting along?"

*

Rosemary Gless was made as comfortable as possible in the small interview room on Vallejo Street, a plastic cup of water in front of her. She refused to phone a lawyer, 'don't need one' she'd said. Four thin strips of neon tubes lit the room, light reflecting off the stainless steel grill of the high window. The grey, metal table with four chairs sat forlornly against one wall. Rogers and Harris sat opposite Rosemary. Rogers asked her to tell them what she knew and he pushed the recorder button as she began.

And she told it as it happened. Her son Doug had phoned the week before to say he'd like to visit Frisco, catch up with some old buddies, take in a club - some name beginning with a 'Q', and see his Ma on the evening of 1 May. It was a Friday as Rosy recollected. She'd already invited her friend Amanda over, but that would be OK. She'd introduce Doug to Amanda, they'd have a chat, then he'd leave to go out with his pals and she and her friend could talk in peace. But it went wrong. Horribly wrong. Rosemary then described in detail what happened next.

The hammer, wrapping the body in an old carpet, taking it up to Muir Woods, the shallow grave, thoroughly cleaning the kitchen, relaying the footpath, getting rid of the evidence . . . and the help she'd received from her good friend, Amanda Gardner. How Amanda had agreed to help, be a part of this heinous crime, get rid of the evidence. In fact, she put it down as being Amanda's fault – if she hadn't turned up none of it would have happened. Rosemary spoke uninterrupted for sixteen minutes, her eyes glazed over most of the time like a China doll. Rogers left the recorder running.

"So Mrs. Gless, hmm, would you mind if I called you Rosemary?" She shook her head. "So Rosemary, Doug became annoyed, in an uncontrollable manner, over what he felt was his – the money left in the will – after the passing of your husband, Geoff? So, while Mrs. Gardner was being held, you hit him with the claw hammer? Then, . . ." Rogers continued, paraphrasing her response, but careful not to put words into her mouth. Each time the detective stopped speaking, Rosemary replied, as full eye contact was maintained during the interview.

"I had to hit him, he would have strangled her! I didn't mean to kill him, though." She wiped her eyes. "I loved him!" The interview continued, with as much detail as Rosemary could recall. She admitted in the frenzy and her panic she couldn't remember everything. *'I was past myself with terror'* was how she put it. Her mind was a blank when it came to the disposal of the head, carpet, hammer, hacksaw and knife, telling Rogers that Amanda had agreed to do all of that. Oh, and get rid of Doug's shirt.

Amanda had brought her black car close to the house and they put Doug's body in the back. They drove up to the woods. There they'd bundled it out of the back and laid it in the shallow hole that had been dug by Amanda for that very purpose. Rosemary thought that Amanda had dumped some items in industrial waste bins along the back of a line of restaurants, but couldn't quire recall which ones . . . and so it went on, with both detectives listening carefully and Harris taking notes, the recorder doing its work.

"Are you saying you don't know where the head is?" asked Rogers. Rosemary shook her head. "It was in your garage fridge, Rosemary." She froze. In the garage fridge? Impossible. Rosemary could not recall when she'd last opened the door of the fridge, but knew there were some cans of beer in there. "Rosemary, are you all right, do you need a glass of water?" A knock on the door was followed by Jim Bell entering the interview room, sheet of paper in hand. The forensic report. Rogers scanned it, and gleaned sufficient detail to be able to continue without turning the recorder off.

"Rosemary, you need to know that the claw hammer in your garage, along with a hacksaw and a serrated kitchen knife with a wooden handle from your cutlery draw all have traces of Doug's DNA on them. Did you use the hacksaw and knife to decapitate your son?" A pause, with no response from Rosemary. "Also, the luminol test shows minute spots of blood in the cracks of your kitchen floor. The beige coloured stowage area carpet from your station wagon has traces of his blood at one side, suggesting that you laid the body across the back with your son trussed up like a Christmas cracker. A bottle of sulphuric acid in your garage was very probably used to damage the epidermis on his fingertips except the tip that's missing! We took a look in your trash can, found a knotted Hershey bar wrapper." Rogers paused for breath. "There was a Hershey bar sleeve found at the crime scene! You know what that says, Rosemary? You even had time to sit down and have some chocolate after you'd buried the body! We have so much evidence to connect you this horrendous act! You did it, isn't that correct, Rosemary?" She was beginning to break down, her breathing becoming more quicker by the second, her face whiter. She denied eating any chocolate and could not recall that she'd put a wrapper into her waste bin. Harris pushed the plastic cup of water in front of her. "And the green and white tape you used to tie his wrists was an unusual industrial type – isn't that correct, Rosemary? Straight out of your garage! We found a roll! No, two rolls. Now, why would Dr. Amanda Gardner get herself involved with all of this? Did you have somebody else in the house, another friend, perhaps? Waiting for your son to arrive. Isn't it time you started telling us the truth, Rosemary? You need to know about ECLAT. Every Contact Leaves A Trace." She straightened up, raised her voice.

"I want my lawyer here. I'm not saying another word until he arrives." Rogers concluded the interview, switched the recorder off and left the room. They still hadn't let her phone Vida Honeywell. He walked briskly along to the office of Marty Kluisters and gave him the short version of events.

"Gardner?" Kluisters mused. "OK, Simon, get the lawyer of Mrs. Gless on the phone and get him in. Better bring Amanda Gardner in for interview, too." Rogers turned to go. "Do you think either Gless or Gardner have anything to do with Jake Bauer?" asked Kluisters. Rogers shrugged as he left the room, then turned.

"Well, we know Jake Bauer was friendly with Caroline Sinclair, and Dr. Gardner had a heated argument with Bauer. What do *you* think?" Kluisters smiled as he stared at Rogers.

" I pay *you* to think, Simon, now get on with it!" The door closed and Marty Kluisters, laying back and folding his arms, felt more satisfied than he had done for a long time. And, by way of a bonus, he didn't have any indigestion.

Meanwhile, Rosemary Gless waited for her lawyer to arrive. Picking up her plastic cup to take a sip, and with her hand being slightly unsteady, a few drops of water fell onto her bright green blouse.

And although *she* didn't know it, the fabric was known as Nylon 66.

44

Saturday was clear, the sun tried hard to shine, but Frisco had a thin blanket of mist cast over it like a giant, grey shawl. The Golden Gate bridge had the tips of the main supports shrouded in low cloud as the air temperature struggled to reach 50F. Amanda had given permission for Jane to take the children to the funfair half an hour's drive away, and each of them had some spending money. Jane had packed some snacks and drinks, and promised ice cream on arrival. Taking her camera, Jane wanted more photos for her college project. Gloria had asked the students to take images that would fit into three categories – Happiness, Colour and Weather. And their interpretation of each one was as wide as they wanted to make it. Jane could take some of the mist and cloud today, maybe sunshine later, the children being happy with their ice cream, and colour . . . that could be anything, but the brighter the better – the chair-o-planes were technicolour!

But as Jane drove her Honda Civic south, with Teresa and Ryan excitedly chattering in the back seat, she wondered if everything was all right between Amanda and Howard. The past few days had been odd somehow. Jane had heard them arguing in the past, but during the last 48 hours they'd hardly spoken to each other. She couldn't be sure if Howard had told Amanda about her questions, or if the estimate for the extension was too expensive, or if Amanda had become suspicious about something . . . but for certain, life seemed quiet in the Gardner household just now. Jane had heard Amanda come home on Thursday afternoon, just after she'd brought the children from school, and thought she'd heard the thlurp of a cork being pulled out of a bottle.

And as Amanda sat with a glass in her hand her mind replayed events . . .

'Hell, I told Rogers what happened! I arrived at Rosy's place at about a quarter to seven. We chatted for a while . .

. you know, family, vacations, Thanksgiving, Christmas, all that. She brought out two glasses of fresh orange juice. Told me Doug was arriving around eight. Said I'd leave her to talk with him. I'd meet him another time.

No, I don't recall the colour of her blouse . . . maybe bright something.

No! I wasn't there when he was there. I told you that.

I wanted some fresh air – had things on my mind. I've got a few difficult cases right now.

Left Nob Hill just after eight, it was getting dusk...almost dark. Drove over the bridge, parked up, listened to classical music. No! I didn't go to Muir Woods.

Must have dozed off . . . next thing I know it's ten o'clock and I had to be getting back.

Howard would wonder where I was. (Or maybe he wasn't really bothered).

Yes, we're clean people! So we get the car cleaned now and again! Is that against the law?

And I got new tyres fitted. So? If more drivers took care of their tyres there might be fewer accidents around here!

Yes, I've seen Rosemary Gless in the hospital...at the Psychiatric Outpatients Clinic actually. I work there myself as you know. She's undergoing treatment but I do not have any details . . .they're confidential. You'd have to ask her doctor.'

"Here we are!" Ryan screamed. "Turn here, Jane, there's a car park there look! Wow, look at that big dipper! Can we go on that, Jane?"

. . .

"OK, guys, take it easy," said Jane. "We've got nearly all day, there's no hurry!" The car was parked, shoulder bag and camera picked up, and car locked. The trio tramped off towards the ticket office on the far side of the car park where Jane purchased tickets with a fifty dollar note that Amanda had given her to cover some of the costs for the day.

Time passed quicker than expected, it always does when you're having fun. Seven rides were taken on the roller-coaster, dodgem cars, and ferris wheel, but Jane opted out of four of them. It was the kids time. Jane set her camera to movie mode on a number of occasions to capture the thrill and excitement of the children as they yelled loud enough to almost burst their lungs.

Ice creams were bought, a different flavour each, and they all had a lick of each others - another bonding gesture, Jane thought, and nobody had a cold or 'flu. In the distance, amongst the now thinning crowd, Jane spotted a guy she knew. It was Arty Jennings, Marie's boyfriend, who Jane had been introduced to some time back. In fact it had been at the fair in Sausalito not long after Jane had arrived in Frisco; Jane recalled that Marie had said Arty liked fairgrounds.

"Hi, Arty," shouted Jane. He turned, surprised that he heard a female voice calling his name. He stopped. Jane walked up to him with Teresa and Ryan in tow. "Hey, good to see you again. How are things?" Arty smiled and told Jane he was fine, but he and Marie had broken up and she was seeing somebody else. Jane introduced the children as a means of avoiding making a direct comment on his news. Arty shook their hands, and they laughed. They rarely shook hands with adults!

"By the way, Jane, I visited Andrew last week in prison. He got sentenced you know . . . five years. Was asking after you, said he missed you." Jane was both thrilled and frightened at the same time. Did she want Arty to give Andrew her best wishes, or regards, or love? "You could always go and see him if you wanted to. Marie has his address." She was caught on the hop.

"I'll see. I'm a bit busy just now. Is that the time?" replied Jane looking at her watch. "Arty, we need to go. Sorry about you and Marie. Take care." And with that they parted, Jane telling the kids it was time to go home. Ryan groaned. He'd wanted another ride on the dodgems, but Jane was insistent.

"We're spent up! Money doesn't grow on trees, you know!" They giggled at a phrase Jane used from time to time, passed down from her Yorkshire-born mum.

On the way back to Hayward, the children were subdued, probably owing to tiredness Jane decided. But it wasn't that. It was because Arty had used the word 'prison' and the children had picked up on that.

"You guys OK? You're both quiet." Teresa replied.

"Yeah, we're fine. It's just that, well, Mum used that 'prison' word yesterday when she came back from town. She'd been seeing somebody important, she said. Wouldn't say who. Then I heard her say to dad something like 'People who commit a crime like that ought to go prison. I don't know who she was talking about, though."

And Jane wasn't sure if she wanted to get in touch with Andrew.

*

Hi Lou-Lou, We need to take it easy. After what you told me. Don't text me on this number any more. Use the other one. H

45

"We had her in, Marty, and she claims that she was only there about an hour. Had a soft drink, talked, Gless was expecting the kid, she left before he arrived. Spoke to the neighbours. It's a quiet neighbourhood, and with it being a Friday some folks told us they had headed away for the week-end. Nobody saw a black SUV. Been speaking to those who live either side – they didn't see the boy come to the house, either. We're going to give Gardner a polygraph test, see what that shows.

Two neighbours thought they saw a two door, silver grey BMW passing the place on that Friday evening – we know Roberts had a car that matched that description. And also, and this is where it gets interesting, Roberts knew the Gless kid, Doug. Both gays, both known around some of the down-town clubs and gay hang out joints. If Doug had anything on Roberts, he might have had a motive to kill the kid?"

"So what's your take on this, Simon? I mean, what you're telling me is that his own mother, and possibly Roberts, murdered that kid in the house up on Richmond Avenue."

"Rosy Gless met Roberts at the Gardner home at a party last November. Because her son was gay I guess she had some empathy for him – you know like, understood him better. She tolerated guys like that. So if Doug was going to visit his ma and be threatening, she might want some protection. Roberts is well built. Strong." Rogers took a mouthful of luke-warm coffee. Kluisters was leaning forward, fingers laced under his chin, belly touching the desk.

"Course, with Roberts still on the run we can't speak to him, but we can talk with Gless and tell her what we think happened. Might confess? They do sometimes." Kluisters grunted meaning 'yes, go on.' "My take is this . . . Doug told his ma that he was going to see her on that Friday evening, and she expected a run in with him. She'd already asked Amanda Gardner over, and didn't want to change that – she'd be there for support. Gless got in touch with Roberts, asked him to be there before her kid turned up. He parked his car away from the house, maybe went round the back door, and he hid in the house. Gardner arrives, stays for an hour, leaves. The kid turns up, gets aggressive, throws a tantrum, Roberts and his ma restrain him. It gets out of hand, then she, or Roberts, digs the hammer into his skull. Blood everywhere, they try to clean up. By now she's passing bricks while Roberts is calm. Stick his body in the Buick station wagon, minus shirt, head in the fridge where they'll remove it later, and try to clean the claw hammer. Don't want to cut the hands off so use acid to remove prints. We know Roberts had been to art school for a year before he quit to become a hospital porter. He probably put the tattoo on the left shoulder blade to lead us astray when the body was found.

When it's dark enough, with Roberts driving, they take the body up to Muir Woods in the Buick. Park up, dig the shallow grave, and drop the body into it. Scrape some earth over it, make it look all natural, and brush the area around there with a leafy branch. Relax a little, it's dark after all, and Gless needs an energy boost. She eats her Hershey choc bar, knots it . . . habit . . . then they drive back to Nob Hill, park the car in the garage, do some more cleaning, Roberts leaves and Gless tries to calm down after what's been one hell of a night for her!" Rogers takes a deep breath as Kluisters leans back, reflecting for a few seconds.

"When can you do the polygraph on Gardner?" asked the Lieutenant.

"We've got her coming in this afternoon. We'll have the results by four o'clock."

Kluisters knew that when people lie they perspire slightly. Their pulse rate increases, breathing quickens, blood pressure rises, pupils dilate. If the client is lying the moving pointer on the machine arm lashes across the paper as if measuring an earthquake.

All additional evidence for the court to consider.

*

Detective Shaun Pomfret was informally discussing matters with Lt. Kluisters, each with a salami and cheese sandwich, in the police station canteen. Two large cardboard cups held cola near to overflowing.

"Say that again, Shaun, about this guy Jepson."

"He gave a statement few days back. Mentioned Roberts being friendly with a woman up on Nob Hill. Er, let me see, Rosemary Gless, yes, that was her name." Kluisters nodded. "And I made some enquiries a couple days back. A neighbour swears that she saw a guy fitting Roberts description was at the house on or around 21 October. Not only that, but I phoned them Cypress Lawn folks . . ." Kluisters held up his hand as if taking an oath.

"Shaun, let's get back to my office. This is too important to talk about here. There are chin-wags and informal chats, and this is becoming more than that." Both finished their sandwich, picked up their drinks and headed back to Marty Kluisters' office. Pomfret followed him in and they sat down.

"OK, Shaun, so you phoned Cypress Lawn . . . what then?" Kluisters laid back and patted his stomach after swallowing two *Tylenol* tablets and taking a swig of *Pepsidol*.

"Yes, I was asking the Director of the firm if he knew who the dame was that went up to the woods with the party that had Hudson's ashes. Scattered 'em around a tree an' all. She had dark glasses on, I ain't seen her before, thought maybe she was blind or something. Turns out it was Rosemary Gless, no less!" Pomfret grinned at the poetic link he'd just made. Kluisters sat up, stifled a burp, and leant forward.

"So, we've got Mrs. Gless scattering Hudson's ashes, Roberts visiting Gless on more than one occasion, Lee

Jepson telling us about the empathy Rosemary Gless had for gays, and Doug Gless who was homosexual and stood to inherit some money. Quite a family affair, in a way." Kluisters continued, like a judge summing up. "We believe Roberts shot Hudson and he's still out there on the loose, and because Mrs. Gless has this so-called 'I understand gays' culture maybe she gets to scatter the ashes when nobody else wanted to do it. One key question is 'Did Rosemary Gless get help from Roberts to murder her son or was it really Gardner?' Simon has got Amanda Gardner in for a polygraph test this afternoon. Talk to him and compare notes, will you? And Shaun," Kluisters took another swig of *Pepsidol*, "ask Simon to give Mrs. Bauer a call. Tell her we're doing everything we can to find her son, Jake. If *he* was gay we might be onto something."

Detective Shaun Pomfret closed the office door as Kluisters gently burped again.

*

She put her handbag and jacket into the locker and slipped the key into her jeans pocket. All she held was her passport. Queueing up at the desk, she had her fingerprints taken on a digital scanner, and her head and shoulders were photographed. Her passport was read and filed by the computer. A group of ten were allowed through the double entry iron gates at a time. Once through, guards frisked them, shoes were removed and checked. She placed her passport into her back pocket and entered the room. The air was slightly dank, a hint of body odour mixed with heady anticipation. Looking around she saw the aisles of tables and chairs, eight rows across, ten tables per row. A man was sat at each table, all wearing the same pin stripe blue and white shirt and black trousers. Around the perimeter of the room were eight uniformed, armed guards. And then she spotted him, second row from the left, four tables back. Number 26. He smiled at her as if to beckon her to come and sit down. Walking slowly toward him, she looked into his blue eyes, then sat down, keeping her hands on the table as instructed.

"Hello, Jane, I'm glad you could come," said Andrew Wilson.

*

Jane didn't know why or how she came to be sitting in front of the man who had lied to her so convincingly. Lied about everything – his possessions, his skills and talents, and also he turned out to be a car thief and a bank robber! He had taken her in hook, line and sinker after she'd been introduced to him at the fairground shortly after arriving in Frisco. Jane didn't know that Andrew had been one of Amanda Gardner's patients. Wasn't aware of his treatment, and his habit of forcing his fingernails into the palms of his hands until they bled. Dr. Gardner would not have revealed patient confidentiality matters to anybody. But Jane knew only too well that what Andrew said should not be believed. He'd let her down . . . all the charm around the Chinese restaurant table, holding open the car door when he picked her up, his politeness . . . and all those bloody lies!

I went to school in Sacramento and got good grades...was captain of the soccer team

I play musical instruments and love Schubert

I have a number of cars but prefer taking the tram to work

And so it went on . . . those damned lies! So what was she doing here? Was she going to hear more crap stories about how well he was doing in prison, how he'd made friends, how he'd impressed the governor . . . ?

But that wasn't the way it turned out, as it happened. Within less than a minute, Jane recognised a reformed character in Andrew Wilson. His blond hair was trimmed, no sideburns, his attitude was less arrogant and he came across as genuinely honest with a pleasant smile. Continuing, he said.

"How are *you*, Jane?" Keeping her hands in front of her and glancing round briefly, she replied.

"Hi, Andrew. I'm fine. And you?" It sounded a bit formal, and Jane wanted to make the meeting relaxed. Smiling, she added. "Hope you're behaving yourself!" Andrew nodded.

"Jane, we haven't got long. They allow thirty minutes per visit. There's something I want to tell you – something you need to know." It sounded slightly ominous. And with that, Andrew Wilson began his story about the evening of 23 April, the date of Billy Shakespeare's birthday.

"A group of us went out around seven o'clock. Down town, to find a couple of bars. Headed to the Blues Bar first. There was Jimmy and me, Caroline, Jake Bauer, they were seeing each other, and a couple of guys and girls hanging on in there. We were messing about, telling jokes, usual crazy stuff. Jimmy and I had done a small job and had a wad of cash but we didn't flash it around – just paid for most of the drinks. No one was driving and the booze flowed, mostly beers. The girls tried some cocktails, mojitos and such. We all got on well, but Caroline mentioned something about Jake and Dr. Hudson. Calling him a butcher or whatever. Hudson went crazy over that, apparently. Jake didn't say much for a while, but you could see he was pissed off with Caroline for mentioning it. Jake was a guy who could hide his feelings, and outwardly he seemed calm. After that I watched them all evening, she cuddled him lots, kissed his cheek – all that jazz. But he didn't show much affection towards her. Heard him say something like she thought more about the doc than of him. Then her attitude changed, maybe it was the cocktails? Around ten o'clock we were all getting off our heads. But it was a Thursday evening and we all had work the next day so we didn't overdo it.

Thing was Caroline told me that Dr. Hudson and his wife were out that evening. Their two kids were staying with an aunt, and they were going to a Shakespeare party being held by an English couple they'd got to know. All

Union Flags, English beer and pies, stuff like that. As we were going our separate ways, Caroline was hanging onto Jake's arm – not sure who was holding who up. Anyway, heard her say she'd get a cab to take the two of them back to Adair Way. Empty house – yeah! Time for a little cuddle or something? We said our goodnight's and then we split. I remember seeing Jake stop a cab and they both got in. Last I saw of him.

Did they both go back to Adair Way? Don't know for sure. One of Caroline's friends told me that they did. So, if they went back there, what happened to him? Nobody saw him after that.

Did the Gardner's come home early and catch them in bed? Maybe the doc or his wife went crazy. Decided to teach him a lesson?

Was there another argument between the doc and Jake? I know the doc had made a derisory comment about his gold earring.

So . . . I don't know what happened.

But you know, Jane, there was something about Caroline Sinclair that scared me."

Jane collected her handbag and jacket, left the locker key at the desk, and walked out into the sunshine. The Pacific breeze felt good on her face as she left the big, grey, stone prison behind her.

Had Andrew Wilson been telling the truth, or was he still a compulsive liar?

46

The lawyer of Rosemary Gless arrived, sweating and out of breath. Wesley Mitchum, working his last few months before retirement from Hardy & Davison, had got to Vallejo Street as soon as he could. Dressed in a dark suit, Mitchum looked every inch the lawyer you saw on some television crime programmes. Tall, greying hairline, suit creased in the wrong places and a brown, worn leather briefcase. His paunch suggested a liking for good eating. Once he'd sat down in the interview room and been given a plastic cup of water, Rogers had switched on the recorder and the interrogation recommenced.

Gless answered most of the questions put to her, repeating some of what she'd already told the detectives. Mitchum was picking up information as he went along – his role was really to prevent Gless saying anything that would incriminate her. But as the interview went on, Mitchum began to feel he was on the losing side. He could only listen out for circumstantial evidence that the detectives were laying on the table. And there was plenty of that. But the main issue revolved around whether Amanda Gardner had been in the house when the murder took place, and, whether Gardner had been an accessory. Or was it Roberts?

Gardner's story differed from that of Mrs. Rosemary Gless. OK, so who's lying? Or, who's telling the truth? The green blouse that Gless was wearing right then hadn't gone unnoticed by Rogers. He was certain it was the one from which fibres had been found at the crime scene; just on the inside edge of a back pocket of the jeans worn by Doug Gless. Harris spoke.

"Mrs. Gless, would you mind if we terminate this interview for a few minutes. We'd like to take two fibres from the blouse you're wearing. We can go into the lab along the corridor or we can take them here."

"Is that necessary, Detective? My client does not have

to remove her clothing without good reason." Harris explained the position, wanting to keep it simple and quick. If truth were known, Gless could not recall what the heck she was wearing on that fateful day. As long as her blouse wasn't damaged, she agreed. It had seen better days so in truth, she didn't care. Remaining seated, Harris saw there was a strand of material, no more than half an inch long, hanging from the right cuff. It was snipped off, along with another fibre, and placed into a small clear evidence bag. Again, with her agreement, one hair was plucked from her head by Harris. Ditto plastic bag. Then Harris left for the lab where the samples were deposited with a senior forensics technician. The detective returned to the interview room. She'd been away for four minutes. Job done.

Further questions were posed regarding her association with Kris Roberts. Gless looked astonished. Her association with Roberts? Her empathy, indeed sympathy, with the gay community of San Francisco was probed. Her husband, Geoff, it turned out was a regular donor to a gay charity in the city. But all of this was on the sidelines . . . because it was abundantly clear that Doug Gless had been murdered in Richmond Avenue on or about 1 May by Rosemary Gless and an accomplice. The evidence was overwhelming but somehow Gless continued to be unable to comprehend it all, her eyes glazing over at times. There was a knock on the door of the interview room. It was the technician.

"They match. Fibres and the three hairs found at the scene. A perfect match," he reported. Rogers confirmed this information for the benefit of the recorder. Gless burst into tears as Mitchum coughed and made some notes. He could see how it all looked to the police, and if he was honest, he could see their viewpoint. But Mitchum didn't know that in another room Dr. Amanda Gardner would be connected to a lie detector in about twenty minutes.

*

Gardner had been taken into the test room by two qualified laboratory technicians who had performed over a thousand procedures. Sitting down, she was linked up to the polygraph machine – a BP cuff attached that also measured pulse rate, a moisture detection band on her arm, respirometer for breathing rate, and the eye pupil dilation device that made it look as if she were wearing an oversized pair of spectacles. The senior technician told her they would begin the test in thirty seconds. Amanda eased her blonde hair back and relaxed as Detective Rogers, who'd terminated the Gless interview, came in to supervise matters.

"Ready?" asked the senior technician. She nodded. The test commenced with several basic questions. 'What's the date today?' 'Who's the president of the USA?' Amanda remained still and composed, answering each question calmly. Readings were checked. The machine was working fine. Then the real testing began. Rogers had a list of nine questions. It was all over in five minutes, ten seconds.

"That's fine, Mrs. Gardner. You'll be hearing from me within half an hour. If you'd like to take a seat in the outer waiting area." He held his arm out like a waiter showing you to your restaurant table. Amanda left the room and made herself comfortable with a glossy magazine and a dollar cup of coffee from the machine in the corner. Fifteen minutes later, after Rogers had spoken with Kluisters and the senior technician, he called Amanda into his office.

"Well, the test went well. Everything appeared normal." He gave little away. "Have you ever taken a polygraph test before?" asked Rogers. She shook her head and smiled. "OK, well, we may be in touch again soon, but you're free to go. Thank you for your co-operation."

Meanwhile, Rosemary Gless had been shown to a cell for an overnight stay, courtesy of SFPD. Wesley Mitchum demanded that his client be treated respectfully, and reminded Kluisters, as if it were needed, that they had 24 hours to charge Gless with the murder of Douglas Peter

Gless or release her. Lt. Kluisters walked into Rogers' office seconds after Amanda had left. Sitting down he spoke.

"Well, Simon, was Gardner there that evening to help murder Doug Gless? What's your hunch?"

"No. I'd say no. She's told us what happened, it stacks up. We did not find anything to link Gardner to the scene of the crime. No hairs, no fingerprints . . . nothing. And not many people can beat a lie detector! Yes, Gless did it, with the help of somebody unknown, but I'd say it was Roberts."

"What about the SUV license plate with 4, 8 and A?"

"Been thinking about that. Just how reliable were the hikers who gave us the details of the plate? Suppose they'd mis-read the plate . . . after all it was dark. Have we been barking up the wrong tree?"

"OK. We'll charge Gless in the morning," said Kluisters. He was going to be home early tonight to see his wife, Letitia. Maybe he'd buy a pizza on the way, but he decided he'd better phone her first. Check what she wanted . . . stay in her good books.

47

"Hi Jane, how are things?" It was Sam. She was taking a break from her desk at Hardy & Davison Lawyers. Jane was talking about Teresa and her latest homework project when Sam interrupted. "Sorry to change to subject, Jane, but I thought you might be interested in something I overheard in our offices yesterday."

"Oh?" Jane stopped chattering. "What was that?"

"Are you sitting down?" Sam lowered her voice. " Did you know that Louise Archer is Priscilla Gardner's sister? You know, Howard's first wife, Priscilla Archer as was. Louise was at the Canyon when Priscilla fell, actually there on the viewing platform. Rumour has it that Howard Gardner had an affair with Louise before that happened. I think Priscilla found out and someone said they believe that she took her own life, right there in front of both of them!"

"My God," whispered Jane, now sitting down in her own room in Adair Way. Sam continued.

"Howard was undergoing psychiatric treatment at the time with his current wife, and although Louise was very fond of him, he ended up marrying Amanda. Louise still loves him, I'd say. She even started to grow her hair and had it dyed blonde to look more like Amanda – allegedly. And . . ." Sam's voice went even lower, "Louise took a liking to Jake Bauer at some party to which she was invited. Caroline was there, too, and wasn't impressed, apparently. Louise isn't that big, but I wouldn't like to mess with her. Somebody else mentioned that she takes judo classes." Jane recalled Louise coming to her help in the underground car park when Jodie Patterson grabbed her. "Listen, Jane, must go. Lots to do in a busy office! I'll call you again soon and we'll grab a coffee or something! Bye."

Did Howard's first wife really jump from the platform in front of her husband and her sister, Louise? Making it look as if she slipped? Too close to the edge. An affair with his sister-in-law? Surely not. And Lou knew Jake, but Caroline hadn't mentioned that. Suddenly there was a knock at the door. It was Katie.

"Hi Jane, how's it going? I guessed you were in – kid's washing out on the line an' all. Well, that smell has gone at last – no more dead bodies for Mrs. Gardner to worry about now!"

*

'I knew from the first time we met that there was something about him. The way he shook hands, the way he acted. He had a certain way, rude sometimes, his words had an edge to them, but he didn't mean much of what he said. I think it was his upbringing. Parents divorced, his mother was left to look after him. Two aunts were particularly unpleasant, and a family friend abused him. But I don't think he was gay.

No, although I could tolerate him at times, eventually I decided that he had to go. He was making things difficult for me, for us – if truth be known, and I began to dislike him. But the time had to be right, and the method, of course. Some folk, mainly the California ex-pats, were celebrating Shakespeare's birthday, and, ironically, the Bard died on the same date that *he* was born – 23 April.

So with it being party time for some, I decided that the time could be right. I hoped there would be an opportunity that evening. I hadn't killed anybody before, but I'd read enough crime thrillers to give me some ideas. And there wasn't only the killing, there was the disposal of the body.

It had to be nice and clean. An injection from an umbrella tip like that Russian spy in London had been given. Or a quick acting poison in a drink . . . or perhaps a tight noose – no blood. I didn't want blood on my clothes. Too messy. Then an easy way to get rid of the corpse. What a lovely word that is, *corpse*. No digging, too much like hard work. Something that was sanitary, clean and wholesome.

That was it then. During the evening, going on into the night, when my opportunity came, I'd murder him and do a good job on hiding the body. Murder... that's a strong word, isn't it? Murder, so final. And, *hiding the body*, I like that.

Hiding the body.
But where?'

48

Wesley Mitchum had turned up at the police station just before eight o'clock the next day. Having briefly spoken with Rosemary's daughter, Samantha, who'd taken the news very badly, he'd spent a restless night going through as much information on the 'headless torso case' as he could. Transcripts by Tom Lederer in the newspapers, video reports on the news channels archives, notes he'd made on Rosemary Gless at yesterday's interview, and the five minutes he'd been allowed to talk with her in private before she was shown to a cell. She'd mumbled something about chocolate bar wrappers which Mitchum ignored – why bother with splinters when you're looking at a plank of wood, for goodness sake?

'Damn it!' he thought. 'She ain't got a chance! What's a lawyer supposed to do when the cards are stacked against you? Not a poker player, Mitchum thought of a Canadian song . . . *'Never hit seventeen when you play against the dealer, for the odds won't ride with you.'* The answer was 'get on and find a chink in the armour.' He racked his brains. There must be something he could hang his hat on? Learning of the lie detector test, he'd asked about the outcome but wasn't told the result. If his client was telling the truth then Gardner *was* there at the house when the evil deed was done. Amanda Gardner had decapitated Doug Gless and helped take the body up to Muir Woods although his client had actually struck the fatal blow, in a sort of defence way. How come nobody had seen the black Audi that Gardner drove to Nob Hill? No one saw them loading a carpet-trussed body into the back? The blouse fibres on the jeans and three hairs found at the scene were conclusive evidence that Gless had been involved. Had she made a poor job of cleaning the claw hammer, and planned to dump the head but forgot it was in the garage fridge? The big trash bins used to hide the carpet and his shirt were long emptied. Hell, it was a forlorn hope that he could get Gless off this one.

At around 8.30 am Samantha Gless walked into the police station demanding to see her mother. Her request was denied. One minute later Mitchum was entering the interview room where Rosemary Gless was being held. Dark bags under her eyes, she was charged by Detective Marty Kluisters with the murder of her step-son, Douglas Peter Gless. *She didn't have to say anything, but anything she did say may be taken down . . .* At the trial held a week later in the senior court in San Francisco, Gless was found guilty. Amanda Gardner was absolved of any involvement in the crime, and Gless was accused of trying to needlessly involve her. Despite the two of them being good friends, her reasoning was unclear. Gardner's account of her evening's activities was accepted, backed up by her husband. Of course, a professional couple like the Gardner's had an excellent reputation in San Francisco. A Dr. Bloomberg from the Psychiatric Outpatients Clinic at SFCH confirmed the treatment that Rosemary Gless had been receiving, and her current medication, was very likely, he stated, to cause her to confuse reality with imaginary concepts.

She was sentenced to death by lethal injection, a triple cocktail of drugs that would render her unconscious, stop her breathing and finally bring the heart to rest. That night Mitchum went out and got blind drunk. Another failure for the hapless, overweight lawyer who should never have qualified in legal matters in the first place. Hardy & Davison couldn't wait for his retirement - there'd be no gold watch for him.

Tomorrow's Chronicle would have fresh front page news that was going to make an impact on a wide population across the 'city by the bay,' no doubt written by Tom Lederer or Louise Archer. But there was something that had never come up in the case. Mitchum had missed a crucial piece of evidence relating to the two knotted Hershey bar wrappers, one found in Rosy's trash can and one at the shallow grave in Muir Woods. Rosemary Gless had a nut allergy!

There was no way she could have eaten a chocolate bar containing almonds . . .

Meanwhile, Sam realised that she should have tried to be closer to her mum over the years. Sam had largely ignored her ma, said things that she regretted.

And hastily spoken words can never be taken back.

*

Detective Shaun Pomfret had spoken with Simon Rogers about Mrs. Bauer, and suggested another follow up phone call. Trouble was, Rogers had no news. It made it worse when you called the mother of a missing son or daughter – they always expected good news. Six months since her boy had gone missing, Rogers had interviewed a number of Jake's friends but after Jane's visit to see Andrew and her call from Sam, the chances were that Jane Lester knew more about the missing guy than Rogers did. She decided not to go volunteering information to SFPD. It was their job, wasn't it? 'Why get involved?' pondered Jane.

In fact, when Jane thought more about it, she realised that she didn't know who she could trust. The people around her were friends. But after comments regarding the couple for whom she was an au pair, Louise Archer's situation, Jodie Patterson's poisonous remarks, Caroline's honest appraisal of matters, Sam's comments and Andrew Wilson's confession, Jane was now confused. Very confused! She was still unsure about Howard and Amanda. Was he really the nice guy that he made an effort to portray? Sometimes when she looked into his eyes she saw fear. And after her court appearance, Amanda seemed brighter, bouncier, more alive. What a difficult time that must have been for her, thought Jane, especially after a good friend accused her of being involved in murder.

Jane had been through a lot. It felt like she'd been in the States at least a year. Never forgetting her main priority, Teresa and Ryan, she wanted to concentrate on them.

Sometimes it was so easy to let her mind wander, but she had to remain focused. Her photography course was occupying her, and Jane was doing well. In a recent exam she'd achieved a mark of 89% - third in the class. She came top in the 'Happiness' photo project that Gloria Rudetsky had set with a shot of the two children at the fairground each licking an ice cream at the same time, their arms interlinked. Jodie Patterson hadn't been seen on the school run, which was a blessing, and Jane hadn't seen the 'Skinny Kid' or 'Gum Chewer' in the photography class for a few weeks now.

None of this would make the local Keighley news, thank goodness, and Jane owed her parents an email, with some photos attached. It was also time to phone Melody Oppenberg for a catch-up. When she did it would all be positive news – how well the kids were doing, their progress at school, the college course, really settling in with the Gardner's, blah, blah, blah. Keep it simple. But Jane would be prepared for any comments from Melody about the recent goings on in Frisco and play them down, tell her she was protecting the kids from exposure to any of the more gruesome aspects of headless torsos - keep them away from the newspapers and avoid news on the car radio to and from school.

Jane didn't need to tell anyone that she'd been to see Andrew, except maybe Sam, although Marty would find out. She wasn't sure if she wanted to go again, but she could always write to him. The visit to the prison had been oppressive. All those visitors to see a bunch of criminals . . . waiting, queueing, being searched, the smell of warm bodies, clanking of metal gates to let you in and out. No, one visit was enough. Andrew didn't have email access, and Jane certainly did not want letters with a prison-franked envelope arriving at Adair Way! She'd leave it for now.

Jane hit the numbers on her mobile phone . . . "Hi, Melody, it's Jane. Just wanted to let you know all's well at my end . . ."

*

Over at Vallejo Street, Lt. Kluisters was sitting with Pomfret and Rogers. They were piecing together information on Jake Bauer. Kluisters had asked Pomfret to get involved as a 'new eye' on the case. Emails and history found on his laptop as well as the names of people he knew had all been followed up but without any positive leads. Three coffees later, Kluisters had to leave for a meeting with his chief. There was a big drugs bust operation coming off within a day or two and Kluisters was heavily involved.

"OK. I'll leave you guys to it. Needless to say, I'm sure that you'll have something for me by the end of the day." That was his way of putting pressure on both detectives. But then that was their job; Mrs. Bauer needed answers soon.

"The more I look at the email transcripts and scan your reports, Simon, the more I see one person's name jumping out at me. There's an email here . . . and the little red notebook there that his ma found and gave you a little while back . . . it's not obvious at first, but with a motive to get rid of Bauer and the wherewithal to do it. I've got a hunch, and I think I know where we should start looking."

49

'That evening I would be on my best behaviour. Act normal, be calm. Talk about all sorts of things I'd usually talk about. Nothing odd, nothing that somebody could later say was unusual for me to make a remark about. And smile, not too much, but just enough to give others the impression I was happy and not concerned about anything. Like murdering him and hiding the body.

Yes, he had to go. He knew something about me that would make things awkward if others found out. That would never do. Why did the interfering little brat go checking up on me like that? And me, in my position! Why didn't he leave things as they were? Just downright nosy, that was all.

No. There was an opportunity coming up and I had to take it.'

*

The doorbell rang. It was half past seven on a Wednesday morning. The children were up, breakfast cereals had been put in bowls, the toast was nearly ready, and the hum of a family preparing for the day ahead filled the house.

"I'll get it!" shouted Howard Gardner. He couldn't think who'd be calling at this time, unless the architect was back, anxious to get something confirmed for the extension.

"Good morning, Dr. Gardner. Sorry to bother you at this early hour, but can we come in?" Detective Marty Kluisters was standing on the front step with Simon Rogers. Beyond them, a plain white van was parked at the kerb. Howard could see two men sitting in the vehicle. It looked as if they were wearing paper suits.

"What's this about?" asked Howard. "My wife hasn't been too well since the trial, and if you've come to ask more questions about that, well . . ." Kluisters quickly held his hand up.

"No, it's not that Dr. Gardner. It's about a missing person. Jake Bauer. We believe you know him?" Howard swallowed hard.

"Yes, I knew him. His girlfriend, our au pair, used to bring him here sometimes."

"You said *knew* as if he wasn't around any more? Past tense?"

"Er, well, I meant I haven't seen him since he was last here." Gardner swallowed again. "You'd better come in." Gardner stood back, holding the door wide open as the two detectives walked in. Amanda looked at the kitchen clock as if to query a visit at this early hour.

"Honey, this is..." She cut him off.

"I know these two gentlemen, Howard. What can we do for you?" Amanda glanced at Jane with her 'deal with the children now' look.

"Let's use my study," suggested Howard quickly, striding out of the kitchen and beckoning the officers to follow him. "Amanda, this way honey." Amanda told Jane to make sure Teresa and Ryan got ready for school as soon as they'd finished breakfast. Jane nodded and forced a smile, picking up the tension in Amanda's voice.

Howard unlocked the door and they entered his study. He pointed to two leather chairs in front of his desk for the detectives, whilst he and Amanda remained standing . . . psychologically more powerful in the situation.

"I'll cut the niceties if you don't mind." Kluisters went for the jugular. "Jake Bauer has been missing since 23 April. He was friendly with your previous au pair girl, Caroline Sinclair, and we know she brought him here on a few occasions. We believe that Bauer and you, Dr. Gardner, had words. Our ICT analysts have checked a number of emails on Bauer's laptop computer and these have led us to believe that there may be evidence in this house that could assist us to clues as to his whereabouts." Howard gave his wife an unusual glance that Rogers noticed. "We have two crime scene officers waiting outside who will be taking a look around in a few minutes.

A search warrant has been issued by the judge. We'll let your au pair take the children to school, and if one of you wishes to stay here during the morning, that's fine by us." Howard looked at Amanda, searching her eyes, asking what the hell was going on.

"OK, I'm not due in clinic until noon. I can stay here to make sure things are all right. Howard, you've got some ops this morning. You go on and keep your surgical commitments. Jane will be back soon and then we can sort out whatever this ridiculous, ludicrous matter is all about." Howard nodded and forced a smile at Amanda who looked as if her last pair of Manolo Blahnik shoes had just been shredded.

They all stood up, Howard leaving his study last to lock the door. Kluisters went to the front door and flicked his fingers at the van. The two white-suited men in the plain police vehicle alighted and walked to the rear door of the van. They took out two large bags; an examination of the Gardner household was about to begin.

Howard kissed the children as he left the house, gave Jane a slightly indifferent look, went out to his Audi Q7 and left for the hospital. Through the hall window Kluisters glanced at the Audi and its license plate. Had one of the hikers really made a mistake? Jane went through her routine – checked the children for their daily needs, teeth brushed, school bags with their homework inside. Jane knew that her journey to school was going to prove to be a challenge. How to explain to Teresa and Ryan what on earth was happening at their home – with two police detectives asking questions about something that had happened regarding a young man called Jake Bauer. A name that they would have known, especially as their previous nanny had first brought him home.

Jane picked up her car keys and herded the two children into her car, shouting goodbye after Teresa and Ryan had kissed their mum. Her au pair training had not prepared her for what was about to be asked. This vortex of darkness, this complicated array of interweaving tales and whispers had seemed unreal. After reading about the Doug Gless case in the Chronicle co-written by Tom Lederer and Louise Archer, Jane began to ask herself if she really wanted to continue being a nanny to the Gardner family.

Amanda had been implicated in the murder of Doug Gless, but had been found not guilty of any part in his killing. Now there were two senior detectives wanting to take a look around the home of the Gardner's . . . what was she going to come back to after dropping the children off at school? Jane wondered if she ought to talk to somebody she could trust. Was it was time to call Caroline? They had some things in common, she liked her predecessor, and perhaps there were more questions to which Jane could get some answers to those things spinning around in her head.

Just what were the Gardner family *really* like?

Did Dr. Howard Gardner have some real psychological issues?

Could Teresa and Ryan be trusted with everything they said?

Was Amanda Gardner a trusted middle American 'down to earth' psychiatrist that seemed friends with everyone?

Did Howard's wife know of his infidelity with Louise Archer?

As Jane was about to leave the house, the two paper-suited guys had started to examine the rooms. She wondered what they would find by the time she got back from Lexington Junior.

It wasn't long before she would know the answer.

50

"Hi, Caroline. I need to talk to you. I feel unsettled. Call me back when you have a minute? Love, Jane." The text message had been sent.

But right then, Caroline Sinclair was on a Greyhound bus heading out of L.A.

*

Kluisters had released the body of Douglas Gless from the mortuary. Spaces on the shelves of the refrigerated body storage unit were always required, so another seven by three feet gap, two feet deep, was ready for the next client.

But who would want to see Doug Gless laid to rest? No father. No mother. Maybe friends? Perhaps Ollie Jackson or Cissie from San Diego, if they were still around? Was Cissie still carrying Doug's baby? Truth was, she wasn't. Doug had told her what he was planning to do – get to find out how much cash he was going to get from his old man pegging out. She was a damned leech, hoping to get her hands on a few thousand dollars with her made up story. But the travellers from San Diego had gone quiet. Maybe they'd gone back there with their tails between their legs?

Kluisters decided that a small announcement in the Chronicle was the right thing to do. Just a few words so that whoever needed to know could see that Douglas Gless was being laid to rest. His body, plus head, would be in a cheap wooden box, a pastor hired to say a few words at a short funeral service, and the casket lowered into a hole and a small wooden cross stuck in the ground above it. The place and date of burial, along with a funeral number, would be logged in the San Francisco Registrar of Deaths file.

A week later, at a small cemetery on the north west side of the city, the flimsy coffin was lowered into a roughly dug grave courtesy of the funeral company. Father Seamus

O'Rourke, slightly smelling of whisky and aftershave, said a few words at the graveside. He slurred his words a little, but nobody noticed.

Standing, watching the casket lowered into the grave, were a handful of people, there more for Rosemary than for her son. Vida and Marie Honeywell, Samantha, an uncle who hadn't seen Doug for ten years, and an old friend of the Gless family who used to visit at Christmas. Sam, who'd hardly had any contact with her step-brother, was sobbing whilst the others maintained their dignity, or tried to. Vida put her arm around Sam who was finding this whole matter very emotional after the recent trial and execution of her mother. There was one other person at the edge of the grave, too.

Amanda Gardner stood just behind the others. A wide brimmed black hat hid most of her face, a black lace handkerchief gently scrunched in her right hand to wipe away any crocodile tears.

As Father O'Rourke ended his prayer, spots of rain began to fall and the small crowd started to disperse. It was another one of those dull, misty days that seem perfect for a funeral, and Seamus O'Rourke needed another drink.

'Such an awful shame,' said Father O'Rourke to himself as he trudged wearily back to the car park.

*

Jane arrived back in time to see the paper suits getting back into their van. There was a SFPD cruiser parked just along the road, and Kluisters and Rogers were sat in an unmarked black Chevrolet on the other side of the road, their heads down. Howard had gone to work, leaving Amanda to keep an eye on things. Jane hurried inside, tossing her car keys onto the hall table.

"Amanda! What on earth is happening?" Amanda looked a ghostly shade of white. Taking a deep breath she spoke in a hushed tone.

"I don't know! They've closed off the utility room, sun

room, and the back garden. We can't even make a cup of coffee – we're not allowed to touch anything! An officer is in the utility room whilst another is hovering between the kitchen and the door into the garden." Amanda had to use all of her self control skills in an attempt not to get flustered or panic. "The two detectives sitting outside seem to having an in-depth conversation. No doubt they'll be back inside very soon."

"Have you phoned anybody, yet?" asked Jane innocently.

"Not allowed! Nor can we take incoming calls." The white van pulled away but within half a minute, another, larger van had parked at the kerb. "Who is this?" Jane could tell it was another NCIS vehicle. Four men got out, one walked to the front door while the others opened the back of the van and began unloading their forensic kit. Amanda opened the door wide, holding it as a neighbour or two stared from over the road. 'Nosy bastards,' thought Amanda.

Jane felt helpless. But what if she wandered along the road and made a call with her mobile phone from half a mile away? Who'd know? The problem was, who to phone? The current activity had not yet spread beyond the Stonebrae Country Club complex in Hayward, but for certain, it wasn't going to take long. She could trust a few of her friends, but wasn't absolutely certain if they'd start to blab. Caroline hadn't replied to Jane's text, and Sam worked in a lawyer' office where people had big ears. Marie Honeywell . . . ditto for real estate agents. It wasn't Jane's place to call Vida – perhaps Amanda would do that later? Then there was Kate, a kind natured woman but with a small panic button in her brain – no, best to leave it. For an instant, Jane thought about Jodie Patterson! Hell, what was her mind doing? She hadn't seen Patterson on the school run for a while, and wasn't even certain if her daughter, Amy, was still there. And thinking of school, Jane had never taken the caretaker, Liza, up on her offer of a confidential chat, her words *'You can trust me, Jane'* reverberating in her head. Was there anybody else . . ?

"Miss Lester." Jane, standing in the hall, jumped. It was Detective Rogers. "May we have your cell phone. We won't keep it long, but right now we would rather no phone calls were made from this property. Mrs. Gardner has handed hers over, and we do not want you to use the house phone until we give you the OK. Do you understand?"

'Understand?' Jane allowed herself a wry smile. His words were plain enough – there wasn't much to understand. Rogers suggested Jane and Amanda try to relax in the lounge while the forensic work was done.

"And no emails until I say so!" said Rogers authoritatively. Kluisters smiled to himself.

"How long is this going to take?" asked Amanda, eyeing the Lieutenant casually as she and Jane stood a few feet away.

"Not sure. Maybe an hour. The four crime investigation scene officers are checking things out now. They're very meticulous. We may even need to come back, depends on what they find," replied Kluisters.

"And just *what* are *you* expecting to discover here, Detective Rogers? Crime investigation scene?" Amanda's tone had changed. "I mean, this had something to do with Jake Bauer, right, but he disappeared about six months ago. Hell, I'm no expert, but no way are you going to unearth anything here that's going to help you with your enquiries!" Rogers stayed calm but picked up on the use of the word 'unearth.'

"We have evidence to indicate that Jake Bauer came back here on the night of 23 April. You've told us that you and your husband were at a party, not arriving home until around midnight. We've questioned some of Bauer's buddies and they saw your previous nanny and Bauer get into a cab, and as far as we know they came here. We don't believe he was seen after that. Now, you don't have to have any of Einstein's genes to realise that things are stacking up, do you?"

"Stacking up! I don't think I like your insinuations, Detective!" Amanda shouted, suddenly reigning herself in as Jane gazed at her outburst. Kluisters continued, but with a mellow voice.

"And, when you arrived home, Mrs. Gardner, you told us that Caroline Sinclair was in her room with the light on but you did not disturb her. You did not find any indication that Jake Bauer had been here – no empty glasses, no beer cans, nothing unusual. No mess of any sort, in fact, nothing out of the ordinary. We checked the cab firms in town and one of them employ a cab driver name Paco who had a drop-off here on the 23 April at a little after ten pm. But there is no trace of a cab pick up from this address on the date in question, nor in the early hours of the following day. You mentioned having a headache, so you went to bed as soon as you got home, but you don't recall your husband getting into bed? Are you certain you know what your husband was doing at that time? And the key question, Mrs. Gardner, is 'did Bauer ever leave here?'"

"What the hell are you saying? My husband had gone back to pick up his cell phone from the party. So Bauer had bloody walked home! Or he called a pal who came to collect him! You need to be talking to Miss Sinclair about this, too!" Amanda was getting furious. "I fell asleep. No, I didn't hear Howard come to bed – so? And our friends will vouch for Howard's trip over to theirs . . ." This was not the best place to be having this conversation, as Kluisters realised, especially with Jane looking more and more embarrassed.

"Let's all calm down, shall we? There are more facts to confirm, and we really don't want to discuss these matters *without* your husband present. Let the CIS guys finish off here and we'll get off the premises." Forty five minutes later, the two detectives, two uniformed police officers and their four colleagues were leaving Adair Way. Kluisters had more thinking to do, a lot more, but it was coming together nicely, he decided.

Meanwhile, her returned mobile phone in hand, Jane

lay on her bed. Amanda had not spoken a word to her since the police had left. Amanda Gardner was a difficult person to read, Jane decided. Very difficult. It should be her that's taking up playing cards! Could Jake's body be right here? For a few seconds Jane had thoughts of entering Howard's study and Amanda's studio, taking a good snoop round, but instantly dismissed them. Then the front door slammed as Amanda left the house to get to her clinic for a noon start. Another round of questions and answers with four clients whose heads were filled with crazy notions and possible thoughts of suicide. 'What a bloody mad world we live in,' mumbled Amanda as she started her Ford Taunus.

Jane tried Caroline again but it went straight to voice mail. There seemed little point in leaving another message. She'd try again in the morning.

51

Kluisters shook the brown bottle and took another swig of *Pepsidol*. Pomfret, Rogers and Harris were sitting in Kluisters office. Four empty cardboard coffee cups needed refilling soon. Although there were several other cases that needed police time, the Lieutenant decided that his team would focus on Jake Bauer today. He sensed they were close and he was going to spend an hour with the trio to pinpoint key issues. He invited Sean Pomfret to begin.

"Well, after you asked me to take a look at Bauer's laptop and his emails, keeping an open mind, I trawled through those between him and Caroline Sinclair. I began to get the impression that he had something on her." Pomfret tried to maintain eye contact with the other three as he spoke.

"Something on her?" interjected Rogers.

"Yes, as if he had found out something about her that she didn't want spreading around. Look at this one . . ." Pomfret looked own at his notes. "I'll just give you phrases or sentences from a few emails between them . . . from him:

'...found you interesting after we first met. You had something about you that I liked, but after checking you out on google I grew concerned...'

Her reply. *'You've made a mistake. I googled myself two years ago and found six people with my name in the Glasgow area alone. You are being silly! I like you!'*

A follow up two weeks later: *'It said on an internet newspaper source that you had been in a borstal for young people in the Gorbals. Where are the Gorbals? Why were you in a borstal?'*

Pomfret continued. "Sinclair refuted his claim. Said he was mistaken. It looks like emails were the only way that Bauer could ask difficult personal questions, although we can't be sure how much of this they talked about together. In spite of their buddies telling us that they were simply good friends, it looks like Sinclair was getting concerned that Bauer has something on her. I think she sees the evening of 23 April as an opportunity to have Jake Bauer to herself in the Gardner household and show how nice a person she really was, maybe putting him right over his concerns about her background, sweet-talk him into forgetting what he's read in some internet news article. She certainly wouldn't want him getting loose tongued after a few drinks. We know they were seen getting into a taxicab around ten o'clock in town and driven to Adair Way and the driver confirms the young couple seemed very friendly on the journey." Rogers was crunching his empty cup. He suddenly spoke.

"And the Gardner's reported arriving home just after the bewitching hour. So Sinclair and Bauer had about two hours together. Alone. Time enough for her to clarify her dubious background, if indeed she really had one in the first place? Perhaps they made love?" Rogers tried to hide a smirk. "Megan, you were going to take a look at her details, weren't you?" Megan smiled, her teeth as pearly as ever.

"Sure. There are seven females with the name Caroline Sinclair within the Glasgow zip code, or post code as they call it over there. Our Caroline has the middle name of Patricia and was born 15 February 1994. She did spend three months in a house of correction on the south bank of the River Clyde in Glasgow for drug offences. Also falsified her au pair application apparently, citing previous child care experience that she did *not* have. Sinclair also claimed to have two A level passes in English and History with an offer of a place at university, but that's false, too. Colleagues in LAPD tracked her down to a rented apartment in a run down part of town near South Westlake Avenue. She's been working washing pots in a Howard Johnson restaurant for the last four months." Kluisters breathed in heavily.

"We need to talk to this girl. Simon, get hold of your friend Harry Daniels in LAPD, bring her up here. Let's have a little chat with Miss Sinclair." Rogers sighed.

"Already tried Lieutenant. Her place is empty. Landlord said she owed $300 on her rent. She has a small Dodge car, but that was parked up round back with two flat tyres. She's gone." Pomfret chipped in again. "But I've got someone checking bus and train stations – she's only been gone 24 hours so let's hope we can get a lead.

"And here's another thing," added Pomfret opening his notebook, "I heard yesterday that Sinclair got a job for two weeks just after she was sacked by the Gardner's. At Quentin's Club as a cloakroom assistant . . . you know, looking after coats and scarves." Kluisters raised his eyebrows as if his IQ wasn't high enough to understand what such a job entailed. "Anyhow, she and Kris Roberts were seen together in an Italian restaurant called Perbacco in California Street one evening while she was still working there by a regular at Quentin's, dining out with *Dr. Hudson's* boyfriend! Apparently, Sinclair and Roberts seemed to be enjoying each others company! You know what they say about a gay man . . ?" Kluisters coughed and then spoke.

"Let's not go there, Sean, what with my stomach being a bit off this morning and that!" Chuckles ensued for a few seconds. "So look, we got some other things to do, but here's where we are with the Bauer case, as I see it.

One, we need to talk to Sinclair. Find out just what went on when she and Bauer arrived at Adair Way and when he left the property – if he did. We have to find her. Megan – ball in your court.

Two, Roberts has a link to Sinclair. It might only be tenuous but *both* of them may have had motives to get rid of Jake Bauer. Although we think Bauer was straight, Roberts may have a reason to have harmed him. Sinclair could have used him? He's out there somewhere. Find him. Simon, your chase.

Three, let's question the Gardner's again about what really happened when they got home on the 23 April, and the early hours the following morning. She says she went to bed, he stayed up, forgot his cell phone and that, but what time did the surgeon get home? Was Bauer hiding in the house? Did Gardner find him sleeping in the garden shed? An opportunity to murder him? Let's check it out. Simon, yours, too. Now, what I can let you know is that the forensic report from our visit to Adair Way was on my desk by 8.25 am today." Kluisters patted the manilla file as if feeling his stomach after a good pizza. "Nothing unusual in this folder. Two hairs from the head of Bauer were found on the utility room carpet, a tea cup had his fingerprints on, and the sole-prints from a pair of size 9 Nike trainers were found on the kitchen floor facing inwards underneath the sink where someone hadn't cleaned the floor properly. The CIS guys removed the U- bend from that sink and collected the contents, irrigating it twice after that to collect any further residue. Chemical analysis revealed traces of mercuric cyanide in several small pieces of undigested pineapple. A few traces of food, including salami and cheese, that had not been flushed through the pipework indicated that possibly a pizza had been consumed two to three hours before the stomach had given up its 'special of the day.' Maybe Bauer was bending over that sink and puking his guts up?

The tea cup with prints had not been washed properly, then replaced in a cupboard where it remained until our recent visit. And we know mercuric cyanide is stored at SFCH where the Gardner's work, and where Roberts worked." Kluisters smiled as he stood up. A satisfied smile. "Let's get some more coffee and move on. Things to do. People to see." Simon Rogers' cell phone beeped. It was a text from Harry Daniels at LAPD.

Sinclair booked seat on Greyhound to Seattle. Used credit card. Left L.A. three hours ago. Bus will be stopping Portland, Oregon 3.25 pm today en route to Seattle. Let me know if we can help. Harry.

52

Kris Roberts never got on well with his twin brother, Mickey. They were always at loggerheads, a real challenge for their mother during the school vacations. But despite that, Kris always protected his twin. No bully got away with hitting or threatening Mickey at school or in the local neighbourhood. Kris would beat some kid up, tell him not to tell his parents or he'd get more, and slap Mickey, telling him to keep out of trouble!

Mickey grew up to be an honest member of society, well, reasonably honest. A bit of stealing here and there wasn't really a crime to him. He joined a gang to feel secure, and his role was to steal hub caps, sell them where he could, and keep the gang in cigarettes. He washed cars at the auto-valet place on the east side of town for a few years, and also worked at the Golden Arches stuffing French fries into paper cones and cooking greasy burgers for San Franciscan's who didn't know any better.

But Mickey didn't seem healthy. He'd get out of breath easily and couldn't run to catch a bus. He was the focus of the PE teacher at school, always on the end of his cruel jibes about lack of fitness, and nicknamed Quasimodo.

The problem was, however, that Mickey had a heart condition. It was never picked up until he went for a routine health check. An operation was necessary; a heart bypass operation had to be performed. And so, at the age of 26, Mickey Roberts ended up in the Operating Room at SF City Hospital. But the operation was not successful. Dr. Gardner didn't have many failures, but Michael Roberts was one of them.

And, ever protective of his twin brother, Kris Roberts didn't like that. He didn't like it at all. Roberts was one to harbour grudges, but he could take his time; had taken his time. He wanted revenge . . . and the time was right.

Now.

*

Simon Rogers had contacted Oregon State Police Department. Caroline Sinclair was met when she left the Greyhound for a comfort break. It was 3.26 pm. Detective Christopherson had explained very little to her except to say that she was wanted for questioning by SFPD in connection with a missing person. Sinclair's luggage was removed from the storage area of the bus and she was taken south to a small town about half way to San Francisco by Christopherson and two uniformed officers. There she was met by Rogers and Harris, convoyed with an SFPD cruiser that contained two police officers. One male, one female. That same evening Caroline Sinclair was being questioned by Rogers and Harris in Vallejo Street station.

"So, Miss Sinclair, you were going to Seattle. Reason?" Caroline told Rogers she'd got a new job working in a primary school. When probed, she hesitated but gave the name of the school. Beaver Junior. "And you owe your landlord three hundred dollars, I believe." Caroline was incredulous, stating she was certain that she had paid a cheque into the landlord's account yesterday. Rogers continued, putting her under constant pressure as Harris threw in a few questions herself. Sinclair denied knowing the whereabouts of Jake Bauer, and had not seen him since the evening of 23 April but she now wanted to put the story straight.

They'd arrived at Adair Way after leaving their buddies in town and picking up a pizza. It was maybe just after ten pm when they'd got out of the taxi. She'd offered Bauer a can of Michelob beer, one of a six pack she'd bought earlier that day. He wanted to know more about her past. Bauer told her that he knew about her stay in a house of correction and wanted to know about her drug habits and anything else she'd been involved with. If she didn't tell him, he threatened, he'd grass on her, be a snitch, tell all her friends. Now that was the last thing she wanted. Her role as an au pair with a wealthy family in Haywood and a nice lifestyle was something she wanted to maintain. Sinclair confessed to falsifying her documents when applying for the au pair job, but it was the only way she'd get it. She also told the two detectives that Dr. Gardner had made advances to her on several occasions, but she always rebuffed his actions. Sinclair was truthful about problems controlling the children, and in a fit of rage had poked Ryan in his leg with a ballpoint pen although, of course, she'd denied it at the time.

Bauer had drunk three or four beers when the situation between them turned ugly. Sinclair stated that she'd tried to be amorous with Bauer – to calm him down – but it hadn't worked. She recalled how he'd begun to slur his speech. He'd gone to the kitchen sink for a cup of water and then began to get angry before he fell to the floor in the kitchen. Checking his pulse which was weak, Sinclair believed that Bauer was messing about, then told him that he could sleep on the kitchen floor for all she cared.

When Sinclair was asked if she thought Bauer was still alive she simply replied 'No idea.' She had left the kitchen and gone to her room. Feeling tired she'd laid down but planned to go back downstairs fifteen minutes later to check on Bauer. Sinclair told Rogers that she'd fallen asleep and the next thing she knew was that she heard the voices of Teresa and Ryan who'd obviously arrived home with their parents. Sitting up on her bed, she waited for the reaction by either Amanda or Howard when they saw Jake Bauer on the floor but there was nothing. No shouting, no raised voices. So, she told Rogers, she stayed in her room until the next morning.

At 9.35 pm Simon Rogers concluded the interview and switched off the recorder. Caroline Sinclair, face ashen, would be spending the night in a cell with a thin mattress and thinner blanket for company. She was offered food but refused, a plastic tumbler of water being all she wanted. It was Friday, 30 October. The interview would recommence in the morning when the two detectives hoped that

Sinclair, under more questioning, would provide more clues as to the location of Mrs. Bauer's son.

Both Rogers and Harris were certain that Sinclair either had murdered, or was involved in the disappearance of, Jake Bauer, and was lying through her teeth. But they needed more evidence.

*

"I'm upset," said Teresa. "Ryan and I were talking last night after we'd done our homework and we are confused!" Teresa sounded so grown up thought Jane. The matter needed a large degree of diplomacy.

"Tell me why you're upset," said Jane in a calm, considerate way.

"Well, it's everything that's been going on over the last few weeks. Mum having been to the courthouse, the policemen coming to the door, the men in white suits coming into the house, Mum and Dad whispering to each other, arguments over the phone between mum and Mrs. Honeywell – not sure what about, Dad getting cell phone text messages and deleting them quickly. It goes on!" Both of the children stared at Jane. Their eyes begged for a response.

"Listen, there's nothing you need to worry about. Your mum *had* to go to court so give evidence in a trial. That's all over now. The policemen were just checking up on a missing person and wondered if your Mum or Dad might be able to help . . ." Ryan interjected quickly.

"Was that Jake Bauer?" Jane was a little surprised.

"Why yes, did you get to meet him?" Teresa chirped up.

"Of course, when Caroline brought him round here. He upset my dad at least twice, and mum suggested she didn't bring Jake back. He never came round again until the night of the Shakespeare party. In April, I think. But I liked him. He'd bring Ryan and I candies."

"How do you know he was here that night in April?

You were were staying with an aunt, weren't you?" Jane's interest was aroused as Ryan replied.

"Well, yeah, but we didn't want to stay all night, I had a bad stomach, so our aunt phoned Mum and they collected us two on the way home. I went into the lounge before I went upstairs to find my teddy bear and saw a packet of cigarettes near a cushion. I remembered Jake smoked that kind and he'd maybe left them there - otherwise Katie would have got rid of them. We went straight to bed when we got home and I saw a light coming from under the door in Caroline's room, but we didn't disturb her. Oh, and . . ." Ryan hesitated. "Underneath another cushion on the sofa there was a little machine."

"Machine? What sort of machine? What did you do with it?" Jane probed gently.

"It's small, I put it in my pocket. It's in a drawer in my room, stuffed in a sock along with the cigarette packet. I just didn't want to tell anybody . . ." Ryan began to sob. Jane hugged him gently as Teresa wiped away a tear. She'd recover the little machine later and dump the cigarette packet somewhere.

"OK, OK. Take it easy, little man." Jane let the seconds pass. Very soon Ryan's sobbing stopped. Jane knew him well enough to believe that he wanted to be strong about the matter. Ryan pulled away, then looked at Jane and held her gaze. "What is it?" she asked.

"And there's another secret. Caroline knew where dad kept a spare key for his study. She must have seen him place it under the large plant pot in the hall because I saw her pick it up one day when I was off school sick and Mum and Dad were at work. She went in a few times – I can see the study door from my room upstairs." Ryan paused. "And we know that Jake is still missing because I heard a reporter from a newspaper telling him on the telephone a while back. One day the phone was ringing, Mum was out, I went to answer it on the other line. Dad got there first and, I know it's wrong, but I listened in. Some girl called Louise was telling him about Jake and something was going to be in the Chronicle. I let Dad put the phone down first, then I did the same and hurried to my room. I've seen them do it on TV crime shows." Jane hugged both of them.

"Look, this is all going to blow over in a matter of days. It'll seem like a bad dream and then we can all get back to normal. Why, I was thinking of going to that big amusement park with you two again – you know, some ice cream. Any flavour you want!" Their eyes sparkled. "So why don't we say that we keep this conversation between us, about the little machine and the cigarette packet and what we've said . . . nobody else needs to know. Listen, it's nearly time for bed, so I'll go get each of you a warm glass of milk, then brush your teeth thoroughly, and tomorrow's another day. What do you say?" Teresa and Ryan nodded. "Promise?" They nodded again. Jane had fulfilled her nanny role and wanted to get to Ryan's sock drawer and one of its contents. As she stood up, Ryan posed another question that took her by surprise.

"Jane, why does Dad have a loaded gun in his study?"

53

The morning of Saturday, 31 October had started off cloudy, but by ten o'clock the sun was burning away the mist; the forecast for the whole week-end was good. It was Halloween, and there was a buzz around the city as children and young adults planned their All Hallows Eve parties. There'd be toffee apples, doughnuts to dunk, sodas and milkshakes, and beers for the adults. If the weather was nice enough, aspiring dad's would consider cooking a BBQ in the back garden and the neighbours would be invited round. Kids would dress up in ghoulish outfits, some of the girls turning into witches for a few hours. But it wasn't only the kids who got dressed up; some adults who got into the spirit of Halloween donned black costumes, probably with a face mask or make-up to heighten the 'fright' factor. And a bonus was that it was a Saturday! Dad's could get stoned and sleep the effects off the next morning.

Because of recent events Howard persuaded Amanda that they'd give a party for the two children, and ask the neighbours on either side to come round. Claire, one of the neighbours with two young daughters, offered to bring some toffee apples whilst Valerie on the other side would bake some doughnuts – caramel and cinnamon – and prepare a large green salad. Both husbands would bring some beers and wine. Valerie asked Amanda if she'd mind if a couple of friends, who were staying over, came round. It wasn't a problem. It would be a nice sized group, and Amanda had suggested they all gather at six o'clock.

With firecrackers going off and people getting into the mood there'd be lot's of people milling around Hayward, most dressed in costumes with masks that made them look like supporting characters in a Stephen King horror movie. There'd be revelry with glitter-stars showering the sky as spooky individuals, carrying a bottle of wine or a pack of beers, would be in party mode as they went from house to house taking part in the fun. That was the way it was on Halloween - being friendly with everyone . . . very friendly. And the Gardner household was going to be in for a surprise.

A real Halloween surprise.

*

On the morning of 31 October Sinclair was still looking pale. After a medical check up the previous evening and again when she awoke, Caroline had eaten a light breakfast. A Bible that she had requested was in her hand as she was taken to the interview room, Rogers and Harris already waiting. Megan Harris sensed that Sinclair had changed. Her demeanour was different, she seemed more positive in her manner, but what Sinclair did not know was that the police were going to use the services of a psychic medium, a Miss Docia Lightbody, who would accompany them to Adair Way. Miss Lightbody had been used on several occasions before and had proved extremely useful in solving a difficult murder case in a derelict, haunted house. Simon Rogers managed to get the agreement of the Chief of Police, a natural 'doubting Thomas,' to employ the services of Miss Lightbody, but if she failed in this particular case Rogers would probably be in for a rollicking from the Chief! He switched on the CD recorder and they began.

Sinclair continued to reiterate her innocence, smiling at times. Despite the insinuation from Harris, Sinclair stated that she had *not harmed* Jake, and certainly not poisoned him as Rogers suggested. How could she have done? She told the detectives that she'd never harmed a mouse; she could never kill anybody. Having tried to be nice to him, Caroline felt Jake a loose cannon and she'd begged him not to put anything on social media. She also then added that Jake said he had 'something to tell her, something important that she may find very interesting' but he never got round to telling her. But Caroline had no idea of what it may have been. When Rogers again asked Caroline what had really happened to Jake, hoping she'd give in and let her conscience override her reluctance to admit to anything, she continued to shrug her shoulders. But seconds later Caroline Sinclair was vomiting over the table and floor, green bile tinged with mucus that ran down her chin and onto her blouse. Rogers switched off the recorder and ordered the police officer standing at the door to get a medic as soon as possible. Detective Rogers began to wonder if Sinclair would be fit enough to visit the Gardner's before Monday. Had she taken something? Did she have any hidden drugs? The news of the use of Miss Lightbody's paranormal skills was yet to be shared with Sinclair, so it couldn't be that.

Rogers' plan, agreed with Marty Kluisters, was that the psychic medium, clutching the hairbrush of Jake Bauer, would be asked to lead the way into the house. He knew it was a gamble but CIS officers had checked all the obvious places in the house. They'd removed partitions around baths, airing cupboard, the loft, and carefully examined the back garden. There was no sign of a body. Rogers hoped and prayed that Sinclair would be true to her word – she'd agreed to return to Adair Way and go through in detail what had happened that evening. But a doctor had refused permission for Sinclair to leave the station until Monday at the earliest. Her temperature was still up, pupils dilated, pulse above 80 . . . she was in no state to be going anywhere until these were back to normal and prescribed some medication and complete bed rest.

Blast!' thought Simon Rogers, 'another damned delay. Kluisters is gonna have my ass!' He'd have to postpone the psychic medium, too.

But then Docia Lightbody probably already knew! Psychics are like that.

54

The dry weather for All Hallows Eve was ideal, a gentle mild breeze blowing in from the Pacific with a partly cloudy sky and a temperature in the mid sixties Fahrenheit. At the Gardner's the fumes of hot charcoal from the barbecue wafted across the garden. Amanda, now wearing a short black cloak and black wig, had set up a half barrel filled with water, green apples bobbing about like buoys on the sea - ready for eager youngsters to grab one with their teeth. A string of sugary doughnuts were threaded on cord between two tall bushes for the children to nibble – hands free! Half a dozen large black candles were placed around the garden to create a scarey atmosphere, added to which were three hollowed-out pumpkins, eyes and mouths aglow. Four broomsticks, decked with black ribbons, were hanging in trees. Claire with husband George, and Valerie holding hands with her partner Waylon, wandered round at a little after six o'clock. Claire's daughters Emmylou and Petula hung onto their mum. Valerie's weekend guests, Johnny & Reeba, were introduced and the group were offered drinks by Amanda as they relaxed on the lawn. Jane gravitated towards Emmylou and Petula who instantly formed a quartet with Teresa and Ryan who began chucking with anticipation of the evening ahead, and all with face make-up that almost cracked as they giggled.

With drinks in hand the adults, all wearing costumes, chatted about a variety of topics – the state of politics, work, forthcoming vacation plans. Johnny and Reeba were a little shy to start, but as the home made rum punch and high strength beers took effect the conversation flowed. Suddenly Amanda nudged Howard and pointed toward the built-in barbecue.

"Oh, yes! Sorry, I need to check on the BBQ. My memory!" Howard adjusted his Dracula fangs and strode over to poke the briquettes before turning over the browning meat.

"He'd forget his home address if it wasn't for his sat-nav!" Amanda added. It raised a laugh, more out of politeness than for the comic value of her comment.

"Any vegetarians?" Howard asked innocently, his fangs clacking. He'd forgotten that Claire was a near vegan. She raised her hand like a schoolgirl needing a toilet break.

"Oh, yes, I forgot Claire. Don't fret, I've put some oiled onion, red pepper and pumpkin cubes onto skewers. There are also half a dozen corn cobs!" Howard burst into singing 'the corn is as high as an elephant's eye' but got a look from Amanda. He'd done his bit in preparation for this evening and was now in a good mood. It began to get dusk around seven o'clock but the garden was adequately illuminated, six solar powered gargoyles having maintained brightness as the darkness descended, and adding to the six large candles.

Howard adjusted the steaks and burgers on the griddle, plus a few veggie skewers, the charcoal now white and hot. The children laughed as each one of them tried to bite an apple in the barrel, Ryan spluttering as water went up his nose. The hubbub at the party was low, and Amanda wondered if one or two other neighbours might pop by. Maybe some of those that had been invited to last year's Thanksgiving party? Both sides of the house were open, with easy access to the back garden so it was 'open house.'

With candles and flickering hollow pumpkins doing their work the atmosphere grew more eerie. It was dark overhead but a few star constellations were visible, and the sound of rockets going off in other parts of Hayward were lighting up the night sky with colour for seconds at a time. The food had been served, with potato and green salads alongside chunky bread rolls. Pumpkin pie was for dessert – what else, and a bowl of whipped cream invited those not counting calories to help themselves. They all did! Amanda had baked chocolate brownies that the children ate heartily, washed down with home-made lemonade.

The Gardner's and their guests became merrier and

noisier, the conversation turning to ghost stories and spiritual events that some of them had experienced. As Johnny was finishing a tale of a headless ghost he'd seen in an old hotel in San Antonio, Texas, a man wandered into the garden. He was wearing a long black, kaftan-like smock, and a face mask. A black beret sat perched on his head, slightly cocked to one side. Amanda recognised him as Willie Schmidt from further along the road.

"Hi, Willie. Glad you could come round. You want a drink?" Willie stopped and looked at Howard. Howard smiled and agreed with Amanda. Seconds passed. "What'll you have, Willie? Beer? Rum punch?" Howard hesitated. "Willie, are you deaf? Come on, what do you want . . . ?"

A gun was slowly raised from under the smock and pointed at Howard. Everyone froze, time stood still. A bullet hit its target. Whup! It penetrated the forehead and exited the other side as the children screamed. Blood slowly oozed onto the lime-green lawn as the half barrel tipped over and the apples were sent flying in all directions.

But it wasn't Willie Schmidt.

And the screaming didn't stop for a long time.

55

On the Monday morning a doctor agreed that Sinclair could be escorted to Adair Way. Megan Harris stayed close to Sinclair as they both got into the back of an unmarked police car as Rogers sat in front with the uniformed driver. Arriving in Hayward twenty minutes later, with no conversation in the car during the journey, Rogers rang the bell at number 31. On seeing the police vehicle, Miss Lightbody waddled the fifty yards to the house from where she'd parked her car. Rogers had already telephoned early that morning to tell Amanda Gardner that he and Harris would be arriving at about 9.30 am with Miss Sinclair and another 'colleague.' He clarified the objective of the visit and that it would be short – probably no more than ten minutes.

Amanda Gardner was on her own, Jane having taken the children to school and been asked by Amanda to do some grocery shopping on the way back. She didn't want Jane there when Sinclair arrived. Amanda opened the front door, stood back and allowed the four to enter, the police driver staying in the car. Miss Lightbody was briefly introduced to Amanda as a 'colleague' that was helping in the enquiry. Caroline avoided eye contact with Amanda, but Amanda's stare drilled into the previous nanny like a laser beam.

'This girl caused so much grief for our family. A liar and troublemaker, she could not be trusted. I rue the day I first set eyes upon her.'

Harris gently tugged at Sinclair's right arm as they followed Miss Lightbody with Bauer's hairbrush gripped in her hand, firstly through the main rooms, then the kitchen and out into the utility room. This was large room, about twenty square yards in area, with appliances such as a fridge, a chest freezer, washing machine and clothes dryer. Shelving held a range of items such as washing powders, old paint tins, white spirit and tools.

Lightbody walked around slowly, muttering quietly, her eyes closed for part of the time. She said she felt an 'emotional coldness' permeating through her as she went from corner to corner, touching one appliance, then another. Lightbody shivered for a few seconds causing Rogers to sneeze as the psychic uttered a shriek that sounded as if someone had stood on a cat's tail. The hairs on Harris' neck stood up. After a few minutes the psychic medium glided across to the chest freezer and tapped it three times with the hairbrush. The two detectives looked at one another.

"In here?" whispered Rogers incredulously. Docia Lightbody nodded. He turned to Amanda. "Do you ever defrost this freezer, Mrs. Gardner?" Amanda explained that it was done twice a year, around the middle of April and again in mid-October but confessed it hadn't been done lately. Rogers lifted the lid of the Frigidaire. Bags of supermarket meat and fish, alongside frozen vegetables, colour-splashed the interior. Crystal rime had formed on most of the products, silvery and shard-like. Miss Lightbody stood back alongside Harris and Sinclair as Simon Rogers began to move bags in an effort to see what lay below.

Amanda Gardner, swayed, felt faint, the events of the past two days catching up with her. Needing to sit down, Amanda moved from the utility room, but before she did Rogers asked if there were any spare plastic boxes, and a pair of gloves? He knew he had to go lower, through the frozen food packs to see what else was in there. Rogers brought three large plastic containers from the garage along with some industrial rubber gloves. The other three stood back as Simon Rogers placed pack after pack into the plastic boxes, working as quickly as possible, the heavy gloves protecting his hands. He felt Sinclair laughing at him, sensed she had been lying, playing mind games with them.

Suddenly Harris stopped, a dark shape appeared further down in the freezer. Removing almost the last of the food packs he saw a pair of open, glassy eyes that were staring right at him. No, right through him. Rogers was looking at the open-mouthed, clothed body of Jake Bauer. With blue, swollen lips he resembled a codfish . . . a giant codfish that had met his end at the hands of a callous killer.

Amanda, on hearing a loud gasp, went back into the utility room and glanced into the Frigidaire. She passed out as Jane walked through the front door with two bags of groceries, but Rogers, hands still gloved, was quick enough to catch Amanda and prevent her head from hitting the cold concrete floor.

'Such an awful waste,' Lightbody murmured to herself as she looked into the glazed marble eyes of the corpse.

*

Once the stiff body of Jake Bauer had been removed from the utility room and loaded into a police van, Amanda Gardner had been made comfortable and had confirmed that she was OK to remain in the house with Jane. The detectives, Sinclair and Miss Lightbody left the house as Megan Harris slipped into the back seat alongside Sinclair whilst Rogers walked to Miss Lightbody's car with her and thanked the psychic for her invaluable help. She knew there would be a suitable reward for her with an 'under the counter' payment.

On the way back to the police station Sinclair felt her neck and uttered an 'oh!'

"I seem to have lost my scarf," she said, "a blue one. Chiffon." Harris reassured her they'd make enquiries with Mrs. Gardner as soon as they got back to the station.

56

The body of Kris Roberts, same height and build as Willie Schmidt, had been removed from the Gardner's lawn by 11.30 pm on Halloween. It had been a terrible ordeal for the family as well as the neighbours, although it later transpired that those living three or four doors away weren't even aware of anything abnormal at the time, especially with noisy fireworks going off.

A police marksman had shot Roberts through the head with a high powered Colt 6940 rifle from an upstairs window in a house in the next road. Lieutenant Marty Kluisters had been in charge of what they termed Operation Witch-hunt.

Lee Jepson had telephoned Vallejo Street at around seven o'clock on the Friday evening and was put through to Kluisters. Jepson had met with Kris Roberts at Roberts' suggestion in a bar down-town. Jepson barely recognised Roberts who had grown a beard since the last time Lee had seen him. He informed Kluisters that Roberts had been drinking, even before they'd met in Jimmy Fivebellies' Bar. He was all talk, mouthing off about the police, how he'd managed to evade them for so long, and how he tried to get to know Rosemary Gless better, be kind to her, get his hands on her money. Roberts had met Doug Gless in Quentin's and knew that his father had left his step-mum a handsome sum and he wanted some of it . . . a new car, a Caribbean vacation . . .

And Roberts blabbed to Jepson about his killing plan. On Halloween, which was Roberts' 28 birthday, he'd go to the Gardner's and murder Howard; shoot him in the head with a handgun. He owed it to his brother, Mickey, whose 'life had been taken by the surgeon' on the operating table. In fact, Roberts took the job as hospital porter to get close to Howard Gardner – watch him, find out about him, plan to end his life for not looking after his kid brother. So with Roberts' plan exposed, Kluisters had placed two of his best marksmen in the bedroom of a house overlooking the rear garden of 31, Adair Way. Although a hard decision for Kluisters, the whole operation had been done with complete secrecy and stealth. Nobody knew that the neighbours, Mr. and Mrs. Evans, had police guests staying for a few hours! And Marty Kluisters' reputation was on the line here – if Operation Witch-hunt had gone wrong he could have been stacking shelves in Wal-Mart until he retired! Their orders had been to maintain vigilance during the Halloween party and expect Roberts to turn up any time.

When a guy wearing a black cloak turned up, then raised a hand gun that was pointed at Howard Gardner they had no option but to shoot. A single rifle shot was enough to kill the assailant where he stood; the Colt bullet that had taken some of his brains away was lodged in a tree four yards behind him and later recovered.

On that evening Jane, with great fortitude, had maintained her composure and rapidly shepherded the four children inside of the house. The party neighbours all had the presence of mind to stay calm, but clearly they were in a state of shock as Amanda ushered them into the kitchen where the neighbours Claire and George had made tea. Howard, shaking slightly, had called the police, not realising that it was them that had carried out the killing. He'd been put through to Pomfret and explained what had happened but Pomfret quickly reassured Howard that everything was under control and gave him a briefing on the police operation telling the Gardner's to have their neighbours return home and keep their doors and windows locked. Howard was so shaken up that he didn't know whether to be relieved or annoyed – relieved that he was alive . . . annoyed that he hadn't been told of the plan.

Jane suggested to Amanda that she sleep in the same bedroom as Teresa and Ryan, the children using bunk beds, whilst Jane could spend the night on a Z-bed. She hardly slept but Jane would be there for the children when they awoke sobbing or crying from a horrible dream. In fact, the whole event was like a dream as Jane lay on her narrow mattress trying to piece together what she'd witnessed. She couldn't. Thoughts raced through her head as if on a continuous loop . . . the things that she'd been told by a number of people about Dr. Gardner, the surgeon. And who the hell was the guy that had been about to shoot him?

Staring at the ceiling, Jane remembered Ryan's comment about the little machine and cigarette packet. As the children lay asleep she went into Ryan's sock drawer and found the Sony micro-cassette recorder, a crumpled Peter Stuyvesant pack next to it. The recorder was empty. She squeezed both into her handbag, settled down and tried to sleep, but Mr. Sandman wouldn't visit her for a while .

Kluisters told the Gardner's that a discrete police presence would be maintained on their property, although he was convinced that Roberts acted alone since Lee Jepson had explained to the police the reasoning behind Kris Roberts objective of an 'eye for an eye.' The party neighbours had left soon after the police arrived, and Kluisters had reinforced with Howard the need to take care of the kids and stay safe.

. . .

So not only was the Halloween party and the week-end ruined, there was more to come. When Jane saw Caroline on the morning of Monday, 2 November, bags of frozen food piled into boxes and the Frigidaire freezer lid open, she soon realised that there was something very serious going on.

But they didn't know that there was a bigger surprise in store. For everybody.

*

As Teresa and Ryan were being cared for at school by an

education department counsellor on the first day back at school after the shooting, the body of Jake Bauer had been removed and taken to the mortuary. It took eight hours for his naked body, covered with a white sheet, to defrost on a trolley. Iced water drip-dripped into a channel as it trickled down a drain. He looked as fresh as the day he was poisoned, six months and one week before. Bauer's clothes were too much like plywood, removal impossible. But on the Tuesday afternoon Dr. Jenkins, the police pathologist, had undressed the corpse and his assistant had poly-bagged the clothes. Detectives Rogers and Harris would be arriving at about 3.00 pm to talk with Jenkins about his findings.

Howard Gardner was at work as normal, another routine heart bypass op, trying hard to put the events of Saturday evening behind him. Word had got round about Kris Roberts. The Evans, the neighbours who'd agreed to help the police, couldn't wait to tell friends and neighbours about the police marksmen who'd holed up in their back bedroom for two hours before the shooting. The news spread like a Californian bush fire and Howard realised that hospital staff were trying to be considerate – not to ask awkward questions or how he was feeling. Karen and Angelina, two of Howard's reliable nurses, had had a quiet word with him before the operation began; they'd reassured him that his skill as a good cardiac surgeon was in no way diminished by events of the past 48 hours. A well qualified heart surgeon, Dr. Stephan Davison, had joined the staff at SFCH from a hospital in Sacramento and was at Howard's side as the procedure progressed.

Amanda had taken unpaid leave of absence from her psychiatric clinical role at the City Hospital, neither was she taking any more appointments in her own practice for the foreseeable future. Existing diary entries were cancelled. She had decided she wanted to be home for the children, be close to them after their traumatic experience, try to become a loving wife and mother, something she'd lost somewhere, somehow along the way.

The two detectives arrived at the mortuary just after three o'clock. Dr. Jenkins had completed the autopsy and had a report ready. He confirmed that Jake Bauer had in fact died from mercuric cyanide poisoning. There was some bruising on the body, mainly the head and upper arms, consistent with being lifted and dropped into the Frigidaire. After the debrief Rogers took a copy of the report and the poly-bag containing the damp clothing as he and Harris drove back to the police station.

Finding an empty interview room, and wearing latex gloves, Rogers laid the items on a plastic sheet on the table. Thin woollen check shirt, grey cotton-twill trousers, boxer shorts, blue socks, and brown leather slip-on shoes. Bauer's Casio wristwatch showed the time as 11.02 pm. Picking up the trousers, Harris checked the pockets. One black leather wallet containing about $30 but no credit cards, a pink handkerchief, a micro-cassette tape, and a folded A4 sheet of paper – a print out of an email. Unfolding it carefully, she read the contents to Rogers who listened as he palmed the small tape.

From: jakebauer123@gmail.com
19 April 2015
To: andrew.wilson@atandt.com

Hi Andy,

Just thought I'd let you know that I've been threatened by Amanda Gardner, the woman who's brat kids Caroline looks after. She and her husband don't have any sense of humour. Just because I called her old man a butcher she took me to one side and said she'd 'do me.' Her very words!

She actually asked me if I knew what it was like to be poisoned! Hell, what sort of a question is that? I'd been there twice and on the second occasion she grabbed my jacket lapel (Caroline was using the bathroom at the time) and whispered to me not to go to her house ever again.

When Caroline came back Mrs. Gardner was as nice as pie. A different personality!

Course I told Caroline, but she said not to take any notice. So there you have it. Sent this email just in case...you never know what's round the corner?

Catch you soon for a beer. Chow,

Jake.

Simon Rogers was silent. He was certain this wasn't on Bauer's laptop when it was examined. Was this copy of an email from Jake Bauer enough to place Amanda Gardner as prime suspect? He looked at the small cassette in his hand, remembering that when he'd searched Jake's room he'd seen a micro-cassette recorder, and a receipt for one, but no tapes.

"We'd better listen to this, Megan." Rogers slipped next door, grabbed a Samsung player and inserted the tape. He pressed Play as they both sat together in the interview room.

Click. *If that excuse for a human being comes anywhere near this house again I swear I'll kill him! Caroline knows how to pick them. Hell! I could send Caroline out to buy some cookies – some reason like that – then we get rid of him. Dispose of the body before she gets back, toss his cell phone in the river... tell her he just upped and left the house and that was the last we saw of him. Howard, are you listening to me? God, you're the one he insulted! He's trash, pond life, and has to be made to pay!* Click.

They were speechless for a few seconds. The silence was interrupted by Rogers' cell phone ringing.

"Simon, Dr. Jenkins here. Sorry, forgot to give you the earring."

"Earring?" asked Rogers.

"Yes, in the clenched right hand of Jake Bauer was a small, gold earring. A teddy bear. I'll have a courier send it over to you straight away. Bye."

57

Amanda Gardner couldn't explain the missing earring. Yes, she confessed to owning a pair of golden teddy bear earrings, bought as a birthday gift for her by Howard, but could find only one of them. The recording and the copy of the email were read in court as Amanda Gardner sat before the jury and a packed courtroom that included Louise Archer, Tom Lederer and a raft of other reporters. Her previous appearance in the case of the murder of Douglas Gless hung heavy with those present, but Judge Rizburger asked the jury to put that behind them. 'This was a case that was to be tried *only* on the evidence as presented' he told the court.

Despite the efforts by the defence counsel, and emphasis on the good character of Dr. Amanda Gardner as a fine upstanding citizen of the city of San Francisco, a doting mother and caring wife, the jury would retire with much to consider. How could they ignore the tape? That was the voice of Amanda Gardner threatening to kill Jake Bauer. The email to Andrew Wilson laid it out – clear as day. And yet, how often do people make threats to carry out an action and never do it? Surely a well qualified and competent psychologist like Dr. Gardner could never bring herself to kill this young man.

When Amanda and Howard got home after the party on that fateful night of 23 April, Amanda had put the children to bed straight away. She noticed a light from Caroline's room but did not disturb her. On returning downstairs Howard told his wife that he'd left his cell phone at the party. He'd decided to go back and fetch it, leaving Amanda on her own for about forty minutes. When Howard got home, Amanda was in bed.

Amanda had told the court that she'd felt very tired that night, and after putting a few things away in the kitchen and getting some bowls and cereals out ready for breakfast, she'd gone upstairs, washed, and got into bed.

She claimed she didn't hear Howard come back in. The next thing she knew, she'd stated, was the alarm going off at 7.00 am. Amanda made it clear to the jury that at no time had she seen Jake Bauer that night. She didn't even know if Caroline had planned to bring him to the house . . . Amanda certainly hadn't been asked.

'Did she know he'd been there?' No.

'What would she have done if she'd seen him in her home?' Told him to go.

'Did she wish him any harm?' No.

And Sinclair's story was simple. Fashionably dressed and looking smart, she said she had taken Jake back after an evening out with friends and had forgotten to ask Amanda if it was OK. They'd had a few drinks in a couple of bars, a pizza, and discussed a number of matters including a possible vacation together somewhere. After arriving at the house, perhaps an hour or so later, they'd argued about nothing and Bauer had stormed out of the house, shouting something about hoping to phone for a taxi. Caroline went to bed, read for a while and fell asleep with her bedroom light on. She thought she had heard the children's voices but may have been dreaming. But that was all. When questioned about the Howard's Audi leaving the property that night, Caroline said that she hadn't heard the car engine start up.

The counsel for the prosecution spelt it out clearly. Mrs. Gardner had planned to get rid of Jake Bauer at sometime for insulting her husband – the tapes and email were unambiguous. Bauer had not left the house after his argument with Miss Sinclair, it was suggested, and after Howard had gone back to get his mobile phone, Amanda had come across Bauer hiding somewhere on the premises - possibly in the garage or in the rear garden at the time the Gardner's had returned. The window of opportunity when Howard left to get his phone gave her the perfect opportunity to murder him. Using her subtle psychiatrist-honed interpersonal skills, the prosecution counsel proposed that Amanda had placated Jake, made him feel relaxed, and then poisoned him with a drink of tea, a tea cup having been found with his prints on it. He struggled with her, and unknown to Amanda, had pulled one of her gold earrings off that ended up in his clenched hand. Shortly afterwards he was dead, the mercuric cyanide having done its job. She'd unloaded the food contents of the freezer and then, perhaps with a struggle, lifted his body into the chest and reloaded the Frigidaire. Tidying the utility room quickly, Amanda then replaced the mercuric cyanide in Howard's study. Only Howard's fingerprints were found on the bottle since Amanda, it was proposed by the prosecution, had worn washing-up gloves, and Howard's stated reason for keeping the white granules was only to use as a rat poison. Amanda had got into bed as quickly as possible and on Howard's return she feigned sleep despite having committed the murder.

The prosecution showed the jury some of Amanda's paintings that she'd exhibited in San Francisco at the California Institute of Art exhibition. When the jury saw 'Grief' depicting a dead woman in a rocking chair, some were visibly shaken. When counsel raised the Doug Gless case and Amanda's court appearance in that, they were chastised by Judge Rizburger, reminding them again, for the last time, not to bring that into the equation!

Detective Rogers had visited Mrs. Bauer with Megan Harris as soon as the post mortem was complete and had informed her of their findings. In fact, Mrs. Bauer, handkerchief in hand, was sitting in the packed gallery anxiously watching the proceedings. Jodie Patterson was amongst them, too, as well as Vida Honeywell and several of Amanda's neighbours. Katie was sitting with her head in her hands for much of the time. Neither Lieutenant Kluisters nor Sean Pomfret were in the courtroom, they had other police work to get on with, but Rogers and Harris sat at the rear observing carefully.

The counsel for the defence brought three witnesses to the stand to vouch for the good character of Amanda Gardner. One was her neighbour, Claire, who told the court what a kind and thoughtful person Amanda Gardner was, without a bad bone in her body. Her kindness was second to none. The other two came from the Psychiatric Department of the hospital, again vouching for Amanda as a caring medical professional who under no circumstances would ever contemplate murder. She was prone to the occasional outburst but she could never, ever, kill. Never administer poison . . .

The whole case had taken eight days during which Jane had worked hard to take care of the children who, naturally, were distressed and full of questions. Jane stayed away from the court, preferring to be there for Teresa and Ryan who, with great bravery, had tried their hardest to soldier on. On the ninth day the jury of twelve retired to consider their verdict. After several hours of deliberation they unanimously came to their conclusion.

"And how do you find the accused? Guilty or not guilty?" asked Judge Rizburger. The jury spokesperson stood, hesitated as she swallowed, and held her hands tightly in front of her.

"We find the accused guilty of murder, your honour."

58

On Thursday, 12 November Dr. Amanda Gardner was sentenced to thirty years at Central California Women's Facility at Chowchilla, California. CCWF is 149 miles south east of San Francisco, a two and a half hour journey by car. Howard and the children, along with Jane, planned to visit as often as they could. The Facility helped women who had committed a variety of crimes; rehabilitation was the core philosophy, with group therapy and education being at the centre of each inmate's stay. The Warden had been there for twenty years and had turned CCWF into a model institution.

The first few weeks of Amanda's internment were sheer hell. Her thoughts of being there for another twenty nine years and eleven months was unimaginable. It would take all of her mental strength to come to terms with her new home. Many hours, when not being encouraged to talk about her crime in the 'open talk sessions' or being lectured on how people ought to live their lives, were spent going through the details of exactly how she had come to be here – in Chowchilla. She continued to deny the accusation and the unbelievable verdict! But the most difficult periods were when some poorly qualified therapist asked Amanda 'why did you kill?'

"I didn't do it," was all she ever replied to this inane question. Amanda's long blonde hair had been shorn – to almost a bob – and her flawless skin began to show wrinkles with no cosmetics to cover her lines. Bouts of crying did little to prevent crow's feet appearing at the edges of her eyes. She became insular, not wanting to take part in any of the pastimes or games sessions, and although painting was offered she declined to pick up a paint brush ever again. Amanda Gardner became a shadow of the young woman who'd arrived in San Francisco, lost forty pounds in weight, and her eyes were getting darker and more hollow as time went by. Eventually, Howard ended up visiting Amanda on his own, the children finding it all too traumatic as they cried themselves to sleep after each trip.

Caroline's lawyer, Gregory Jennings, had put in a claim against the SFPD for unnecessary harassment and stress during her interviews. It transpired that *she was* on her way to Beaver Junior School to take up a janitorial position when she was removed from the Greyhound bus without good reason and her landlord in L.A. *had received* his cheque for rent owed. Sinclair was awarded $250,000 damages and had never been so well off! On Monday 23 November, she was flying first class from San Francisco to Prestwick, Glasgow after contacting the Beaver Junior School to withdraw from her new job. The flight attendant on the America Airlines Boeing 747 had offered her champagne as she lay back and listened to soothing, classical music in her headphones. She didn't get her scarf back but what's that compared to a quarter of a million bucks?

The sun shone through the cabin window, shutter partly lowered, and glinted off her necklace as she sipped from the glass flute. Opening her handbag, she brought out a small black velvet pouch. Inside were two teddy bear golden earrings. Smiling, she recounted how they got there.

The whole plan had been easy. So easy. Caroline had purchased a pair of earrings from Swarinski's jewellers identical to those owned by Amanda. How gullible Amanda had been earlier in the day when Caroline had said how nice the teddy bear earrings would look at the Shakespeare party that evening. And Amanda wore them! How easy it had been for Caroline to put one of her own earrings into Jake's clenched hand after she had poisoned him and lifted him into the freezer. The following morning, when the house was empty, Caroline had gone into Amanda's jewellery box and taken one of her gold teddy bears which she hid in the black velvet pouch, along with the other one of her own. And Amanda had never missed it, or, if she had, it was never mentioned.

One spoonful of mercuric cyanide in a single can of beer had been enough to kill Bauer, and Caroline had carefully disposed of the empty can the next day. She didn't know that a copy of an email and a micro-cassette were in his possession, and neither did Caroline know that on one of his visits Bauer had left his recorder running under a cushion on the lounge sofa while she and Bauer drank tea in the kitchen. He'd gone back to remove the tape, quickly slipped it in his pocket but had been interrupted by Howard and slid the Sony back under the cushion. The recorder remained there until Ryan had found it.

Caroline had worked quickly and efficiently on that evening, leaving the utility room and kitchen exactly as they had been left when the Gardner's went out, except for the cup that Jake had filled from the kitchen tap and used to take two analgesic tablets for a headache. Caroline had replaced it in the cupboard unwashed. And although Caroline had gone to her room before their return, she'd hardly slept that night, the little oiled cogs in her head moving continuously with a gentle whir. Her story had to be clear . . . and simple. And it was.

*

Caroline Sinclair had sent Amanda Gardner to the CCWF for a very long time. After a further six months of visits by Howard, he began to to see Amanda less and less. He told Teresa and Ryan that their mother wasn't well and it would be better if they sent a nice letter every month. But they never got a reply. At Christmas they all made the journey to Chowchilla and spent an hour with Amanda. She'd lost more weight and her features were becoming haggard.

A family photograph taken in happier times at a funfair sat on the lounge mantelpiece and was the only visual reminder for them. Jane almost, but not quite, became a surrogate mother to the children until she returned home on Friday 19 August the following year after her twelve month period as the au pair girl to the Gardner family.

During long winter evenings, Howard sometimes wanted to talk to Jane about his past life. Sitting in the lounge, he would turn the TV off and just open his heart. She would sit and listen to stories about his first wife Priscilla, his relationship with Louise of whom he was fond, and his regrettable contact with Jodie Patterson. Howard, after a couple of whiskies one night, confessed to straying to a house of ill repute within his first week at SF City Hospital. Jodie was the madame of the house and blackmailed him for a long time. When he and Patterson were seen by Jane entering an elevator in the shopping mall car park, he was making his final payment to her.

As far as Priscilla and Amanda were concerned, he loved them both equally he would tell Jane, but he didn't say much about Louise Archer. Howard also confessed, and was very apologetic, that he never took up bridge. He'd conned Jane and she'd believed him. Jane became concerned, too, when Howard mentioned things he'd already told her on more than one occasion, but when Jane reminded him simply could not recall telling her.

Jane had completed her photography course, Gloria Rudetsky awarding her a distinction. Three of Jane's photographs were hung in the college, proudly signing each one before they were framed.

Before leaving San Francisco, Jane said her goodbyes to friends. Sam, Marie and Katie all got extra strong hugs. She'd never been to see Andrew in prison but wrote him a long letter a week before she left, enclosing a yellow slip of paper from a Chinese restaurant. Howard had been more formal, shaking Jane's hand before holding her gently to him for a few seconds and thanking her for all that she had done . . . and apologising for the bad times and the lies. Jane had met with her counsellor, Melody Oppenberg, for a final debrief three days before she left the city. Over a Starbucks coffee she told Melody the whole story, saying she was sorry she hadn't been more truthful about what had happened at Adair Way. Melody's jaw dropped several times as Jane gave a full account.

Teresa and Ryan cried their hearts out as the cab driver lifted Jane's luggage into the trunk of the Chevrolet, then headed for the airport after Jane had hugged the children. Jane promised she would skype them regularly and send postcards from places she visited. That helped the tears subside but their little hearts would ache for a very long time.

Howard continued full time at the hospital for a few more years before he decided to reduce his hours in order to spend more time at home. A rich uncle had left Howard and Amanda two million dollars in his will so Howard could manage financially, although the house extension was never built. Howard and the children occasionally visited the CCWF where Amanda regained some weight, her face filled out, she had grown her hair longer and dyed it black. He had proposed down-sizing, and, with Amanda's agreement, Howard and the children moved into a house in a different part of the city although still within an easy commute to SFCH and Lexington Junior school. St. Mary's High School, where Teresa and Ryan would complete their education, was on a school bus route from their new home. Howard took on a full time 'home help' soon after moving in who was able to combine being a nanny, keep the home clean and do the laundry. Maybe be a companion?

Jodie Patterson became a loner, was rarely seen in the city now, and Vida Honeywell got on with her own life. She and her daughter, Marie, became closer. And although Vida had visited Amanda once, the trip was too traumatic for her and she never went again. Katie wasn't needed now. She'd told Howard she would be happy to travel the extra distance to clean and do the washing and ironing but Howard refused her help. And Katie, being the good person she was, kept a lot of her secrets about Dr. Gardner to herself. Liza Freeman, the school caretaker at Lexington Junior, was killed in an early morning hit and run accident.

The police never found the driver or the car. Ironically, it was within a hundred yards of the school gates.

Andrew Wilson served half of his sentence. When he came out of prison he always claimed to have seen a vision of the Virgin Mary and he took that as a sign from God that he had to mend his ways. A lapsed Catholic, Wilson was to spend three years training to be a priest with the church and would use his experience talking with inmates in some of California's worst institutions. Father Wilson, as he would become, carried the scars on the palms of his hands until the day he died, always a reminder of his dark days.

When Jane got home she was warmly welcomed by the local community. Her mother, Jenny, had talked positively about her exploits in San Francisco and news had spread around Keighley. She was hailed a heroine when folk heard about her care of the children under gunfire on Halloween, although she often wondered how much her mum had embellished the news! Jane went to university and, after gaining a degree in English literature, became a crime writer. Within four years she would have three books published by Penguin, one of which - *The Sky Above The Mud Below* - sold over two million copies, half of them into the US market.

Jane would send a signed copy of each one to Ryan and Teresa which they'd always cherish.

59

Despite the thirty year sentence, it became apparent that Amanda Gardner would probably serve less than half of that – with good behaviour. With time to think and reflect on events, Amanda repeatedly went through that fateful evening of 23 April, like a tape on a figure of eight loop. In her mind there was only one killer, and that was Caroline Sinclair. The nanny had brought him to the house, poisoned him and dumped the body in the freezer before she and Howard had returned from the party. *'She must have done it!'* A voice in Amanda's head kept repeating it. The bitch had been clever enough to buy another pair of teddy bear earrings and made certain that the Sony tape and printed email were on him when she shut the freezer.

But as time passed Amanda changed her ways, took part in social events, even helped with the open talk sessions . . . almost became a model prisoner. She used the gym, took up painting again, but chose outdoor scenes as her subject rather than the dark, horrific images that had been in her head for a long time. Certain privileges were allowed . . . use of a computer for example, limited to one hour per week, but no access to email. She was able to google a host of facts, scan unlimited topics, and research almost everything and anything.

Amanda became interested in Scotland, and Glasgow in particular. What a delightful part of the world it appeared to be. Rolling hills, coastline, culture. And it wasn't difficult to find out about people who lived there – so much information . . . and it was time to start planning.

Amanda calculated that when she was released, in about 2030 or perhaps earlier, Caroline Sinclair would be in her mid thirties and, Amanda assumed, probably still living in Glasgow; it wouldn't be too difficult to find her. Closing her eyelids, Amanda pictured herself – dressed in plain dark clothes with flat shoes, shorter black hair, and a pair of horn rimmed spectacles. Sinclair would never recognise her and she'd be able to get nice and close. Really close. Using some of her uncle's inheritance, which Howard had placed into a trust fund, she would fly to Prestwick airport with a new passport in the name of Mandy Jean Raskoff, her maiden name, and pay cash for everything - no trace left.

And, with ideas from some crime novels in the prison library, Amanda would kill her. She mentally toyed with her plans and that made her smile, eyes still closed. A slow agonising death . . . perhaps poison? How ironic. A fine needle on the end of a small umbrella 'accidentally' pushed into her leg as they passed each other, an apology quickly made as the perpetrator scurried off. Then, a young woman would be found dead . . . in a quiet side street . . . After the little 'accident' Caroline Sinclair's heart would soon stop beating . . .

Stretching her arms upwards and breathing out, Amanda decided to go use the gym for an hour before starting a new watercolour painting after lunch. Perhaps things weren't so bad after all when you had something to look forward to . . . like seeing Caroline Sinclair again.

Although the day had started out dull, the sun was shining brighter now in Wrangler blue skies over Chowchilla as Amanda Gardner used a rowing machine, her muscles toning up nicely

. . .

One summer's day over in Vallejo Street, about a year after Jane had left the USA, Detective Simon Rogers took a phone call from Miss Docia Lightbody.

"Hi, Detective Rogers, Docia Lightbody here. Do you have time for a brief chat?"

"Sure, what's up?"

"Well, I've been stroking a blue, chiffon scarf, it's here on my knee now. Not so much stroking as caressing it. Well, it . . . somehow got into my bag . . . that time we were looking for the Bauer boy over in Hayward. I'm getting vibes from it. Strange vibes . . . I think we need to talk. And soon."

Detective Rogers thanked Miss Lightbody, wondering what she may have gathered from the scarf? He recalled that Caroline Sinclair had lost a scarf on their visit, but how come Lightbody had it anyway? Sipping his coffee, Rogers thought 'why not phone Dr. Gardner at home - maybe see how his wife was coping up there in Chowchilla, see if Dr. Gardner had a different view on past events in Adair Way back in September 2015, get any views from him at all before the overweight psychic came to visit?' Checking the new telephone number for Dr. Gardner in his notebook, Rogers punched in the numbers.

"Hello, Dr. Gardner's residence. Louise speaking. How may I help you?" Rogers knew that voice.

"Louise. Is that Louise Archer? This is Detective Simon Rogers . . . is that you, Louise . . . from the Chronicle?"

"Why yes. Hi, Simon – long time no speak." Not since the Doug Gless case, she recalled.

"You on another story or something . . . ?" Was there a scoop on Gardner?

"No. I'm Dr. Gardner's new live-in housekeeper . . . and I've left the newspaper . . ."

'Well, well. Just like some dreams . . . they fade and die,' thought the detective as he wished her luck and put the phone down.

The End

Acknowledgements

As usual my grateful thanks go to my wife, Nora, for her comments, feedback and constructive criticism, and for finding the correct word when I couldn't. Also for agreeing to use her photograph for the front cover.

Thanks, too, to those who added their own thoughts that made me consider various aspects of the novel, especially an up and coming young author Cameron Jackson.

This story was partly inspired by my good friends Paul and Jenny Lister who live in France, and whose daughter, Helen, went to the US to be an au pair girl. This novel is a work entirely of my own imagination and in no way reflects what may have actually taken place during her time as an au pair!

Any incorrect factual details in this story can be heaped at my door. I hope there aren't too many!

Last, but by no means least, this book is dedicated to the memory of a dear friend, Lorrie Honisett, who left us in April, 2016. I hope you've found everlasting peace in the arms of the angels, Lorrie, and that *your* candle has made heaven a little brighter. I'm sure it has. God bless you.